# Cat's Claw

*Alex Matthews*

INTRIGUE
PRESS

For information, please contact Intrigue Press, P.O. Box 27553, Phila-
delphia, PA 19118, 215-753-1270.

ISBN 1-890768-22-7

First Printing 2000

Grateful acknowledgment is made for permission to reprint a line from
the comic strip *Sylvia* © 1998 by Nicole Hollander. Used by permission. All
rights reserved.

Library of Congress Cataloging-in-Publication Data)

Matthews, Alex.
    Cat's claw / Alex Matthews.
        p. cm.
    ISBN 1-890768-22-7
        1. McCabe, Cassidy (Fictitious character)--Fiction. 2. Women
psychotherapists--Fiction. 3. Chicago (Ill.)--Fiction.  I. Title.

PS3563.A83958 C38 2000
813'.54--dc21                                            99-088369

10  9  8  7  6  5  4  3  2  1

Other books by Alex Matthews
*Secret's Shadow*
*Satan's Silence*
*Vendetta's Victim*
*Wanton's Web*

For my husband Allen, who makes all things possible.

Many thanks to all the people who helped in the birthing of this book: my husband, Allen Matthews, whose fourth career has become book promotion; my editor, Chris Roerden, who would not accept less than my best; my fellow critique group members, Nancy Carleton, Jan Fellers, Carol Hauswald, and Denise Stybr, who faithfully refused to let me get away with anything; my publicist Barbara Young, who applied her vast energy and enthusiasm to book promotion; my fellow DL member, Betsy Fraser, who named my fourth book; Barbara Lakey, a sibling from SinC who provided consultation on car vandalism; Melissa De Vries, who educated me about guardianship; Penny O'Leary, another DL member who answered my questions about phone records; Audrey Abbott, also from DL, who informed me about Medicare fraud; Chicago Police Detective Anne Chambers and Oak Park Commander Robert Scianna, who tried to set me straight about police procedure. Everyone gave freely of their time and expertise. Where errors exist, they are mine.

# Cat's Claw

# 1. Raised Blinds

***Early Spring***

"Olivia Mallory is a real challenge." Cassidy McCabe muttered to herself as she stared out her dining room window at the neighborhood cat lady's house across the street.

Starshine, the small calico sitting on the teak table in front of Cassidy, pricked her ears and fixed enormous green eyes on her human, a look she used whenever she wanted attention. Cassidy, never able to resist the cat's wiles, jiggled her fingers in front of the calico. Starshine attacked instantly, drawing a bead of blood on Cassidy's forefinger.

She jerked her hand away and sucked the wound. Wondering why she never could seem to remember that cats had claws, she picked Starshine up and gently deposited her on the floor.

Her gaze returned to the house across the street as she brooded over the problem she was having in establishing a relationship with Olivia, a relationship essential to accomplishing the cat-related mission she'd set for herself. *Here I am being my most helpful, charming, empathic self,* she thought, *and there are still times the woman barely speaks.* Although, she had to admit, there had been an amazing, totally un-Olivia-type breakthrough the week before.

*Right. I've been doing backflips to be nice, and now Olivia's actually granting me the privilege of doing her a favor.*

*You're doing yourself a favor. She's going to let you feed her indoor cats while she's away on business, which means you actually get to step foot inside her house—something you've been dying to do for ages.*

The more Cassidy thought about it, the more she realized she really was making progress. A few days earlier she'd gone into Olivia's backyard at feeding time and her forty-something neighbor had surprised her by starting a conversation. Eyes glistening, Olivia had pointed to an emaciated feral, one of many strays fighting over food bowls on the stoop, and said, "This cat's dying. It won't be long before he just disappears and I never see him again." Cassidy had looked at the sick cat and blinked back tears herself.

Plunking her elbows on the table, she continued to gaze at the cat lady's bungalow, a charcoal frame facing the north side of Cassidy's corner two-story. Olivia had lived in her house alone and put out food for the colony of feral cats that collected around her stoop since before Cassidy moved onto the block.

Cassidy noticed a couple of kittens pouncing in Olivia's driveway, two new additions to the six or so adult cats that clustered in the yards belonging to Olivia and the man in the corner house to the west. *Oh shit, first litter of the season.* Heaviness settled on Cassidy's shoulders. *Time to launch my cat rescue campaign. Which, like most of the projects I misguidedly get myself into, is undoubtedly going to prove way harder than I expect. And I won't be able to do it at all unless Olivia gives me permission to tramp through her yard catching kittens.*

Starshine, overriding Cassidy's objections, had taken up residence with her more than two years ago, and in the interim Cassidy had gradually metamorphosed into a cat person. Attached as she was to the calico, she found she could no longer ignore the sufferings of the wild felines across the street, whose ranks were regularly decimated by disease and cold winters.

As Cassidy watched, the cat lady's rusted-out Cavalier turned into the driveway, causing the kittens to flee. Her car appeared every evening at close to six and left every morning before Cassidy had enough coffee in her system to shake off her beginning-of-the-day fog. Olivia went out in the evenings and on weekends, but Cassidy had never seen another person go in. And she had never seen any of the slatted, horizontal blinds that covered every window opened or raised.

*She ought to live on a moor, have Heathcliff as a lover. An Oak Park bungalow, dinged-up car, and feral cats just don't cut it in the gothic romance department.*

It was only since deciding to tackle the colony of ferals that Cassidy had become a cat-lady watcher. But from the time she'd first moved into her house, it had been impossible not to notice the woman's reclusiveness and the excess cats.

Olivia climbed the steps to her main entrance, located on the west side of the house, and disappeared through the door. She did not look up or wave, did nothing to acknowledge she had neighbors. She behaved, in fact, as if she were cut off from every other human on the planet, even though Cassidy, by dint of extreme effort, had managed to establish a tiny thread of connection.

*Used to think it was only old ladies who gave up on people, turned to cats for company. But once you actually looked at her, boy, were you surprised.* Even from across the street Cassidy could tell that Olivia was slender and youthful, a clearly attractive woman. Up close, she discovered Olivia also had creamy skin, fine features, and dark, shiny hair pinned up in back.

The kittens, one orange, the other tiger striped, raced out from the bushes beneath Olivia's front window. The April light was thin and pale, the sun not yet delivering any real warmth. But small bumps on the branches of Cassidy's corner maple told her that spurts of greenery, dandelions, and more kittens were on the way.

*What does Olivia do all alone in there? How can she stand never looking outside?* Wanting all the light she could get, Cassidy kept her own windows as uncovered as modesty would permit, sometimes more than modesty quite liked. Although the bungalow was in good repair, the closed blinds and Olivia's isolation made it seem Dickensian, a picture forming in Cassidy's mind of dead flowers, cobwebs, and motes of dust floating in the gloom. She muttered, "That, and the stink of cat pee soaked into every floorboard."

*You're not certain her cats've done unauthorized peeing. Could smell like roses for all you know.*

As if any cat lady doesn't have a feline-fragrance problem.

She heard the back door. *Zach's home. Wonder what kind of carryout we're having tonight.* She went into the kitchen to see Zach Moran coming around the oak room divider, a bag in hand. As she started toward him, Starshine raced in behind her, tangled in her legs, and sent her grabbing at the refrigerator to keep herself upright.

The calico sprang onto the counter and glared in outrage at her human, who had offended by thrusting legs into the cat's path.

The large old kitchen was badly in need of an uplift, its gray linoleum floor curling at the seams, the ancient linoleum countertop so worn the color was nearly gone. On the east side of the room, an oak cabinet stood perpendicular to the wall to serve as a divider between the kitchen and the waiting area she had set up for her home-based psychotherapy practice.

Placing his bag on the dining room table, Zach said, "It's nice to be greeted but don't fight over me." Cassidy's housemate was just under six foot, wide through the shoulders and chest, with smooth dark hair and an easygoing expression. The carryout bag emanated delicate stir-fry aromas.

Cassidy set the table while Zach put out four white cartons. They sat kitty-corner from each other and dished up food. Her voice grim, she said, "I saw the first kittens."

Zach chewed absently, gazing into space.

"You know, kittens?" she tried again.

He gave her a blank look.

Jumping onto the end of the table, Starshine intently observed every forkful that went into Zach's mouth. Cassidy said, "She doesn't even like Chinese."

"But she hates being left out."

"Where were you just then? You didn't hear a word I said about the kittens." She watched him make a mental effort to switch gears and focus on her.

"Sorry, I was thinking about a call I got today. There's this small-time dealer, Reno, who's been snitching for me ever since I blew the whistle on some cops who seriously punched him out."

*My hero—defender of downtrodden dope dealers.* Propping her chin on her hand, she gazed fondly at his bronze-skinned face, a jagged scar running across the left cheek.

"Police brutality is practically a non-story around here. But what Reno told me today—that a couple of cops are running a major dope ring out of one of the clubs, and these same two cops shot a dealer on the street for refusing to hand over his heroin bag—now that's front page."

*Don't like this. People who swim with piranhas sometimes get eaten.* "My preference'd be something a tad less dangerous, but I know you'd never pass up a story as big as this."

"If it ever gets to be a story. The word of a loser like Reno isn't evidence, and proving anything against a couple of cops won't be easy. Anyway, you were saying something about kittens."

"You know, capturing all the litters and taking them to no-kill shelters."

He lowered his chin, his face skeptical. "There you go, tilting at windmills again. Those cats are feral. Feral means wild, remember? They do not come when you call 'kitty kitty.' Nobody can get near them."

Her jaw tightened. "What? You think feral cats are more hard-core than those killer cops you're planning to go after?"

He slanted his head toward the window, then turned to face her again, his blue-gray eyes amused. "Can't imagine why I ever try to talk you out of anything. I certainly know by now how useless it is."

She licked a stray piece of rice from the corner of her mouth. "You do it for the same reason I do. Right now I'm fighting an urge to say that going after dirty cops is insane. We both have an unfortunate tendency to try to straighten each other out."

He ran his hand down the arm she had propped on the table. "I don't want to straighten you out. I like the curves." His shaggy brows drew together. "Instead of telling you not to play Don Quixote, I ought to be telling myself."

Half rising from her chair, she dropped a kiss on his eggroll-tasting mouth. "One of the things I love about you is that you throw yourself at windmills, but just as you're ready to leap into space, I want to grab you and pull you back."

He smiled. "Exactly how I'm feeling about your feral cat campaign."

"Yes, but don't forget the coup I pulled off last week."

"Coup?"

"Remember, a couple of days ago I was helping Olivia feed the ferals and she mentioned she had to spend next week in L.A. getting trained in a new software program. So I, of course, volunteered to feed both the outdoor *and* the indoor cats. She came up with every excuse in the book to avoid letting me into her house, but she's so timid I was able to argue her down. I'm hoping that if she lets me inside and nothing bad happens, she'll start to develop a little trust."

"I can't believe it. I thought the place was under some kind of quarantine. Besides, isn't she your basic paranoid wacko?"

"Paranoid? Definitely. Assuming anyone knows the difference between paranoid and realistic any more. But I don't think she's seriously wacko." Cassidy tilted her head. "At first I thought she had a schizoid personality disorder. Schizoid sounds like schizophrenia but it's totally different. A schizoid has no interest in relationships. Just doesn't care about people."

"But you obviously didn't stick with that theory."

"She's scared is all. She has a real longing for connection but she's afraid to let anyone near her. So the right diagnosis is social phobia, which means only slightly wacko."

"The shame of it is, she could be a real babe if she gave it half a try." His mouth stretched into a mock leer. "I might hit on her myself if I hadn't gone and gotten married."

Cassidy smiled warmly at Zach, images popping into her head of the two of them standing at the altar in a small chapel, the party afterward at their house, the honeymoon in Mexico. Pulling herself back to the present, she said, "Olivia's not your type. It'd take a year to get to the first kiss."

"You think she's a virgin? Nah, couldn't be. Virgins over forty don't exist."

&#8476;     &#8476;     &#8476;

On Saturday Olivia gave Cassidy a key for the side entrance and took her inside to introduce her to the three indoor cats. Cassidy was disappointed to discover that she'd been right about the smell, wrong about the dead flowers, cobwebs, and dust motes. The interior was merely old and tacky, not mysterious, and the stench even worse than she'd expected. On her first day in the house alone, she felt an urge to go upstairs and peek into Olivia's bedroom. But after giving herself a strict lecture on her neighbor's right to privacy, she succeeded in avoiding the offense.

On the final feeding day, her virtue was rewarded with a nearly guilt-free glimpse into the upstairs rooms. Upon opening the door, she suming Olivia must have returned a day early, Cassidy briefly debated whether to call from the first floor or simply go up, then followed her impulse and climbed the carpeted staircase to a short hall at the top. Olivia's lacy-mauve bedroom was to the right, her darkly paneled office to the left.

Olivia stood at the far end of the office in front of a filing cabinet, her back to Cassidy. She had the second drawer pulled all the way out and was digging in back of it.

"Olivia? I hope you don't mind that I came upstairs but I heard the music and—"

Her neighbor's shoulders jumped wildly. She spun around and bumped the drawer closed behind her. "Cassidy. I should have called to tell you I finished early." Olivia hurried out of the room, closed the door, and hustled her downstairs.

Cassidy wondered briefly if her neighbor was hiding something, then decided it was just Olivia being her normal scared and secretive self.

# 2. Cold Blooded, Perfume-Tainted Jerk

***Late Summer***

Two staccato rings came from the bell at the back door, used primarily for the therapy practice. Sitting at her desk in her upstairs bedroom, Cassidy glanced through the window at darkness. *Nine-thirty. Can't be a client on the wrong day. You never schedule anybody this late.*

Feeling some minor twitches, the uneasiness she always experienced in response to after-hours knocks or bells when she was home alone, she trudged downstairs through the soupy heat outside the air conditioned bedroom.

*Burglars don't ring,* her no-nonsense voice declared firmly.

*Home invasion three blocks away. Your own garage broken into last week,* her anxiety-voice whispered back.

Not giving in to timidity, she hastened through the dilapidated kitchen and around the oak room divider. Olivia's face stared in at her through the window in the back door, causing her to halt briefly in surprise.

*First time in twelve years she's ever come near my house.* Cassidy opened the door. Her neighbor, graceful and willowy in a long, filmy skirt, stood haloed by the opal light shining down from the small canopy overhead. "Olivia." She read the brightness in the woman's almond eyes as panic. "What's wrong?"

Ducking her head, Olivia said in a soft, halting voice. "I'm sorry to bother you so late. And it's probably . . . there's probably nothing to it. I'm always getting myself all worked up and then it turns out to be just my imagination." She turned to face her own house on the opposite side of Briar, the street that ran along the north side of Cassidy's property. "It's . . . well, it's the light. You see that light in the bedroom?" Her right hand fluttered, the sapphire ring she always wore giving off a hazy shimmer.

Stepping out into the muggy August air, Cassidy gazed at the yellow square beneath the peaked roof. "It was off when you left?"

"I thought I turned it off but maybe I didn't. Anyway, when I drove up and saw the light, I . . . well, I started imagining things." Wisps of chestnut hair, straying from the knot in back, fell around her hollow cheeks.

*That shuttered house'd make me imagine things too.* Although younger than her neighbor, Cassidy felt a maternal tug. *You should bring her inside, feed her hot chocolate, make her come live with you till she's willing to tear down those blinds. Zach could look but not touch.*

"Always better to be on the safe side. We can get a cop over here right away. He'll go through the house, make sure everything's all right."

Olivia's hand flew to her throat. "Oh no," she said, the panic stronger now. "I don't need the police. All I need is for you to watch from your stoop while I go inside. If everything's okay, I'll come to the door and wave."

Cassidy's brow furrowed. "The Oak Park cops are really nice. They always *want* you to call, even if there's nothing to it."

"No, please, I never would've come over if . . . well, if I thought you'd do anything like that."

"Okay," Cassidy said, her voice level, "then I'll go in with you." *Even if the stink does knock me over.*

Olivia shook her head emphatically. "No, really, I can't let you do that." Twisting her hands, she said in a nearly inaudible voice, "This is so embarrassing. If there is somebody in the house, well I'm afraid . . . afraid it won't be a stranger."

"You think it's somebody you know?"

"I made a terrible mistake. There's this man, you see. Not somebody I'm interested in, just somebody who's having . . . having a hard time. I got to feeling sorry for him, and I just . . . I acted on impulse. I did something I should never've done.''

Cassidy's eyes widened in amazement. "You let him stay with you?"

"Just for a few days. I told him he had to find someplace else right away. But the problem is,'' her doe-like eyes darted up from under her brow, checking Cassidy's face, "I gave him a key. Then I got scared. I realized what an awful mistake I'd made, so I told him he couldn't come back.'' She shifted her weight. "But he's still got the key.''

*Didn't ask me for her key back either. Afraid to ask anybody for anything?* "You have any reason to think he'd hurt you?"

"I guess not. He probably wouldn't.'' She sounded doubtful. "He's really just a gentle giant now.''

"Giant?"

"Yeah,'' Olivia almost smiled, "he's really enormous.''

*Here she is, scared of everything that moves, she gives some guy her key.*

Probably why she did it. You see it all the time. Person goes way off to an extreme in one direction, then backlashes in the opposite direction. She probably got so sick of being afraid to do anything she went overboard on being reckless.

"Okay, I'll stand here and watch while you go inside. But if you're not out in about one minute, I'm calling the cops.''

Olivia started toward her house. In the narrow strip of lawn fronting the tall, pitched-roof dwelling, two large ferals observed as the woman crossed Briar, wraithlike in the pale light from the street lamps. The sixty-something widower who lived in the corner house came out to take his two Dobermans for a walk. George Brenner hated the ferals and had been feuding with Olivia over them for years.

The cat lady went through her side entrance just off the driveway. As she moved from room to room, lights appeared behind closed blinds, marking her progress. In a short time she reappeared and gave Cassidy a wave.

*Well, isn't that nice. She actually came to me for help. I guess all that time I've put in helping her feed the ferals wasn't a waste after all.*

&#8279;&#8365;  &#8279;&#8365;  &#8279;&#8365;

Two weeks later on a Saturday night, Cassidy drove east on Briar past Brenner's house on the corner, Olivia's house next to his. She was coming home from a party hosted by a psychiatrist friend. *After nine. Should've left sooner, even if the guy does send a lot of clients your way.* She pulled into her garage at the far end of the lot. *The Cougar's in front so Zach's still here, but he'll be taking off on his nightly prowl in about an hour.* She gritted her teeth. *And you've got to make him talk before he leaves.*

She yanked down the garage door and plodded toward her back gate, feet sore in burgundy pumps, silk dress clinging damply to her legs. Even this late in the evening, humidity thickened the air, making it hard to breathe. Bathed in the warm city glow, tall elms and spacious houses created a Hallmark card vista in front of her, while screeching radios and wailing sirens leant a jarring sound track in back. The traffic noise came from Austin Boulevard a block to the east, the border between her security-minded suburb and the crime-ridden neighborhoods of West Chicago.

*Can't stand what he's doing.*

Won't be that long. Besides, he told you up front it'd be bad and you said you could live with it.

*Didn't say it'd be this bad. And I lied—I can't live with it.*

Starshine, who spent far too much time hanging out with the feral cats across the street, came racing to greet her. The cat rolled on the sidewalk, making seductive noises to entice her human into lavishing compliments and attention.

Cassidy sat on her heels to respond, then noticed a movement out of the corner of her eye. Standing, she stared at Olivia's house. The blinds covering the picture window in front had disappeared. *My God! She raised them. Actually raised her blinds.* For the first time ever, Cassidy could see inside her neighbor's living room from the street, the scene illuminated by a low-level interior light.

Olivia, her back close to the window, was facing an indistinct figure on the opposite side of the room. Feeling a prickly sense of alarm, Cassidy focused intently on the person in the background, but his distance from the window made it impossible to get a clear view of him—*or her—can't tell if it's a man or woman.* She squinted, straining for details. *Hardly a giant. Maybe not even as big as Zach.* She hugged herself tightly, feeling more and more disturbed.

Only reason Olivia'd raise the blinds is to send a signal. Or make it so public the guy'd be afraid to touch her. Cassidy sprinted across Briar and rang her neighbor's bell.

Olivia pulled the door partially open. Standing with the left side of her body behind it, she peered around at her visitor. "Oh, Cassidy. What is it?" The woman's voice, always a little tremulous, seemed more shaky than usual, but Cassidy could not tell if it was from fear, surprise, or something else.

"I saw the blinds go up."

"I . . . well, I raised them."

"Is something wrong?"

"No, not really. I've got . . . there's someone here and this person . . . said it seemed . . . it seemed a little dreary." Getting that one sentence out appeared to leave Olivia drained.

Moving slowly, the way she would with a frightened child, Cassidy started to open the screen door. She said in a low voice, "Why don't I just come in and make sure everything's all right."

Olivia's hand went to the base of her throat. "Oh no. Really, you can't. I'd be so . . . I'd be too embarrassed." Her skin was chalky.

Embarrassed? This some kind of romantic interlude? But why raise the blinds? Bringing her face up close to the screen, Cassidy tried to determine if the emotion on Olivia's face was embarrassment or fear. She whispered, "Do you need help?"

Olivia shook her head.

"Are you sure?" *Oh shit, what do I do? Barge in? Walk away?*

"Really, I'm fine. I don't . . . I don't need anything." The door closed quietly in Cassidy's face.

Returning to her own side of the street, she gazed into Olivia's now empty living room. *Call the cops?* She pictured herself saying to a skeptical uniform, "I know she said she was okay but you have to check because she raised her blinds."

*Because she raised her blinds. Because she's Olivia and she never wants anybody to see inside her house and she'd never have opened up her living room unless she were in danger. Because she gave her key to this guy and now she's afraid of him.* Sucking in one cheek, she shifted her weight.

You're blowing things out of proportion, her no-nonsense voice cut in. Imagining things, the way Olivia does. The way you're doing with Zach. Making a federal case out of his going too far to get a story.

But maybe Olivia is in danger. Maybe you just want to ignore it so you can go have it out with Zach. She watched a middle-aged black woman, her arms filled with bags, plod wearily toward her on Briar.

Probably just what she said. A little romance. And about time too. Gave some man her key, panicked because she's never had a boyfriend before, then got up her nerve and invited him back. He hated the house being all closed up—just like I would—so she raised the blinds to make him happy. Then I rang the bell and she felt like I'd caught her in the act. The living room remained empty, the yellowish light illuminating the house's out-of-date interior, the space reminiscent of a fifties movie set.

Way to go, Olivia! You just have at it, and if the guy turns out to be a jerk, I'll give you a free session.

Mrorrr! Starshine called indignantly from the back stoop. Cassidy had offended on two counts: first, in ignoring the special greeting Starshine had dashed over to bestow, and second, in failing to provide a timely door opening.

Cassidy went through the gate, opened the door, and scurried to put out fresh food, hoping that her effort at appeasement would bring about rapid feline forgiveness. *If Zach's as much of a jerk tonight as he's been the past couple of weeks, we're going to have a blow-out that'll leave me needing megadoses of catly TLC.*

A sense of dread—thick, viscous, spreading like torpid black oil—infused her body as she contemplated the fight she was about to start. Starshine took two bites of fishy smelling food, gazed at her warmly, and extended her nose for a nosekiss.

Cassidy touched her lips lightly to the pink nose, then turned slowly toward the stairs at the opposite end of the house.

*Can't stand what he's doing.*

You know he's not going to stop. And you also know—if you go at him the wrong way, he won't talk at all. You want him to stomp out of here mad, leave you to spend another sleepless night waiting till dawn for him to show his face?

She climbed to the second floor, Starshine's furry little rump bouncing ahead of her, then paused in the short hall at the top. Zach's office and the extra bedroom were to the right, their large master bedroom to the left. The cat disappeared in the direction of the waterbed and other assorted comfortable furniture.

Cassidy gazed into Zach's office, her chest tightening, a low buzz starting in her brain. He sat with his back toward her tapping computer keys. Although he had to have heard her coming up the stairs, he refused to turn around, refused to acknowledge her in any way. *Been this way for days.* Before he started his undercover investigation, he'd never failed to greet her when she came in.

Clenching her teeth to keep accusatory words from pouring out, she proceeded into their bedroom and slammed the door. The large room contained an executive desk in each corner of the north wall, a waterbed, and two dressers. Starshine lolled amidst piles of paper on Cassidy's desktop, her luminous green eyes fastened on her human as if to say, "Now you just sit down and tell me all about it."

Dropping into her swivel chair, Cassidy pounded one fist on an unopened managed care packet. "I don't get it. Why's *he* acting pissed? He's the one screwing up here, not me."

Eyes growing more alert, Starshine swiped at Cassidy's hand.

"What're you doing? Telling me not to have this fight I'm itching to have? I suppose you want me to do what you do. Turn my back and pretend he doesn't exist."

*That's your therapist part talking. The part that knows it's better to keep your mouth shut till you calm yourself down, better not to go in swinging.*

She took several deep breaths, then looked at Starshine. "Okay, I'll talk first, attack later."

She went to his doorway and waited for him to look in her direction. Having changed his appearance to go undercover, he now sported an image completely foreign to her. He'd slicked his hair back into a small ponytail and grown a three-day stubble, black threaded with gray, to make his scar less visible.

After thirty seconds, she gave up. "You speaking to me tonight or not?"

Keeping his eyes on the monitor, he replied, "I'm busy."

"We need to talk."

"Not now."

Gritting her teeth, she held back a full minute before speaking again. "When you crawled into bed this morning, you reeked not only of alcohol and smoke, you were also wearing someone else's perfume."

She watched over his shoulder as words formed on the screen.
8/23. Saw N & B at The Zone between 1 & 2:30.
They talked to Randy, Zeke, and H, plus two other guys
I haven't met yet.

She said, "What the hell's going on with you, anyway?"

He swiveled toward her, his face remote. "I'm not getting into this. You have a nasty habit of going into snits over women who are totally irrelevant and I'm tired of defending myself. At this point, I don't care what you think."

A sick feeling came over her.

"What I'm doing is extremely dangerous. I have to be as focused and clear headed as I've ever been in my life, and I can't afford to let your little temper tantrums distract me."

She flashed an image of the two of them in bed, Zach's body wrapped around hers, his voice soft in her ear. *Three weeks ago. It's only been three weeks.*

"What's happening to us?"

"I'm undercover, that's what. I told you it'd change things for a while."

"You've never been like this before." She pressed both hands to the sides of her head, which felt as if it would burst. "I can't stand it. I just can't."

He rose, his blue-gray eyes regarding her coldly, an icy indifference she'd never seen in him before he started on this story. "I'll get a hotel room till this is over. It'll be easier on both of us. You won't have to deal with my associate's perfume and I won't have to deal with your hysterics." He brushed past her and started downstairs.

Hugging herself tightly, she watched his rigid back disappear around the L in the staircase. She sensed panic floating around her like a cloud, but her anger held it at bay. *Never had hysterics in my life. And never been pissed without a damned good reason. And this reason is the best damned one of all.*

She rocked up and down on the balls of her feet, one part of her wanting to march into the bedroom, slam the door, and let him go, the other wanting to pursue him downstairs.

*No pleading or crying. You won't be one of those pathetic women who follows her man from room to room begging for crumbs.*

Yeah, but you might make one more stab at reasonable discourse. Zach's been a really good guy for over two years. Just because working undercover's turned him into a cold-blooded, perfume-tainted jerk is no reason to throw away a good relationship.

She found him in the kitchen next to the sink, a full tumbler of bourbon in his hand, no ice, no water, just bourbon.

Stopping right inside the doorway, she folded her arms beneath her breasts. *He drinks that and tries to drive, you'll have to call the cops on him.*

Their eyes met briefly. His, she noted with relief, no longer held that strange coldness she'd seen upstairs.

"Don't worry, I'm not going to drink and drive. I started to dig out a suitcase, then thought maybe I'd just stay home and get quietly blasted." Taking a long swallow, he emptied the glass into the sink. "But that's not such a hot idea either, considering the paper's on my ass to get this thing wrapped up." He sighed. "I suppose the only other option is to talk, since getting divorced over a story would be stupid."

She released a long breath. Moving closer, she wrapped her arms around him. "Even though you're being a complete jerk, I love you too much to let you get away."

His hands slid around her back. "I guess I've been counting on that."

Tilting her head backward, she received a kiss on the forehead. "So, you going to tell me whose perfume you brought home last night?"

He sighed again.

"When I've asked about women before, you've always been will-ing—not eager but at least willing—to explain yourself. So," she paused, almost afraid to ask, "why all the reluctance this time?"

His arms tightened around her. "I have to be this other person from ten till dawn, and this guy I have to turn myself into is somebody you wouldn't want anything to do with. When I'm being him, I have to do things that, in the light of day, I don't much like."

Her shoulders stiffened. "Such as?"

"There's this girl, Heather. She's a heavy doper, and I've seen her hanging with those two cops I'm after. So I started hitting on her, and she let me know, in no uncertain terms, she'd be perfectly happy to take me up on any offer I cared to make."

"So what are you offering?"

Running his fingers through her auburn hair, he placed his hand on the side of her face and drew her cheek up against his chest. "She hasn't pinned me down yet." He paused. "No, scratch the 'yet.' I didn't mean that." He paused again. "I don't know quite how to explain. I flirt with her, tell her she's hot, just generally play along. She does a lot of coke, and now and then I buy little bags off her, go in the john, and flush it."

"I thought you had to present yourself as a non-user or the cops wouldn't take you on as a dealer."

"Yeah, but Heather wouldn't trust me if she didn't think I was getting high with her at least to some extent." His brows drew together. "Anyway, after I get her warmed up, I talk about needing to establish the right connection so I can make this big score. She's also a major boozer, so I keep the drinks coming, and then around three or four I pour her into a taxi and send her home."

"What's she look like?" Cassidy asked, her voice tight. "How old is she?"

"Twenty-five. She looks like a dissipated model."

"What does playing along mean?"

She felt his body go tense. "I told you—I'm tired of defending myself."

She waited, her stomach knotting.

"Okay, if you really want to know, I have to handle her to make it seem real. That's what people in these places do. I grope her a little, cop a feel. But that's as far as it's going. I'm not planning to climb into bed with her."

Cassidy squeezed her eyes shut, remembering times when he'd made her crazy touching her like that. Her teeth ached. She took a step back. "Does she turn you on?"

He sighed, looked at the floor, shook his head. "I really wish you wouldn't ask questions like that. The truth is, I'm not totally immune to having her drape herself all over me, but she's so messed up she can't get out three consecutive sentences. She'd bore me to death in less than a week."

"Why her? Why not somebody else?"

"Nobody else is motivated to do me any favors. She wants something from me, so she's willing to give me what I want, which is an introduction and a character reference."

Anger flashed through her. "What she wants is for you to sleep with her or pay her rent or something else equally unacceptable."

"Yeah, but I'll get the introduction and that'll be the end of it. Maybe I'll show my gratitude by giving her a referral to rehab."

"This is what you have to do to bust those cops?"

"This is what I have to do."

*I can't stand it.*

You have to. He's doing what he's got to do and you have to be able to both stand it and understand it. Looking away from him, she forced herself to breathe deeply. After a long time, most of the tension drained away. "Okay."

"Okay? You mean you're not going to pitch a fit and demand that I stop?" He gave her a quick hug. "How'd I get so lucky as to find you?" He looked at the floor, then raised his eyes to her face. "I knew I'd have to tell you about Heather at some point, but I was expecting a major battle and just didn't feel up to dealing with it."

Scowling, she crossed her arms. "So you reverted to your standard I-just-won't-mention-it approach. The one you use for everything you know I won't be happy with."

"It's more like I couldn't shake off this attitude the undercover guy has. I know this is hard on you and I don't like having to put you through it. I wish I could just walk in the door and get this other guy out of my head, but it isn't that easy."

"You've been feeling guilty, haven't you? That's why you've been so hostile."

Putting his hands on his hips, he gazed into space, then looked at her again, his eyes puzzled. "I know I've been irritable but it isn't guilt. It feels more like you're in my way somehow." He shook his head. "But that doesn't make sense. You've been more than reasonable about everything."

"No guilt?" she asked, unconvinced.

"The only way I can do this is by staying in character as much as possible, and I assure you, this other persona is not encumbered by trivialities such as guilt. He's out to score some serious coke, and he has no objection to messing around with any bimbo who might pave his way to getting it.''

A slight shiver ran down Cassidy's arms. ''If this other guy's taken possession of your mind and body, how can you predict what he might do?''

A look of intense concentration came over Zach's face. ''That's what makes it so tricky. I have to play this role and stay in character, and at the same time, the reporter that's after a story has to hold on tight to the reins.''

*The reporter? What about the husband who vowed to be faithful?*

He suddenly broke into a sheepish grin. ''Sounds like I've gone over the edge, doesn't it? What am I dealing with here? Undercover syndrome?''

Following him upstairs, she indulged in a brief fantasy of showing up unannounced at The Zone and checking out for herself what playing along meant. *Nobody tells the exact truth. They always doctor it a little, if only to make themselves feel better.*

She was enormously curious, but Zach, knowing all too well what she was capable of, had said he never wanted her to go there. Having her surprise him could throw him off his stride, disrupt him, make him forget for an instant who he was supposed to be.

Half an hour later he was dressed in a black, open-throated silk shirt, gold vest, and skin-tight designer jeans—his clubbing costume. Cassidy watched from her desk chair as he poked a tiny diamond stud through his earlobe. *Change is astonishing. Not just the clothes. His whole demeanor. Zach's always detached, laid back, never entirely serious. This other guy's intense, determined—ruthless, even.*

As the other guy went through the doorway, he tossed her a steely look.

*And he definitely doesn't like me.*

&#8478;  &#8478;  &#8478;

After Zach left, Cassidy moved to the waterbed, pulled her knees up tight, and wrapped her arms around them. A picture popped into her mind of her first husband standing in a meadow, straight and tall as a maypole, a bevy of bare-limbed maidens dancing around him.

*Oh God, here you go again, back around the same old track.*

Stop! her voice of reason commanded. *This is not the same thing*

*all over again. Kevin lied constantly and was an incorrigible woman-
izer. Zach tells the truth, even when he doesn't want to, and there's
never been the least hint of other women.*

Jumping onto the bed, Starshine wriggled into her lap, began
kneading her chest, and purred riotously. Cassidy heard the phone ring
in Zach's office. It was on the same line as her desk phone, but they had
turned off the sound in the bedroom to accommodate Zach's need for
daytime sleeping. Not wanting to talk to anybody, she didn't pick up.

Scratching Starshine's cheek, she gazed at the montage of gold-
framed pictures across from the bed. Nearly a dozen family photos filled
the dusty-rose wall above her chest of drawers. In the center she had
added a large wedding picture showing Cassidy with Zach's eighteen-
year-old son, Bryce, to her right and Zach, his face beaming, to her left.

*Yeah, but this isn't Zach I'm dealing with here. It's a hostile,
remorseless subpersonality that wants me out of the way.*

You're a therapist, remember? You understand these different parts
and how to work with them.

This change in Zach was not totally unfamiliar to her. She'd known
of other people who experienced sudden shifts in personality after being
dropped into new situations. Her mother, dowdy, disapproving, and
anti-male for as long as Cassidy could remember, had found herself a
boyfriend and abruptly become a giggling, girlish coquette. Then the
boyfriend dumped her and she'd reverted to her old demeanor. Cassidy
had seen people in the midst of divorce regress to hormone-driven
adolescents for a brief period, then return to normal after their lives
stabilized again. She'd swung in the opposite direction after her own
divorce, a part that was scared of being hurt again keeping her away
from men until Zach pushed his way into her life. Clearly, this hoodlum
side of Zach was what he needed to survive in the environment he
currently inhabited.

*But this is only a part, not his real self, and it's not going to win.
There's no way I'm going to allow this diamond-studded, coke-buying
creep to hijack my husband. I just have to stop torturing myself and
think about something else.*

What sprang to mind was the image of a white-faced Olivia
standing half hidden by the door in the house across the street. Cassidy
hurried downstairs, turned off the lights so she wouldn't be seen, and

stared at her neighbor's bungalow. Olivia's blinds were down again. The living room window was illuminated, the upstairs window dark. *Nearly eleven. Her lights are usually all off by now.*

That prickly feeling started in her chest again. Even though she wanted to believe that Olivia was enjoying a romantic liaison, it just didn't fit. Olivia, who was afraid of her own shadow, who would die of embarrassment if people even suspected she had a lover, would never raise the blinds and stand next to the window with her boyfriend on display in the background.

*Only reason she'd do it is if she was afraid of the guy on the other side of the room. The guy she gave her key to.*

But Olivia was afraid of everyone, so the fact that she was frightened didn't necessarily mean that the guy was out to do her harm.

It could be that Olivia'd given her key to a nefarious character, he'd arrived with malice in mind, and she'd raised the blinds, hoping he wouldn't hurt her in plain view of the street.

*If that were the case, why get rid of me so fast?* Visualizing Olivia as she peered out from behind the door, Cassidy suddenly realized that the figure from the living room could have been holding a gun to her neighbor's head.

Or it could be that the guy with the key really was a romantic interest, and when Olivia raised the blinds it was just her paranoia coming out. She could've invited him over, then the minute he got amorous started thinking rape. *She did say she has a habit of imagining things.*

A beat-up sedan parked in front of Cassidy's house, its rap music rattling her window. The music stopped. A white man disembarked and started ambling toward Austin Boulevard.

If Olivia's visitor was a bad guy, Cassidy should call the cops instantly. If he was a lover, she should stay the hell out of it.

*There's no way to tell. Whichever choice I make is bound to be the wrong one.*

Cassidy dashed upstairs and plunked into her swivel chair to try and figure it out. Starshine, sitting on the desk, scratched her ear.

*The most important thing is to make sure she's safe. Give her a call. If she answers, you don't have to worry.*

She dialed and counted rings, hanging up at number twelve. Her skin felt clammy. Did this mean she had to call the cops? *Olivia will hate you forever if you do.*

Cassidy still had the key. *If you open her door with a key, it's not breaking in. Considering you can't raise her on the phone and have reason to worry about her safety, going inside is not such an unreasonable thing to do.*

She stood and looked down from her north window onto Olivia's side entrance, the streetlight making it clearly visible. A large white tom sat on the porch. Bamba, Olivia's inside cat, a feline Cassidy had made friends with when she'd fed the indoor pets in the spring. These were cats that never went outdoors.

*Something's definitely wrong. You have to get inside that house and see if Olivia's all right.*

Cassidy pictured herself all in black like a cat burglar sneaking into the bungalow. *If he's a criminal and he's still in there, it could be dangerous.*

The calico picked up the coiled phone cord, sat tall, and placidly munched on it.

*I've done things like this before and never gotten caught. Besides, the chances are he isn't still around.* She slid a pepper gun into her waistband, dug the key out of her drawer, and took off.

&#8486;    &#8486;    &#8486;

As she stepped out her back door, Starshine zoomed ahead of her, racing halfway up the trunk of a parkway elm and sliding back down. Cassidy gripped the stoop's wrought iron railing and stared at the light seeping through the blinds across Olivia's front window. The locusts were droning, an unremitting buzz as loud as her lawnmower. Although the night air was warm, she shivered slightly.

Staring at the closed blinds, Cassidy told herself firmly that the odds were slim that anybody would be watching from behind them. She took a deep breath and marched across the all too well-lit street, up Olivia's driveway, and around the Chevy.

Yowling loudly, Bamba came running toward her. Cassidy gritted her teeth at the noise and scooped the cat into her arms to shut him up.

She stopped in front of the door, put Bamba down, and inserted her key in the lock. Since all she had was the key to the side entrance, she could not go in the back as she would have preferred. Olivia's reason for restricting her to the side door, Cassidy was certain, was that the feral feeding station on the back porch made that area the worst smelling place on the lot. She guessed that at least some part of her neighbor's reclusiveness was due to the cat pee problem.

She pushed the door open, allowing Bamba to race in ahead of her. As she stepped into the foyer, she started breathing through her mouth in reaction to the stench. The closed-up house still held the heat of the day, the foul-smelling air so heavy it felt like walking into a swamp.

Sidling along the rough plaster wall to her right, she peeked around it. The living and dining rooms were empty. She heard the distant sound of a toilet flushing. *Damn. Either Olivia's still up or the guy's still here.* After a long wait she saw an enormous figure—*a mountain man*—stumble through the kitchen doorway into the dining room. Retreating to the door, she flattened herself into the corner, a position that rendered her nearly invisible. She heard unsteady footsteps take him into the living room, followed by the creak of ancient plastic as his body settled on the yellowed sofa-covering that had protected the faded brocade furniture for untold decades. She waited several seconds, then moved along the wall to peer into the dimly lit living room again.

The mountain man sat on a sofa against the wall opposite the window. He was bent almost double, hands clamped to the sides of his head. The reek of alcohol and a fainter stench of vomit assailed her. *Bet he just emptied his guts into the toilet.* A wine bottle lay on the floor together with several needlework pillows she had previously seen piled on the rounded, Victorian sofa.

*Not a mountain man. Just looks like one with that long straggly hair, torn plaid shirt, enormous shoulders. Actually, more like a homeless person.* She pictured Olivia's face, eyes bright with panic, as she'd told Cassidy someone might be in her house. *Why the hell give her key to a bum like this?*

Deciding that a man who could barely hold his head up posed no real threat, Cassidy came around the entryway wall to stand in front of him. "Where's Olivia?"

# 3. Mountain Man and Mental Status

He moved his head carefully, squinting at her out of red-rimmed eyes. A few strands of greasy, iron gray hair stuck to his forehead. "Who're you?"

"A neighbor. If you don't tell me where Olivia is right now, I'm calling the police."

"Don't ask me." He let out a deep-chested, rattly cough. "I've been passed out God knows how long." He shook his massive head. "Is it late? Maybe she went to bed."

*Could she be asleep?* Cassidy knew the house lights usually blinked off at ten. *Maybe Olivia and this guy had an argument. She got scared and raised the blinds but he really wasn't threatening her. She went to her room, he crashed on the couch.*

"You ever want to go on a drunk, stay away from cheap red wine." The toe of one filthy tennis shoe nudged the bottle. "Guzzling anti-freeze'd be better than drinking that goddamned Thunderbird shit."

Cassidy examined him closely. *Really huge.* She remembered not being certain whether the figure in the living room was male or female. *How could I've had any doubts? This man's so big boned, he could never pass for anything but a guy.*

She glanced around the room, searching for evidence of damage or violence. Except for the mountain man's presence, everything appeared the same as when she'd been inside before. *Probably the same as when Olivia was born. Right here in this house. And the poor woman never escaped.* Cheap reproductions in elaborately carved frames hung in perfect alignment on the faded cabbage-rose wallpaper. A new television, the only object clearly purchased by Olivia herself, sat on its cabinet against the east wall, an old recliner positioned in front of it. Not a speck of dust. Everything in order.

*You just fabricated a life-threatening situation out of a briefly uncovered window and a guy too drunk to do anything worse than collapse on the couch.* She had two feelings at once and couldn't tell which was stronger, the wave of relief or the sense of being incredibly stupid.

The man hacked out another long cough.

*You should check the bedroom, make sure Olivia's safe, then get on out of here.* But a strong tug of curiosity held her in place. *How on earth did she ever get involved with this guy in the first place? Olivia's probably never going to speak to you again anyway. Long as you've already blown it, might as well see if you can get him to talk.*

"When did you come in?"

"Been drinking at least two days, lady. You think I have any idea when I arrived?"

"You must've scared the wits out of her when you walked in drunk."

Sitting straighter, he made an effort to focus on Cassidy. "Don't know if she was here or not. I might've come in earlier, before she got home."

*Really doesn't remember what he did.* She tilted her head, wondering what tack to take. "I haven't seen you around before. Have you and Olivia known each other long?"

"Why don't you ask her?" He blinked a couple of times. "No, wait. Don't say anything. She doesn't want people to know about me."

"Look, I'm her friend. I help feed the ferals. Since I found you drunk on her couch, you might as well explain how the two of you got together."

He stared at her in silence for several seconds, then said, his voice growing crisper, "She doesn't have friends. And she really doesn't want me talking about this."

*Looks like your average wino but doesn't exactly talk like one. No ain'ts or she-don'ts. Bet he's got some education.*

"If you won't tell me, I'll have to go wake Olivia. Because as far as I know, you're not supposed to be here."

"Shit." He rested his forearms on his legs. "Oh hell, why not? I don't much like secrets anyway. Secrets get you into trouble." He gazed at the floor, then looked up. "I was in Menard. She started writing me there a couple of years ago."

*Menard? That's a prison. Olivia had a convict pen pal? Does that mean he is dangerous after all?*

"Anyway, by the time I got out, it seemed like we'd known each other forever." He glanced at the closed-up window, then back at Cassidy, his brow furrowing in confusion. "But what're you doing here? She never lets neighbors in."

"I didn't think she let men in either." The tape of the suddenly exposed living room played in her mind again. "I was in front of her house when the blinds went up. I saw Olivia standing close to the window and . . ." She'd been about to say, "and you in the background," when it hit her. *This man's too big. Couldn't've been him.* Blinking, she gave her head a slight jerk. "And somebody standing in the background."

"Never would've happened." He shook his large head. "She'd sooner play Lady Godiva down the middle of Lake Street than raise those blinds. I've tried to get her to do it but she refused." He paused. "This dark old place gives me the creeps. It's like living in the hole."

Cassidy looked him in the eye. "She raised them because somebody scared her. To make it public so the person in the background wouldn't do anything to hurt her."

*Sound awfully sure of yourself for somebody operating out of pure guesswork.*

*Yeah, but why else would she do it?*

"You bring another guy in with you?" *Why ask? He doesn't know what he did.* "Or give out the key? Didn't you do something that scared her? You're not even supposed to be here. She told me."

"Yeah, but then she changed her mind." He pressed the heel of his hand against his forehead. "You have any idea what my head feels like? Why are you asking all these questions?"

*Olivia bringing this guy into her house is like a canary inviting a cat in for tea.* She felt the same maternal stirrings she'd had when Olivia came to her door two weeks earlier. "Because I don't want to see her taken advantage of."

"Of course you'd think that." He sighed heavily. "You probably won't believe this, but Olivia means the world to me. I don't know why I'm telling you. . . . Actually, I do know. I'd like to make you understand that telling Olivia you saw me here would not be in her best interest."

*This guy's good. Could be a used car salesman, voice ringing with sincerity as he gilds lemons into lilies.* "Okay, make me understand." She perched on the edge of a wingback chair, the plastic squeaking as her weight came down.

"When I went to prison, I thought my life was over. I figured I'd get out and just drink myself to death because there wasn't anything to live for anyway. Then Olivia started writing and I began to think there might be something for me after all. I joined AA and swore to myself that when I got out, I'd do my damndest to stay sober and prove to Olivia I could rebuild my life."

"Well, apparently you didn't succeed." She stared at the small brown stain on the threadbare carpet where drops of wine had spilled from the bottle.

He covered his face with his hands, sat without moving for a long moment, then looked up, his hooded eyes glistening. "I don't need you to tell me how bad I screwed up. This is my second relapse in eight months. The first time she got really scared, told me to get out of her life. But the next day I went to a meeting, got back on track, and after a while I was able to make her see that it was only a slip, that we could put it behind us and move on."

"So now you've gone on another bender. You came in drunk. You can't remember anything. There was somebody else in the house with Olivia when she raised the blinds. Probably some lowlife you brought in with you. And you want me *not* to tell her she should dump you ASAP?"

His eyes filled. Swiping the back of his hand across them, he said, "I'm not going to let this happen again. I'll go to meetings every day if I have to. Olivia's all I've got. My only reason for staying sober. If you tell her you know about me, the embarrassment'll be too much for her."

Picturing the look of panic on Olivia's face when she'd suggested calling the police, Cassidy winced.

"She's like this tiny, frightened bird perched in the palm of my hand, always fluttering her wings, ready to fly away. If she finds out you saw me here, she'd probably never be able to face either one of us again. Do you really want to see her crawl back into her shell? I can't guarantee I'll be able to take care of her—God knows I've got my own demons to fight. But if you stay out of it, there's at least a chance she might be able to have a life. Maybe together we could both have a life."

Although his eyes were faded and bloodshot, he met her gaze straight on. *Shouldn't've listened. You started off feeling like a mother tiger ready to yank Olivia out of his clutches. Now you're feeling like you ought to forget you ever met him.*

"The problem is, I can't just silently tiptoe away. I saw somebody else in here."

He shook his head. "That doesn't make sense. She never lets anybody in. Maybe it was me you saw."

"This guy wasn't anywhere near your size. So since I know somebody was here, I have to make sure he didn't do anything to her. I'll try to be quiet, but she may well see me. Which would probably be for the best, since secrets really *do* get you into trouble."

"Look, I really appreciate this." He let out a long sigh of relief. "She takes sleeping pills so there's a good chance you can get a quick peek in the bedroom without waking her." He stood, flexed his shoulders, squeezed the back of his neck. "You go check. I'll straighten up in here. If she's sleeping like I think she is, we can both get away without her knowing." He sighed. "Then tomorrow I can start trying to patch things up again." He reached for the pillows.

Cassidy started to turn, then saw something that riveted her gaze to the floor. A gun. It had been underneath one of the pillows and now lay in plain sight about a foot from the west end of the sofa. She pulled the pepper spray from her waistband, extended both arms, and pointed it at his face. "Don't touch that."

Shock registered on his features. "That's not mine. I didn't bring it in." He rubbed his eyes with his fists. "At least, I don't think I did. I never want to have a gun in my hands again."

*Again? What happened the last time?*

She wondered if his whole story could've been bullshit, if he might already have killed Olivia, be planning to kill her. Studying his face, she saw alarm growing in his eyes. *If he did do anything, he doesn't remember. Now stop worrying about yourself, go find Olivia.*

Cassidy pivoted and raced upstairs, his footsteps coming close behind. Olivia's bedroom was uninhabited, the bed neatly made, everything in its place.

Cassidy and the mountain man stared at each other.

He said, "Maybe she left the house."

"Her car's in the driveway."

"Jesus, we've gotta find her."

He started toward the stairs but he was still a little wobbly and Cassidy was faster. She swerved around him, dashed down the staircase, through the living and dining rooms, and into the kitchen. The basement door on the far end of the east wall was open. Cassidy had seen it before but had never gone down. Bamba sat beside an empty dish watching her.

The mountain man stopped just inches behind her. He spoke, his raspy voice coming from well above her head. "You stay here while I check it out."

"No," she said sharply, realizing she would vastly prefer to follow his suggestion but had some vague fear that if Olivia was dead or injured he might contaminate the evidence. Pushing against her own resistance, she crossed to the door, switched on the light, and gazed downward. The section she could see, the half flight to the landing, was empty. She could feel the large man hovering over her shoulder. Anxiety flashed through her at the thought of his huge hands slamming into her back, knocking her down the stairs.

At the landing, she peered cautiously around the corner of the L. Spotlighted under a bare bulb, Olivia's body lay in a pool of blood near the bottom step. Cassidy gasped and went numb.

A guttural moan came from the man behind her. Shoving Cassidy aside, he lumbered down the remaining stairs.

"Stop!" she yelled. "Don't touch her. If she's still alive, you could make it worse."

She watched helplessly as he lowered himself onto the concrete floor and cradled Olivia in his arms. From the awkward, stiff-limbed response of the body, Cassidy realized he could not make it worse because the worst had already happened. *All he'll do is destroy the crime scene.*

Hardly aware of her movements, she returned to the kitchen and picked up the receiver of the rotary phone on the counter. She stared at the dial as if she'd never seen one before. Watching her fingers poke awkwardly at the holes, she noted how strange it was not to be able to feel her hands or any other part of her body as it moved through space. It took a few tries, directing her hand entirely by sight, but eventually she managed to dial the numbers—9-1-1—and recite the address, adding as an afterthought, "It's Olivia's house. She's dead. The mountain man picked her up even though I told him not to."

Replacing the handset, she saw that all three of Olivia's cats now sat near their empty bowls, Bamba in the middle, an orange female on either side. They clumped together, not moving except for their constantly swiveling ears, their wide, anxious eyes fixed on Cassidy.

She removed a bag of dry nuggets from the cupboard and filled each dish, then sat on the floor beside them as they ate. "What's going to happen to you?" she asked, a terrible sadness coming over her as she contemplated the fate of the orphaned cats. "Olivia won't be here to take care of you any more. Nobody to pet you, brush you, talk to you." Tears brimmed in her eyes and trickled down her cheeks.

&#8486;  &#8486;  &#8486;

Cassidy sat in the back seat of a police car parked in front of the house. She had just delivered a summary of the night's events to the beat cop behind the wheel, a young black guy with a touch of attitude who'd introduced himself as Officer Barnes. Several other uniforms had congregated on the sidewalk, their squads extending from the corner halfway down the block. Cassidy's initial numbness was gone, replaced by a large lump in her stomach. *Numb was better. Sometimes it's good not to feel.*

Pushing a thick tangle of auburn hair back from her face, she said, "You're going to call a detective, right?" *See if you can get the one guy on the force who knows you. Maybe Manny'll take you seriously.*

He twisted around to look at her. In the dusky light, she saw a flash of annoyance cross his face. But he recovered instantly, the respectful attitude demanded of Oak Park cops sliding back into place. "Yes, ma'am. We'll have a couple of detectives over here in a few minutes."

"Is Manny Perez on tonight?"

"I wouldn't know."

Making herself sound humble, she said, "Manny's a friend of mine, and it'd really mean a lot if I could talk to him instead of a stranger. I mean, I'm feeling pretty shaky and a familiar face sure would help."

*Last time you saw him he chewed you out for playing lone gun.*

*Yeah, but he wasn't really mad. And he probably won't treat me like an interfering civilian who doesn't know what she's talking about.*

Speaking into his radio, the cop asked for Perez. "Neighbor who found the body says she's a friend of yours. Lady by the name of McCabe. She asked if you could catch the case."

Five minutes later a Ford sedan parked in front of Cassidy's house. Manny Perez and his partner, Lou Waicek, exited from the vehicle and joined the uniforms, who'd clustered in the driveway behind Olivia's car.

"You stay here," Barnes instructed as he went to join the newcomers.

He spoke to the detectives briefly. They disappeared into the house for a while, then returned to huddle with the uniforms again.

She peered into the squad behind hers, but with trees blocking the street light, it was too dark to see into the vehicle's back seat. *Wonder how the mountain man's holding up.* Barnes had appeared first, followed almost immediately by a second officer. The two cops had dragged the mountain man away from Olivia's body, then deposited Cassidy and the big man in separate cars.

She knew that any woman who started writing to an inmate was asking for trouble. Convicts who corresponded with lonely ladies usually had only one thing in mind: exploitation. Anyone who thought otherwise had failed to do their Ann Landers homework. *Majority of cons are sociopaths. And any sociopath worth his DSM diagnosis can charm your great-grandmother's wedding ring right off your finger.*

Majority doesn't mean all. The mountain man's not a sociopath—I'd bet my own wedding ring on it. She touched the gold and garnet circlet Zach had placed on her finger.

*You think therapists are immune to sociopathic wiles? You think you can't be conned just like anybody else?*

*There's no way he faked his reaction to seeing Olivia's body. And when he talked about wanting to get sober so they could have a life together—I've never heard anything that sounded more genuine.*

*That doesn't mean he didn't shoot her. He could have killed her in a drunken rage, gone into a blackout, and still been grief stricken when he saw the body.*

She went through the whole scenario in her mind, looking at it from all angles, trying to be as objective as possible in her assessment of the mountain man's innocence.

The figure in the living room was too small to be the drunk on the couch. Olivia had raised the blinds because she felt endangered by the unknown figure. She'd appeared shaken when she answered the door and the odds were the unknown person was standing behind her.

*It doesn't make sense to think the other person scared Olivia into opening the blinds, left the house, and then the mountain man killed her.* Cassidy shook her head. *It couldn't have been him.*

She scanned the activity around her. Police radios crackled. Mars lights flashed. People gathered in small clusters in the street. A teenager from the house south of Cassidy's poked his head in the car window to ask what had happened.

"Police said not to talk about it."

Tuning out the external noise, she shut her eyes and replayed the large man's voice in her mind. "Like this tiny, frightened bird perched in the palm of my hand." Sorrow welled up in her again: for the cats who'd lost their human, for the mountain man who'd lost his reason to get sober; for Olivia who'd lost her life just at the point when there might've been some love in it.

*And you could've stopped it,* yelled the voice that railed at her every misdeed. *Soon as you noticed the slightest hint of danger, you should've called the cops.*

*And why didn't you?* She knew that a preoccupation with her own concerns—the cat rescue project, the confrontation with Zach—had caused her to minimize the risk.

Clenching her teeth, she stared at Olivia's house in an effort to stop the accusatory voice clanging in her head. A large gray feral skulked through the bushes in front of the window. She watched intently, trying to determine which one it was. Olivia had given them all names, and during the months Cassidy'd joined her neighbor for the nightly feeding, she'd heard their stories and come to know them as individuals. *Gotta be Milton.* Milton was the granddaddy of the colony, an old tom with a gimpy front paw and a stump of an ear. But maimed though he was, the elderly cat still showed more gumption than any of his progeny.

Her whip-cracking voice screamed louder. *How could you be so selfish? Raising those blinds was a signal. If you'd only gotten it, she wouldn't be dead.*

Dropping her chin, Cassidy wished she could go hide in the basement the way she had as a child when her mother was mad.

*No point wallowing,* a calmer voice stepped in. *You made a terrible mistake. All you can do now is try to rectify it.*

She gazed at the cops conferring in the driveway behind Olivia's Cavalier. Perez, tall and lean, stood about ten feet away, his back to the squad car. Waicek, short and blocky, faced her, arms crossed over his chest. Barnes and two other uniforms filled out the group.

*How can I rectify anything with Olivia dead?* Her throat thickened. She pressed her fingertips to her temples. *Don't let it get worse. Find a home for her cats. Make sure the mountain man doesn't get convicted.*

She watched Milton creep around in front of Olivia's car.

*Need to check on the mountain man, see if he's okay. Cops won't let you near him. Perez might if you give him a good enough reason.*

As she started toward the group of police, Barnes called out to her, "Ma'am, you need to stay in the car."

Perez, wearing an elegant silk suit, turned to face her. "Sorry, Ms. McCabe, you'll just have to wait it out."

She stopped a yard's distance from Perez. "I've been trained in crisis intervention and mental status evals." *All of three role-plays in a class once.* "So it occurred to me I might be able to help by assessing the man I found in her house."

Waicek, the junior detective, had moved up next to Perez, his manner as unyielding and opaque as his refrigerator-shaped body. Compared to Perez's afghan sleekness, he reminded her of a churlish bulldog. He said in a curt voice, "Thanks, but we got our own people to do that kind of stuff."

Swallowing her anger, she maintained an even tone. "Yes, but none of your people are here. Won't you be interviewing that guy soon? Seems to me it'd be useful to know if he's psychotic or delusional before you start."

Perez stroked his jaw. "You could make that determination on the spot?"

Looking through her as if she wasn't there, Waicek said, "The guy's psychotic, I think we'd notice."

She fixed her gaze on Perez. "Sure, if it's full blown, you'd know. But a little delusion? Hard to tell. You could talk for hours and not pick up that his version of reality is slightly askew." *And you're going to ferret it out in ten minutes?*

"You're giving us quite a pitch, Ms. McCabe. Why so eager to talk to this guy?"

"I'd like to make sense out of what happened tonight. If he's paranoid and/or hearing voices, it could explain a lot." *Oh how the lies roll off. You don't for a minute think he's crazy. You just want to dig out everything you can in case you have to figure out who really did it.*

Perez regarded her thoughtfully. She noted that his angular, strong-boned face had a grim cast to it she hadn't seen before. There was no scarcity of crime in Oak Park, but it did not happen often that people were intentionally made dead. Although Perez was a seasoned detective, this might be his first time out as primary on a homicide.

"I suppose it wouldn't hurt. If the guy's looking at the world through weird-colored glasses, I'd just as soon know up front."

"Yeah, but she's not authorized," Waicek objected. "We can get the crisis worker from family service."

"Why get the crisis worker out of bed when we've got a social worker right on the scene? Besides, the last one we got from family service was an intern. Didn't know squat."

*Neither do I when it comes to mental status, but I bet I can fake it better than the intern.*

Perez looked at her. "Okay, let's do it. But you absolutely can't discuss the case—you got that?"

Waichek gave a disgusted snort. "If you're gonna mess around with the suspect, I'll get the guys started canvassing." He and the three uniforms walked away.

*Think you can nudge Perez a little further?* "Uh . . . as long as I'm talking to him, would it be okay if I asked about Olivia's next of kin?"

The detective's brows drew together. "What's that about?"

"I doubt that she's got anybody, but if she does, I'd like to write a note. Tell them how I found the body." *Plus a few other things there's no need to mention.*

"Hmm." He made a noise deep in his throat letting her know she was pushing the limit. "I guess it'd be all right."

They went to the squad where the mountain man was being held in back, a beat cop watching over him. Perez asked the uniform to step out, then ushered Cassidy into the front. She knelt on the car seat overlooking the back rest so she could face the mountain man, who'd crammed himself in by slanting his knees to the side, hunching his shoulders, and tucking in his elbows. Up close, the foul mix of alcohol, bad breath, and body odor made her stomach clutch. Perez seated himself behind the wheel and flipped on the dome light.

Cassidy took a deep breath. *You got yourself into this. Now let's see if you can approximate an evaluation.*

"Well," she said, "how you doing?"

"Just fine and dandy." His flat tone minimized the implied sarcasm. Although his face was fleshy, he had straight, well defined features, and his hooded eyes, red and watery though they were, displayed a gleam of intelligence. Noting the directness of his gaze, Cassidy began to see why Olivia might have been attracted.

"Why are you here?"

"I'm a social worker. I'd like to talk to you."

"A social worker, huh? I thought you were a neighbor."

"I'm both." She shifted slightly. "You going to hold it against me that I'm a social worker? I guess a lot of people in the prison system don't have much use for them."

He smiled fractionally. "Nah, I always liked the bleeding-heart types myself."

"What a night we've had." She chose her words carefully, wanting to touch on their shared experience without crossing into the forbidden territory of case discussion. "I can't begin to imagine how terrible this's been for you."

He raised a hand to shield his eyes.

*Acknowledging a person's pain usually makes it more intense but you still need to do it.* She said, "My name's Cassidy McCabe, and I'd like your permission to do an evaluation."

"Evaluate what?"

"Suicidality and orientation to reality."

"No and yes." He let out another phlemy cough.

"No, you're not suicidal and yes, you're oriented?"

He nodded.

*Quick and bright. Just what I expected.* "How can you tell if you're oriented to the same reality as the rest of us?"

"The name's Jake Streeter. I don't know what day it is 'cause I've been bingeing since Wednesday." He shook his head. "Damn! Talk about silver linings having black clouds. You know what got me started? A winning lotto ticket, that's what." His mouth turned down at one corner. "Now there's a piece of damn irony. After eight months with only one slip, I win twenty-five dollars on the lotto, everybody at the restaurant says you've got to celebrate, and off I go like the dumb shit I am."

"Okay, Jake, you know your name. You don't know what day it is. How 'bout telling me who's president?"

"Clinton's president, the Republicans've locked down Congress, and Olivia . . ." he lowered his head so she couldn't see his face, "and Olivia's dead."

# 4. Lonely Old Lady and Glomming Privileges

She raised both hands, palms out, to stop him. "Can't talk about what happened or Perez'll send us to our separate rooms."

"Sorry."

"Ever had a psychiatric hospitalization?"

"I'm not schizophrenic, not bipolar, not on meds, and I only get paranoid when I drink. I'm just a flat-out drunk who never even had sense enough to check himself into rehab."

"Well, you certainly breezed through this evaluation of mine. What are you, anyway? A psychiatrist?"

"I used to be a history teacher at Purdue but I've changed professions. My current employer is Popeye's Chicken on Madison."

She heard a slight sound from Perez, which she took to be a suppressed chuckle. "Tell me about the paranoia when you drink."

"Paranoia." He met her gaze, then looked away. "You think that's what happened? I got paranoid and killed her?"

She heard the fear in his voice. *Afraid he did it?* Raising her hands quickly, she said, "Can't talk about it. So, you've been paranoid in the past, is that right?"

"I don't think it was real paranoia. More like rationalization and denial." He sighed heavily. "I suppose you want me to tell you about it."

"Would you?"

"It happened in my previous life. Before everything fell apart." He paused. "Before I made everything fall apart." His gaze moved off into space and stayed there so long she began to wonder if he had some kind of dissociative disorder.

Finally he went on. "I killed my best friend. I thought he was having an affair with my wife but he wasn't. He kept coming around the house, badgering me about my drinking. He said Marion had asked him to talk some sense into me but I refused to believe it. I had to invent some other, perverted reason for his showing up all the time. So I convinced myself that he and Marion were sleeping together." A look of anguish came over his face. "And then, the next time I went on a drunk, I got hold of a gun and shot him."

*God, what would it be like to be inside this man's skin?* She tried to imagine how it would feel to know you'd killed a friend whose only crime was visiting too often in his effort to help. *Like drinking carbolic acid for breakfast every morning, that's what.*

"And you *aren't* suicidal? How do you manage not to be?"

"Pure cowardice. When I was awaiting trial, I used to entertain fantasies about offing myself but I never had the balls to do it."

"Were there any other times you thought somebody was your enemy, somebody was against you?"

He gave her a small, sad smile. "When I'm sober, people usually like me. Even when I'm polluted, my fellow drunks welcome me into their clan."

"Ever think of yourself as a special person?"

"Actually, I was beginning to think of myself as someone who might be able to break down Olivia's walls. I suppose there's a certain hubris in that."

"No voices? No hallucinations?" She thought a moment. "Ever have blackouts when you're not drinking?"

"Sorry to disappoint you, but none of the exotic labels apply." The sad smile reappeared. "All you've got here is a garden variety drunk who's just won himself another all-expense paid trip to a quaint little villa downstate."

Cassidy searched her brain for other lines of inquiry but no questions marched up and declared themselves.

Perez cleared his throat. "You done?"

*Oh yeah, I know.* She glanced at the detective. "Next of kin?"

He nodded.

She said to Jake, "You happen to know if Olivia had any relatives?"

*Not likely, considering I haven't seen a single visitor in the past twelve years.*

"Yeah, there is one. An aunt—lives right here in Oak Park. The name, um . . ." he rubbed his forehead, "Esther Dvorak."

*An aunt who never comes to the house? Doesn't care for cat pee?* "Were they close?" Cassidy asked quickly, sneaking it in before Perez could cut her off.

"I'm not sure how to call it." He moved his large head from side to side. "Sometimes Olivia made it sound like they were tight. Other times, she seemed almost to hate the woman."

Perez said, "Okay, guys, that's enough." He stepped out and opened Cassidy's door. "Sorry, but I've got to take you back to the squad." As they walked toward the car she'd been in before, he added, "I gather we don't have anything to worry about."

"Not at the moment, although I wouldn't rule out suicidal impulses in the future."

Perez opened the squad's passenger door but instead of getting inside she turned to face him. "If I'd called the cops the minute the blinds went up, this probably wouldn't've happened."

Leaning in slightly, he said, "Don't beat yourself up. You did better than most."

*Hate that condescending, don't-feel-guilty attitude.* "Anyway, there're a couple of things I'd like to do for Olivia. To make up for not calling sooner."

He stood straighter. "And would these by any chance be things better left to the police? You're not planning on giving us any trouble this time, are you, Ms. McCabe?"

"I'd like to look after Olivia's cats, see if I can find homes for them. That is, if the aunt doesn't want them. Her cats were like children to her." *Are you nuts? Digging up takers for Starshine's cuddly kittens almost did you in. How'll you ever get rid of three full grown, less than adorable felines?*

"So you want the cats." His tone let her know that he was humoring her, that he had a murder to solve and cats were the last thing on his mind."

"No, I don't want the cats. But if animal control picks them up, they'll be euthanized. What I'd really like is to feed them at Olivia's place for a few days while I try to find new homes. How long will her place be sealed?"

"Until after the autopsy. We might be able to unseal it as early as tomorrow."

She leaned against the police car. "So if it's okay with the aunt, I could leave them in their own house while I look for new owners?" *You're definitely not taking them home with you. Starshine'd have conniptions and your place'd start smelling like Olivia's.*

"Once we turn the key over to the aunt, whatever happens at the house is between you and her." He paused. "You said there were two things."

"I'd like to go with you when you break the news to the aunt."

The expression that came over his face was: What the hell's the matter with you. The word out of his mouth was: "Why?"

She screened out her first three responses. *I want to meet the aunt. I want to come back later and pump her. I want to find out who that other guy in the living room was.*

Instead she said, "Since I work with people in crisis, I could help ease the shock."

"Let me think about it." He turned and headed toward the house.

Sliding into the car, she knew she was in for a bad night. *Just past midnight. Going to be up till dawn and most of it's going to be waiting time.* Waiting ranked right up there with root canals on her list of least favorite things. Waiting for Perez to finish at the crime scene, waiting for someone to take her statement at the police station, and the worst, waiting for Zach, not knowing if he would appear as the supportive guy who loved her or the hostile guy who wanted her out of his way.

&#8359;   &#8359;   &#8359;

At one a.m. Perez came to get her. "When offered the choice of giving a death notification or letting you stand in for him, Lou decided he could tolerate a little irregularity."

Buckling herself into Perez's blue Ford, Cassidy said, "Would you let me be the one to say the actual words?"

He flashed a grin, his straight white teeth dazzling against his café au lait skin. "You really ought to see a shrink about this guilt problem of yours."

*What's wrong with you? You've got no experience in this kind of thing. Informing someone of a murder—even an aunt who never visits—what a miserable job to take on.*

*Punishing yourself. You should turn Catholic so you could do it right, Hail Marys instead of assuming guardianship for cats and becoming a bad-tidings bearer.*

She glanced at Perez, remembering how impressed she'd been when he handled a case involving one of her clients. He'd struck her as a classy kind of guy, surprisingly empathic, with a taste for elegant attire that far surpassed her own second-hand, shades of purple wardrobe. After interviewing her, he'd issued an invitation to lunch, which she'd declined, even though at the time her relationship with Zach appeared to be on the skids. Since then, she'd occasionally wondered, especially during times like this, if rejecting the detective and sticking with Zach had constituted a wrong-turn in her life.

*What with Zach groping bimbos, maybe you ought to reconsider. Look at this as a second chance at Perez, see if you can lure him into bed.*

*I'd never pull it off. I'm doomed to remain forever locked into the pitiful role of the cheated-upon, never destined to move up to the more prestigious role of cheater. Unfairly coded with true-blue, loyalty-bordering-on-insanity genes.*

Perez parked in front of a brick house set close to the sidewalk, its windows dark, its lawn flat and treeless, the property well lit by a nearby street lamp. Beside the dwelling was a detached garage, a small sedan in the driveway. The house was located in the three-block strip of village domain between the Eisenhower Expressway and Roosevelt Road. This narrow band was looked upon as something of a stepchild, its houses smaller and more humble than the dwellings in the main section of Oak Park. The more snobbish-minded thought of this corridor as an adjunct to Berwyn, a community many Oak Parkers looked down on as ethnic, blue-collar, and conservative, not nearly as progressive and urbane as the village.

*The main downside to being an Oak Parker is how full of ourselves we sometimes get.*

Approaching the small front porch, Cassidy noticed weeds growing through cracks in the concrete walk. It reminded her that her own weeds had started spreading like germs ever since Zach went from yardman and helpmate to undercover narc.

The doorbell was missing, two wires protruding from a hole where it should have been, so Perez banged on the oak front door with his fist. Within a minute the porch light blinked on and a male face appeared in the door's window. Perez flashed his badge and the door opened.

A man in a beige robe, early thirties, stared at them drowsily. He had thick brown hair that stood out in odd clumps from sleep and a pleasant boyish face. Giving his head a shake, he said, "What's going on?"

Perez asked, "Is Esther Dvorak here?"

"She's asleep. What is it?" His voice faltered slightly. "Something wrong?"

*Nobody ever wants to see a cop at their door in the middle of the night.*

"May we come in?"

The man stepped aside. They entered a small living room with a kitchen to the right. Perez introduced himself and Cassidy, then asked, "Are you Ms. Dvorak's son?"

"I'm her caregiver. We're not related." He paused. "My name's Danny Kline."

*A live-in caregiver?* Cassidy scanned the scruffy old sofa, the paper bags piled in corners, the cracked side window. The air was thick and musty, reminding her of sludgy, green water. *She one of those rich old ladies with bats in the belfry and money under the mattress?*

Perez asked, "Anyone else living here?"

Danny shook his head. "She's a widow." Worry flickering in his light blue eyes, he added, "You still haven't said what this is about."

The detective glanced at the hall leading to the rear of the house. "I'm afraid we have some bad news. Is Ms. Dvorak an invalid?"

"Bad news? But she doesn't have anybody except Olivia." A startled look came over Danny's face. "It's Olivia, isn't it?" His expression clouded with anxiety. "God, I hope it isn't serious. Olivia always seems so . . . I don't know . . . delicate, not quite able to cope." He tugged the belt of his robe tighter, then let his hands fall to his sides. "I'd hate to see anything happen to her. And Esther—why she'd just fall apart."

"So, is Ms. Dvorak confined to her bed or could she come out and talk to us?"

"I'm sorry, I didn't answer your question." Danny said in a clear, educated voice. "Esther's not an invalid at all. She comes and goes whenever she wants. Still driving, even. But she gets pretty confused at times and she does need someone to make sure she takes her medication."

*A professional sounding guy like this handing out pills?* Creasing her brow, Cassidy asked, "So, is this your full time job?"

"Actually, I've almost got my degree in architecture. This is just an arrangement that happened to work out for both of us. I get free room and board plus pocket change. Esther gets her grass mowed and the looking after she needs."

Perez slid his hands into his jacket pockets. "Is she at risk for any kind of medical emergency if she hears about the loss of her niece?"

"The loss? Oh my God! You mean Olivia's dead?" His face twisted. He looked away, apparently struggling for control. After a moment he took a deep breath and returned his gaze to the detective. "Her heart's sound. Ester's going to take this really hard but it won't kill her or anything."

He turned and disappeared into a rear hallway, emerging minutes later with his hand beneath the elbow of a tall woman who appeared to be in her seventies. Wearing a shapeless robe over a thin cotton nightie, Esther had a doughy face with stringy gray hair, a lumpy nose and long upper lip above a large-framed, amply-bosomed body.

Assessing the two figures, Cassidy decided that both were what she would call average. *Either one could've been the person I saw.*

As Danny guided her toward the sofa, the elderly woman demanded in a rusty-hinge voice to know why he'd gotten her up in the middle of the night. He settled her on the ratty cushion, then stood off to the side.

Cassidy glanced at Perez, who signaled with a nod that she could step in. Sitting beside the old woman on the crumb-littered sofa, she introduced herself as Olivia's neighbor. The hunched body next to her gave off a sour, unwashed odor. *Why do you do these things to yourself?*

Esther's colorless eyes moved constantly. "Something bad's happened, hasn't it?" Her voice went screechy with alarm. "You gotta tell me. What is it? What's happened?"

"Why don't you let me hold your hands?"

She allowed Cassidy to grasp her clawlike talons.

"That's right. Now take a deep breath, just like I'm doing."

Esther followed her lead.

"That's good. Now just keep breathing." Cassidy drew in a lungful of air, exhaled, and said, "I know this is going to be very painful . . ." Her words took on the same slow cadence as the rise and fall of her chest. "But Olivia's been hurt—"

"What is it? What happened?" Esther's voice dropped to a lower pitch, mirroring Cassidy's.

"Somebody came into Olivia's house . . . with a gun . . . and shot her."

"She's not dead, is she?" Esther jerked her hands loose, then grabbed Cassidy's right arm, her knobby fingers digging in. "Oh God, oh please, tell me she's not dead."

Danny headed for the kitchen.

"I'm sorry to say she is." Patting the hand on her arm, Cassidy added, "This must be a terrible shock."

"Uh, uh, uh . . ." Esther let out small hiccoughing sounds, the noise children make when on the verge of crying. Her hands grasped vaguely at the air.

Danny returned to kneel in front of Esther, wrapping her arthritic fingers around a glass of water. She gulped greedily, then clasped her arms around the young man's neck. "She's dead, Danny. Our Olivia's dead." She buried her face in his shoulder and sobbed loudly.

Rising on his knees, he rubbed her back and made soothing sounds. When she finally quieted, he perched on the sofa arm next to her and held her hand.

"Oh Danny, I'm so glad you're here. What would I do without you? Olivia was the only one left and now she's gone."

Pulling her hand out of his, Esther turned to Cassidy. "He's a sweet boy, but it's not the same. Olivia was my sister's child, my own blood. And these men, they never really understand. Now you'd understand, wouldn't you, if I needed someone to talk to? You're a sweet girl, I can tell. You care about people, like my Olivia did."

*She wants glomming privileges. You don't need twenty calls a day from a lonely old lady.*

*Can't you show a little compassion? Besides, you're planning to pump her for information.*

Esther's callused, sandpapery hand started stroking Cassidy's arm as if she were a pet. Cassidy cringed slightly but didn't pull away. The old woman said, "Your skin's so soft, just like mine when I was young." She chuckled. "You wouldn't know it now but I used to be quite a looker. Men were falling all over themselves. What did you say your name was? Carrie something?"

"Cassidy McCabe."

"Such a pretty name. Will you call and talk to me on the phone sometimes the way Olivia did? And bring me treats? Olivia always used to bring me kolacky and I'd make tea." Her voice turned pleading. "You'll come see me, won't you?"

Cassidy felt the same pang she experienced whenever her mother wanted something she was reluctant to give. "I'll call you tomorrow," she said firmly. "Now there's one other thing. You know about Olivia's cats, don't you?"

Esther's voice turned venomous. "She should never've started feeding those strays. Disgusting." She made a spitting sound. "They ruined her nice house. I told her not to but she wouldn't listen."

*She just flipped. Turned on a dime. Went from victim to persecutor in the blink of an eye.*

Removing the talonlike hand from her arm, Cassidy laid it in Esther's lap. "Olivia gave me a key and I'd like to go into her house to feed her cats for a few days. Would that be all right?"

"You should let them starve. Filthy creatures. There's no reason to waste good food on them."

Unclenching her teeth, Cassidy said in an even tone, "May I have permission to go inside and feed her cats?"

Esther hesitated, then said, "Oh, all right. You will call, won't you?"

Stepping closer, Perez told Esther he was sorry for her loss, then added, "As soon as the house is unsealed, we'll need to turn the key over to someone who can take responsibility for her property. Do you feel up to handling that or is there someone else we should give it to?"

She brushed at the air with both hands. "I don't want nothin' to do with that disgusting place. All those cats—it stinks like my grand-daddy's outhouse."

"Then who could act on your behalf?"

"You can throw the key away for all I care." She turned to Danny. "I'm tired. I don't want to talk about it anymore. You go make some tea so I can get back to sleep." Standing, she turned her back on Cassidy and Perez and started toward the hallway.

"Ms. Dvorak," Perez said in an authoritative tone, "I need the name of someone who can take charge of Ms. Mallory's property."

Danny, now standing also, said, "That would be her attorney . . . uh, Carl something or other. He was her godfather and he handled all her affairs. I can get his name and number for you."

Turning toward Danny, Esther said, "I'm sleepy. You go fix my tea first."

Danny patted her hand. "Olivia's been murdered and we have to take that seriously. Let me give the detective the information he needs, then I'll make your tea."

   &#8359;  &#8359;  &#8359;

Perez's Ford pulled into the parking lot facing village hall, a yellow brick structure erected in the early seventies. Cassidy approved of the building's sharp angles, large round windows, and canted exterior walkway. She also approved of the purpose behind its placement in the southeast section of the village, the area most at risk for white flight when the new hall was constructed.

Back then, Oak Park's future was still very much in doubt. The west side of Chicago had recently undergone a devastating, block by block change from middle-class white to inner-city black. Some Oak Parkers were fleeing to the far west suburbs. Others were crusading for civil rights and open housing. The leadership, taking a middle ground, vowed to manage integration, to oversee a gradual, gentle change from solid-white to integrated.

By investing millions in a dramatic new municipal building a mere two blocks west of Austin Boulevard, the government had made it clear it was putting its money where its mouth was.

   &#8359;  &#8359;  &#8359;

Cassidy sat at a table across from Perez in the brightly lit, window-less interrogation room. She talked and he took notes. "I'm convinced

Jake didn't do it. He probably came in and passed out some time before Olivia and the killer even arrived. Either that or he met the killer at a bar and brought the guy into the house with him." She tried to read Perez's strong-boned face but his expression remained impassive.

"So what would be the motive for this other person killing her? There's no sign of robbery. We'll check for rape but from the looks of the body I'd say the shooter never touched her."

"Maybe robbery was the intent but the killer didn't find anything worth taking." She pictured Olivia standing at her back door, the stone on her finger glimmering under the porch light. "Her sapphire ring was the only thing I know of that had any value. Was it still on her hand when you examined the body?"

He shook his head. "No jewelry of any kind. Was she wearing the ring when she answered the door earlier?"

"I couldn't tell. But I've never seen her without it."

"Maybe it'll show up somewhere in the house." Leaning back in his chair, Perez tapped his pen against the pad. "You say the deceased never let anybody in except Streeter, and there's no sign of forced entry. I suppose it's possible the ex-con could've brought somebody in with him, but unless we have a serial killer on our hands, we're back to robbery as the only motive. So why shoot her and not ransack the house? If we eliminate the stranger-from-a-bar theory, how would this other person have gotten in?"

"He waited for her car, intercepted her, and either persuaded or forced her to take him inside."

"I've got officers canvassing the neighborhood. Maybe we'll come up with something to corroborate your statement."

"This person would not have been out pacing in the middle of the street."

Perez sat forward, apparently ready to end the interview.

"Look, I've given you two solid reasons for taking Jake off the suspect list. First, the fact that someone other than Jake scared her into raising the blinds, and second, the fact that the ring appears to be missing. If it doesn't turn up in Jake's pocket or her jewelry box, then it had to be somebody else who removed it."

"How much time elapsed between when you talked to her at the door and when you came back later to go in the house?"

She thought for a moment. "About an hour and a half."

"Plenty of time for Jake to whack her, take the ring to a fence, come back in and collapse on her couch."

"That doesn't make sense."

"You expect drunks to make sense?"

"So, are you going to ignore my statement about the other person in the house and put all your effort into building a case against Jake?"

"This is neither a witch hunt nor a Ken Starr investigation—if there's any difference between the two. We'll proceed as always, which means gathering all the available evidence before we charge anybody." He closed his notepad.

*But what if nothing else turns up? What if they've already got everything they're going to get?*

"I have one more question. If it turns out that Jake's fingerprints are on the gun, he doesn't remember what happened, and I'm the only one who saw this other person, would you go ahead and arrest him?"

"I suppose it's your theory that the killer shot the Mallory woman while Streeter was unconscious, then put Streeter's fingerprints on the gun."

"The only reason for the gun to show up next to the sofa is that the killer intended to frame Jake."

Perez gazed into space.

*Least he's not blowing you off. Manny's a good cop. You should get out of his way, let him do his job.*

*Yeah, but the last time I saw him, doing his job meant trying to nail the wrong person.*

Perez's intelligent brown eyes met hers. "It wouldn't be clear-cut. The prints and the blackout would weigh against the con, but you're a reliable witness and we'd have to take your statement into account. At this point I couldn't call it."

# 5. The Cat Lady Vacancy

It was nearly three a.m. by the time a squad car dropped Cassidy off at her back gate. The lights were on in Olivia's house and a sedan with EVIDENCE TECHNICIAN printed on the side was parked in front; except for that, everything appeared normal. Starshine bounced down from the stoop and ran to greet her, then trotted off to do her bug-jumping dance in the shaggy grass. The yardwork had gone undone ever since Zach started his dirty cop investigation, and even though the growth typically slowed during the midsummer dry spell, three weeks was long enough to turn a tidy lawn into an incipient prairie.

*Zach won't be home for at least another hour. Falling asleep's about as likely as John Grisham's developing writer's block.* She felt edgy and wired, as if she'd been mainlining caffeine, her thoughts spluttering and disconnected.

Standing on the stoop, she called "Kitty, kitty," then watched the calico continue her lovely, graceful arcs as if Cassidy hadn't spoken. *Starshine's ignoring you. The ferals never come.* The fuzzy workings of her mind rendered up an odd thought. Now that Olivia was gone, would she, as Olivia's assistant, have to take on the mantle of neighborhood cat lady? Would she be required to get eccentric and weird, live alone, and devote her life to feline tending?

*Best to take a pass on the cat-lady vacancy, but that doesn't mean I have to let my old buddies starve.*

She went inside to get the gallon jug of dry food she'd used to augment Olivia's supply. Cassidy had assumed her neighbor had money, having seen a lawn service truck arrive year after year to whisk Olivia's yard into a state of manicured perfection. But after they'd started talking, she'd learned that Olivia made only a small salary as a lab tech and in fact lived in a state of constant desperation over finances.

The lawn service, in Cassidy's opinion a luxury, was deemed a necessity by Olivia, whose yard and house constantly overwhelmed her. After hearing about her neighbor's money woes, Cassidy began making sizable donations to the supply of little brown nuggets so greedily gobbled by the ferals.

Locking the door behind her, she felt a sharp and familiar pang in her right ankle. She kicked at Starshine, who raced off to crouch in the grass and await another opportunity to jump her. Cassidy scowled at the calico. "You think socializing with the ferals is fine for you, but you don't want me going anywhere near them. You especially don't want me giving them food. Which you think belongs entirely to you. Actually, you think everything belongs entirely to you."

Ever since Cassidy'd begun assisting with the nightly feeding, Starshine had done everything in her power to express opposition. Any time Cassidy picked up the dry-food jug, she was vulnerable to sneak attacks.

She started toward the bungalow, her stomach twitching nervously. As she crossed Briar, the calico dashed ahead, then abruptly zoomed in front of her feet, clearly attempting to trip her. Watching every step, Cassidy proceeded up the short drive and around the rusted Cavalier. As they approached the gate between the house and the garage, Starshine dropped into her low-slung stalking position, ready to go to war with the ferals over ownership of Cassidy and the dry food, which she refused to eat when it was poured into her bowl at home.

Pausing, Cassidy pictured an indistinct figure, average height and weight, slinking through the gate and flattening itself against the garage. *Came up behind her just as she was unlocking the door. Forced her to let him inside. Saw Jake out cold on the sofa and decided a drunk guy'd fit very nicely into his scheme.*

She went through the gate into the shadowy yard. Enclosed by a six-foot fence with overgrown bushes sprawling around the edges, this space made her feel almost as claustrophobic as the shuttered house. But Olivia had needed her fence and her blinds, and both had proven useful when it came to sneaking in a very large, very noticeable man on a frequent basis.

Cassidy knew exactly the route Jake had taken. He'd entered the alley at the north end of the block, come into the yard through the alley gate, and gone into the house through the back door. The only person who could have seen him once he was on Olivia's property was the widower next door whose second-story windows overlooked Olivia's yard. And the widower, a member of the village fire and police commission, hadn't seen him, because if he had he would've called the cops.

Hearing a low growl, she looked down to see Starshine on the ground ahead of her pointing her flattened, jungle-cat body at two ferals who'd just appeared on the porch feeding station. Scanning the yard, Cassidy observed several other stealth-creatures melting away from the black spaces beneath the shrubbery. Whenever Cassidy or Olivia came to feed them, they crept one by one out of their hiding places and moved silently toward the bowls on the porch.

Starshine, no more than half the size of a full-grown feral, puffed her fur, arched her back, and took mincing sideways steps, her performance accompanied by an awesome display of snarly noises. The other cats paid no attention. The small calico had been throwing hissy fits since Cassidy's first trip to her neighbor's yard but had the good sense never to stray far from her human's feet.

Breathing through her mouth as she approached the foul-smelling porch, Cassidy rattled food into the assorted bowls, then got out of the way as the cats pushed, shoved, and bit an occasional ear in their frenzy to grab it up. A half-grown tiger-stripe, one of the two kittens from the first litter of the season, bapped the nose of a cadaverous feral, the sickly-looking feline skulking off to wait until the melee calmed down. Olivia had told Cassidy that the striped cat was female, and that her sibling had disappeared shortly after leaving the nest. *The life of a feral, unlike the life of a spoiled and pampered Starshine, is no cruise on a luxury liner.*

Homeless cats led a dire and precarious existence. They died of lingering diseases. They died of cold. They ate dinner on the porch at night and were never seen again. The desperation of their lives was what had spurred Cassidy to spend her summer stalking kittens. With the help of Olivia and Zach she had captured all but the first two, delivering them to shelters where generous volunteers rid them of fleas and ringworm, accustomed them to human contact, then sent them off to new homes.

The tiger-stripe rubbed her body against an orange tom, flicked her tail, and jumped down from the porch. Cassidy wished she could reach out and pet her but knew the least movement in the cat's direction would send her flying.

A late arrival emerged from the darkness, a familiar tom with an unsteady gait and a stub of an ear. Sitting erect a few feet from the bottom step, Milton stared straight at her. As she gazed into his wide, iridescent eyes, she had the eerie feeling he was reading her mind.

*What with Olivia's murder and these new catly responsibilities you've inherited, your unconscious is going nutso. You better get out of here before you see Scully and Mulder walking through walls.*

She returned to her house, Starshine jauntily leading the way, and wrote a note for Zach:

> Olivia was murdered and I found her body. I need to talk. I'd appreciate it if you could dispose of the undercover guy and get your normal self back in control before coming upstairs.

&#8483;   &#8483;   &#8483;

Cassidy sat in bed with a book, her eyes on the words, her mind elsewhere. Starshine, curled next to her, raised her head, stared through the open doorway, then trotted downstairs. *Zach's home.* The bureau clock said four-thirty. She wondered how long she'd have to wait before he shed his jerk persona and arrived in the bedroom.

*Hate what he's doing.*

*Oh, that's good. He'll come upstairs all ready to be comforting and you'll bite his head off.* Knowing that when she approached him the right way, Zach was quite good about talking, she forced herself to tune down the volume on her resentment.

At five-fifteen Zach walked into the room carrying two glasses of his usual bourbon and soda. She studied his face, noting with relief that the familiar, easygoing expression was back in place.

"How you doing?" He handed her a glass.

"It's morning. I never drink in the morning."

"It's nighttime for me." Dropping his clothes on the floor, he sat on the bed and pulled his knees up tight. She came around to rest her back against his bent legs, her body slanted so their faces were merely inches apart. As she moved closer, she picked up all the usual clubby smells, including something minty she didn't recognize and the musky perfume that had aroused her old jealousy demons the night before. *Don't say anything,* she warned herself sharply. *Nagging won't help.*

Taking a swallow, she realized she was glad he'd simply given her the drink without her having to admit she needed it. "What a night." She shook her head dazedly. "I met a drunken mountain man, I sat and cried with Olivia's orphaned cats, and I looked into the eyes of a feral who read my mind." She went on from there to recount the evening's events.

When she finished, Zach lowered his brows and said, "Olivia had a convict pen pal? She gave him a key and let him stay at her house?" He shook his head. "What the hell was the matter with her?"

"At first I couldn't believe it either, but now I see it makes perfect sense. When I was trying to make friends with her, she kept swinging back and forth. Sometimes she'd seem delighted to see me, like she was lonely, almost desperate for company. Then she'd get scared and act really suspicious, as if she thought I was out to steal the gold from her teeth."

"Okay, I get it. She could feel connected through the letters but figured she'd never have to see the guy face to face. But then, why didn't her paranoia kick in once he was out?"

"I'll bet she fell in love with the fantasy the letters created in her mind while he was safely behind bars. Then, when he was released, how could she resist seeing him? I'm sure there were times she did get scared. I even saw her panic once because she thought Jake was in her house. But since he thought of her as this frightened little bird, he undoubtedly was cautious in his approach. And even though she went through the same kind of swings with him as she did with me, her urge for closeness was winning out."

Starshine jumped up and climbed onto Zach's chest, her motor throbbing.

He gazed into space. "You know, I think I can relate. Before you came along I was doing similar swings, just not so extreme. I liked having a girlfriend around for sex and Saturday night dates, but as soon as she wanted anything more, I was off and running." He began massaging the back of Cassidy's neck. Starshine, who preferred her humans to remain immobile during her occupancy, abandoned Zach's chest, retreated to the foot of the bed, rolled over and went to sleep with all four paws in the air.

"You haven't done your backing off routine in ages. But now I've got this hostile part to contend with." She frowned and chewed on her lip. "You know, I think I could cope better if I had a little more understanding of how you go in and out."

He shook his head slightly. "When I'm getting ready to turn myself into this wannabe dealer, I have to erase all my normal thought patterns. I've got to put you, Starshine, the job out of my head and get myself to thinking like this two-bit hood who wants to be an operator. The kind of guy I'd prefer to see locked up. But then, once I'm into it, it takes on a life of its own that's hard to shake."

"So how did you pull out tonight?"

"Sat on the porch, sipped a drink, blanked out my mind. When I'm doing the undercover gig, I have to be totally focused, so getting relaxed is how I turn it off."

*Drinks too much.*

*Look—you decided a year ago—it's not a problem.*

*That was before he started spending every night in a place where all anyone does is drink and drug.*

Shortly before they were married, Zach's life had been turned upside down by the arrival of a teenage son he didn't know existed, the murder of the boy's mother, and a homicide investigation that centered on Zach as the chief suspect. Despite extreme stress, he'd navigated that period without letting his primary vice get permanently out of control. His ability to rein in his drinking after the crisis was over had convinced her it was not something she needed to worry about.

She pressed her lips together, trying not to ask, but it slipped out anyway. "How much *are* you drinking?"

He said in a gentle voice, "We've been over this before."

"I know, but I need reassurance. I'm feeling very insecure."

"It's not that much. I'd like to cut loose and just party along with the others, but I've decided not to and I won't. I've also decided not to do anything I couldn't tell you about, which is why you don't need to worry."

"I trust *you* completely but the undercover guy's another story." She stared through the north window. A pearly light had risen, illuminating the thick leaves on her maple, and behind that, the peaked roof of Olivia's house. "This guy's my enemy and I need to know what I'm up against."

He rested his hand on her thigh. "You're beginning to sound really weird, you know that?"

"It's been a really weird night."

"I'm sorry I wasn't able to be with you."

She felt a sudden stinging at the back of her lids. "It's good for me to handle things on my own for a change."

"Why should you? You're not alone any more. Neither of us is."

She laid her outspread hand on his chest. "I've missed you. I feel like such a baby, whining about it when it's only been three weeks."

"It's been too long for me too." Drawing her closer, he said, "I've missed our time together. Missed touching you, holding you." He brought his mouth down against hers. "Missed making love."

ಐ  ಐ  ಐ

Afterward they lay together, her face on his shoulder, their legs intertwined. Turning his head away, he muttered, "I need a cigarette."

It struck her as odd, since he'd quit before they met and seldom mentioned it. But, having more urgent matters to consider, her mind veered off in another direction.

*You didn't tell him everything.*

*Too late. Both too tired. Sleep first, talk later.*

*You're just trying to weasel. You promised not to go behind his back any more. Besides, if you sneak around and get in trouble, you won't be in any position to yell at him when he does the same.*

Separating herself, she rose on one elbow. "I probably ought to mention that I'm thinking of doing a little checking around on my own. See what I can find out about that person in her living room. I can't just stand by and watch Jake get convicted, you know." Sighing, she continued. "And I really feel like I ought to do something about the ferals and the house cats too." She paused. "I suppose you think this is more than any sane person would take on."

"Well, no one's ever accused you of being sane, have they?" He lay on his back and stared at the ceiling. "I don't need this now."

She gritted her teeth briefly, then said, "This has nothing to do with you. I was merely informing you. Because you've been irritated on previous occasions when I failed to give proper notification. I don't expect you to *do* anything."

Rolling onto his side, his eyes concerned, he said, "What in the world would make you take so much on yourself?"

"I just feel like I need to do it."

"C'mon, Cass. That's not good enough."

"Mostly it's feeling responsible, feeling like I could've prevented it."

"You know that's ridiculous, don't you?"

Her eyes filled. "Zach, when those blinds went up I had this really strong gut feeling that Olivia was in danger. Then I talked myself out of it because I wanted to get on with that fight I was itching to have with you."

He ran the back of his fingers over her cheekbone. "I really don't like the idea of you investigating a murder when I won't be around to work with you or make sure you're okay." He paused. "Are you certain you're not doing this to get even?"

She took a moment to focus on the different voices inside her head. "Actually, there is a connection with you, but it's just wanting to distract myself, needing to keep my mind from conjuring up unpleasant images." A picture of Zach with a reptilian, Lolita-like creature wrapped around him popped into her head.

Shifting onto her stomach, she jammed a pillow under her chest. "There's also a piece that has to do with Jake. There's something about him that draws me. This sense of the terrible price he's paid for killing his friend. If he ends up believing he murdered Olivia too, it'll be all over for him. He did a dumb thing going off on a binge like that, but he doesn't deserve to have the rest of his life ruined because of a relapse. I want to see him cleared."

"You're basing an awful lot on one quick glimpse from across the street. We've all had the experience of remembering something as bigger or smaller than it really was. If you were to go on the stand and testify that this vague figure you saw through the window couldn't've been the ex-con, you'd get ripped apart."

She replayed the tape in her mind. "Jake would fill out Shaquille O'Neal's clothing quite nicely, whereas I doubt that the person in the window could've been any bigger than you." She shook her head. "I admit my memory is a little fuzzy and I could be off by a few inches. But it wasn't Jake. I'm sure of it."

෯      ෯      ෯

Milton was conducting a seance in Olivia's backyard. The feral cats sat in a circle, Cassidy and Starshine among them, a tall candle in the center. An image separated itself from the flame and floated in her direction. It was Olivia's ghost, a gauzy, diaphanous shroud drifting around her. The transparent figure placed a round mirror in Cassidy's outstretched hand. Gazing into the glass, she saw a series of faces: Bamba, Milton, Jake, the Lolita-like girl, and Zach. As Zach's face disappeared, the mirror went black.

She knew Olivia was sending her on a mission but had no idea what it was. Raising her eyes, she saw her neighbor's form start to fade. "Wait," she called, but Olivia and the candle blinked out. The ferals fled. She remained on the dry, prickly grass, alone except for Starshine, who jumped up and began attacking her bare toes.

The muffled sound of the phone ringing in Zach's office across the hall pulled her out of her dream. She kicked Starshine away from the foot she had carelessly left sticking out from under the sheet. Nine-thirty. She slipped out of bed, taking care not to disturb her sleeping husband.

A short time later Cassidy sat at the dining room table inhaling the fresh-brewed aroma steaming up from her purple cat mug. Staring across Briar, she watched a pregnant orange and white feral basking in a patch of sun in Olivia's front yard. Daisy, working on her second litter of the year.

As Cassidy raised her mug, she noticed that her hands were shaking. Lack of sleep. It made her body wobble and her brain short circuit.

Another cat chased Daisy out of her little square of sunshine. *What to do with the ferals?* Having called all the shelters in the Midwest, she knew they were overfilled already. Nobody was willing to take adult ferals which, unlike the kittens, could not be socialized. Zach had insisted that the only sensible recourse was to call the village animal control and request that the animals be put down, but neither of them had really wanted to do that.

Starshine jumped onto the table and sat across from Cassidy.

She said to the calico, "If I stop feeding them, they'll starve. If I keep filling their bowls, I'll be perpetuating the problem. If I call animal control, I'll be handing down a death sentence."

Taking a large swallow of creamed coffee, Cassidy felt it work its way through her system, the caffeine throwing on neural switches as it went. *The possibility exists, you might actually make it through the day.* Sunday morning. *Thank God, no clients to face.* After less than four hour's sleep, she wasn't sure she could remain coherent throughout an entire session. Her client load typically dipped during the summer, and right now she was quite happy not to have more than ten sessions scheduled for the upcoming week.

Diligently licking the side of one white forepaw, Starshine scrubbed her triangular face: one ear orange, the other black, a small pink nose.

A squad pulled up across the street. The driver spent a few moments at Olivia's side entrance, headed around toward the back, then returned to his car and left.

"Well, the house is unsealed. Which means I can take food to her indoor cats as soon as I'm able to drag myself back over there." She reached across the table to scratch Starshine's cheek, receiving a love bite in return. "Which also means you'll be attacking me again unless I'm able to keep you inside. And that's something I've never had any great success at."

*You should go feed those poor kitties.* She remembered the smell, the heat, the horror of finding Olivia's body.

*What you really should do is leave the country until the cats are disposed of, the house is sold, and Zach's put his hoodlum phase behind him.*

She was halfway through her second cup of coffee when she saw a white van park in front of George Brenner's house. Printed across the side of the van were two orange words: Animal Control. A man in a police uniform went up to the small canopied porch and rang the bell. A moment later Brenner came outside to stand beside him. Both men looked in the direction of Olivia's property.

"Oh shit!" Sprinting across the street, Cassidy hurried to join them. The two men backed up against the wrought iron railing to make room for her.

"Good morning, Ms. McCabe." The shiny-pated widower greeted her with a friendly expression. "I understand you were in the thick of things last night." Brenner's narrow face took on a properly downcast look. "Shame about Olivia."

"Do you think so?" *'Course he doesn't. He's hated her for years.* Staring at Brenner's trim figure, she decided he would fit quite nicely as the unknown person in Olivia's living room.

Drawing in his chin, Brenner looked at her oddly.

*You realize how off-the-wall you just sounded?* Not able to stop herself, she said in an accusatory tone, "You called Animal Control."

# 6. A Dive Down the Rabbit Hole

The pink-cheeked animal officer, regarding Cassidy as if her next trick might be speaking in tongues, took a half step back.

"Yes, of course." Brenner scowled. "It's like living next to the city dump, having all these cats around. I can't imagine why I put up with that woman—" He stopped, shook his head, then continued in a milder voice, "I've been deferring to Olivia for years, even though these strays are a blight on the neighborhood. There's nothing to be done except have them euthanized. A more humane solution, actually, than putting them through another Chicago winter." He gave her a stern look. "Now I know you've been helping Olivia feed them, but I hope you're planning to be more reasonable about getting this problem resolved than she was."

*Why are you attacking him? You've beaten your head against the wall trying to find some other alternative and come up empty.* "I'm sorry." Using her best rapport-building voice, she said, "I know you've been very patient. And I agree, the cats can't stay where they are. But I'd like a little time to see if I can find a shelter that'll take them." *You already tried. There aren't any.*

The animal officer addressed her in an earnest voice. "It really is better to put them out of their misery." He went on to tell her everything she knew already, his argument in favor of euthanasia merely increasing her determination to prove him wrong.

She gazed directly at Brenner. "Give me three days. If I haven't found a place by then, you can call the animal officer"—*little twerp that he is*—"and have him do it."

"I don't know why I always let women get around me." Brenner lowered his brow. "Okay, but on Wednesday morning the cleanup begins."

The animal officer said, "I'll have to start by trapping, and that always goes faster if they're hungry. So please refrain from feeding them for at least twenty-four hours before you ask me back."

ʊ    ʊ    ʊ

Just as she was coming in the back door, the phone started to ring. Racing across the kitchen, she lifted the receiver off the wall.

"I'm Carl Behan, Olivia's attorney." The voice was flat and lifeless. "I understand you're the one who called the police."

"It must've been awful, getting the news in the middle of the night the way you did." Starshine wandered in and began rubbing against her ankles.

A pause. "I just can't believe it. The whole thing seems incredible. The police tell me they found a drunk in her house and they think Olivia actually let him in."

"I'm still reeling myself."

"Well, I wanted to thank you. She was my goddaughter, you know." He cleared his throat. "If you hadn't noticed something was wrong and called the cops, the killer would've gotten away and God knows how long it might've been before . . . well, before anybody found her."

*Doesn't sound like Perez told him I was in the house, saw everything.* "Did the detective mention that I'd like to feed her indoor cats?"

"He might have. I wasn't able to take it all in." Behan paused. "You mean you want to adopt them?"

"I was thinking more along the lines of leaving them at Olivia's and bringing food over." Starshine, not getting a response, nipped her knee.

"I guess that'd be all right. I'll have to drop off a key."

"I already have a key." There was a silence, which she took to be stunned. *Just as I would've expected. She hoarded information, giving out teaspoonfuls on a need-to-know basis. Bet we all heard different stories. People as powerless as Olivia usually keep a tight lock on the one thing they have control over—the dispersal of data.*

His voice turned suspicious. "She gave you a key to her house?"

*No, I tunneled under the street, came up through her basement, and stole it.*

"She left a key with me so I could feed her indoor cats when she went on that business trip last spring." Cassidy leaned against the kitchen doorjamb. "What I'd really like is to find someone to take them in." She let it hang for a moment. "Can you think of any prospects?"

He let out a dry chuckle. "You're kidding, right?"

*Don't care if he is grieving. Sounds like an arrogant bastard.*

She gazed through the window above her sink into the kitchen belonging to the Steins, her neighbors to the south. Cassidy's window provided a view of the back half of the Steins' house and yard. "Well, then, I'll just have to see what I can come up with." *He's her godfather. He should take the cats. You hardly knew her.*

*Yeah, but I'm the only one dippy enough to care about them.*

"Speaking of cats, I suppose I ought to do something about those strays she collected."

Now it was Cassidy's turn to be stunned. "She told you about the ferals?"

"Not in this lifetime." He chuckled again. "She never would've admitted what a problem she'd created by feeding the neighborhood strays. But I used to visit the house before her mother died, so I had the opportunity to both see and smell the cats firsthand. Her mother was very unhappy about it, but she couldn't get Olivia to stop any more than I could."

*I never noticed this guy visiting.*

*Maybe before you moved in. Besides, you didn't go around spying on your neighbors in your pre-cat-rescue days.*

Behan added, "After her mother was gone, Olivia began insisting we meet elsewhere. She never came right out and said she didn't want me at the house, but it was obvious she was manipulating to keep me away. Probably because I always read her the riot act over those goddamn cats."

"You don't need to worry about the ferals. Somebody here will take care of them." *Now if I can only figure out a way to make that somebody be me.*

Hanging up the phone, she pulled out the dry cat food jug and set it on the counter, then remembered what the animal officer had said about not feeding before trapping. *On the absurdly optimistic premise that you're going to come up with a last-ditch rescue, you better hold off on filling their little tummies.*

At sight of the jug, Starshine sprang onto the counter, flattened her ears, and began nattering at her in an irritated tone.

Standing next to the sink, Cassidy stared at her neighbor, Dorothy Stein, weeding her vegetable garden. The sprawling tomato plants were neatly staked and bore a bounty of gleaming red fruit.

*Why can't you be normal like Dorothy? Here she is, supermom of the century, married to an AT&T exec, works a full-time outside job on top of a full- time homemaker job, never even whines. But no—you have to marry an overzealous reporter, let Starshine walk all over you, see clients, and solve mysteries while your weeds grow like Bill Gates's assets.*

Putting the unopened jug away, her mind went back to chewing on the feral cat problem. "What did I not follow up on? Who did I forget to call?"

*Sheryl Thomas.*

Sheryl was president of the Oak Park Animal Care League. Although Cassidy had called the shelter, she had never talked to Sheryl directly to see if her old friend had any insider tips.

The thought of her former schoolmate brought a smile to Cassidy's mouth, ironic rather than amused. Sheryl's family had moved to Oak Park in 1970, a time when the village was trembling on the verge of integration, with many residents feeling highly threatened by the arrival of blacks. Sheryl, a radiant, pecan-colored beauty destined to become homecoming queen in her senior year, was placed in Cassidy's room at Lincoln Grade School.

The part Cassidy considered ironic was her mother's reaction. Acting as if Sheryl was a bubonic-plague carrier, Helen had issued dire warnings about the ostracism Cassidy would incur were she to so much as speak to the "new little colored girl."

Cassidy decided not to tell Helen that three weeks into the school year her daughter, always introverted, sat alone at lunch while the outgoing Sheryl was surrounded by a throng of new friends. But as popular as she was, Sheryl was never a snob, and so eventually the gregarious black girl invited the lonely white girl to join the group.

Although not close friends, Cassidy and Sheryl chatted like old buddies whenever their paths crossed. Pulling a tattered red and yellow telephone book out of the drawer beneath the wall phone, Cassidy looked up Sheryl's number.

"Hey, Cass, how you doing?" a cheery voice answered.

"Not bad, although from your point of view a one-cat household probably seems deprived." The last time they'd talked, Sheryl was fostering four adult cats plus a mother and her litter. "You ever find homes for those kittens you had?"

"Which ones?" Sheryl laughed, a full, rich sound. "This cat house of mine has a revolving door. So, you're cat deprived, are you? I sure can fix that in a hurry."

"Starshine refuses to give up her status as only cat." Cassidy gently nudged the calico away from the shoe lace she'd just untied. "What stories do you have for me today?" she asked. Sheryl was a walking cat-shelter newsletter, full of inspirational tales of injured creatures who'd been snatched from death and taken to the shelter.

"Here's something to break your heart."

*Just what I need to top off the orphaned house cats, doomed colony, and soon-to-be-arrested mountain man.*

"One of the volunteers brought three kittens to my door, so tiny they still needed bottle feeding. They were found in an abandoned garage, dehydrated and nearly starved." She sighed. "Well, we lost one. But this tiny little girl perked up right away. Wouldn't you know it? The so-called weaker sex always turns out to be tougher in the end." She laughed. "And this other little bro here, he's touch and go."

"Sheryl, you are a true hero."

"Aw shucks," she said, parodying her down home roots. "If I stopped today, by tomorrow night you'd have your own houseful of foster kittens."

*No, I wouldn't. I'm not self-sacrificing enough. And not quite obsessive enough either. Just enough to take on the house cats and strays.*

Cassidy said, "Since we're on the topic of cat rescue, I've got some ferals in my neighborhood that're going to be put down if I don't find some shelter to take them."

"Well," Sheryl began speaking in a breathless tone as if imparting state secrets, "you've just tapped into the best underground railroad for cats—and I mean every kind of cat you can think of—that exists anywhere." She lowered her voice. "It turns out we have this little-known resource in Oak Park named Harve. Now this rescue operation of his is strictly independent, so if you run into any problems, just remember, he has no official status."

*Warning me he's difficult.*

"Anyway, Harve is one of the few people I've ever known who could implement a deathless cleanup of an entire colony."

"How does he do it?"

"I'll let him fill you in on the details."

"Harve who? What's his number?"

"The guy probably started out with two names but he seems to have lost one along the way." She recited his number. "But don't expect to get him on the phone. For some reason I don't understand, it's always off the hook."

"Are you sure this is a real person, not just an imaginary companion? Maybe you should come sit on my couch for an hour."

"Harve's a real cat fanatic. I don't know how we'd get along at the new shelter without him. But any time I want to reach him, I have to go bang on his door because all I ever get is a busy signal." Sheryl reeled off an address. "You be sure to knock real loud now 'cause his hearing's not what it used to be."

Figuring exercise might compensate for loss of sleep, Cassidy hauled out her old wreck of a bike. Whenever she was able to persuade Zach to go cycling with her, he pestered her about replacing it, but she'd grown fond of the old rattletrap and wasn't ready to give it up yet.

By the time she reached Harve's house, the sweat pouring into her eyes and the weakness in her knees forced her to admit that the idea of taking a mile-long bike ride in August had to be the product of a diseased mind. Standing astraddle her bike to wipe her brow, she scanned the asphalt-sided house, the sloping wooden porch, the downspout dangling tipsily from one corner of the roof, and the battered pickup, a cap over its bed, sitting in the drive.

*Bet he's got a page-long list of code violations and a housing inspector yapping at his heels.* Before Zach came into her life, she'd had run-ins with the village housing department herself and knew how relentless the inspectors could be.

She parked her bike at the foot of the sagging wooden steps. Chunks of wood, a rusty saw, rocks, dirt, and three wobbly, homemade cages littered the floor of the porch. *Considering how Sheryl raved about him, this can't be as bad as it looks. Besides, as the former dandelion queen of your block, who are you to judge?*

After knocking and waiting, knocking and waiting, the door was finally opened. A sour smell of garbage wafted out from the dark interior. A short, pudgy man, clearly the recipient of senior citizen discounts for a couple of decades or more, frowned up at her. "Who are you? What are you doing coming on my property and disturbing the peace?"

"Uh . . . I'm a friend of Sheryl Thomas. She said you run an underground railroad for cats."

"I told her to stop sending people. I'm too old for this." Stepping out onto the porch, he hiked himself up to sit, feet dangling, on the wide plank railing. With his large bald head, a few strands of hair combed straight back over the dome, pink cheeks, and sausage-shaped body, he reminded her of someone she'd seen before, but she couldn't think who.

Cassidy folded her arms beneath her breasts. "You actually know of a place that'll take feral cats?"

"Under special circumstances they might. But I don't want the word getting out. If too many people know about them, folks'll start driving up there to dump their pets." He shook his head. "I don't get it. How can people just abandon their animals like that?" His heavily lidded eyes gazed into hers as if he expected an answer.

"But they will take ferals?"

"Well, the little cats are easy."

"Little? These aren't kittens."

A sly gleam came into his ancient, colorless eyes. "Jill used to have this big cat she kept in the house 'cause he was so old and sick. But he died a while back."

*Is this guy trying to put something over on me? Or is he just a few instruments short of a band?* She said cautiously, "Is there something unusual about this lady keeping her old cat inside?"

"How many people you ever run into who got themselves a lion in the living room?'' Letting go with a sharp cackle of laughter, he slapped his overalls-covered thigh.

*Maybe Harve isn't the answer to your prayers after all.* Gazing past him at the battered black pickup with its contrasting blue fender, she asked, ''So why would she keep a lion in her house?''

'' 'Cause she's Jill.'' He burped out another giggle. ''That's what Jill does. She rescues big cats and keeps 'em in cages on her Wisconsin farm. Calls it JES—Jill's Exotic Sanctuary or something. I'm not sure. Can't quite remember.''

He hopped down from the railing and went to sit on the top step. She eased down beside him, the weathered wood feeling corrugated beneath her cotton-clad rear. She hoped she wouldn't get splinters.

Harve added, ''Jill, she doesn't do anything else. Her whole life goes to taking in every goldurned lion or tiger in the country that's outta luck. I'm glad these mangy old cats don't have to get sent to the gas chamber, but I gotta tell you, I think poor old Jill's gone 'round the bend.''

*Sheryl says Harve's a cat fanatic. Harve says Jill's gone 'round the bend. Standing next to this crew, my little obsession about Olivia's cats and the mountain man doesn't seem strange at all.*

Cassidy explained about the cat colony, then asked, ''So, do you think she'd be willing to let the ferals join her farmland menagerie?''

''Under the right circumstances,'' he said, his face going sly again.

''What circumstances?''

''Well, you see, buying food and building cages ain't cheap. No it ain't. Not by a long shot.''

''You're saying I'd have to pay her to take them?''

''She never charges nobody.'' He gave her a wide-eyed, innocent look. '' 'Course she does take donations.''

''How much would she need?''

''She's got maybe fifteen, twenty big animals, plus a slew of house cats. What kinda money you think it takes to run an operation like that?''

*I have no idea. Not even a glimmer. And he's not about to enlighten me either. He's going to wait and see what I offer, then up the ante.* ''How 'bout a hundred dollars?''

He picked up a pebble from the step and sent it gliding in a long, smooth arc onto his parched lawn. ''I dunno if I'm up to this job or not.''

She gritted her teeth for thirty seconds, then said, "One-fifty?"

He tossed a second pebble after the first. "I gotta tell you, Jill's knocking herself out trying to take care of those animals and raise money at the same time. That poor woman never gets a break. No she doesn't."

*You're being grossly manipulated here. If you said you were broke, he'd probably do it for nothing.* Glaring, she offered two hundred.

"Yeah, okay. What with you being so generous and all, I could probably accommodate you on the ferals."

*Just what we don't need. Zach's put out a ton of money for his investigation, which the* Post *may or may not reimburse, and here I blow another couple of bills on creatures everybody else regards as one step up from vermin. Zach's right. I am nuts.*

*He'll think saving the cats is crazy, but he won't blink twice at the money.* Having grown up with wealth, Zach had taken on the mission of liberating Cassidy from her poverty mindset.

Harve explained that, due to the nocturnal nature of cats, he always did the trapping at night. He said he would arrive at Olivia's in the early evening and set up the four traps he owned. As each cat was captured, he would slide it out of the trap and into a cage he'd built in the bed of his pickup, then reset the trap. At dawn he'd catch a few hours sleep, then drive the ferals up to Jill's Wisconsin sanctuary.

"But if one cat sees another getting caught, won't the observer cat refuse to go into the trap?"

"Maybe. Maybe not. Depends on how hungry they are."

"If you don't catch them all tonight, will you finish tomorrow?"

"Look, lady, I'm eighty-seven years old. Used to be I could keep going two, three nights in a row. Now I put in one all-nighter, it takes me a week to catch up. I'll get what I can, but the rest'll just have to stay where they are."

"You mean, there's nothing we can do for any of the ferals you miss?"

His voice went gruff. "Can't save every goldurned stray in the country."

*Wishes he could. That's why he sounds angry—because there's so much he can't do.*

On the hot ride home, she realized who Harve reminded her of. *The*

*Tweedly twins.* He closely resembled the illustration of Tweedledee and Tweedledum in her *Alice in Wonderland* from childhood. *And visiting Harve was like taking a dive down the rabbit hole.*

ಶಿ     ಶಿ     ಶಿ

Although it was past noon when she returned home, Zach was still asleep. She showered, then decided she could no longer postpone feeding Olivia's indoor cats. She left a note for Zach, gathered up the dry food jug and some small flat cans, then headed across the street.

As she opened her neighbor's door, Cassidy braced herself for the bad smells and bad memories she knew would engulf her upon re-entering this house of the drunken mountain man and dead Olivia. The smells hit first: pungent odors of cat urine and human blood. Then came the heat. With windows permanently closed and no air conditioning, it was like walking into a steambath.

She set the cat food down on the chipped formica countertop as Bamba came squawking to greet her. Wanting to do something special for the orphaned cats, she'd planned to give them some of the nasty, fish-smelling food Starshine adored. But now, with Bamba rubbing against her ankles and the other two peeking from the doorway, Cassidy began to wonder if improving the cats' diet was such a good idea.

*Indulge them once, it's a treat. Indulge them twice, it's an entitlement. Cats develop new entitlements even faster than your mother. Do you really want these three felines you've taken under your wing turning up their collective noses at little brown nuggets the way Starshine does?*

Bamba sat next to an empty bowl and looked up at her out of sorrowful green eyes, or at least eyes that through some trick of projection appeared sorrowful to Cassidy. Seized with the need to ameliorate his sadness, she offered up the pricey food.

When she'd fed them in the spring, the two females had dashed out to eat, then disappeared, but Bamba had climbed all over her to get attention and petting. She sat on the floor, knees bent, and waited. After gobbling a few bites, the white tom came to stand on her chest, front feet planted on her shoulders, head held high, eyes gazing regally down into hers.

"Getting one-up is obviously a guy thing." *You never allow human males to treat you this way. Why put up with it from felines?*

*All cat owners get inured to abuse from their furry little tyrants.*

When Bamba'd had all the petting he wanted, he walked away, obviously through with her. *Amazing the gender similarities across species' lines.* She stood, thinking she ought to go but feeling unfinished. What she wanted to do was look around.

*Maybe the police missed something.*

*Yeah, right. Heroine finds clue dumb cops missed.*

A picture flashed into her mind: Olivia in the upstairs office in front of a filing cabinet, its second drawer pulled out. That's where Cassidy had found Olivia on the last day of her cat feeding stint when she'd followed the music and come up behind her neighbor unnoticed. As soon as Olivia had become aware of her presence, she'd hustled Cassidy away from the office.

*Up to something. Caught in the act. And now, if the police haven't carted the files away, you can find out what that something was.*

The metal cabinet stood against the office's north wall next to a blinds-covered window. Beneath the window was a gouged-up mahogany desk, a calculator and a square glass jar filled with red and green gummy worms sitting on the desk's tidy surface. A straight-backed chair was pushed into its kneehole.

Cassidy raised the blinds, releasing a cloud of dust that brought on a sneeze, then opened the cabinet's second drawer. Three-quarters of the drawer was crammed with old paper: receipts and bank statements dating as far back as fifty years. Behind these she found about a dozen files tied with a thin cord into a single packet.

She definitely intended to read the files but wasn't sure if she needed to stay in this oppressive little room to do it. *Much rather take them home and be hassled by my own cat instead of Bamba.* However, she realized she might need to hand them over to the police later, and if Manny found out she'd walked off with them, he would not be pleased.

*Considering you're on the verge of all sorts of other infractions, why not endure the bad air and play it safe on this one?*

She sat at the desk, untied the cord, and read through the file tabs, each of which was labeled with a name, address, and phone number. *Well, what do you know? I rated my own file.* Inside the folder she found newspaper accounts of her crime-solving exploits along with handwritten sheets of paper arranged according to date, the earliest at the front.

The first had been written in March:

I swear that woman's stalking me. Every time I step foot outside my door, she comes running over to babble about cats. The thing I can't understand is why she's doing this now, after ignoring me all those years. Uncle Carl says there's no law to stop her. Wish to heaven I knew what she was after.

*My God! I thought I was being friendly. She thought I was stalking!*

As Cassidy skimmed over the pages, she realized that some of the significant events were missing, such as the first time she helped feed the ferals. *Olivia must've been as erratic with her record keeping as I am with my client files.* The final note said:

I made a terrible mistake. Told Cass about giving Jake the key. I could just die. But where does she get off judging me? She let that shady reporter move in before they were married.

*You weren't judging her. Well, maybe a little. You always think you've got people pegged. This just goes to show how someone as secretive as Olivia can keep things hidden, even from a sharpie therapist-type like you.*

Bamba jumped onto the desk and sprawled across the files, attempting to cover as much paper as possible with his body.

"It's all about power, isn't it? Whenever you cats succeed in preventing a human from doing what they want, you win."

She pulled a folder out from under him. This one was on Olivia's doctor. The next three were neighbors. The handwritten notes presented a commentary on each person's activities, along with expressions of anger over perceived slights, such as her doctor's nurse having called to report on a blood test when Olivia thought the doctor should have cared enough to call personally.

Gazing through the window, Cassidy clasped her hands behind her neck. *You knew she had to be full of resentment. People as timid as Olivia always are. You take anybody who goes around bending over backward to be docile, peel away the skin, on the inside they're seething with rage. Passive-aggressive to the hilt. Sometimes just plain old active-aggressive.*

Sunlight played on the leaves of a maple near the window, bringing out nuances of color ranging from mint to olive. From the alley behind Olivia's yard she heard the whump, whump, whump of a basketball hitting asphalt, then a deep male voice. "That was a friggin' foul and you know it. You can't count that shot. Here, gimme the ball, man."

She read Jake's file, which held no surprises.

Next she opened the file on Esther's caregiver, Danny Kline. The earliest remarks, dated three years ago, indicated that Olivia was gleeful at having found a competent person willing to accept a minimal salary in exchange for a place to live and the flexibility to pursue his degree.

Danny's a godsend. Doesn't seem to mind Esther's ugly disposition, which absolutely amazes me. If he's there, I won't have to run and fetch all the time. And with Esther living on next to nothing, she can actually pay him out of her social security.

At a later point, however, Olivia reported that Esther had accused Danny of stealing her jewelry.

She doesn't have anything worth taking. This must be just another of Esther's lies.

But Olivia's final note showed a change of heart:

I suspect Danny is stealing after all. The trouble is Esther likes him too much to fire him. As a matter of fact, I don't know how I'd get along without him either. This is a serious problem. I don't know what to do.

# 7. Collaboration and a Confession

Cassidy said to Bamba, "Boy, it sure didn't look to me like there was anything in that broken down house worth hauling away." *Old coins, a stamp collection? Heirloom china in the attic?*

She pushed Bamba off the desk to make more room for laying out the files. He landed neatly, leaving a puff of white fur in his wake. Separating Danny's file from the others, she drummed her fingers on it. *Olivia must have been Esther's beneficiary. Which meant, if Danny was stealing from the aunt, he'd also be stealing from her. Given Olivia's anxiety about money, the thought of Danny chipping away at her inheritance would've made her crazy.*

*Would she have had the gumption to confront him? Go all out to get him fired?*

Cassidy gritted her teeth in frustration. *Too many unanswered questions.* She didn't know if there'd been any actual evidence of theft, and she also didn't know if Olivia had talked to Danny or anyone else about her suspicions.

*So, why keep files on everybody?* It went back to power. Since Olivia, unlike Bamba, was too timid to exert control directly, she had to do it indirectly through the files. In her real-life dealings with people, she always took a one-down stance. But by keeping a record of all the embarrassing, dumb, and sometimes illegal stunts people pulled, she could feel one-up in private.

And there was also an element of protection. If Cassidy ever gave her any trouble, Olivia could produce documentation of what she saw as stalking. Even though most of what Olivia had recorded was of no interest to the police, it would give her the sense of having ammunition to use against anyone who gave her a hard time. Cassidy sighed. *What a sad case.*

Standing, she made a half-hearted attempt to open the window but didn't succeed. *These old wooden jobbies never budge.* Looking down at the backyard, she paused to watch the tiger-stripe feral playing with an orange cat in the afternoon sun.

The next two files contained insignificant comments about people Cassidy didn't know. The one after that was on Carl Behan, Olivia's godfather and attorney. Cassidy got the impression that he was the person Olivia turned to for help of all kinds, even though she whined about his not doing enough for her. Cassidy closed the file with the sense that Behan, who'd come across as arrogant to her, had served as a kindly father figure to his goddaughter.

Picking up the calculator, Cassidy turned it over in her hands, noting the MED TECH label on the bottom. *Much as she liked to get the goods on everybody else, it appears she wasn't above a little office pilfering herself.*

Cassidy opened the file on George Brenner, the fire-and-police-commission widower Cassidy had argued with that morning. This file, fatter than the others, documented their decade-long feud over the ferals. Now that Cassidy had calmed down about the fate of the colony, she was forced to admit that George had a number of very good reasons for wanting Olivia to stop feeding strays. Page after page recounted their run-ins on the topic, and as Cassidy read through them, she found her sympathies falling on the side of the man whose air had been befouled and property devalued by the accumulation of cats.

Then she came across a note dated a year earlier that made her not want to sympathize with him after all.

> I was in my yard and heard George through the back fence. He was bragging to a friend about having bought a black market, fully automatic Uzi for his collection.

Cassidy didn't know which guns were prohibited by federal law, but if Brenner had acquired his Uzi through the black market, she assumed it must be illegal. Upright citizen George would have a high stake in not getting caught.

*Would our civic-minded neighbor really collect illegal guns? Or was Olivia crazier than I thought?*

The final note was of particular interest in that it showed Olivia's nontimid side. *Nobody can be a mouse all the time.* And it also showed that at least one person might have had a motive for murder. The note said:

George yelled at me today. Told me if I didn't get rid of the f-ing cats, he would. I was so mad I yelled right back at him. Said I knew he could get in big trouble for owning those guns of his and even more trouble for shooting them. I told him if he ever harmed any of the animals, I'd have my attorney talk to the FBI. But he could be killing the cats one by one and I wouldn't know it.

A memory sprang to Cassidy's mind of a time when she and Olivia were watching the ferals eat. Olivia had looked up at George's house and said, "You probably won't believe this—nobody ever believes me—but I've seen George shooting a pistol out of his window up there. I'm sure he was trying to kill one of the cats but I never found any bodies, so maybe he isn't a very good shot."

Cassidy had stared first at the window, then at Olivia. "Police-and-fire-commission George? Are you sure you actually saw him do it?"

"I knew you wouldn't believe me."

Olivia was right. Cassidy hadn't believed her. But now, reading his file, she wasn't so sure.

*No proof of any of this. Could be pure delusion.*

*She had the facts right where you were concerned. Okay, so the word "stalking" is a little extreme. But you look at it from her point of view, your sudden intense interest must've seemed a bit odd. "Stalking" or "making friends"—it's all in the eye of the beholder.*

*Yeah, but that isn't any reason to believe this congenial guy who puts in volunteer time for the village is not only a collector of illegal guns, but worse yet, a cat-killer. Possibly even a* pet *cat killer.*

It also isn't any reason to believe he's not. Being high-profile and public-spirited is no guarantee of righteous behavior. She envisioned George standing at his window firing an Uzi at Starshine. The picture made her so angry she had to grip the edge of the desk to keep from flying over to his house and demanding to know if he hunted cats for sport.

Placing Brenner's folder on top of Danny's, she created a separate stack for people who might have had a reason to do Olivia harm. She stood and stretched, then wandered across the hall to Olivia's bedroom. A lace doily, porcelain lamp, and stack of romance novels graced her neighbor's nightstand. *Don't think I've ever been in a house that had actual doilies before.*

About a dozen greeting cards stood on an open shelf, five bearing Jake's signature, the remainder Carl Behan's. *This could be the sum total of cards she received in the last decade.* A moth-eaten teddy bear leaned tipsily against the pillow on the twin-sized bed. Cassidy's throat tightened, the cards and the teddy bear bringing home to her the extent of her neighbor's aloneness.

She returned to the desk and opened the file on Edwardo Mirandez, the owner of Olivia's yard service firm. The first note went back to June of the previous year.

> Lawn's all splotchy and he's killed my beautiful lilac. I argued with him yesterday. Said I'd pay half the bill now, the rest when he replaces my lilac and makes my yard green again. He claims the grass is ruined because of the cats urinating on it, but it's never been this bad before. Also says the snow killed my lilac. I think the real problem is, he's incompetent. That's why his fees are so low. Should've gone with someone in the business longer, except I just don't have the money.

In July the hostilities escalated.

> Caught me getting out of the car. Actually threatened to kill my shrubs if I didn't pay the whole bill right away. But I've been giving him half every month, which is what keeps him coming back. He even swore at me. Disgusting little wetback. I said I'd see to it he got sent back to Mexico where there won't be any rich Americans to cheat. These people are all illegals. I'm sure Uncle Carl can take care of it.

*Well, Olivia's aggressiveness coming out again. I'll bet she was never so happy as when she had a threat to hold over someone's head.*

There were no more entries until April of the current year.

> Found a note under my door asking if I wanted to sign up for the same yard service again. The new owner's Luis Cordova. Since Edwardo got deported way back last summer, maybe this Luis person doesn't know about the fight we had. I shouldn't do it—Luis is probably just as bad as Edwardo. But their rates are so much lower and I just don't have the money for anything else.

The final note indicated that she had signed a contract with Luis and the service was acceptable.

Cassidy had just picked up another file when the doorbell bonged. *Shouldn't be anybody ringing the bell. Zach's the only one knows I'm here. The cops, the attorney, Esther—they'd just walk in. So it's gotta be Zach.* If it was, she didn't need to hide the files. But on the general principle that unforeseen shit happens frequently, she stuffed them into the drawer before going downstairs.

Opening the door, she gaped in surprise at the familiar wiry figure on the porch, the elderly woman's gnarly face surrounded by the smooth fall of a Lauren Bacall wig.

"Gran! What are you doing here?"

Her grandmother, shorter than Cassidy's five-two and sturdy as a steel spring, responded to the query with three of her own: "Who's that guy who answered your door in his bathrobe? What've you done with Zach? And why in heaven's name are you over here in this stinky old house?"

In an effort to divert her, Cassidy said sternly, "You didn't answer my question."

"I'm here to find out why you haven't returned any of the fifteen messages your mother left on your machine over the past twenty-four hours. If I can't give her a good explanation when she calls my cell phone"—she dug the new toy out of her purse—"she'll drop out of her Branson bus tour and hitchhike home."

Cassidy sighed. "It's a long story."

"That's what the guy in the bathrobe said."

*No way out of it. If you don't account for yourself to Gran, you'll have Mom back home and breathing down your neck.*

Taking her grandmother across the street to her own house, Cassidy settled the tiny woman into her therapy office, the only first-floor room with air conditioning, then headed into the kitchen to make coffee. She moved slowly, buying time to think through how much she ought to reveal.

*Why not all of it? One of Gran's friends died recently. You know she's grieving, even though she tries to hide it. Hearing about adventures always perks her up.* She turned the dial on the grinder, setting off a loud rumble.

*This isn't an adventure. Zach's investigation is off-the-scale risky, and nobody'd call what you're doing exactly sensible either. Gran's got enough on her mind. No need to add to her worries.*

*She isn't half the worrier you are. She'd not only love getting the scoop, she'd insist you cut her in on the action.* Cassidy put a clean filter into the basket and added coffee grounds.

*Well, why not? Every time you get involved in crime solving, she begs to be included. And the truth is, she's dug up some amazing information. You need to be distracted from Zach's dope dealer part, she needs to be distracted from her friend's death.* A smile lit Cassidy's face at the thought of spending more time with her spunky little grandmother.

She carried the coffee into her office. As she placed a mug in her grandmother's hands, she flashed an image of Esther's arthritic talons. Although the skin was thin and translucent, Gran's stubby fingers remained as straight and well formed as ever.

Cassidy sat in her director's chair across from Gran, a low wicker table holding a potted coleus and a tissue box between them. Gran, clad in a white shirt and red shorts, perched on the sectional that curved around the room's two outer walls. Above the sectional the east window showed burgeoning, sunlit trees.

Gran's bright eyes nailed her. "So what do I tell your mother? She wanted to give you an umpteenth reminder about this trip she left on today. When I took her out to breakfast this morning, I had to practically sit on her to keep her from marching up to your door and demanding to know why you hadn't returned any of her calls. Considering you've got this slick new guy hanging around, it's a good thing she didn't."

From the curious look on her grandmother's face, Cassidy could tell she was dying to know why Zach had transformed himself into a stubbly-faced hood.

"Hmmm." Cassidy took a sip from her purple mug. "I think it might be best to say the machine malfunctioned."

"I knew it!" Gran banged her fist on her knee. "Zach's in disguise and the two of you are up to your ears in some new investigation."

"This is different. Zach's working on a story for the paper and he won't let me near it." Rubbing a finger over her garnet wedding ring, Cassidy felt a momentary sense of loss. In the past she and Zach had always worked together, and now they were being pulled in separate directions.

"So who's Zach pretending to be?"

"Johnny Culver. He's a kid Zach used to smoke dope with in high school. Johnny did a little jail time for dealing, then he and his family moved to Athens, Illinois." Cassidy reached over to straighten the coleus. "Whenever Johnny gets himself in trouble, he calls Zach for money, and my nice guy husband always gives it to him. Zach's attitude is, there but for the grace of good genes go I."

Scrunching her forehead, Gran wagged her head from side to side, causing her smooth, blond hairpiece to slip slightly to the left. "Does Zach look like this Johnny person?"

"Not really. But Zach worked out this cool idea for passing himself off as Johnny. A few months back, Zach got Johnny to spread the word that he'd inherited a chunk of money and was heading out to Chicago in search of a drug supplier. He told everybody he was planning to set up his own little dealership in Athens—a modern version of the good old American dream." She set her mug on the table.

"Zach used Johnny's ID to replace a 'lost' driver's license. They traded cars and Johnny left town. Then Zach came home and began ingratiating himself into the local drug scene. He's got these two dealers he's after, and he's spent the past few weeks trying to get next to them."

Gran pulled the wicker table closer and propped her gym shoes on it. As the table moved, creamed coffee sloshed out of Cassidy's mug. *One of the nice things about wicker is it matches my shade of coffee so well.*

Her grandmother said, "Two dealers? Why these two guys in particular?"

*Should I tell her?*

*Why not? Her circle does not include narcs and she's not likely to worry. She'll simply assume that Zach will, of course, prevail. Which is exactly what you should do.*

"Because they're cops. Zach has a lot more tolerance for crooks selling dope than cops doing it. Especially when they steal it from the little guys, jack up the prices, and sell it on the night club circuit."

"So he's gonna bust those lowdown cops? Well, good for him." Her gaze met Cassidy's, then moved away. "Long as he's buddying up with all these dope dealer-types, you don't suppose he could bring me a sample of that cope they're always talking about, do you?"

Cassidy looked at her askance. "You're kidding, right? You don't really mean you want to do *coke*."

"Well, I thought it wouldn't hurt just this once. Everybody makes such a fuss about drugs, it seems a shame not to even know what it's like to get high." Her voice turned wistful. "It must be an awful lot of fun or people wouldn't be getting themselves in so much trouble over it."

"I don't think that'd be a good idea." *Not hardly, considering one of Zach's problems may be proving he didn't buy any for personal consumption. Or the consumption of his grandmother-in-law, either.*

"Oh well, at least I'll get to hear about it when he's done. So, getting back to the not answering messages part . . ." Gran looked confused. "The reason you don't return phone calls any more is that Zach's busy being Johnny Culver and running down sleazy cops."

"We turned the telephone ringer off and moved the answering machine into Zach's office so he can sleep during the day. I've been forgetting to check the machine because it's in the wrong place, and I especially forgot it last night because I had a lot going on."

Gran shook her head. "It's too bad he won't let you in on it. You could be his moll and I could be the grand moll."

"It's just as well. I've got my hands full right now. Last night, Olivia—across the street—was murdered, and you know the cops, they've got the wrong guy and on top of that I've got to find homes for her cats and the ferals."

Gran's face brightened. "There's been a murder? And it's got feral cats in it? Of course you're going to poke around a little to see what you can find out." Her voice went stern. "Well, you better let me help or I'm gonna be really peeved."

*Why not?* "Actually, I could use some assistance." Cassidy started telling Gran about Olivia's death, but before she got very far into it, she heard Zach's footsteps in the kitchen. Her shoulders tightened, the tension she experienced whenever she faced the prospect of another encounter with the part of him that didn't like her.

He stepped into the doorway, setting off the same small jolt of surprise that still hit her whenever she saw his unshaven face and slicked back hair. The coldness in his blue-gray eyes made it clear that the undercover guy was back in charge, the man who'd made love to her last night locked away somewhere deep inside.

Glancing briefly at the two of them, he said, "Well, I'm off."

Cassidy didn't reply.

"See you later," Gran responded uncertainly. After he left, she added, "That Johnny Culver, he isn't much of a talker, is he? I bet you're not too happy with Zach bringing his work home with him like this."

Cassidy gazed through the window behind Gran's head at a flock of starlings busily flapping in and out of the small tree in her yard. "I think I might've preferred an advanced case of toenail rot to seeing my husband go club crawling all night, spend his days in scummy bars, and treat me like the invisible woman in between."

"I know this is none of my business, but I hope you don't get too mad at him. I'm sure he wouldn't be acting this way if he didn't have to."

"Yeah, I know." Sighing, Cassidy gazed into the small face dwarfed by thick curtains of blonde hair on either side. Despite the sagging skin, her grandmother's lively eyes and brisk movements conveyed a sense of agelessness. "Well," Cassidy said, "let me finish the story."

When she was done, Gran said, "I'm sure sorry I can't take any of those cats off your hands, but you know I get real bad allergies anytime I'm around them very long."

Cassidy smiled fondly at her grandmother. "Believe me, that's the only reason I wasn't begging you to take all three."

"Since we'll be working together, let's you and me go read the rest of those files."

"Considering the guy in the corner house could be watching her property, I think it'd be best if I'm the only one seen going in and out."

"Then you should bring the files over here so I can read 'em too."

"What I *should* do is hand them over to Perez."

Disappointment clouded Gran's face. "But then he'd tell you to stay out of it, wouldn't he?"

"Unfortunately, that's the dilemma. If I give him what I've got, he's going to be pissed that I searched her files in the first place and even more pissed when he finds out I'm talking to these people. But if I don't, I'm withholding evidence and preventing the cops—the guys who actually know what they're doing—from having access to all the information."

"Well," Gran said, her tone not matching her words, "of course I don't want to see you get into any trouble."

Cassidy stood up. "I'll call Manny. If they're still pursuing all possible leads, I'll confess to being a busybody and take my lumps."

Heading into the kitchen, she lifted the handset off the wall. Perez was not in so she asked for the commander. He said, "The suspect signed a confession early this morning."

# 8. An Impudent Little White Wine

"Jake signed a confession?" *Oh my God. Did he do it? He couldn't have. Olivia raised her blinds because she felt threatened by that person in her living room.* Putting her hand to throat, she asked, "What's going to happen to him?"

"He'll be arraigned Sunday. If he's denied bail, which seems likely, he'll be transferred to Cook County."

"When can I see him?"

"He should be able to have visitors some time next week. Just call 1-800-425-JAIL to see what his visiting day is."

*Dammit, Jake, why'd you have to go and confess to something you can't even remember?*

Cassidy plopped into her director's chair. "He confessed."

"You mean he *did* kill that woman after all?"

"No, I mean that for some reason I can't comprehend, he told the police what they wanted to hear. The confession can't be genuine because one, I'm certain it was somebody else who scared her into raising the blinds, and two, I'm convinced he was telling the truth when he said he didn't remember anything that happened the whole time he was there."

"Maybe it came back to him."

Sitting straighter, Cassidy blew out air, trying to quell her irritation so it didn't get directed at Gran. "When people experience alcoholic blackouts, their memories usually don't return. It's not like having an image stored in your brain you can't retrieve. In a true blackout, the memory never gets recorded so there's nothing to bring back."

The phone rang and she returned to the kitchen to answer it.

"Where were you?" Esther's querulous voice demanded. "I've been calling and calling and nobody answers. Danny's at the library and I'm here all alone. I know you told me something happened to Olivia but I can't remember what it was and I need you to tell me again."

Cassidy responded in a neutral voice, "I said I'd phone. If you want me to talk to you, you'll have to wait till I call." It had not been an easy lesson to learn, but she now knew there were some people who always pushed the limit, and the only way to deal with them was to draw a firm line and stick to it.

"But I don't remember. You have to say it again."

*Pure manipulation. You show the slightest weakness, you'll have a pest for life.* "I think you do. Now tell me what happened to Olivia."

"No I don't." Her tone rose hysterically. "I'm just an old lady. I can't remember things any more."

"If you don't tell me, I'm going to hang up." Standing straight and stiff, Cassidy gazed through her kitchen window at Dorothy Stein stirring a pot on the stove next door.

Esther said slyly, "Somebody shot her. She's dead."

Hearing not the least hint of sorrow in the woman's voice, Cassidy felt her stomach twist in revulsion. "I don't have time to talk now. I'll call you later."

She returned to her office just as the clock on the windowsill chimed three times. "Why don't I finish reading the files, then we can strategize afterward."

"I'll pick up something at Erik's," Gran said. "You can come to my place when you're through. And don't worry about your mother. I'll tell her you're real busy right now but you'll call her later on at her motel."

They went out the back door together. Waving as Gran drove off in her red Chevy, Cassidy returned to the stack of unread files.

ဆ    ဆ    ဆ

Cassidy skimmed the first entry, dated almost a year earlier, in a file labeled SHELBY ONKEAN:

Received a letter from my daughter today.

Cassidy's jaw dropped in surprise. *Her daughter? Zach said Olivia couldn't be a virgin because virgins don't exist over forty, but it's more like, they don't exist after childbirth. Not unless the mother went shopping at her neighborhood sperm bank, which doesn't seem to be the case here.*

The file continued:

Shelby just passed her twenty-third birthday. I've wondered for years what I'd do when she tried to contact me. Now she has, and I don't think I can bear it.

The daughter's letter was clipped to the note. It indicated that Shelby, raised by her father in Maine, now worked at Channel 11, having come to Chicago expressly to develop a relationship with her mother.

*Poor kid. I can't imagine any mother who'd be harder to get close to than Olivia.*

As it turned out, the issue had not been one of getting close but of gaining access.

She keeps calling. Before this, the only people who ever called were Esther and Uncle Carl. But I hang up on her. I don't understand why she doesn't quit.

Staring through the grimy window at Olivia's maple and the bright blue sky behind it, Cassidy was aware of a growing dislike for her neighbor.

*First it was the lawn guy she got deported. Now it's her own daughter. Kids separated from their moms at birth usually have a real yearning to get to know them. Yet here's Olivia, just slamming down the phone. How could she be so caring with cats, so heartless with humans?*

*Aren't you being a little heartless yourself? People like Olivia need all the energy they can muster just to get from day to day. There's no way of knowing how difficult a simple conversation with her daughter might have been for her.*

Cassidy picked up the glass candy jar and gave it several hard shakes, rearranging the red and green worms.

*Here you are, reading her innermost thoughts and judging them. How good would you look under similar scrutiny?*

It suddenly hit her what an egregious breach of privacy she was committing. *God, I hope her ghost isn't looking over my shoulder.*

*What you're doing isn't nice, but it also isn't an ethics violation. And you're certainly not going to let a small thing like a guilty conscience stop you.*

The notes continued:

After three months of trying to make me talk on the phone, Shelby waited in front of my house and forced me to speak to her. I was amazed at what a beautiful girl she's grown into. Nothing like me at all. She wanted us to have dinner and I agreed.

After this there were several notes reporting Olivia's mood swings as she flipped between moving closer to her daughter and running away.

*Least she's consistent. Same damn thing she pulled with you and Jake. But it must've driven the daughter nuts. Olivia was right to give the baby to the father. She had no more ability to mother a child than to sing at the Met.*

A more recent note indicated that Olivia's sapphire ring had become a topic of mother-daughter discussion. According to Olivia, the ring had been passed down through several generations of the Onkean family, and Shelby was on a mission to reclaim it. The next note said:

When we were at dinner, she kept sneaking glances at my finger and one time she even tried to touch the ring. She isn't interested in me at all—just the sapphire. She's greedy and conniving. I don't want to see her any more.

*Could the daughter have killed her mother for the ring?*

The last note in the file bore an early July date:

She's a wretched girl. Bitter and mean. She's been bullying me beyond belief to get at my ring. But Bobby gave it to me and she has no right to it. After what she did tonight, I don't want anything to do with her ever again.

Closing the file, Cassidy ran her thumbnail along a small crack in the mahogany desktop. She'd often heard clients describe the pain of maternal rejection. *And Olivia's rejection of Shelby was about as blatant as it gets. First as a newborn, then as a young woman wanting to connect with her mother. Even if Shelby was a grasping little bitch, she couldn't have deserved that much rejection.*

Cassidy could not imagine committing matricide over a ring. But, rejection being one of her own personal hot buttons, she could imagine that sufficient quantities of it might make her want to kill.

Standing, she wiped sweaty palms on her lavender shorts and paced out to the hallway. Although one part of her was determined to read every single word, another part was beginning to feel disgusted with Olivia's tawdry secrets. She stared at three framed reprints on the wall, each a sticky-sweet picture of kittens. Clenching her lips, she marched herself back to the desk and opened the last folder, a file labeled EVELYN WENTWORTH.

The first note, dated nearly three years earlier, announced that Evelyn had bought out the previous owner of the lab where Olivia worked.

Old Burzak was a regular guy but this Evelyn's always got her nose in the air. She doesn't like anybody very much, especially me.

Another note read:

I heard her whispering to Patsy today. She said I was slow and stupid, and she doesn't know what to do with me. She's so unfair. I can't help it that everything's changed since I first started. And this new software—it's all so hard. What if she lets me go? I'd never be able to find another job.

Cassidy raised her eyes to look out at the tree. *What an awful life Olivia had.*

*There you go, feeling sorry for her again. What's it going to be—sympathetic or disgusted?*

The final note was dated two months before Olivia's death.

I've got her now! Proof she's been commiting Medicare fraud. With what I've got here, she'd never dare fire me.

This entry was clipped to a sheaf of papers which appeared to be claims paid by the government.

If Evelyn knew Olivia had the forms, that could easily constitute a motive for murder. But there was nothing in the file to indicate that Olivia had ever confronted the lab owner, or, taking it a step further, attempted blackmail.

Olivia was not, however, a perfect record keeper. Cassidy knew this because of omissions in her own file. So it was possible Olivia had threatened her boss but failed to write it down.

*Shit! Why didn't she lay it out explicitly either way? A message from beyond the grave. Maybe even a ghostly finger pointing at her boss. "I told Evelyn I was going to the authorities and she said she'd see me dead first." Or, less satisfying but at least clear-cut, "I never said a word about the forms." Damn it, Olivia, why didn't you spell it out for me?*

Cassidy placed Evelyn's folder on the stack with caregiver Danny, fire- and-police-commission George, lawn-service Edwardo, and long-lost Shelby— all people with reason to wish Olivia harm. Replacing the others in the drawer, she retied the questionable five, tucked them under her arm, and headed toward the stairs. *Okay, this is it. Infractions start now.*

She smiled inwardly, remembering how she had ragged at her first husband, Kevin, and after that at Zach, over their non-law-abiding ways. *Never realized until recently you have such an aptitude for it yourself.*

As she reached the bottom of the stairs, she heard the thunk of the side door closing. Her first impulse was to turn around and race back up to the office. *Don't run. Be cool. You're here to feed the cats.* She straightened her back and started toward the door, coming face to face in the entryway with a man in his early sixties.

They regarded each other for about thirty seconds, the man looking very powerhouse-Madison-Avenue with his expensive sport jacket, upswept white hair, and aggressive stare.

Cassidy forced herself to meet his eyes and not speak first, knowing that if she unclenched her teeth, flimsy excuses for her guilty presence would start pouring out.

"Well," he said slowly, "you must be the neighbor."

She nodded. "And you're Carl Behan, the man I talked to earlier."

He gave her a fractional nod but did not offer his hand or unsquare his shoulders as he would have if the showdown were over. The problem, of course, was the files. She had absolutely no recourse but to hold them under her arm in plain sight, and until she satisfactorily explained why she was removing them from the house, she and the attorney would be locked in place, sniffing each other out like wary cats.

Thinking fast, she said, "I'd been trying to convince Olivia to find some place to send the feral cats. I even made up files on various animal shelters around the country and insisted that she take them, although I suspect she did it more to humor me than anything else." *Is he going to buy that dumb story about the files and give us a graceful way out of this staredown? Or up the ante by demanding to see them?*

Taking a minuscule step back, Behan dropped his shoulders slightly. Cassidy felt almost giddy with relief.

"Well," he said. "I just stopped by to check out what needs to be done in the house in order to sell it."

She heard a fly buzz overhead. *I'll bet Behan could be useful. He's known Olivia forever. Bound to have information you don't, and there's nothing in his file to make him a suspect.*

Shifting her weight, she said slowly, "There are some things regarding Olivia's murder I'd like to discuss with you. Would you be willing to come to my house and let me tell you more about what happened last night?"

His body stiffened. "Her death hasn't been easy for me and I don't see that rehashing it would serve any useful purpose."

"Would you consider it useful if I could convince you that the police have arrested the wrong man?"

A fat black fly, akin to the ones that swarmed around the bowls on the stoop, flew into her face. She fanned it away.

"Really, Ms. McCabe." Behan's voice was condescending, his expression similar to the one that came over Zach's face whenever she said something he considered totally nuts.

"I know I sound like some flake who's overreacting to just having seen her first dead body. But I'm not." Looking past his wire-rimmed glasses into his dismissive blue eyes, she continued. "Do you remember the news story about an Oak Park therapist capturing a psychopath who'd been infecting women with HIV?" *All over the news for days. Not likely he'd forget.*

"You're not that same therapist?"

"I am." *Long as I had my fifteen minutes, I might as well use 'em.*

"Well." He smoothed an eyebrow that curved elegantly above his narrow glasses. "I've been feeling this sense of shock ever since that detective—Montez or something—got me up at three a.m. What I'd like to believe is that it's all over, that the police have it all sewn up." He paused for a couple of beats, then met her gaze. "But since you showed yourself to be reasonably savvy in that other situation, I suppose I can't just ignore what you have to say."

ॐ　　ॐ　　ॐ

Finishing her story, Cassidy studied the aristocratic figure who sat in approximately the same place on her sectional that Gran had recently vacated. He gazed out the north window, his fine-lined face unreadable. *He's a lawyer. What do you expect?* He was distinguished in a regal, Jason Robards sort of way, but his aloofness annoyed her.

"Sorry," Behan said in an amused tone, "I'm not convinced." He smiled slightly. "Here's a man who's killed before in a drunken rage. He somehow managed to entice Olivia into becoming his prison pen pal, then sweet-talked her into giving him a key. Last night he pulled a gun, and that frightened her into opening the blinds. You were so surprised at seeing her window uncovered you misjudged his size and jumped to a wrong conclusion." He paused. "And as far as the ring goes, your detective's right. He could have removed it from the house, then returned and passed out."

*Could that be how it really happened?*

She heard Jake's voice in her mind: ". . . like a tiny, frightened bird." *He didn't do it. He may have been drunk out of his mind, but he didn't kill her.*

"If this guy's so cold-blooded, why would he confess?"

Behan gave her a patronizing look. "Happens all the time. You'd be amazed at how often a good interrogator can squeeze a confession out of a career criminal." He eased forward on the rough-textured cushion. "Now if you don't mind—"

"What kind of lawyer are you?"

"Used to be defense. I'm retired now."

The sand-blaster sound of an unmuffled car crawled slowly past her office. She said in her firm, therapist voice, "Wouldn't my having seen a much smaller man in her living room, plus Jake's description of an alcoholic blackout be sufficient to create reasonable doubt?"

Behan smiled broadly.

*That wolfish grin. Bet that's exactly how he looked when he was just on the verge of trouncing the prosecution.*

"If I were his defense attorney, I'd have no difficulty bringing in a not-guilty verdict. That doesn't mean he didn't do it."

"But doesn't my account at least raise a reasonable doubt in *your* mind?"

He frowned, apparently not pleased at having his legal opinion challenged. She held his eyes until he moved them to the window.

"All right," he said curtly. "There's some possibility the man's innocent. But what does that have to do with either one of us?" His voice turned ironic. "I suppose this is a lead-in to a plea for a pro bono defense for this poor ex-con of yours."

"Olivia loved her cats. She might even have started to love Jake." Cassidy paused. "And I think you loved Olivia—in a father-daughter sort of way."

He slanted his face toward the window again.

"When Olivia and I were feeding the ferals, she opened up to me quite a bit. I happen to know there were several people who had a reason to be angry at her. Maybe even want her dead. Jake had no reason at all." Cassidy leaned slightly forward. "All I want from you is help in figuring out which of these people would've been most likely to go from anger to murder."

He looked at her coldly. "She didn't open up to anybody."

*Time to drop a name. Wonder if he knows she had a baby? Or that the baby grew into a young woman who thrust her unwanted self into Olivia's life?*

"One of those angry people was her daughter, Shelby."

"Her daughter?" He reared back in surprise. "She never would've told you about the baby."

"I'm a therapist. People say all sorts of things to me they wouldn't to anyone else." *That was slick. You didn't even have to lie.* "Considering how ambivalent Olivia was about seeing Shelby, it's hardly surprising she'd need somebody to talk to."

"Seeing Shelby? What are you saying?"

Cassidy told him.

"I knew she had secrets but *this* . . ." He shook his head. "Well, I have to give you credit. The only time she admitted any of her problems to me was when she wanted something fixed."

Embarrassed at the unwarranted praise, Cassidy dropped her eyes briefly, then looked up and said, "Assuming there's at least a possibility Jake didn't do it, who else might have?"

"This is ridiculous."

"I know," she said sweetly. "But since I've already wasted so much of your time, humor me with a few minutes more. Don't concentrate on it or try to figure it out. Just see what pops into your mind." *The unconscious—a lot more reliable than reason.*

He gazed into space for several seconds. "There is somebody who might actually be violent enough to do a thing like this." He shook his head. "But he's probably out of the country."

*Lawn-service Edwardo.*

Behan explained that Olivia had come to him for help after Edwardo threatened her. Initially the attorney had advised her to pay her bill and fire him. But when Olivia insisted the man was dangerous, Behan agreed to talk to him.

"I went to the lawn service office expecting to simply hand over some extra money and send him on his way. But as soon as I mentioned Olivia's name, the man went berserk. From the crazy way he started talking, I decided he might be pretty unbalanced. So I pulled some strings and had him deported." He paused. "I suppose it's possible he swam the river again, returned to Chicago, and decided Olivia was to blame for all his troubles."

"How tall is he? What's his body build like?"

"Larger than most Hispanics. Pretty bulked up, like he worked out. I'd say as tall and heavy as your average Anglo."

"Then it could've been him."

"Damn." He smoothed his eyebrow. "Up until a couple of minutes ago, I really was thinking of you as just another overwrought female. I assumed the reason you and Olivia hit it off so well is that you shared a similar, shall we say, overly imaginative sense of the world." He gave her a smile that was more human than any she'd seen from him before. "But now, I have to admit, you've got my attention."

"I don't suppose there's any way to find out if Edwardo's back in the country?"

"Not really. Although it wouldn't hurt to do a little surveillance at the office where I talked to him before."

"Is there anyone else you can think of?"

His eyes narrowed. "There's one other possibility." He shook his head. "No, that doesn't make sense. Now I'm the one letting my imagination run away with me."

*Who is it? Tell me. Don't leave me hanging.*

*Be cool. You start getting emotional, he'll just disqualify you as an overwrought female again.*

               ဢ     ဢ     ဢ

Gran opened the door, her blonde pageboy neatly in place. "I laid in a supply of peanut butter cups in case you didn't have time to buy any yet."

Stepping inside the pale peach foyer, Cassidy gave her grandmother a hug. "I picked some up already but it was sweet of you to think of it."

"The food's all ready to go." Gran led her past a bleached oak dining room table heaped with books, newspapers, and magazines. "I stopped at Erik's and bought a couple of those humongous sandwiches that fall apart when you try to get your mouth around 'em. Plus I picked out an impudent little white wine with an oak-flavored finish—whatever that means—to wash 'em down." Gran whisked through the swinging doors into the kitchen. "Unless, of course, you'd rather have the complex Pinot with the wild berry flavors."

"So, you've taken up wine tasting, have you?" Cassidy pulled the straps of the tote containing Olivia's files higher on her shoulder.

Gran arranged their sandwiches on cherry-red plates, then set the plates on wooden trays laid out with wine glasses, silverware, and extra napkins. "You know that gourmet food store on Oak Park Avenue? Hemingway's Table? Well, I started some wine classes there, but I'm afraid my palate's too old to learn any new tricks. I can't tell the difference between the hoity-toity, five-dollars-a-sip vino and the cheap brands I've been buying for years at the Famous."

Taking a bottle of French wine from the refrigerator, Gran carried it to a metal contraption that stood two feet high on the counter. The apparatus, with its baroque, cast-bronze centerpiece, reminded Cassidy of a small medieval torture device. "What on earth is that?"

"It's my fancy new bottle opener." Gran inserted the top of the bottle into the center of the machine, then cranked a long, curved handle forward. Groaning slightly, she said, "The best thing about this gadget is, I'm probably going to build up a big old arm muscle 'cause this handle here's so hard to turn."

Cassidy pulled the uncorked bottle out of the device, filled their glasses, then shoved the bottle into a silver ice bucket sitting next to the trays.

Gran added, "I bet that Hemingway's manager thinks he's got a customer for life. But I've had about enough of his fancy booze paraphernalia. I'm ready to go back to the Famous where I don't drop a bundle every time I walk in the door."

"Living room?" Cassidy asked, picking up a tray.

"That's the only place I have to sit that isn't a mess."

The living room was stylishly decorated in shades of sand and rose. A stone fireplace took up the north wall, with a seating arrangement on the opposite side of the room. They set their trays on a square glass coffee table, a mound of paper in the middle, then settled into large cushy armchairs facing the table.

Silver-threaded, saxophone-style jazz issued from an entertainment center to the right. Off in a corner stood a small trampoline Cassidy had always intended to test out.

"Aren't you gonna try that impudent, oak-tasting junk?"

Cassidy took a small sip. "I'd say it's more like audacious or brash."

"Bet you forgot to eat again, didn't you?"

"Six peanut butter cups." Cassidy gazed at the three-inch tall sandwich, her stomach making greedy noises but her brain not sure how to tackle it. Wrapping a napkin around the bottom half, she picked it up with both hands and took a huge bite. Juice dribbled down her chin and arms. When her stomach had received enough food to end the audible complaints, she laid the sandwich on her plate and scrubbed up with the extra napkins.

"You uncover any more suspects in those files of hers?" Gran asked.

"As it turns out, Olivia had more potential enemies than I ever would've guessed." Pushing aside the pile of catalogs and loose paper, Cassidy placed the files in the center of the coffee table. "Although, if I'd had my clinical wits about me, I would've recognized that, given her extreme timidity, she's exactly the type who'd be likely to have an enemy or two."

"You mean, being timid gets you more enemies?" A puzzled look crossed Gran's face.

"Being hypersensitive can cause a person to make enemies, and timid people tend to be hypersensitive. I should have made the connection sooner, since a lot of timid, hypersensitive people show up in therapy."

"Is that like being hypersensitive to strawberries and getting an allergic reaction?" Taking the top piece of bread off her sandwich, Gran applied a knife and fork to the cheese, ham, bacon, tomato, avocado, and sprouts that lay beneath it.

Cassidy smiled. "Actually, that's not a bad comparison. Hypersensitivity means taking things personally, being thin-skinned. Sort of like being allergic to the tiny, little insults you or I wouldn't notice." She sipped wine, leaned back in the large, comfortable chair. "Hypersensitive people go through life feeling hurt or angry a lot of the time."

"But how could you have known if Olivia didn't tell you?"

"Because people fall into distinct personality types. If I'd given much thought to why Olivia was so timid, I might've figured it out. You see, the reason people are timid is that they assume other people are angry, critical and rejecting, so they try to be invisible to keep the anger, etc. from being directed at them. And the reason they make this assumption is that deep down inside, they're angry, critical, and rejecting themselves."

"I'm always amazed at how you figure people out. Sort of makes me wish I'd gotten a degree in psychology myself." Gran hopped up and trotted into the kitchen, returning with the bright new ice bucket. She topped off their glasses.

"Gran, you are a natural psychologist." Cassidy smiled warmly. "You don't need any degrees." She picked up her sandwich but before she could get it to her mouth a tomato slice slipped out the bottom and landed on her grape-colored tee. After cleaning up the mess, she decided to dismember the remains the way Gran had done.

Cassidy continued. "If you want to understand people, here's a simple rule of thumb—just pay attention to how a person views his fellow humans, because whatever they say about other people is the way they are themselves." She stuck a forkful of ham and cheese into her mouth. "For instance, you always see people as kind and generous, which is exactly how you are."

"Well, and so are you. You help all your clients and even get along with your mother, which is sorta like making friends with a porcupine."

"Funny how I always feel better around you. Maybe I should move in till Zach's investigation is over." She took a sip of wine, leaned back in the soft chair, and closed her eyes, suddenly realizing how tired she was. *What I'd really like to do is to empty that impudent little bottle and sleep in this nice big chair for about twenty-four hours.*

She remembered that Harve was due at Olivia's soon. Forcing herself to sit up, she glanced at her watch. Six-thirty. She put her tray on the floor and picked up the files.

"The advantage to Olivia's hypersensitivity is that it motivated her to keep a close watch on anybody who ever gave her any trouble. I think the odds are high that the killer is somebody from these files right here. All we have to do is figure out which one." *All? As if you could ask and they'd tell you. Nothing to it. Easy as getting politicians to keep their pants zipped.*

Rummaging in her pile of loose papers, Gran pulled out a pen and notepad. "Let's go over the list. We can put our heads together and see what we come up with."

Gran, who savored gossip almost as much as she relished new adventures, was a great source of information about local residents. But since her grapevine seldom extended past village boundaries, she had nothing to contribute regarding the daughter or the lawn service guy.

Cassidy picked up the next file from the stack. "How about George Brenner?"

Gran's face lit up. "Everybody knows about the Brenners. George's father was a hero in World War II. Then, in the sixties, he got into his own personal war against integration, and he was about as far from a hero as you can get. There were a lot of people back then having fits about the village not being all white anymore, and he was one of the worst."

"What did he do?"

Gran rested her chin on her fist. "He wrote some purely hateful letters to the editor, and he ranted and raved at village board meetings about how we should build a wall at Austin Boulevard. I think he even made bomb threats against some of the new families moving in."

Cassidy dug around in Gran's pile, found a pen and began making notes on the back of an envelope. "That was George's father?"

"Yep. Now as for George himself, he was never such a problem. I seem to remember he went off to be a school teacher somewhere. Anyway, after he retired, him and his wife moved back to Oak Park and surprised the dickens out of everybody by buying a house only a block away from Austin Boulevard. None of us could figure out if he was trying to make up for his father's bad behavior, or if he'd simply come to terms with all the changes. But as far as I know, he's not any kind of troublemaker like his daddy was."

*Or maybe he is, but a secretive one, not the loudmouthed kind like the senior Brenner. Maybe he learned from his father's mistakes and so he's taking a quieter approach to glorifying guns and violence.*

*Or maybe every word in the file is pure delusion and Brenner's just a civic-minded guy who doesn't like cats.*

Putting Brenner's file aside, Cassidy filled Gran in on the Medicare-fraud boss, then related Olivia's belief that Danny Kline was stealing from her aunt.

"Esther!" Cassidy reared up straight. "There's no file on Esther. Considering how difficult she is, Esther's the number one person Olivia should've kept notes on."

"I sure would've expected her to have a file on that weird old Esther."

"Jake said there were times Olivia actually seemed to hate her aunt. So why wouldn't there be a file?"

Gran's knee jiggled in excitement. "You think Esther stole it? And if she did, does that mean Esther killed her?"

# 9. Climbing the Tree

Cassidy pictured the old woman shuffling into the room, Danny's hand beneath her elbow, then zoomed in on the knobby fingers digging into Cassidy's arm. "Esther's probably one of the few people Olivia would've voluntarily let into her house. But whether the aunt'd be mentally and physically capable of murder is another story." She drew her brows together. "I wonder if Esther'd be able to get those thick fingers of hers around a trigger? And as to motive . . . I can see the aunt killing someone spontaneously, in a fit of rage. But it's hard to imagine that she could hold onto an idea long enough to plan it out and execute it."

"Maybe Olivia didn't keep a file on her after all." Gran's face puckered in thought. "Maybe she'd been living with that old fishwife's temper tantrums for so long she didn't even bother writing 'em down."

"Fishwife?" Cassidy grinned. *Haven't heard that since I was a kid. Probably more PC than the word I would've used.* "I take it you've met the aunt?"

"Esther, she's almost ten years younger than me, but a lot of people I know have had run-ins with her. She's always trying to get away with something. There was one time I worked on a township committee handing out Thanksgiving food baskets, and Esther, she tried to pass herself off as a poor, penniless soul, even though everyone knows her house is paid for and she's got her social security."

Cassidy gazed at the round trampoline in the corner, wishing she could curl up and go to sleep on it. Pushing her half-empty glass away, she fished a peanut butter cup out of her tote. *Maybe a hit of caffeine and sugar'll get me going again.*

"That Esther." An uncharacteristically sour look came over Gran's face. "She always knows how to get what she wants. Here she is, she doesn't have any big health problems, and she finagles a way to get this good lookin' young guy to take care of her.'' Gran stood to pull the black wine bottle out of its icy nest.

Cassidy noted the elegant design of the chalice-shaped bucket. ''Speaking of good looking young guys, on a scale of one to ten, how would you rate that Hemingway's manager?''

Gran's eyes sparkled and her mouth clamped into a tight line, an expression Cassidy read as I'll-never-tell. She pointed the bottle toward Cassidy's glass.

Putting a hand over it, Cassidy asked, ''You know anything about how Esther got Danny to work for her?''

''The way I heard it, that poor Danny Kline had to quit school to take care of his mother when she came down with Alzheimer's. Seems like his mom was a real sweet person and he just didn't have the heart to put her in a home, so he stuck it out till she died. Then he ended up owing a bunch of money for her medical expenses. Well, by then he must've been in a big hurry to get his degree, so I guess he made himself a deal with the devil.''

*Gran almost always sees people in a positive light. She must* really *not like Esther.*

Her grandmother gazed at the stack of files on the table. ''You think you could leave them here and let me go through 'em?''

*Medicare forms, only thing that's really official.* She removed them from Evelyn's file. ''I think I better put these in my safe-deposit box, but you can keep the rest.''

Noticing that the evening light was turning warmer, she added, ''Well, I better be going. I have to meet Tweedledee or Tweedledum—can't tell which—for a trapping party.'' She picked up her tray, carried it into the kitchen, and started putting silverware into the dishwasher. ''If it doesn't work out with the Hemingway's manager, I'll set you up with the Tweedly twin.''

''If you don't stop fussing with those dishes,'' Gran said severely, taking a glass out of her hand, ''I'll expect a home cooked meal out of you the next time we get together.''

''Okay, you win.'' Cassidy stopped loading and dried her hands on a towel.

"So what's next?" Gran held the bottle up, eyeing the four remaining inches.

Cassidy removed the bottle from her grandmother's hands, recorked it, and deposited it in the refrigerator. "First thing tomorrow I'm going to pay a visit to daughter Shelby and boss Evelyn and inform them of the murder."

"What about me?"

"You can find somebody to take three cats."

ༀ      ༀ      ༀ

Sitting on Olivia's side porch, Cassidy felt the sting of a mosquito on her upper arm. She slapped it, then dug at the itchy colony of small bumps on her calf. The stink of cat spray mingled with the late summer smells of overgrown bushes and flowers.

She was listening for the metallic clang that would announce the springing of the first trap. When it came, she fully expected to see Starshine's small face staring back at her from behind steel bars. *So damn curious and greedy. She's bound to be the first one to try to steal the tuna.*

The calico, who'd appeared out of nowhere to streak through her legs and escape from the house as Cassidy was leaving, had been at her aggravating worst all evening. During the entire time Cassidy and Harve were setting traps, Starshine had emitted yowly noises and harassed her human. When they'd finished their task, Harve had gone to read under his pickup dome light, Cassidy had settled on the concrete porch, and Starshine had disappeared into the darkness, either to sniff out the tuna-bait or spy on the strays.

*She gets herself trapped, maybe I'll send her off to Wisconsin with the ferals. A stint as a barn cat, no humans at her beck and call, might raise her consciousness. Make her aware of hunger, poverty, homelessness.*

*Raise a cat's consciousness? The only thing that ever gets raised is their expectations regarding personal service from their two-legged valets.*

Hearing a steel door clang, Cassidy hurried toward the trap they had set in George Brenner's yard. As she came around the back of Olivia's car, she glanced at the widower's brick two-story, a porch the size of Cassidy's stoop in front, a small maple hugging the southeast corner. The three-foot long trap—Cassidy had been relieved to discover the traps were not homemade—sat beneath a shrub next to the porch.

"Guess we caught us our first stray," Harve said, his sausage-shaped figure bobbing toward her.

*Let's hope it's a stray.*

She heard a swishing sound from somewhere near the porch. A feral cat, evidently panicked by their approach, zipped up into the maple.

"Well, goldurnit." Harve, coming to stand beside her, aimed his large flashlight into the branches overhead. "We got us one cat in a trap, another in a tree." The swinging beam landed on the half-grown tiger-stripe, the one remaining feline from the spring's first litter. The cat's large eyes glittered at them through the leaves.

Feeling fur against her ankles, Cassidy looked down to see Starshine high-stepping through the grass at her feet. She made a grab but the calico leapt delicately out of reach.

Turning to Harve, Cassidy asked, "Is the tiger-stripe likely to come down?"

"Maybe, maybe not. She might just sit out the party, stay in her tree all night." He turned the light on the trap, illuminating a pumpkin-colored Daisy, sides bulging with her second litter of the year. The terrified stray crouched in the far corner.

Hunkering down next to the cage, his rough voice going gentle, Harve said, "Now don't you worry, little mother. I'm gonna take you to a place where your kits'll be warm and safe."

He stood abruptly. "Well, come on. Let's get going. We gotta get this here mother cat in the truck so we can catch us the rest of 'em critters."

When the trap was reset, Cassidy borrowed the flashlight to check on Tigerstripe again. The cat had settled into a crotch between two branches midway up the tree.

"You won't be able to catch her if she stays up there." Cassidy paused, then continued, thinking aloud. "If I climb into the tree, she'll just go higher. But maybe I could poke at her with a yardstick and scare her into jumping down."

"Might work, might not. Nobody ever knows what a cat's gonna do. No they don't."

She studied the tree, its first crotch at least four feet off the ground.

Although flexible and slender, she'd never made any effort to develop upper body strength. *Well, here you are, thirty-nine years old, going to find out if you can pull yourself up into a small, easy tree. Is there no end to the tests life puts you to?*

She ran home for a yardstick, then returned to stand next to Harve, looking first at the tree, then at Brenner's house. The two picture windows in front, uncovered during the day, now had wooden shutters drawn across them. Light from behind the shutters indicated he was probably still awake. Her proper behavior voice urged her to ask permission, but after what she'd read in his file that day, she couldn't bring herself to face him.

She wrapped her arms around the lowest branch and walked her feet up the trunk. After considerable huffing and puffing, scraping and bruising, she managed to straddle the branch in an upright position. As she climbed into the center of the tree, Tigerstripe inched farther out onto a slender branch of her own.

Hearing a series of irritated mrups from below, Cassidy looked down to see Starshine, who clearly disapproved of her human chasing strange cats into trees, yapping out her annoyance.

"Hand me the yardstick."

Cassidy took it from Harve and jabbed at the feral. The cat jumped to a lower branch and Cassidy jabbed some more. As sinuous as a snake, Tigerstripe glided from branch to branch, moving generally downward. She finally made a great leap to the ground and disappeared.

Lowering herself cautiously, Cassidy got her own feet back on the ground, leaned against the trunk, and wiped her forehead. She had wanted to attend the trapping long enough to satisfy herself that feral cats actually would set foot in ominous steel boxes. But now a great yearning for the comfort of her bed came over her. She pulled herself up straight, shifted her weight, and darted a glance at Harve.

"You got something to say, spit it out."

"Well . . ." Holding her watch up to the streetlight, she saw that it was ten o'clock. "I was just wondering how much longer you'd like me to stay and help."

"Whoever said I needed help? I just let you hang around so you could see how it's done. That way you can take over after I'm gone." He brushed at his thighs. "You get on home now, get outta my way."

She had to restrain an urge to hug him. *I'll just have to introduce him to Gran. I'll just do that. Yes I will.* She pictured Gran in her Hedy Lamarr wig holding hands with Harve in his overalls. *Even if he does look like a Tweedly Twin, he's gotta be a better catch than that price-gouging Hemingway's manager.*

She took a backward step toward Briar. "You'll cross off the cats you catch and leave the list on my porch?" She had given him an inventory, each feral designated by color and markings, so she'd know for sure which ones made it safely to Wisconsin.

"Said I would, didn't I?"

She was heading across the sidewalk when a new idea occurred to her. "If you don't get all of them, how about leaving a baited trap in Olivia's backyard?"

"What would you do with one of them ferals if you caught it? You'd have to handle it yourself, 'cause I'm not driving back to Wisconsin. No, sirree, I ain't doin' that."

She thought fast. "I could have it neutered, then release it." *Or maybe, let it live in the extra bedroom.* She was shocked that such a subversive thought would even enter her mind. *You can't do that,* she told herself firmly. *Starshine would never allow it. You've already got way too much going on, and it'd be cruel to force an outside cat to live inside.* The idea was patently absurd.

&#8278;   &#8278;   &#8278;

She was almost ready for bed when it occurred to her that she still hadn't listened to her messages. Crossing the hall into Zach's office, she sat at the extended dinette table he used for his computer and pushed PLAY.

Her mother's voice began in the middle of a sentence. " . . . hoping you'll have breakfast with us." *Oh shit. The machine's screwing up.* When she rewound the tape and tried again, it started with an earlier, skipped message, ran through the "have breakfast" message, then continued with a number of others.

She compiled a list: one call from a client, five from Esther, twelve from Helen. The messages from her mother complained that Cassidy was not returning her phone calls, had forgotten about the Branson tour, and overall was not the daughter she should be.

*The one good thing about cat rescue and murder is, they don't leave room for filial guilt.* Cassidy returned to the bedroom, lay her head on the pillow, and fell instantly asleep.

ഇ  ഇ  ഇ

Something tugged at her consciousness, warm and familiar, a pleasant nibbling sensation that drew her gently up from her sleep-shrouded depths. Light seeped through the thin skin of her eyelids. She felt a hand on her shoulder, then the warm, soft something again. *Kisses. Kisses on your neck.*

She rolled over on her back but refused to raise her lids.

"You might as well give up because I'm not going anywhere."

Opening her eyes, she pulled herself into a sitting position.

"What are those marks on your arms?" Zach asked.

"I had to climb a tree to get the tiger-stripe down."

Zach, as naked as she was, sat on the bed next to her. He smelled like toothpaste and shampoo, a big improvement over the other scents he'd been wearing lately. Starshine jumped up and settled at their feet.

"What are you doing here?" She yawned broadly, pushing snarled hair out of her face.

"I sleep here, remember?" He pulled her into the crook of his arm. "Sorry to wake you at this ungodly hour but I've got some things I'd like to talk about."

"Why now?"

"Well, for one thing, it's easier to get back to myself when I'm done for the night than when I'm gearing up to go out. For another, I wanted to tell you how much it meant to me, our making love last night. These are things I might not be able to say outside of bed."

"Does that mean we're going to do it again?" she asked sleepily. *Who wouldn't choose love over sleep? Married people, that's who.*

He laughed. "Don't worry, I'm not going to ask you to spread your legs every morning at five a.m."

"Spread your legs?" His terminology shocked her into full wakefulness.

"Sorry. I guess crudeness rubs off."

"Well, if you're going to bring home language like that, I don't think I'll let you play with those clubby guys"—*or girls*—"any more."

"What I wanted to tell you is, before I went undercover I had this sense of you and I always being on the same wavelength. Sort of like we could talk in code. Then I took on this Johnny Culver persona and had to cut myself off from you. Which led to this three-week dry spell, and my drifting farther and farther away. Making love last night reminded me how important it is for us not to ever let anything get between us."

*Now that was worth waking up for.* She rubbed her cheek against his arm.

He kissed her hair. "That's the mushy stuff. The part I probably wouldn't say at the dining room table."

She turned her head to smile at him.

"The second part is more pragmatic." He reached around to pick up something from his nightstand, then laid it on the sheet in front of her. A phone. "Since I know you're headed in the direction of doing stupid, dangerous things—the kind of thing I wouldn't mind if I were doing with you but hate having you do alone—I want you to promise you won't go anywhere without this phone."

"You're right. The phone's a good idea."

"And that you'll call me—anytime day or night—if something comes up."

Turning her head sharply to the left, she stared at her paper-littered desk. *Calling for help puts you one-down. Dependent, less able to take care of yourself than Zach. Or anybody else who walks around with a penis waggling between his legs.*

"If the situation were reversed, would you promise to call me?"

"A year ago, when I was a murder suspect, I promised not to leave the house without you, remember?"

"Oh, yeah—I guess you did." She paused. "Okay, I'll call if I need anything."

"Except for my being so schitzy right now, I'd say we're making progress." He rubbed the back of her neck. "Now tell me what you've been up to."

She detailed what she'd found in the files. "Do you think it's possible George Brenner really is collecting illegal guns and shooting cats?"

"I'm a reporter. You're a shrink. Is there any form of deviant behavior that would surprise either one of us?"

"You've got a point."

"If Brenner *is* firing guns out his window, he's definitely not somebody you should mess with." He laid his hand on her thigh. "If you can hold out another week or so, I might be able to catch him with a pistol in his hand on infrared film." He shifted around to look at her directly. "How about it? Will you make nice to the guy till I'm available to work on this with you?"

"I'll try." *Make nice to Brenner? Yuck!*

Chilled by the cold air blowing from the AC unit, she pulled the burgundy sheet up over their legs. "I also had an interesting conversation with Olivia's attorney, Carl Behan. Do you know anything about him?"

"He's legendary for cutting loose violent offenders. It's my impression the guy is corrupt, ruthless, and very well connected. His win record is amazing."

"I have to admit, I kind of liked him. At least, after I saw how much he cared about Olivia, I did. I mean, I could tell he was arrogant and full of himself, but he was also really grieving."

Zach grinned. "The downside of being a shrink. You feel sorry for everybody, including the cats."

"Empathy does create strange bedfellows." She cast a sidelong glance at her own bedfellow, who was currently looking rather strange himself. "Now tell me more about Carl Behan."

"Let's see, what do I know about him." He scratched his jaw. "He was a mob attorney a long time ago, but then he stopped taking wiseguy clients. This was before I started at the *Post*." His eyes narrowed. "There's a story rattling around in the back of my head about why he stopped. Something I heard from the guy who had the crime beat before me." He stared off into space.

"Okay, now I've got it. There was a time maybe fifteen years ago when two mob families were shooting each other up. Behan got a hit man off who belonged to one of the families, then the other family planted a bomb in his car. Only they missed Behan and blew up his daughter instead."

"Oh God!" She remembered getting the impression from Behan's file that he'd served as a father figure to her neighbor. "So maybe that's why Olivia was so important to him."

"Seems like Behan went through a hard time after that. His wife left. He quit the law for a while. I think I may've heard he had a friend who kind of nursed him through it, got him started working again."

"I bet that was Olivia's father."

"Unfortunately, this story does not have a nice, sappy ending. After Behan got back on his feet, he stopped representing Mafia scum, but his door was open to every other kind. He may not have put any more hit men back on the street, but he got a lot of rapists, killers, and other assorted vermin out of doing jailtime."

"Too bad. I see mob hit men as serving a legitimate function. Pest control for the human race." She remembered another question she needed to ask. "Did you notice if Olivia's murder showed up anywhere in the news?"

"Not with the Cubs actually winning a game, hurricane Hilda pounding the Carolinas, and three kids shot by the Latin Kings."

*Good. That means Medicare-fraud Evelyn and long-lost Shelby probably won't know about it until I deliver my face-to-face bulletin. Unless, of course, one of them killed her.*

# 10. Med Tech and Channel Eleven

Itchy little bumps on the back of her knee roused her. *Don't scratch.* She gritted her teeth, rolled over, and looked at the clock on the bureau. Six-thirty, and she was as wide awake as if she'd already absorbed her usual morning infusion of caffeine. Evidently some combination of deep sleep, Zach's sweet words in the early dawn, and the to-do list buzzing in her head had worked the magic of instant alertness.

*Good thing, too, considering how much you need to accomplish before your four o'clock client.*

She hurried down to the front porch, Starshine running ahead of her. The clipboard she had given Harve awaited her on the wicker couch. Carrying it into the kitchen, she noted that of the nine cats listed, all but two, Tigerstripe and Milton, were crossed off.

As soon as she had the coffee dripping and food in the calico's bowl, Cassidy headed toward her rear entrance to check on the trap Harve had agreed to leave baited in Olivia's yard.

The cat beat her to the door. Sitting with her body plastered against the wood, she looked up and said a coaxing Mwat.

"Curiosity wins out over food, does it?" Cassidy gazed down at Starshine, noting that her sides had acquired a slight bulge. "But then, with Zach coming in at dawn, you're probably double dipping on breakfast."

Reaching for the knob, she hesitated, wondering if she should make Starshine stay in the house. *Trying to keep her inside is like hiding the bottle from an alcoholic. All it does is make her more devious.*

Cassidy opened the door and crossed to Olivia's backyard, the calico dodging between her feet as she went. She found the tiger-stripe in the trap, her skinny body pressed against the far end of the steel box.

Starshine pranced sideways up to the cage.

Sitting on her heels, Cassidy gazed at the frightened, hissing animal. The gray striped coat, like that of all strays, was ruffled and scruffy, but her face was beautiful, a white mask with a distinct black outline around the large, dilated eyes.

"You are such a brat." Cassidy swatted at Starshine, who moved just out of reach and continued her gleeful victory dance.

Cassidy addressed the feral, "You think this is bad, just wait till you meet the vet."

After feeding the indoor cats, she loaded the trap into the Toyota. Her plan was to drop Tigerstripe off for neutering, then pay Olivia's boss and daughter surprise visits at their workplaces.

She showered, then slipped into the bedroom where Zach was still asleep. Assessing tree-climbing damage, she noted scrapes and bruises on her arms and legs. *If I'm going to face two professional women on their own turf, I better look my best.* She took a long-sleeved, violet linen dress and matching leather bag out of her closet, an ensemble Zach had insisted on buying for her. The bag alone had cost nearly as much as she was used to spending at her resale shop for an entire season's clothing.

Ever since moving in with her, Zach had been bent on upgrading her house, yard, and apparel, everything except his own wardrobe, which, during normal times, he refused to expand beyond jeans and black tees. Not liking to see him spend so much money, she generally tried to resist. But he overruled her and bought things anyway.

She went downstairs to call the vet on the kitchen phone, but the recorded message told her the office would not open until eight. Standing in the dining room doorway, she gazed at Olivia's yard, aware that the place seemed empty and desolate with no cats out sunning on the grass. It suddenly struck her that Olivia's death had made no difference at all in the appearance of her property, whereas the ferals' departure had left it looking lifeless and abandoned.

Cassidy poured a second cup of coffee and sat at the table to ruminate over the Tigerstripe-Milton problem.

*You dump Tigerstripe back outdoors, she might starve. Or get shot.*

*She won't have any more regular meals coming her way unless you take up the cat lady position. Which you absolutely aren't going to do. If you were to collect another colony, Zach'd be fully within his rights to lock you in the attic, treat you like Rochester's wife.*

*Well, then, the only alternative is for you to drive Tigerstripe to the sanctuary. And as long as you're going that way, you might as well catch Milton and take both cats up to live with the lions, tigers, and bears.*

Raising her purple mug, she traced the Laurel Burch cat design with a burgundy fingernail. She would hold off on Tigerstripe's delivery until she'd captured Milton also. And if the old tom proved a little trap-shy, if he did not surrender instantly, Tigerstripe would have to endure a brief sojourn in the extra bedroom.

She pictured the tiger-stripe perched on the pile of boxes Starshine had used as a refuge from her kittens when they were hounding her into near starvation. *Oh God, I wonder if ferals understand litter boxes?*

At eight o'clock she dialed the vet again and explained her feral cat situation to the girlish sounding voice on the other end of the line.

Cassidy asked, "Can I drop her off right away?"

"That'd be fine. If you get her in now, you can pick her up after four today. But since she's a stray, she'll also need FELV and FIV tests before she has contact with any other animals. And she'll have to have her shots, of course."

"Oh, right." Cassidy had no idea what the two acronyms meant but she did know about shots.

"What's your cat's name?"

"Uh, Tigerstripe . . ." She paused, realizing the name didn't quite fit. "No, wait, make that . . . Tigger." Picturing the perky yellow animal from her childhood Pooh book, she smiled. *Wouldn't it be nice to see that poor, scared feral turn into a bounce-a-day Tigger?*

Cassidy asked, "So, how much is all this going to run?'

"Oh, it won't be bad," the voice chirped. "Not more than two-fifty."

She groaned inwardly. *Two hundred to Harve yesterday. Another two-fifty on your credit card today, and double that when you bring Milton in.*

With her client load so low, she wouldn't be earning enough to

*Well, obviously, anybody rude enough to disturb this woman's busy phone schedule ought to pay penance by cooling their heels.*

In front of Cassidy was a small waiting area with a partition behind it to separate the public area from what she assumed to be the lab. She could see three doors, one across the waiting area to her left, the other two along the wall to her right. *Three doors, the tiger and the lady. Only this time the tiger is the lady.* Cassidy fastened her eyes on the receptionist and stayed where she was.

Speaking into the phone, the receptionist delivered Cassidy's message. She hung up and said, "Ms. Wentworth's busy. You wanna see her, you'll have to make an appointment like everybody else."

*Damn. I don't want to come back later and I do want to get to her first with the news about Olivia's murder. On top of that, I'm sick of being treated like a peasant in a bread line.*

"You tell her," Cassidy enunciated distinctly, "if she doesn't see me now, I'm going directly to the authorities."

The woman blinked uncertainly. Her eyes flitted to the door on the opposite side of the waiting room. Pivoting, Cassidy strode across the intervening space, her low-heeled sandals clicking against the tile floor. She opened the door, marched inside, and closed it behind her. A blond woman glared at her from the other side of the desk.

"Why did you do that?" Evelyn said, her voice irritated. "Now I'm going to have to call security." She spoke into her desk phone. "Send Joe in here right away."

Cassidy lowered herself onto the side chair's cracked vinyl cushion. "Olivia Mallory was murdered Saturday night."

The lab owner's expression changed not at all. *Already knows about it? Incredibly good at masking? If she is guilty, wouldn't she at least pretend to be surprised?*

Evelyn picked up the phone again. "Tell Joe I won't be needing him after all." She was angular and handsome, her straight blond hair chopped at jaw length. From the lines at her mouth and eyes, Cassidy guessed her to be in her fifties.

She spent a long moment inspecting Cassidy, the blond woman's gaze moving over her as if searching for some small flaw—dandruff on her shoulders, a thread dangling from her hem—anything that might discredit her. Cassidy was glad Zach had bought her the expensive

cover the extra expenses. Zach would pay it without complaint, but even now that they were married she hated needing financial bail-outs. Especially when his current investigation had to have put a strain on his budget too.

*Having Kevin keep you in debt all those years was like sliding down a never-ending greased pole. But being a kept woman is only slightly better.*

      ဢ     ဢ     ဢ

Cassidy had just stepped out her back door when she heard Starshine calling from across Briar. Moving in the direction of the feline cries, she said, "Kitty, kitty." No cats anywhere.

Stopping in the middle of the street to listen more carefully, she decided the cat's tone was more plaintive than panicked. And it seemed to be coming from somewhere above her. She hurried over to Brenner's maple and looked up.

Starshine's triangular face peered down from a crotch about eight feet off the ground.

"What on earth are you doing up there?" *Imitating. She saw Tigger do it, so now she's gotta try it out herself.* Cassidy had read somewhere that cats mimic each other's behavior, but since Starshine was an only child, she'd never witnessed it before. "Okay, I can see that you're an outstanding climber. Even better than Tigger. Now be a good kitty and come on down." *How ridiculous. When did "be a good girl" ever work on you?*

Starshine sat tall and said Mrup. Cassidy took it to mean *fat chance.*

"All right then, you just stay up there. What better way to take off a few pounds than sitting out meals in a tree."

Putting her hands on her hips, she stared at the calico, an uneasy twitch starting in her stomach. *Brenner won't do anything to her as long as she's in plain sight of the street. It's only his back window he shoots out of.*

Her gaze skimmed the front of his house. A large picture window on either side of the porch, a row of smaller windows upstairs.

"Nothing's going to get me up that tree again," she said adamantly. "Certainly not in a linen dress. And not when I have a ton of things to do between now and my four o'clock client." She started toward her car, then turned back for a parting shot. "You're not fooling me. I know damn well that what climbs up *can* climb down."

∞      ∞      ∞

She dropped off Tigger at the vet, locked the Medicare forms in her safe-deposit box, then turned her car toward the Chicago neighborhood where Med Tech Lab was located.

Mentally reviewing the file on Evelyn, she remembered Olivia's comment that the lab owner was unwilling to pay a living wage. This gave Cassidy an idea for another task Gran could take on. At the Augusta-Austin stoplight, she fished her new phone out of her purse.

"I just got my own cell phone, so for once I've caught up with you," she said in response to her grandmother's greeting.

"Mostly all I use mine for is fielding your mother's calls."

The light turned green. "Oops, now I have to negotiate traffic and manage the phone at the same time. And here I'm the one always complaining about drivers with mechanical devices glued to their ears."

"You just tell me what you want and we can hang up."

"Do you think you could get a credit report on Evelyn Wentworth?"

"You bet. Did you know you can dig up all kinds of financial dirt about people on the Internet now? Scary, isn't it?"

"Scary but useful. Although I wouldn't have the least idea how to do it myself. Oh, and there's one other thing." She pulled a notepad out of her purse. "Call this number and find out when Jake Streeter has his visiting day."

Snapping her phone shut, she continued east on Augusta, leaving her middle class suburb behind and driving into a gang-ridden, all-black section of the city. The change from Oak Park to Chicago was immediately apparent in the dearth of greenery, which grew in such abundance in the village. Once she crossed over into the Austin neighborhood, trees were sparse, parkways trampled, and grassy yards in short supply.

Cassidy used Augusta for eastbound travel because it was one of the few noncommercial thoroughfares, and therefore less clogged with busses, trucks, and double-parked vehicles. She passed through some sections that looked reasonably well-kept and residential, although many were marked by graffiti, iron-gated doors, and abandoned cars.

She moved slowly along in rush hour traffic, the sunlight slanting

into her eyes. A woman in the battered sedan ahead of her stopped suddenly, causing Cassidy to slam on her own brakes. A teenaged male who stood on a corner a few feet from her Toyota gave her a long stare. Cassidy locked her doors and crammed her expensive handbag on her lap beneath the steering wheel where it would not be easy to grab.

∞      ∞      ∞

She located the address she was looking for on Division just west of Ashland, a Hispanic neighborhood in the beginning stages of gentrification. The laboratory was housed in a squat, concrete-block building, its front unbroken except for a steel door with a sign above it and a tinted glass window several feet to the left. She parked and considered her options.

*Flaunt your knowledge of the Medicare fraud? Evelyn would deny it unless you tell her about the forms. And it's a little early on to bring out your one and only big gun.*

*So what do you think you can accomplish here? You can watch to see how surprised she seems when you tell her about the murder. You can drop a hint that you know her guilty secret. About the most you can expect is to get a reading on her reactions, because from what Olivia said in the file, this is not a lady who's likely to invite you in for a little heart-to-heart.*

Stepping into a dimly lit interior, Cassidy was momentarily stopped by strong laboratory smells: a powerful mix of chemicals and body wastes. A middle-aged black woman behind the reception desk wa engaged in what sounded like a personal phone call. Cassidy waite several minutes. Finally the woman ended her conversation and beg digging in a drawer. "Help you?" she asked without looking up.

"I'm here to see Ms. Wentworth."

"You got an appointment?"

"I have something to say that'll be of interest to her. My nar Cassidy McCabe."

The receptionist, who wore a yellow knit top that would looked good on her if she'd been two sizes smaller, picked up of papers, tapped them on the desk to neaten the edges, repla stack, and squared it with a corner. "Take a seat. I'll see available."

dress. At last Evelyn said, "Well. Who are you? And why did you come bursting in here to tell me about Olivia?"

"I'm her neighbor. She talked to me quite a bit about what was going on here at her job."

The lab owner's green eyes wavered slightly. *Knows something. Of course she does. She knows she's committing fraud and now she suspects you know it too.*

"You didn't answer the second part about why you're here."

"That's true."

Evelyn rested a silk-clad elbow on her metal desk. "You're not going to explain why you felt the need to drop that little bombshell of yours?"

*This woman is very good at intimidation. Bet she has everybody here jumping. She might even have me jumping if it weren't for the forms.* Cassidy smiled. "As I said before, Olivia told me all about her job situation."

"And what was that? That she was close to being fired?" Evelyn jiggled a pencil between her manicured fingers. "If you came here expecting to see me get all maudlin and remorseful for wanting to dump poor Olivia, I'm afraid I'm going to have to disappoint you."

"I doubt very much that you would have fired her."

"You know, there really isn't any reason for me to be discussing personnel issues with you." Smiling coolly, she tilted her head. "Now, are you going to leave willingly, or shall I have Joe escort you out?"

ﾊﾟ        ﾊﾟ        ﾊﾟ

Cassidy got in her car and started north toward Chicago's public television station, the daughter's place of employment. *Well, that was a bust. You probably should've made an appointment, put on a docile face, and sucked up.* But she could tell from the rigidity in her spine that she would never have been able to make herself do that. *Now the best you can hope for is, she'll see you as a threat and won't be able to let it lie.*

*Right. If I'm lucky, she'll show up at my house with a gun.*

ﾊﾟ        ﾊﾟ        ﾊﾟ

Driving to a far north section of the city, Cassidy located a tall black cube announcing the entrance to the Channel 11 building. Ignoring the "authorized parking only" sign, she stashed her Toyota in the deep lot in front of the sprawling brick structure. She went inside a glass-domed entrance and climbed a flight of widely-spaced, floating stairs. *Must've designed these things with Michael Jordan in mind.*

The spacious reception area contained a row of black leather chairs, three television screens showing public television programming, and at the far end, a glass wall and door. Cassidy approached a well groomed woman behind a long counter, gave her name, and asked to speak to Shelby Onkean. After talking into her headset, the receptionist informed her that Ms. Onkean would be out shortly.

Minutes later a striking young woman in black leggings and a long blue tunic, one large button at the top, came through the door. Gazing at Cassidy out of dark-fringed, inquisitive green eyes, she said, "You must be Cassidy McCabe."

"And you're Shelby." *Could be a model except she's not languid or vacant enough.* Cassidy offered her hand and the young woman gave it a firm shake. She remembered reading in the notes that Olivia considered her daughter not to be like her at all, but Cassidy could see some resemblance. *Same fine, dark hair. Similar features.* The difference was in the expression and the body language. The daughter had a sparkle in her eyes, a lilt in her voice, and a jauntiness in her manner that Olivia had lacked.

Shelby tossed long, curly hair over her shoulder. "So, am I supposed to know who you are? If you're a vendor, you're talking to the wrong person."

*This is not going to be fun.* Cassidy met the daughter's gaze. "I'm a friend of Olivia's and there's something I need to tell you."

"Olivia?" Shelby took a step back, an angry light flaring in her eyes. "What's going on? Did she send you here to talk to me?"

"You'll understand soon enough," Cassidy said grimly. "This is going to take some time. Do you have an office where we could close the door and not be disturbed?"

Shelby twisted the button at the top of her tunic, her face suddenly wary. "I'm just a lowly PA. We don't have offices."

"PA?"

"Production assistant. Well, I don't have an office but one of the producers is out today. Maybe we could park ourselves in his place." Her eyes narrowed. "Can't you give me a hint?"

Cassidy released a small sigh. "This is not good news."

Shelby's features tightened in a slight, nervous frown. "Well, okay. You'll have to wear a visitor's badge." The receptionist handed Cassidy a clip-on plastic rectangle. Shelby led her through the door, which clicked as the receptionist unlocked it, then took her downstairs into a basement area made up of open spaces, corridors, and a warren of offices. Borrowing a key from another woman, Shelby headed toward a door in the middle of a long hallway, unlocked it and took Cassidy inside.

The windowless room was small, stuffy, and anonymous. Two wooden chairs stood in front of a desk. They each took a chair, turning them so they faced each other.

"You like working here?" Cassidy asked.

"I'm on my way to becoming a film maker and this is a good place to start." She paused. "So, what's this about?"

Cassidy took a deep breath. "Shelby, your mother's dead."

"What?" Her green eyes widened. "She can't be dead. She wasn't even sick. At least, if she was I didn't know it. How could a perfectly healthy person just die?"

"She was murdered. The police have a suspect in custody."

"Murdered?" Shelby shook her head vigorously. "No, it can't be true." She rose abruptly and went to stand in front of the closed door, her back to Cassidy. "How could she do this?" the daughter demanded angrily. "Go and get herself murdered. It's so unfair! The last time I saw her we had this big fight. I never even got to talk to her again." She wrung her hands for several moments, then covered her face. "Oh God."

"You're right, it is unfair. You should have had more time with her."

"I don't know why I'm crying. I hardly even knew her." Her voice choked. "I hate to cry."

"Maybe that's why this hit you so hard. Because you didn't get to know her." Cassidy rose and laid an arm around Shelby's shoulders. "Come sit with me a minute while you pull yourself together." Moving her chair next to the other woman's, Cassidy fished a packet of tissue out of her purse and put it in the daughter's hand.

"Why don't you tell me what's making you feel so bad. Sometimes it helps to put things into words."

Damp lines made tracks down Shelby's finely contoured cheeks. "It's too late now. I'll never get another chance." She pressed the tissue beneath one eye, then the other. "I'll never find out what she was really like. I'll never know which version was true."

# 11. A Tea Party

"Which version?" *Thank God, no rule in the ethics book against covert therapy.*

"You know, Dad's or Grandma's." Her teary gaze focused on Cassidy. "What am I talking about? Of course you wouldn't know."

"Your dad and grandmother had different versions of what Olivia was like?"

She nodded. "Dad always said it wasn't Olivia's fault, but Grandma was pretty bitter about the way she dumped me on him." Shelby shook her head. "I'm talking too much. I have this bad habit of letting everything that's in my head come pouring out my mouth." She gave Cassidy a weak smile. "I'm sure you didn't come here to listen to my problems."

*Oh, but I did.*

"I was Olivia's friend and I'm also a therapist. I'm used to people telling me things. Maybe, if you explain the two versions, I could help you with it."

"Did you talk to my mother? I mean really talk?" Shelby pulled out another tissue and wound it around her index finger.

"She told me about your wanting to see her. She didn't say much about the past."

Shelby gave her an intense look. "Did she say anything at all about why she gave me up?"

Cassidy shook her head. "Is that what the two versions are about?"

"When I was just a few days old, my father took me to live on my grandmother's farm in Maine. From the time I was little I used to hear them arguing about Olivia—what was wrong with her that she never wanted anything to do with me."

"How did your father and Olivia happen to get together?"

"Dad came to Chicago to go to med school at the U. of C. That's something he always wanted—to be a doctor. He didn't have any money but he got scholarships and worked a lot of part-time jobs. He was in his last year when he met this pretty secretary." She stopped and began shredding the tissue.

"And Olivia got pregnant."

Shelby looked down at her hands. "I'm not sure I should be telling you this."

"What do you think would be best? To stop or go on?"

"I feel so confused." She let out a deep sigh. "I guess I'd kind of like to talk. And if you're a therapist, maybe you can help me understand."

"I'll do my best."

"Okay, this is the story I heard." She closed her eyes briefly. "Olivia really, really wanted Dad to marry her. My father said she was just young and scared and didn't know what to do. And I can understand that. Back then things were harder."

"But your grandmother sees it differently?"

She sighed again. "My grandmother says she wanted to marry a doctor. At any cost."

"She thinks Olivia deliberately got pregnant?"

Shelby stared into her lap, then raised her head, her eyes brimming. "My father said it was his fault. You see, he felt so guilty about the pregnancy he agreed to marry her, and she was really happy and excited. But then he realized he couldn't go through with it."

"He backed out."

Her hands twisted together. "And by then it was . . . it was too late to do anything."

*This child grew up knowing the only reason she was born is that it was too late to get an abortion.*

"Olivia said she couldn't handle dealing with a baby, that she was going to put me up for adoption. My father didn't want to just turn me over to strangers so he quit school and took me back to Maine."

Turning her head to stare at the wall, Shelby pulled out another tissue and dabbed at her eyes. Following her gaze, Cassidy noticed that the beige paper was lumpy and stained, with a triangular tear near the corner.

Shelby brought her eyes back to Cassidy. "Dad never blamed Olivia. He always said that as a med student, he should have taken responsibility for making sure she didn't get pregnant. Even though he had to drop out of school and ended up with all those debts to pay, he never made me feel guilty about it."

*But she does or she wouldn't have mentioned it.*

Cassidy shifted on the hard wooden seat. "But your grandmother blamed her."

"She said Olivia never cared about anything except catching herself a doctor-husband."

"And you came here to find out whether your mother was simply young and scared, or the conniver your grandmother said she was."

"Dad always told me it shouldn't matter. He died over a year ago." She blinked back more tears. "He said that at this point, nobody knows what really happened, not even Olivia. He said I should put it behind me and concentrate on the future." She paused. "And I'm sure he's right. I'm sure that's what I should be doing."

"But you can't." Cassidy sighed. "That's how a lot of us are. We have to make sense out of our history before we can move on into the future." *And the sad thing is, most people's future is some kind of reworking of their past. No matter how hard they try to escape, if they never understand it, it sticks to their feet like a shadow.*

Shelby's eyes filled again. "You mean, you don't think it's crazy for me to come here and try to force my mother to talk to me?"

"Not at all. You deserved that from her." She paused. "So you weren't able to sort out which version of Olivia was the truth?"

"She refused to talk about the past."

Cassidy reached for Shelby's hand and held it between both of hers. "People are very complex. Whatever they do, there's usually more than one reason for it. My guess is, both versions are true. Olivia was afraid of everything. She probably had a desperate urge to find somebody to protect her, and a doctor must have seemed like an ideal husband. She might even have deliberately gotten pregnant, but that doesn't mean she didn't care about you. She probably felt scared, angry and over-whelmed, all at once. And she also knew she didn't have the resources to be a good parent. By giving you up, she made it possible for you to grow into the strong, competent young woman you are today."

Shelby gazed into space, then shook her head. "Why does every-thing have to be so damn complicated? What you said sounds right but I still feel confused."

"You need time for it to sink in."

"Actually, I think talking did help." She smiled weakly. "Are you going to send me a bill?"

*Ask her about the ring. Now—while she's feeling grateful and open and in the mood to talk.*

*While she's vulnerable, don't you mean? If you take advantage of this poor girl's grief, you'll be every bit as bad as the TV newshounds you're always railing against.*

Cassidy pressed her business card into Shelby's hand. "I'd like for us to talk some more. Will you call me tomorrow?"

&#9702;&#9702;&#9702;&#9702;&#9702;&#9702;

It was only eleven when Cassidy crossed Austin Boulevard back into Oak Park. Not having eaten, she called her grandmother and suggested they meet at the Buzz Café. Bouncing ideas off someone like Gran or Zach always helped her to problem solve.

*Look how much you've accomplished and it's not even noon. You should get up every morning at six.*

*My voluntarily becoming conscious at six again this decade is about as likely as Madonna's being chosen poster girl for the religious right.*

Inside the Buzz Café, Gran waved at her from a table near the front. The decor of the coffeehouse, located in the Harrison Street artists' colony, reflected the neighborhood it inhabited. Cassidy approved of the green and grape color scheme as well as the large variety of original art hanging on the walls. Sliding into a wooden chair, its surface splattered with brightly painted flowers, Cassidy noticed that the wig Gran wore today, a mousy bob, was more subdued than usual.

"I hope that plain hair of yours doesn't signify a drop in mood."

"I'm being inconspicuous. Seeing as how I'm working a case, I didn't want to call attention to myself."

The restaurant owner, Laura, a woman who didn't look a day over twenty but ran her shop as if she'd been doing it for decades, greeted them warmly and took their orders.

As soon as Laura turned her back, Gran leaned forward and said in a conspiratorial tone, "You first. I'm dying to hear what you thought of the suspects."

"I liked Shelby. Evelyn was overbearing and callous. Unfortunately, my opinion has no bearing at all on their guilt or innocence."

The owner brought lattes. Gran held her glass up to admire it. "Ordering latte always makes me feel like some hotshot yuppie insider. You should see me sidle up to the Starbucks' counter and tell 'em I'll have a hazelnut, single shot, regular-sized, skinny. I spent hours memorizing my routine."

Cassidy brushed her fingertips across the polished oak table. "You have a real knack for being an insider. Too bad it didn't rub off on me."

"Now that's just silly and you know it. You don't need to be an insider. You've always had a sense of who you are. Why would you care about getting inside anybody else's world when you've got this nifty little world of your own?"

Cassidy remembered wishing she could be normal like her neighbor Dorothy Stein. "Okay, I don't want to be an insider. But I would like to stop putting myself in the path of dead bodies, killers, and feral cats."

"But that's just part of being you. When you were three, you got stung all over 'cause you tried to put a dead wasp back in its nest. Now here you are all grown up, and your curiosity and that old need to fix things is still getting you in trouble. Not to mention you married a man who's every bit as trouble-prone as you. And I don't for a minute believe that either one of you would have it any other way."

*Would you really trade lives with Dorothy?* Zach's words about not letting anything get between them played in her head, and she decided that living on the edge might not be all bad.

"Okay, you win. I'll cancel that personality transplant I had scheduled for tomorrow."

Laura brought them heaping salads and bowls of steaming, homemade soup. Inhaling the rich, tomato aroma, Cassidy told Gran about her morning. "Even though I'd love to take Evelyn down a notch or two, I can't give her much of a rating on the suspect-scale unless I can prove she knew Olivia had the forms."

"The daughter doesn't sound like she'd rate very high either. Considering you ended up liking her, she probably isn't gonna turn out to be the kind of cold-hearted girl who'd kill her own mother."

"And she wasn't wearing the sapphire ring. Now that would've given us an honest to God clue. Although I have to say, I'd rather pin the murder on some really unpleasant person than that nice Shelby." Poking a spoonful of soup into her mouth, she gazed at a gauzy, blue and lavender watercolor of a unicorn.

Gran sprinkled salt on her salad. "Well, I got a good start on the credit report. I found me a web site and gave 'em my credit card number, so it's in the works. They're gonna email me the scoop on Evelyn in a day or two. And as to Jake, we can visit him at Cook County anytime tomorrow." She shuddered. "I hate to even think what goes on down there."

*Rape, bondage, torture. And probably a few other things beyond the imagination of the noncriminally minded. Thank God Jake's big enough to take care of himself.*

"Gran, you're a whiz."

"But that's not all."

Sitting back in her chair, Cassidy looked at her grandmother in amazement. "You have more?"

"All I got right now is an idea. But it does give us something else to look into." She gave her short hairpiece a slight adjustment, obviously preening.

"C'mon, spit it out. You already have my undying admiration."

"I was reading over the files and it popped out at me that before the daughter came along, Olivia never got phone calls from anybody except Esther and her godfather. So I thought, if Olivia'd gotten herself in a fight with somebody, maybe some of the fighting was over the phone. And it might show up in her telephone records."

"Shelby said she hadn't spoken to Olivia since the last time they were together, which was over a month ago. So if anybody other than Carl or Esther showed up in the records, it would be evidence of something going on between that person and Olivia." Cassidy drummed her fingers on the table. "That's a great idea, except the only way I know to get phone records is through a cop, and I doubt that Zach's old girlfriend is in the mood to do me any favors."

"I bet Irma could do it." Gran's old eyes sparkled. "She's got this high mucky-muck job over at Ameritech. I helped her out quite a bit when her mother was dying, so I think she might do a little something for me."

Jabbing a forkful of salad, Gran raised it halfway to her mouth. "'Course, I realize this is a long shot. The killer might've just pounced on Olivia without any warning. Or at least without any telephone warning."

"Yeah, but it certainly could be the case that a fight'd been brewing beforehand. And some of that brewing could've occurred over the phone. If you can get those records, I'd sure like to see them."

ಬ     ಬ     ಬ

Mrorrr! Cassidy heard it the instant she opened her car door. A forlorn howl coming from Brenner's maple. *Don't go over there. It'll just encourage her.* Cassidy marched resolutely into the house. Zach was already gone but he'd left a note on the dining room table.

Cass,

    I made the mistake of picking up the phone and got stuck listening to your mother. I swear she had me on the line for fifteen minutes before I could insert a single gotta-go.

    You also had two messages on the machine, both from some batty lady named Esther. She wants you to drive to this bakery at 5325 Cermak, buy kolacky—apparently that's the only place that does it right—take them to her house and have a tea party with her. I'd recommend you stay as far away as possible. You've already got your mother—you don't need Esther.

    I don't mind your rescuing feral cats but taking on dingy old ladies is going too far.

Gotta go buy some dope.
Love,
Zach

*Good thing he's so liberal in regard to ferals, since Tigger'll be ensconced in the junk-room spa by the time he gets home.*

She stared out the dining room window at a bunch of kids tossing a football back and forth in the middle of Briar.

*How're you going to handle Esther? You did, after all, promise to call.*

*Yeah, but whatever you do, she'll want more. Give her a phone call, she'll want a visit. Give her a visit, she'll be ready to move in.*

The football sailed through the air in a perfect arc. A girl in front of Brenner's place jumped high and caught it.

*You have to talk to her. There is, after all, the little matter of the missing Esther file. Not to mention the other little matter of the possible Danny thefts.*

*Okay, so I have to talk to her. But a visit might net more than a phone call. She's so flaky, if she did kill Olivia she might just be dying to tell me about it. Especially if I bribe her with kolacky.*

*That takes care of Esther. Now what about your mother?* The guilt she'd warded off the night before began to creep back in. She trotted upstairs, dug out the hotel number, and succeeded in catching Helen in her room. Cassidy apologized for not calling sooner, then paid penance by listening to twenty minutes of complaints about the bus's faulty plumbing, her seatmate's incessant talking, and the uncomfortable bed in her room.

After hanging up the phone, she started off for Esther's. As she stepped out her back door, the woebegone cries from across the street drew her like a magnet. She went to look up at the small, tricolor face peeking over a crotch in the tree's upper branches.

"Not ready to come down yet?" Cassidy remembered that Tigger was due to return from the vet as soon as she finished with her four o'clock client. If the calico was still in the tree, she would be watching every step Cassidy took from the car to the house. The sight of *her* human carrying a trap containing another feline into *her* house might just be enough to spark a long-term tree-oriented sit-in. And in addition to the problem of bringing Tigger into the house, there was also the problem of night falling and the proximity of Starshine's maple to the cat-shooter's second-story window.

"Damn! Why didn't you yowl at Zach and get him to go up after you?"

*Because you're the one she's mad at. You're the one who betrayed her by pursuing another feline up the tree.*

"You are a mean, spiteful, envious cat." *Isn't that a tautology?* "I'm not climbing that tree just to prove I don't love Tigger more than I love you." Heading toward the Toyota, she realized that her sense of conviction about not going up the tree was waning with the hours of the day.

Cassidy stopped to pick up a second cat box and extra litter, then drove south on Oak Park Avenue toward the bakery Esther had indicated. Waiting at the Lake Street light, she gazed at Scoville Park, its corner ablaze with three huge plume-like crimson and yellow flowers curving aloft on six foot stems. Growing in front of a flat, rectangular sculpture, the vivid, overblown blossoms looked like feather boas a giant clown might wear.

She went east on Cermak Road, a wide thoroughfare running through Cicero and Berwyn, two suburbs that had once been primarily Bohemian but now were changing to Hispanic. She located the bakery, then turned north and drove into a parking lot directly behind the storefronts, a wide strip where el tracks used to run. Pulling into a perpendicular slot, she entered the bakery through its rear door. Wonderful bread and pastry smells made her salivate like Pavlov's dogs.

She bought a bag of kolacky, then went to Esther's bungalow. Stopping in front of the house, she noticed a small, late model Dodge sitting in the driveway. A freshly washed, deep purple sedan, its amethyst tone glowed brightly in the afternoon sun. She remembered Danny saying that Esther still drove.

*Would Esther ever run her car through a car wash? Hardly seems likely. But then you wouldn't've pegged Olivia as the convict pen-pal type, either.*

She mounted the porch steps. Since two loose wires were all that remained of the bell, she opened the screen to knock on the inside door. A pile of mail lay on the threshold. She slid it into her left hand along with the bakery sack and banged on the thick oak panel with her right. After a long wait, Esther's face appeared in the window and the door opened.

"Oh, sweetie, you came to see me. What a nice girl!" The clawlike hands grasped Cassidy's arm and drew her inside, where the interior air hung thick and muggy. From the tug of Esther's hands, she got the sense that the aunt was fairly strong. Cassidy winced at the body odor given off by the old woman.

"You brought my kolacky. Now us girls can finally sit down and have ourselves a nice chat over a cup of tea." She snatched the sack from Cassidy's hand, nearly causing her to drop the envelopes. "And you even picked up my letters for me."

Esther grabbed for the mail but something Cassidy had seen made her resist. Turning her body to block the older woman, she fixed her gaze on the top envelope, addressed to Ruth Kravitch at Esther's street number.

"This one came to the wrong house." Cassidy gave the rest of the mail to Esther. "I'll write a note on it and drop it back in the box."

Dumping the other pieces on the coffee table, Esther sidled closer to the envelope in Cassidy's hand. "Oh, don't bother with that, sweetie. You just leave it here and I'll have Danny take care of it."

Her eyes narrowing, Cassidy read the return address, a bank in Berwyn. "Why so eager to get hold of Ruth Kravitch's mail?"

Crossing her arms, Esther pouted. "I don't gotta tell you nothin'."

"Then I'll take the letter and go."

"Promise you won't say a word to nobody?"

"You're beginning to make me very suspicious, you know that?"

A sly look came over Esther's face. "It's a secret from my old man. John, he don't know nothin' about it."

Her brow creasing, Cassidy stared into the lumpy face with its thin gray hair, beaklike nose, and long upper lip. *Danny told us her husband was dead.* "Tell me about the secret."

Esther lowered her voice. "John won't give me his whole paycheck like he oughtta. Men are supposed to give all their pay to their wives to run the house with. But I fooled him. I snuck money out of his wallet and saved it up till I had a *thousand* dollars." She paused, clearly expecting Cassidy to be impressed.

"That's a lot of money to save."

"A whole thousand. Then I went to the bank and opened my own account under my middle and maiden name." A fierce look came over her face. "So that envelope's mine and you gotta give it to me."

Handing it over, Cassidy watched the envelope disappear into the pocket of the aunt's shapeless gray skirt.

"Now you gotta promise you won't tell John."

"Okay, I promise."

"That's a good girl. Now let's you and me go make us some tea." Esther drew her into the kitchen. A formica table piled high with bulging paper bags stood near the front of the room. The aunt went to the stove in back to turn on the gas beneath a grease-coated aluminum teapot.

Moving the bags to one end of the table, she laid down two chipped, rose-patterned plates. Cassidy placed a round, puffy pastry on each dish as Esther bustled about making tea in small, porcelain cups.

After they were seated, Cassidy picked up her cup, inhaled the minty fragrance, and said, "I understand you still drive."

"You bet I do. I can go anywhere I want, and nobody's ever gonna take my license away either." Talking around a mouthful of pastry, she added, "That car out there's mine, dearie. Ain't it a beaut?"

"If you can drive, why send me to the bakery?"

"It's just polite to bring something when you go visiting."

"It's also polite to discuss mutual friends, so I'd like you to tell me more about Olivia."

"I don't wanna talk about her. She was mean to me."

Cassidy nibbled the pastry. "You must be mad at her then."

"It was her that was mad. I told her I was gonna leave the house to Danny and she got so mad she wouldn't speak to me."

"Did you do anything to hurt her?"

Esther slurped her tea, spilling some of it into the saucer. "You wanna know who shot her? Maybe Danny did. Those two were always fighting over the house. But it's my house and I can leave it to anybody I want."

"You think Danny might've killed her?"

"Why don't you ask him?" She bellowed out Danny's name. "He's taking a nap. He was out late last night visiting his girlfriend."

A moment later Danny came to lean against the doorjamb. Putting a hand over his mouth, he yawned broadly. "I'm sorry. I don't mean to be rude." He blinked several times. "You're that social worker who came with the detective, aren't you?" He scrunched his forehead. "I'm sorry, I can't seem to recall your name."

"Cassidy McCabe."

"She wants to know if you killed Olivia," Esther said loudly.

His mouth tightening, he huffed slightly. "Now Esther, you know you shouldn't say things like that." He glanced at Cassidy. "She likes to get a rise out of people."

"Actually," Cassidy said, choosing her words carefully, "Esther was telling me that you and Olivia used to fight over the house."

Looking at Esther, he said, "You really knew how to give Olivia a hard time, didn't you?" He turned his gaze on Cassidy. "Whenever she couldn't get Olivia to do what she wanted, she'd threaten to leave the house to somebody else—her neighbor, the priest, me. She never meant it, of course, but it used to drive Olivia crazy."

Tea dribbled from Esther's saucer onto her ragged beige blouse. Danny crossed the kitchen, grabbed a towel, and mopped her up, talking as he went. "I don't think Esther really meant to hurt Olivia. It's just that she'd get lonely and bored and then she'd want to stir something up. And poor Olivia. She tended to overreact and that added fuel to the fire. I don't believe Esther ever had any real understanding of just how sensitive her niece was."

*Esther's a tough case when it comes to drumming up empathy. I suppose if you take care of somebody long enough, you end up either bonding or abusing, and it looks like this guy's more of a bonder. If I had to live with a pain in the butt like Esther, I might go for abuse myself.*

Esther scowled at him as he returned to stand in the doorjamb. "You hated Olivia. You know you did. Remember how you yelled and cussed at her over that watch?"

"Esther," he chided gently, "why are you trying to confuse Cassidy with these stories you're making up?"

"Because she wants to know who killed Olivia."

*Thought you were being subtle. That weird old Esther wouldn't have a clue what you were up to. She saw right through you.*

# 12. Climbing the Tree Again

Danny's eyebrows rose. "I thought they had somebody in custody."

Making her best attempt to sound amused, Cassidy said, "Uh . . . Esther's mixing things up. All I did was ask why she was so mad at her niece."

He nodded. "Well, as you can see, Esther's moods change from minute to minute."

"You tell this nice girl here how you got in that big fight with Olivia over the watch," Esther demanded.

"The watch." Sighing, he raked his fingers through longish brown hair that grew in arcs above his head. From the slump in his shoulders and the weariness in his eyes, Cassidy had the sense he was carrying far too heavy a load.

*Depressed. These types who go way overboard doing for others usually are. After taking care of his mother all those years, he probably doesn't know how* not *to take care of old ladies.*

Brushing powdered sugar off the front of her violet dress, Cassidy said, "What about the watch?"

Danny looked at Esther. "You own a very expensive Cartier watch, don't you?"

She nodded.

"And how did you get it?"

"Won it in a contest."

Danny shook his head. "The story's different every time. In one version her husband gave it to her. In another she inherited it from a cousin." He shrugged. "It really doesn't matter where it came from. It's just too bad the way she used it to create a ruckus."

He paused, then sighed again. "Poor Olivia. Whenever Esther was in the mood to make trouble, Olivia got the brunt of it. I think the poor girl had been so intimidated her whole life that any time Esther'd start something up, Olivia would either crumble or go ballistic."

"I didn't start something up. It was you yelling and cussing at Olivia that started it."

"So what happened?"

"The band on Esther's watch was broken so she had me drop it off at the jewelry store. Apparently she forgot it was in for repair and went looking for it. When she couldn't find it, she called Olivia and said I'd stolen it."

Cassidy rubbed flakes of powdered sugar between her fingers. "I can certainly see Olivia getting upset over a thing like that."

"It took me awhile to find the receipt, and by the time I did she was so worked up she couldn't seem to make any sense of it. She threatened to call the police, fire me on the spot, all sorts of things."

"It wasn't Olivia. It was you. You were the one yelling and cussing."

Cassidy met his gaze. "Olivia threatened to fire you? Weren't you at least slightly tempted to beat her to the punch and just leave?"

"Esther's a lot like a rambunctious kid. As long as you don't take her seriously, it isn't a problem. And by staying here, I can avoid having a ton of debt when I get out of school."

Cassidy smiled. "You're way more easy going about Esther's little games than I could ever be."

"Well, I kind of like old people. I'm planning to be one myself some day. Now the trick of it is, you have to never let someone like Esther get away with anything. So, to clear the record about the yelling and cussing . . . " He looked straight at the aunt. "Esther?"

She stared in the opposite direction.

"Esther, if you don't answer me, I won't bring you any more kolacky."

She looked at him.

"Who was yelling and cussing about the watch?"

The sly look returned to her face. "Olivia was."

ಬಿ      ಬಿ      ಬಿ

It was nearly two when Cassidy parked across the street from Brenner's maple. With her window down, Starshine's poignant cries came through quite clearly. *Considering you're destined to lose all contests of will anyway, might as well get her down before you commit the next offense—bringing Tigger home from the vet.*

After changing into her jeans, she went on a reconnoitering mission to try to figure out where Brenner might be. She strolled to the corner on her side of Briar in an attempt to peek inside his picture windows, but his house was set higher than Olivia's and all she could see was his ceiling.

She crossed Hazel at the corner, then proceeded north, still on the sidewalk opposite Brenner's place. His attached garage, to the north of his house, was not visible from any point on her property, so she never saw his car coming and going.

Her little jaunt revealed that his small black Honda was sitting in the drive. *He's home. Does that mean I have to ask permission?*

She didn't want to make nice as Zach had instructed her to do. She didn't want to discuss it. She just wanted to climb the damn tree and get it over with.

*If he's not looking out the window he'll never know. Unless I fall out and he has to call an ambulance. In which case I'll be injured and he'll have to feel sorry for me.*

Looking up from beneath the maple, she saw Starshine in a crotch about six feet above her head. "Okay, I'll do penance for last night's offense. Then I'll bring Tigger home, an even worse affront. Which undoubtedly will trigger a new cycle of revenge that'll make tree climbing seem like a day at the beach."

She shook her head. "Was it just yesterday I told myself I wasn't as much of a cat fanatic as Sheryl or Harve?"

Casting one more glance at Brenner's windows, she boosted herself into the first large crotch, then stood upright to gaze at the calico, who stared back from a point just out of reach. *How the hell do you think you're going to catch her? And if you do, how will you ever get a struggling cat down without precipitating a crash landing for both of you?*

As Cassidy hoisted herself onto a higher branch, Starshine moved up also. Feeling a mere step away from the ER, she hauled herself into the thin upper branches while Starshine effortlessly maintained the same distance between them. At about fifteen feet off the ground, Cassidy recognized that the next branch would never hold her weight. Hanging on with both hands, she stopped to get her bearings. She stood about a yard from Brenner's house, his second-story windows a little above her head, his picture windows beneath her.

She looked down into his living room: a wingback chair, two Victorian sofas, a marble fireplace, a shelf unit against the wall on the far side of the window.

She experienced a sudden jolt of recognition. A black metal object crammed between the shelf unit and the wall set off twitches in her stomach before her mind could even register its name. A handgun.

*Well, isn't that clever. Close at hand for bad guys. Out of sight for visitors. Hidden away from everyone except the occasional trespasser in the tree.*

A flicker of movement in the window above snagged her attention. At least, she thought she'd seen movement. Now, scanning the second-story windows and finding no sign of life, she wasn't so sure.

*Did Brenner really pop up, then instantly disappear? Or is it just your imagination going on overdrive? Could be nothing more than an attack of nerves brought on by this incredibly blatant, right out in plain sight, peeping Tom act of yours.*

She stared into Starshine's wild black eyes. "I'm outta here. And if you choose to stay, I will install Tigger in your place and she will become the reigning queen of the house."

Climbing down, she experienced a new appreciation for Zach's refusal to remain in relationships that were bad for him.

As she started for home, she heard a Mwat—not a yowl, just a normal catly comment—from the tree. Starshine bounced to the ground, then trotted ahead of her toward the house.

ço        ço        ço

The calico gobbled her food on the kitchen counter, then sat tall, awaiting praise for her cleverness at manipulating her human.

Although Cassidy was in no mood to reward Starshine for her tree-climbing exploit, she did want to end this episode on good terms because she knew the next episode, fetching Tigger from the vet, was sure to incur serious catly wrath.

She spent a couple of minutes stroking Starshine both physically and verbally, then shut her in the basement. Aggrieved howls came from the other side of the door. *You weren't so simple minded as to expect silent capitulation, were you?*

&#8734; &#8734; &#8734;

After her four o'clock client left, Cassidy picked up Tigger, parked in front of her house, then lugged the heavy steel trap across the enclosed porch and up the hot, humid staircase. Panting, she set the trap down on the floor of the extra bedroom. A junk room in its first incarnation, a kitten nursery in its second, a crash pad for Zach's son in its third, the space was now empty except for three stacks of boxes. Windows lined two walls, with a long radiator stretching across the far side of the room.

She opened the trap door and stepped aside. Tigger crouched at the end of the long box, not moving except for her wild black eyes and swiveling ears.

Cassidy put out food and water, then filled the cat box. *This creature's never seen litter before. What makes you think you can deposit her in a bedroom and she'll suddenly acquire toilet training? Is this the first step on the downward spiral of house befoulment, social isolation, and cat-ladydom?*

Sitting crosslegged on the scuffed hardwood floor, she thought about the evening ahead. *Nearly six. Clients at seven and eight.* Zach typically appeared in the early evening to type notes and rest until he left for his club at ten.

She had two decisions to make: what to do about Starshine and what to do about Zach.

Starshine, whose intruder alarm had probably gone off the instant Cassidy removed the trap from the Toyota, would, upon release from the basement, race upstairs and try to break down Tigger's door. And an assault on the feral's territory clearly would not decrease her sense of terror at being dropped into a foreign environment.

*If only Starshine didn't have to find out. Probably exactly what Zach was thinking when he tried to avoid telling you about Heather.*

But she couldn't keep Starshine in the basement forever, and the longer the cat was locked up, the greater her grievance would be. *You can let her out during your break between sessions.* That way Cassidy would not have to witness the initial storming of the bedroom door, and Zach would be available to handle the cat wars.

*You being a tad passive aggressive here?*

*So what if I am? I have to put up with his hoodlum part, he can put up with Starshine's temper tantrums.*

The what-to-do-with Zach item was really more a question of what to do with Cassidy. She now understood Zach's hostility and his feeling that she was in his way. If he needed to erase all his normal thought patterns in order to turn himself into JC, her presence would make that harder to do.

*So the best choice would be to take my unwanted presence and go elsewhere. Which—considering what a joy it isn't to be in the same house with JC—would be doing myself a favor as much as him.*

Since she still had two unfinished tasks, feeding Olivia's indoor cats and setting the trap for Milton, finding a place to go would not be a problem.

She wrote a note for Zach explaining Tigger's presence and her absence.

Just before seven she returned to Tigger's room to check on the feral. The trap was empty, the tiger-stripe nowhere in sight. Cassidy went to the far wall and looked down. Tigger, squeezed into the four inch space between the radiator and the wall, twisted her head to stare up out of huge, frightened eyes.

&#2347;   &#2347;   &#2347;

After finishing with her clients, Cassidy remained at Olivia's until Zach's Cougar was gone from its parking spot by her back gate. Returning home, she heard Starshine yowling as she neared the stairs. The calico came tearing down, tried to trip her on the landing, then ran back up to throw herself against Tigger's door.

Cassidy stood in the hall to watch as Starshine went on screeching and banging. "Don't make me lock you up again. I don't want you any madder than you are already, but I'm not letting you keep me awake all night either."

She washed her face, brushed her teeth, and tried to read, hoping Starshine would wear herself out, but the attack continued. Finally she grabbed the calico and put her in the basement.

When she went back into Tigger's room, the feral was once again behind the radiator, but the litter had been used and the food bowl was empty, several little brown nuggets scattered around it. *Thank God, an embarrassment of cat pee won't force me to put a quarantine on the house after all.*

She was just turning to leave when a tricolored streak flashed through the open door and zoomed to the back of the room. Starshine skidded to a halt at one end of the radiator, the end pointing toward Tigger's tail. The calico peeked behind it, then disappeared into the narrow corridor that had become Tigger's refuge. Seconds later, she came backing out to prance around the room, a mouthful of dark fur clamped in her jaws.

"I've really had it with your mean, selfish, princessy ways. You do one more thing to torment Tigger or me and I'm throwing you out. Let *you* get a taste of homelessness, see how you like it."

*Starshine wouldn't stay homeless—she's got too much chutzpah for that. She'd go sit on some other dip's doorstep, get them to take her in.*

*Besides, it's your own fault she's in here. You were in a hurry, didn't shut the basement door tight. You know she opens any door that isn't closed all the way.*

Cassidy lunged for the calico but Starshine raced between her legs, crossed the hall, and ducked behind the waterbed, her own refuge of choice.

Closing Tigger's door, Cassidy went into the bedroom. "I'm sick of cats," she muttered, tossing her clothes into the overflowing laundry basket. "I should ship them both to Wisconsin, live out my days in cat-free peace and harmony."

She crawled between the sheets and closed her eyes. Within a minute, she felt Starshine move from the foot of the bed to her usual spot near Cassidy's head, where she curled into a ball and began a low, rumbling purr. Cassidy reached out to scratch behind the cat's ear. *Next time you piss Zach off, you should forget talking it out. Just purr in his face and that'll make it all better.*

ༀ     ༀ     ༀ

On Tuesday morning Cassidy was drinking coffee at the dining room table when the phone on the kitchen wall rang.

"This is Shelby. You asked me to call." The voice was brisk and professional.

*Bet she's sorry she opened up so much. Now she has to put on her best in-charge, strong-woman demeanor, make me think she's not really that sad, vulnerable little person I saw yesterday.*

"Sounds like you're feeling better." Cassidy stretched the coiled phone cord so she could sit back down at the table. Outside her dining room window, the weather was gray and drizzly.

"It was nice of you to spend time with me." Shelby paused. "And I called because I said I would. But I really don't want to talk about it any more."

"You don't?"

"I was a wreck all day yesterday. And then this morning I looked at my puffy eyes and said to myself, 'You're not going through the rest of your life moping because your mother didn't love you.' "

"No, of course not."

"Every encounter I ever had with that woman, I went away so mad I couldn't think straight. And now, even with her dying, it's like she's pulled the rug out from under me one last time. Well, I'm not going to let her keep doing it." Her voice bristled. "This is it. It's over."

"You've decided not to think about her any more, and here I'm about to ask you to do something that'll pull you right back in." Cassidy could almost feel the young woman stiffen on the other end of the line.

Shelby asked, her voice defensive, "What do you want from me?"

*I want you to tell me about the fight you had with Olivia. And I want to help you come to terms with the rejection you experienced from your mother.* "I'd like you to pay me a visit and let me tell you what I know about Olivia."

"Why?"

"It's an affliction therapists have. We go through life with this aberrant need to process things. And we also go around assuming that everyone else should process things too. It drives my husband nuts."

Shelby let out a small laugh. "It's nice of you to offer but—"

"I understand all the reasons you don't want to. But you did come to Chicago for the express purpose of getting to know her, didn't you?"

"Well, yes, but that was—"

"I can tell you things about your mother you won't hear from anybody else. I can explain some of the strange, contradictory behavior that made you crazy. If you walk away now, if you leave this last stone unturned, you'll always feel unfinished about it."

A long silence. Starshine strolled into the kitchen looking for a second breakfast. Upon finishing her first, she had immediately trotted back upstairs to begin her day's work of trying to open Tigger's door.

Shelby said, "I've had enough crying."

"I understand you're tired of hurting. But the crying won't kill you. And if you don't hear me out, your regret at not having finished the task you set out to do will last a lot longer than your puffy eyes."

She sighed deeply. "When would you like me to come?"

"Thursday night at eight."

        ဢ       ဢ       ဢ

Cassidy went upstairs to feed Tigger and check her messages. One from her mother, two from Esther, a client cancellation, and a couple of hangups. She did not mind the cancellation at all. It meant no sessions until six that evening. *You can spend your whole day chasing suspects.*

The hangups, however, reminded her of Zach's son, Bryce, who often failed to leave messages. A year ago Bryce had rung their doorbell and announced to Zach that he was a seventeen-year-old son Zach had never known existed. Bryce had started off hating his father for having abandoned him, then later come to accept that Zach really hadn't been aware of the pregnancy. During the intervening year, Bryce and Zach, with considerable nudging from Cassidy, had succeeded in establishing a tentative relationship.

*Except we neglected to warn Bryce that Zach was going under-cover, so now Bryce hasn't heard from him in weeks and doesn't know why. Which is going to take us two giant steps backward in terms of getting Bryce to believe that Zach could ever be a father.* She sighed. *Relationships are so damned difficult. It's a wonder everybody doesn't end up alone with their blinds drawn and their doors closed.*

She was downstairs in the kitchen when the phone rang a second time. The caller was Olivia's godfather, Carl Behan. He said he was in the neighborhood and would like to confer with her about the lawn service deportee. Cassidy put on a fresh pot of coffee, then called her grandmother to schedule their visit to Cook County jail for later that morning.

ဆ     ဆ     ဆ

The back doorbell rang. Cassidy went into the waiting room where Carl Behan stood, resplendent in an open-necked shirt and perfectly tailored blazer and slacks. *Doesn't even have a job to go to, still manages to look more professional than either you or Zach on your best days.*

"Is this your casual attire?"

"I don't want to get sloppy." He sniffed the air. "That coffee I smell?"

They settled in her office, each with a steaming mug in hand. He said, "I don't have anything conclusive, but I'm seeing enough smoke to start thinking those Mexicans must have a fire going somewhere."

"What happened?"

"At five a.m. I parked half a block from that hole-in-the-wall storefront office where I found Edwardo last summer. There's a new name on the sign—Cordova—but everything else looks the same."

"Did you see Edwardo?" She gazed out the window at an overcast sky starting to show patches of blue.

"Somebody who could've been Edwardo pulled up in front of the office, sat there a few seconds, then drove away. About fifteen minutes later a different guy, smaller than Edwardo, walked up to my car, introduced himself as Luis Cordova, and asked if I needed help. This guy was too friendly, too eager to strike up a conversation with a stranger." Placing his mug on the wicker table, Behan leaned back and pushed his wire-rimmed glasses farther up his Roman nose.

"You think Edwardo went in the back door, then sent Luis out to talk to you?"

"I was sitting there reading a newspaper. There was no reason for Luis to approach me. If they'd left it alone, I might've gone away thinking Edwardo was still out of the country."

"Why would they react like that?"

"Edwardo got rattled. After all, I'm the one who had him deported. He probably thought he recognized the car but couldn't be sure it was me, so he sent his brother Luis out to see if the driver was a lawyerly-looking gringo. He might even have hoped Luis could get me to tell him why I was there."

"They're brothers?"

"Half-brothers. Only Luis is a citizen—born here, I think. I had one of my PIs do some research on Edwardo last summer."

Sipping her coffee, Cassidy gazed at the light as it turned from gray to pale gold. "There must be some way to find out for sure if he's back."

"I'm going to have an investigator photograph all the members of Cordova's crew. If I'm not able to make a positive ID myself, I'll take the pictures around to Immigration." He smoothed one eyebrow. "If Edwardo's dumb enough to be back working at the same place, I'll find him."

"Of course, the fact that he's here wouldn't automatically make him a suspect."

"No, but if you persuade your convict pal to recant, I can make it clear to the DA why he doesn't want to prosecute this case. Once I explain that I'm taking on the defense and I have you as a witness, plus a good alternative suspect, he'll be ready to drop it. Then I'll talk to your detective friend about Edwardo. Given the way he went crazy when I mentioned Olivia, I don't see him standing up under interrogation."

Hope bubbled up in her chest. "I never could've done this by myself. I'm so glad I was able to convince you."

"I didn't say I was convinced. I'm just considering the possibility." Smiling, he moved his legs sideways in the narrow space between the sectional and the wicker table.

"There's one other thing I'd like to ask."

He raised his brows.

"Can you tell me anything about why Olivia was so scared and shy?"

"I thought you were the miracle therapist with all the answers."

"I'm sure I never said that."

"No, but that's what you implied." He gave her a smile with some real warmth to it. "However, if I'd been in your place, I would've played it the same way."

"What happened to make Olivia so afraid?" Cassidy heard shrill, teenaged voices arguing on the sidewalk outside her office.

"Olivia's father, Fred, got what he wanted in a wife, and his daughter paid for it by losing any chance she might've had for a normal life." He gazed out the north window.

"Fred and I grew up in the fifties, and when the time came for us to get married, the feminist revolution was just getting off the ground. Now if you ever tell anybody I said this, I'll deny it, but the idea of women turning the tables on men scared the shit out of most males of that era."

She grinned. "This is not a news flash."

"No, I suppose not. Anyway, Fred wanted a quiet, docile, fifties kind of wife who would encourage his ambition and stay out of his way, and he was able to pressure Donna, who was pretty much that kind of person anyway, into sliding right into the mold. So from Fred's point of view, everything was fine. Except he came to find out, not so long before he died, that throughout their marriage Donna'd been desperately lonely and unhappy."

*You've seen clients with depressed mothers who wanted their kids to take care of them.* "So I bet Donna turned to her daughter for comfort, and Olivia got the message it would never be okay to grow up or leave home."

"That's pretty much it."

"And how did she come to be your responsibility?"

"Fred was dying and he was leaving behind an extremely dependent wife and daughter. He asked me to watch out for them, so I managed their financial affairs, and I also made myself available to Olivia whenever she had some problem she couldn't handle."

"Like Edwardo."

Behan gazed out the window again. "I didn't mind doing it. I knew Olivia could be overly imaginative—paranoid even—but she also had a sweet side that came out whenever she felt completely safe." He picked up his mug, took a swallow, put it down again. "She liked to be helpful. She liked to be kind to people she didn't feel threatened by—which obviously applied to only a few individuals in her universe." He paused. "I went through a bad period once and she was very nice about simply sitting in the same room with me. No talk, no chatter, just a companionable presence." He closed his eyes briefly, a wave of sadness coming over his face.

"Well," he got to his feet, "you are a miracle therapist, aren't you?" He handed her a business card. "Give me a call if you come across anything new."

ช    ช    ช

Gran was waiting on her large open porch when Cassidy pulled up in front of the frame bungalow. As her grandmother hopped into the Toyota, Cassidy was surprised to see that for once Gran's sparse white hair was uncovered.

"What? No wig?"

"I figured you wouldn't want to introduce me as your assistant detective, so that means you'll be stuck explaining why you brought some little old lady along on your jail visit. That'll be bad enough without also having to explain ridiculous hair. So I decided this time out I'd go as just a normal granny."

Cassidy laughed. "You couldn't be a normal granny if your life depended on it. And you don't have ridiculous hair—well, okay, you do, but I wouldn't want you any other way."

Taking the Austin Boulevard entrance ramp, she drove east on the Eisenhower, settling in behind a white sedan with a small brown dog bouncing around the back seat.

Gran turned sideways to talk to her. "I got the credit report back on Evelyn Wentworth. That woman's had so many money troubles these past few years, I almost feel sorry for her. Even though she got uppity on you when you went to tell her about Olivia's murder."

"What kind of troubles?"

"Well, first she had a divorce six years ago, and then she had a bunch of judgments filed against her. The debts must've done her in 'cause four years ago she went bankrupt and had to sell off her business. She owned some other lab before this one."

"A failed marriage, a failed business, and a bankruptcy. That's enough to put almost anyone into a desperate frame of mind." She paused. "And even with the extra money she's skimming off Medicare, the lab she's got now doesn't look all that prosperous."

Gran's mouth puckered in concentration. "If she thought Olivia was gonna blow the whistle on her, I can see where she might do almost anything to stop her."

# 13. Cat Hater and a Break-In

"What a sticky situation," Cassidy said, passing a church bus filled with black women in colorful finery. "Evelyn can't go the bankruptcy route again because of the seven-year rule, so if Med Tech fails she'll have a ton of debt and no income." She shook her head. "Now how am I going to find out whether or not she knew about the forms?"

"You'll think of something. You always do."

Cassidy exited at Sacramento, then drove south on California to the Cook County complex, made up of several jail divisions and a criminal court building. The complex, commonly referred to as Twenty-sixth and California, extended from Twenty-sixth to Thirty-first Street, where a relatively new building housed the division Jake was in.

California was divided into two one-way streets with a dreary looking park in the middle. Cassidy cruised a good fifteen minutes before finding a meter with no car in front of it.

She and Gran walked up to a large white building set back a good distance from the street. Inside, Cassidy was surprised to find the jailhouse architecture quite attractive. The waiting area, with its vaulted ceiling, circular front, and vast, open interior, reminded her of an amphitheater. The cavernous space was empty except for two banks of marble benches and a counter in front.

At the counter Cassidy informed a female officer that they'd come to see Jake Sheffield. The officer said they could not go inside until enough visitors had arrived to form a group. When five other people had gathered, they were taken through a metal detector, patted down, then led to the visitor's room, a narrow corridor lined on one side with a row of stainless steel stools in front of a white counter with telephones on it. Behind a glass barrier, the prisoners awaited the incoming group.

Jake towered above the others, including one man with the height and musculature of a heavyweight boxer. As Cassidy approached she realized that, were it not for his size, she wouldn't have recognized him. The mountain man she had seen on Olivia's couch three days ago was gone. With his iron-gray hair cut short, eyes clear, and posture upright, he now resembled, even in prison coveralls, the college professor he'd once been.

*Oh, Jake, don't give up on yourself. Don't insist on believing you killed Olivia just because you're drowning in guilt over shooting your friend. I've done the hair-shirt routine a few times myself, and it never buys you anything.*

She perched on the stool in front of him and picked up the phone. Standing beside her, Gran leaned her head toward the receiver to listen in.

"Cassidy McCabe," Jake said in his genial bassoon, "you do show up in the oddest places. First you catch me on Olivia's couch and claim to be a neighbor. Next you appear with your cop buddy and tell me you're a social worker. Now here you are at Cook County in the guise of a visitor. What're you up to, anyway? Applying for a job as my guardian angel?"

"Why the hell confess to a crime we both know you couldn't possibly remember?"

His broad forehead creased. "Maybe that blackout story I gave you was pure bullshit."

"Cut the crap, Jake. I'm a social worker. I know about alcoholic blackouts."

"Then you also realize there's no way to prove which time I was lying—when I said I didn't remember or when I said I did."

Cassidy was momentarily distracted by the occupant of the stool to her left, a skinny black woman in her forties wearing a ten-inch skirt and six-inch heels. Her high-pitched voice poured forth a string of ingenuous curses, her hands, the fingers tipped by long red nails, moving in rapid accompaniment.

Dragging her attention back to the man in front of her, Cassidy said, "Why confess, Jake?"

Watching his face, she saw the bravado drain away, a look of defeat taking its place. "If booze could make me kill the person I care about most, then jail's the place I need to be." He paused. "I do okay in the joint. I don't have any trouble staying sober. I never hurt anybody. When I was in Menard, I did some work with literacy, taught a few classes." He lowered his gaze. "The teaching I did on the inside was a lot more worthwhile than anything I did after I got out."

Cassidy said, her voice low and intense, "You didn't kill her. You think you did but you're wrong."

His head reared back in surprise.

"And I happen to think your relationship with Olivia was extremely worthwhile. If she'd lived, you might have changed her life." Cassidy went on to tell him about the person she'd witnessed in the living room and the disappearance of the sapphire ring. "So you see," she concluded, "the killer had to be somebody other than you."

"Evidently Perez doesn't agree with you."

"What's more important right now is whether *you* agree with me."

He shook his large head. "I don't know. I can't reorient that quickly." He gazed into space, then focused on her again. "Is that why you're here? To talk me into unconfessing? And who's your friend? You haven't introduced us yet."

"This is my grandmother, Mary McCabe. She's always wanted to see Cook County."

He frowned. "You brought your grandmother here to see all the freaks behind bars? Sort of like a trip to the zoo?"

"Jake, c'mon."

"Okay, I'm sorry. I know you're trying to be helpful. Which is probably what's getting under my skin. Accepting help is something I've never been particularly gracious about."

"All right, then you help me. I need you to take back your confession. I know of someone else who may have done it, but I doubt that Perez'll even talk to him unless they reopen the case."

Jake frowned. "You shouldn't be involved in this."

"You want me to ignore the fact that I know you didn't do it? Jake, it's really important for you to tell the truth. Now will you please explain to Perez that your confession is bogus?"

He looked down at his left hand, drumming against the counter, then raised his eyes to hers and shook his head. "I assume you've already told all this to the police and they weren't willing to throw out my confession on the basis of your statement. As for me, I have my life all planned out. Cook County may be a hole, but Menard ain't so bad. No temptations, no relapses. Nobody to fall in love with. Nobody to die on me. So, Ms. Bleeding-Heart Social Worker, you can just go do therapy on your clients and leave me alone."

*Persuade Jake to recant, Carl said. That's all you have to do. Just talk him into it. As if the man didn't have his own weird sort of death wish.*

Gran, who'd had her ear up close to the receiver, grabbed the phone out of Cassidy's hand. "You have no business talking to Cass like that. You want to play the martyr and throw your life away, and that's just taking the easy way out. But it's not gonna do you any good. Cass isn't going to quit. She's going to find the real murderer whether you like it or not." Gran returned the handset to Cassidy.

The woman next to her suddenly started yelling in a squeaky, Minnie Mouse voice. "You flea-bitten, dickheaded, son of a hoe." She slammed down the phone and wobbled out of the room on her stiletto heels.

Jake watched her go, then looked at Cassidy again. "Your grandmother's right. There's no reason for me to be insulting. It's just that I had it all clear in my head, then you come along and try to turn everything around."

"Will you at least consider taking back the confession?"

"I'll think about it." He smiled. "But don't expect any great change of heart."

"You're being very difficult, you know that?" She paused. "How about helping me with something else then? I need to know who might've had a reason to show up at Olivia's house with a gun."

"You're not going to give up on this, are you?" He shook his head. "Well, if the killer is somebody other than me, I guess I'd want to see him caught." He gazed into space a moment, then gave Cassidy a direct look. "I don't suppose Olivia mentioned any, uh, blood relatives other than the aunt?"

"You mean her daughter?"

"So you know about that?"

Cassidy nodded.

"Okay, then I guess I might as well tell you. I knew there were certain people Olivia resented, but the only real fight I'm aware of is the one she had with her daughter. She didn't go into much detail, just said it was pretty bad. Then, a week or so later, the daughter sent a letter, and Olivia was so upset she actually showed it to me. It was pretty strongly worded. I guess you could call it a hate letter. Olivia saw it as some kind of threat, but I thought the daughter was just blowing off steam." He shrugged. "That's the only specific incident I know about."

*See if you can find out that other little thing you want to know.*

That's getting really nosy.

*Since when did that ever stop you?.*

"Jake, I know this is none of my business, but there's something I'd like to ask. I keep thinking about Olivia, trying to understand her. I know she was afraid of almost everything. So what I wanted to ask is, was she able to overcome her fears enough to become physically intimate?" She paused. "I hope she was. I'd like to think she at least had that."

"That certainly is none of your business." He smiled. "But since you're one of the few people who cared about her enough to even be curious, I'll answer it anyway." He shifted on the stool. "We weren't having sex yet but we were moving in that direction. It was slow going. Every time I'd take a step forward, she'd withdraw and make me stay away a few days."

"You deserve a medal for patience. I could never have handled all those mood swings of hers."

"As I said before, there was a degree of hubris in what I was doing. After all, here was this beautiful woman with minimal experience and I was the one destined to awaken her sexuality. She was Sleeping Beauty. I was the prince."

*Wants to be the white knight, the helper. Can't stand being the helpee. You've had a few problems with that yourself.*

"And you don't think what you were doing was worthwhile?"

"Not if I killed her."

As she turned to leave, her therapist voice nudged her. *You're romanticizing. You want to believe that love conquers all, that awakening Sleeping Beauty was a worthwhile enterprise. The truth is, Jake was doing all the wrong things. He was so busy trying to fix Olivia, he neglected to fix himself.*

ᴆᴗ   ᴆᴗ   ᴆᴗ

Cassidy dropped Gran off, then headed home. Driving east on Briar, she passed George Brenner walking his two Dobermans in the direction of his house.

Inside, Cassidy sat at her dining room table, chin propped on her hands. Starshine came down from her post outside Tigger's door and jumped onto the table to greet her.

"I think I need to talk to Brenner," Cassidy said to the cat.

Mwat. Starshine gazed into her eyes.

*You promised Zach you wouldn't confront him. Well, you haven't. Climbing his tree and spying in his window—even if he did see you— doesn't qualify as confrontation.*

Cassidy wiggled her fingers on the table. Starshine, apparently in a benevolent mood after her victory of the previous evening, bapped at them with sheathed claws.

"Besides, nobody was there when I looked up so I don't think he really saw me. I was just being overly imaginative, as Carl would say."

Losing interest in the conversation, Starshine went back upstairs. *Probably excavating a tunnel under the door.*

Zach had urged her to make nice to Brenner, and the more she thought about it, the less it seemed like such a bad idea. If she could put the cat-shooting allegation out of her mind, she might even be able to work herself into an apologetic mood over her bad behavior at his door the other day.

*Apology—that's the ticket. An apology will get me in the door, and once inside, I can move on to matters more related to murder.*

ᴆᴗ   ᴆᴗ   ᴆᴗ

"What can I do for you, Ms. McCabe?" Brenner looked at her through his screen door. Just behind him two dogs jumped up and down and barked a lot.

"There's something I'd like to talk about and I'm wondering if I could come inside to do it."

He opened the screen door. "I hope you don't mind the mess. Since I live alone, I don't have anybody telling me to pick up my socks."

"I don't mind messes. I have several of my own." As she came through the door, one of the dogs leapt at her, its paws landing on her chest and nearly knocking her over. She held her breath against the doggy fumes, raised an arm to shield her face from the large tongue slathering towards it.

"Sorry about the dogs." He grabbed their collars and led them off through the dining room. While he was gone, she surveyed the living room. It had a white marble fireplace in the center of the north wall surrounded by a formal seating arrangement, two hunter green brocade couches at right angles to each other and a striped wing chair. The wall unit with the gun behind it turned out to be a cherrywood bookcase holding leather-bound volumes interspersed with ceramic ginger jars.

"This is very nice," she said when Brenner reappeared.

"My wife had a real flair for decorating." He sat on one of the sofas, scraped dog hair from the cushion and held it up to show her. "Unfortunately, I don't have my guys trained all that well."

Taking the other sofa, Cassidy folded her hands in her lap. "I'm sorry about the way I came storming over when the animal officer was here."

"I'm sure you were just upset about Olivia's death and wanted to protect her interests. As it turns out, you seem to have solved the stray cat problem, so I guess that evens the score."

"When I thought about it later, I realized what an aggravation it must have been living next door to those cats."

His lip curled slightly. "Well, you know what that space between the houses smells like. The cats sprayed everything. I don't see how I'll ever get rid of the stench."

"I'm amazed you put up with it so long. What stopped you from calling animal control years ago?"

"Olivia had a fit every time I suggested it. I guess I just couldn't bring myself to do something that would've upset her so much."

Taking stock of Brenner's kindly expression and genteel attire, an expensive-looking knit shirt and slacks, she found herself not believing that this grandfatherly man could be shooting guns out his rear window. But his next few sentences changed her mind.

"My wife was a cat lover." Cassidy heard a distinct note of distaste in his voice. "She had two of them, used to insist they sleep with us." His voice picked up speed. "In fact, I suspect she preferred the cats to me when it came to bedtime. If I'd had Olivia's stray cats euthanized, I think my wife might've sent a lightning bolt down from heaven to strike me dead." He laughed a little too loudly.

Smiling uneasily, Cassidy noticed that his gray eyes were boring into hers with an unusual intensity. *What am I seeing here? Just a hot-button reaction to cats? Or something deeper? Personality disorder brooding and resentment, maybe.*

"What about you? Do you make your husband sleep with that kitty-cat of yours? Are you one of those women who prefer cats to men?"

*This is getting very strange.* "Actually Zach's about as fond of—"

His gaze moved away from her face, his speech returning to its normal tempo. "Your husband works for the *Post*, doesn't he? You know, those stories they've been running about the failure of the Chicago school system are really unfair to teachers. I taught shop in Cicero for thirty years, and I'm here to tell you, no matter how hard the teachers may be trying, if kids don't want to learn, they can't be taught." He stopped abruptly. "Hey, I'm really off on a tangent, aren't I?" He went to lean against the white mantle.

"It's living alone that gets to me. I go for days without talking to a soul, then some innocent person like you starts up a conversation, and I can't stop babbling."

*Diagnosable? Or just lonely and eccentric? You don't have nearly enough data for a solid assessment.*

She said, "It's hard when you don't have anyone to talk to on a regular basis." *No need to mention your habit of confiding in your cat.*

Cassidy picked up a throw pillow, orange flowers against a black background, and laid it in her lap. "Well, what've you heard about the murder? As a member of the fire and police commission, do you get insider information?"

"Not through any official channel, but I do have a friend in the department who lets me take him out for beer on occasion. From what he tells me, it's all wrapped up."

"One thing I wondered about was her sapphire ring. Did the police ever find it?"

"No sign of it. They canvassed neighborhood pawn shops but it never turned up." Leaning forward, he rescued a chew toy from under the sofa and placed it on the dusty cherrywood coffee table in front of him. "But I wouldn't make too much of the ring if I were you. Unlike television, in real life there frequently are some loose ends."

"Did you see anything the night of the murder?"

"When I took out the trash at eight-thirty, I noticed an unfamiliar white van parked by the side of the alley a couple of houses north of here. The cops questioned everybody on the block but nobody knew who it belonged to. Probably just some teenagers from the other side of Oak Park making out in the back."

ಬ    ಬ    ಬ

Leaving Brenner's house, she noticed a group of teenaged boys on the parkway in front. A black kid and a white kid were wrestling playfully on the ground, a third standing nearby to cheer them on.

*Teenagers usually stay pretty segregated. Good to see these three acting as if they're colorblind.*

When are you going to achieve colorblindness yourself? Wouldn't it be great to look at three kids and not even think about race?

She was passing through the kitchen when the phone rang. Lifting the receiver from the wall, she heard Zach's son, his voice angry, on the other end. "Is Zach there? Why haven't I heard from him? What's going on?"

"Hey, Bryce, how about a little polite conversation before you start yelling at me?"

"He never answers at the *Post*. Where is he? Have they canned his butt or what?"

"He's working on a story. Doing research outside the office." She stretched the cord across the kitchen to pull a bag of peanut butter cups down from one of the cabinets. Cradling the phone between her head and shoulder, she unwrapped the Reese's and set it on her palm, ready to pop into her mouth as soon as Bryce was done haranguing her. *You deserve to be harangued. You should've told him.*

"For a month? C'mon, Cass, don't try to dick me over."

"I'm sorry. I know it wasn't right for him to just drop off the radar screen like that."

"You're sorry? Zach's the one who didn't call. I suppose hanging out with a teenager must be pretty boring for a hotshot reporter like him.

Well, it's okay by me. I've got better things to do with my time than drive out to Oak Park."

"You think this is all about you? Now that you're a college freshman, you're suddenly the center of the universe?" She nibbled at the edges of the chocolate.

"If it's not about me, what is it? Is he screwing up again?"

She gazed through her window into her neighbor's kitchen where a boy about Bryce's age was doing homework at the table. "What do you mean 'screwing up again'? "

"You know, like he used to. Doing drugs. Getting arrested."

"That all happened before you were born."

*Poor kid. Of course he thinks Zach's going to create some huge mess, then disappear on him.* "Bryce, the only reason you expect Zach to screw up is because that's what everyone else in your life has done. Everybody you ever cared about has made some terrible mistake, then abandoned you by dying."

"Don't psychoanalyze me," he said fiercely, the same words his father had been known to utter from time to time.

"Zach is the only stable—well, relatively stable—person you've ever been connected with. It was a small screw-up on our part that we neglected to tell you he'd be out of touch for a while, but the truth is, he really is working on a story."

"You still haven't explained anything." He sounded mollified but not willing to let it go.

"Okay, I'll fill in the blanks but not on the phone. You have any hot dates for Saturday evening around five?" *Get him in and out before Zach comes home. Running afoul of JC would not serve to strengthen my argument in favor of Zach's good character.*

"Who's buying the pizza?"

"You. Super large. Everything except anchovies."

    ঙ   ঙ   ঙ

That evening she had clients scheduled from six till nine, leaving her with only an hour to spend avoiding Zach. Killing an hour at Olivia's fussing over the indoor cats would not be bad at all.

After her last session, she went to the waiting room closet and took out the jeans, keys and cell phone she'd stashed there earlier. She changed in the client bathroom, then headed toward Olivia's. Starshine, who'd spent the day with her paw beneath Tigger's door, was nowhere around. *You can actually walk across the street without fear of attack.*

Worried that she had not seen Milton since the night of the murder, she decided to check the trap she had set in the backyard before going inside. She passed through the gate between the house and the garage into the thick darkness of the fenced yard. Glancing up at Brenner's second story, she was relieved not to see him at any of the windows. *Given how he acted today, the sight of him staring down at you would not be reassuring.*

She let her gaze wander over the yard, then back up to the stoop. That's when she saw it. A jagged hole in the back door window. *Oh shit. Somebody's broken in.*

Moving farther from the house, she gazed up at Olivia's office window. A thin beam of light appeared briefly, then disappeared. *A penlight. Somebody searching for a file. But they won't find it because you've already made off with all the files worth taking.*

She pulled the phone out of her pocket, stared at it, tried to think. If she called 9-1-1, the police would arrest the intruder and Manny would have to question that person about the murder. If the intruder was Edwardo, Manny might get the truth out of him.

But of all the suspects, Edwardo—Olivia's lawn service guy—was the least likely to know about the files. *It's going to be somebody else.*

If Manny interrogated one of the others and they did not confess, the person would be charged with breaking and entering and that would be the end of it. Except that the intruder's vigilance would go skyrocketing and he or she would probably never speak to Cassidy again.

*The important thing is to see who comes out that door. I can always tell Manny later if I have to.*

Stuffing the phone back in her pocket, she located a spot near the fence that provided a good sight line to the door. Crawling into the bushes, she sat cross-legged on the hard, prickly ground. She fanned her hands, trying to keep the mosquitoes away, but she could feel them biting the exposed skin on her face and arms. The clean smells of grass and flowers mingled with the stink of cat urine. She waited a long time. Her legs cramped and a small ache started in her lower back.

*Here you are watching a crime in progress and not reporting it. If*

*Manny ever finds out all that you've been up to, he won't be granting any more favors in this lifetime or the next.*

It occurred to her that Zach might not be altogether pleased with her either. *This is not taking risks. You're sitting here in the bushes getting eaten alive to make sure you're not seen and you're not uttering one sound when the person comes out. You can't get any more cautious than that.*

Finally she saw the door move inward. Evelyn Wentworth, dressed all in black, crossed the small porch, went down the walk toward the alley, and passed through the gate at the rear of the yard.

# 14. A Scream in the Night

Standing, Cassidy brushed herself off. *You wondered how you were going to find out if Evelyn knew about the forms. Well, now you have your answer.*

But if Evelyn killed Olivia, why not take the forms the night of the murder?

Cassidy ran through a possible scenario in her mind. Evelyn had used a gun to force Olivia to let her in. Then she'd found Jake passed out on the couch, the blinds had gone up, and a neighbor had rung the bell—enough to give any novice murderer the jitters. Evelyn hadn't known how long Jake would remain unconscious or whether Cassidy would call the police. Having already waved a gun in Olivia's face, she'd also felt she couldn't afford to leave her employee alive.

Evelyn had gotten scared, killed Olivia, planted Jake's prints on the gun, then bolted, undoubtedly hoping the police would arrest the drunk and nobody would go through Olivia's papers. She must have planned to return later and search the house. Then Cassidy had hinted that she knew about the fraud, and that had increased the lab owner's urgency.

Cassidy checked the trap and found it empty. Going inside the house, she squatted down to pet Bamba, who raced up to greet her. After putting out food, she leaned against the sink and watched the three cats eat.

*Nice theory but no proof. And no idea how to get it.*

Manny's the one who should be doing this, not me. The police could search Evelyn's house, hold her at the station, grill her, trick her into confessing.

She wondered again if she ought to turn her findings over to Manny. *Too risky. He'd tell me to butt out, and Evelyn's stellar motive would not override a confession, a murder weapon, and fingerprints.*

So now what?

*Time for a little escalation. Confront Evelyn. It's not much but it's all you've got.*

      ဢ      ဢ      ဢ

She returned to her house and climbed to the upstairs hallway, where Starshine lay in front of Tigger's door, one leg stretched beneath it, trying to jiggle it open.

Cassidy placed a call to report the break-in, not to the police but to Carl Behan, who said he would have the window repaired first thing in the morning. Remembering that she hadn't checked the answering machine all day, she plunked down in the chrome and vinyl dinette chair in Zach's office and pushed PLAY.

". . . and I need to know if you're going to be able to see me off tomorrow morning or not."

*Oh shit. Another mangled message.*

Her mother's call must have come in on Saturday. It was now Tuesday night, and even though Cassidy had played the tape several times in the intervening days, this message had not previously shown up. The machine was not just cutting messages short, it was also losing them. She rewound the tape and played it again but was not able to retrieve the beginning of her mother's lament.

Cassidy chewed on her lip, wondering what else she might have missed. The worst would be calls from clients. *But everybody knows answering machines are not infallible. If a client doesn't hear back, you'd think they'd try again.*

The device needed to be replaced but she was reluctant on two counts. She would much prefer to have Zach, the house expert on electronics, sort through options and make the selection. She also was falling back into her old habit of worrying about money. After Zach had taken over bill-paying, her tendency to fret over finances had abated, but it was starting up again.

*Zach's got to be spending a small fortune at that club of his, buying drinks for Heather and bags of coke he tosses in the toilet.* Clamping her lips together, she pictured him handing his editor an expense report citing thousands of dollars for booze and drugs. *You just put out several hundred for Harve and the vet. Now an answering machine? Boy, will you not want to see the next credit card bill.*

She knew a reliable answering machine was a necessity. She could not afford to lose client calls.

*But it's only missed a couple of messages from your mother,* her rationalization voice whispered seductively. *Messages that didn't matter anyway. You can let it go a few days longer.*

The last thing she did that night was feed Tigger, who remained in hiding behind the radiator. As Cassidy went out, she made sure to close the door firmly behind her.

೮೦    ೮೦    ೮೦

A nerve-shattering scream jerked Cassidy out of a deep sleep. As she hauled herself into an upright position, hairs stirred on the back of her neck.

It sounded like a child but she knew it wasn't. *Cat fight. You've heard it before. But first time you've heard it coming from inside your house.*

Two a.m. She jumped out of bed, pulled a long tee over her head, and turned on the hall light. Tigger's door was open. *Oh shit. Whatever made you think, just because Starshine's never been able to open tightly closed doors in the past, her persistence wouldn't pay off this time?*

Tigger's room was empty, although a clump of dark fur bore testimony to Starshine's success at having grabbed one more mouthful of fur before the tiger-stripe fled. Howls erupted sporadically from somewhere below. Putting on slippers, Cassidy went down two flights of stairs to find Starshine in the basement carrying on like a banshee in front of a section of open-backed metal shelving crammed with junk.

Cassidy recognized immediately that, given the way the feral could glide from shelf to shelf, removing her from her new hiding place would be impossible. As if to demonstrate, the calico leapt onto the left side of the third tier, disappeared behind a suitcase, and reappeared on the right side of the fifth.

*If Starshine were serious about defending her territory, there'd be blood and fur all over the place by now. Considering Tigger's twice her size, I hope the fact that Starshine hasn't jumped her yet means Starshine's going to avoid head-on collisions, limit herself to rear end attacks when Tigger's jammed behind a radiator and can't turn around.*

Releasing a heavy sigh, Cassidy considered the possibility of being stuck forever with a stealth cat living in her basement shelves. The only way to get her out would be to retrap her, and Cassidy had no idea what the odds were of the feral making the same mistake twice. *I'd have to be starving to go back into a steel box that'd clanged itself shut, locked me inside, and led to my being pursued by a calico fury.*

Jumping down from the second shelf, Starshine prowled back and forth, fur puffed, snarly noises coming out of her mouth.

*Wonder if she feels the same about Tigger as you felt about that woman you found in bed with Kevin. You threw a fit back then just about as demented as what Starshine's doing now.*

Guilt started to ooze up over her betrayal of Starshine but she tamped it firmly down. *Humans are allowed more than one cat, unlike husbands, who are required to forsake all others.*

Seeing that the cats were unlikely to kill each other, she carried down the extra litter box, then went upstairs, leaving doors open behind her in hopes that Starshine would abandon her war games and come sleep with Cassidy.

She crawled back into her king-sized bed, which seemed way too large and empty with neither Zach nor the calico beside her.

 める　める　める

The next morning, Wednesday, Cassidy found Starshine in the dining room peering intently into the four-inch space between a corner shelf unit and the west wall. Cassidy gazed into the crack but saw nothing. Looking into the crack on the other side, she discovered Tigger, head facing the corner.

*It's a stand-off. Starshine goes in from the front, she'll have to deal with teeth and claws, which, thank God, she seems to be choosing not to. She goes in from the back, Tigger'll race out the other side, find herself another place to hide.*

Cassidy moved on into the kitchen where a cat-food mess awaited her. Starshine's bowl had fallen from the counter to the floor, splattering dollops of canned food on the cabinet and linoleum. *Damn. Another early breakfast from Zach.* Wondering if the cats had staged a food fight, she grabbed paper towels and went down on her hands and knees to wipe the floor. Starshine trotted up, extended her nose for a nosekiss, then sat to watch the cleanup, her demeanor a study in catly innocence.

As soon as the food-spill was gone, Starshine began talking about a second breakfast. The calico inhaled a small portion, then returned to the corner unit, Cassidy following to see if the feral was still there.

She wasn't. Starshine sniffed where Tigger had been, then dashed upstairs in pursuit of their phantom visitor.

*What have you got yourself into? Bringing Tigger into the house was definitely not one of your brighter moments.*

Think of it as entertainment for Starshine. Eventually you'll have to smoke Tigger out, but in the meantime you've got more pressing matters to deal with, Evelyn being at the top of the list.

She had two clients in the morning, another at one. When her afternoon session was over, she would set out to revisit Med Tech Lab.

ഌ     ഌ     ഌ

Cassidy was just seeing her second client to the door when she heard the roar of lawn service machinery start up on the other side of Briar. She went into her dining room and gazed through the window at a familiar red pickup, trailer attached in back, CORDOVA'S LAWN SERVICE lettered across the side.

*If Edwardo killed Olivia, would his half brother Luis continue grooming her yard?*

If Luis didn't know about it, he would. And even if he did, he might figure they'd be better off keeping everything the same than suddenly disappearing .

As long as she had a break between clients and the lawn service crew was right there, she decided it would make sense for her to take pictures herself instead of waiting for Carl's investigator to do it. She had recently finished a photography class and was sure she could handle it. *But you have to have an excuse. Those Mexicans would not take kindly to an Anglo woman playing paparazzo for no good reason.* She folded her arms, sucked in her cheek, and thought about it.

The final class project had been to create a photo essay. One had been on the homeless. Another on babies. Cassidy had put together a composition on hands.

*Men at work. My mission is to create an essay of males doing their jobs. That's so plausible I'd even believe it myself. It definitely ought to buy permission for some in-their-face shutter snapping.*

Knowing that Cordova's team would cut through the yard like

locusts in under an hour's time, she hurried upstairs, grabbed her camera and headed across Briar.

Inside Olivia's backyard she checked the door, pleased to see that the broken window had been boarded up. Behan, it seemed, was no slouch at getting things done. Next she scanned the four men wielding ear-blasting machines. Three had the short stature she associated with Hispanics. The fourth, the man behind the mower, was taller and heftier, large enough to have been the figure in Olivia's living room.

*Would Edwardo come back and work on her lawn after she had him deported? If he killed her, he wouldn't have to worry about her recognizing him. Even if he didn't, he knows she's never home during the day.*

Cassidy stepped up close to the edger guy, cupped her hands around her mouth and shouted above the roar of the machinery, "Who's the boss?"

He pointed to the man running the trimmer.

She went over to him and yelled, "I need to talk to you."

Looking up, he gave her a beaming smile. His face was round, the nose broad and lips full, but his radiant grin lent a rough-hewn attractiveness to the coarse features.

She jerked her thumb toward the sidewalk across Briar. "Let's go over by my house so we can hear each other."

"Sure thing." He crossed the street beside her, a hint of swagger to his rolling gait. He was broad-chested, burly-armed, and showed the slight swell of an incipient beer belly.

They stopped beside her office window, standing inside the solid block of shade from the house. The parkway trees cast a dappled, shifting shadow across the surrounding street and sidewalks. He brushed his hands together, then swiped at his pants, sending off a spray of grass like a scared cat shedding hair. "I bet you wanna sign up Cordova so your place'll look as good as your neighbor's." He winked. "Maybe even better. For such a pretty lady, we might work extra hard."

"Maybe next spring." She smiled back. "Right now, I've got a favor to ask."

"Sure thing. I always do favors for pretty ladies." He twisted his head to glance back at Olivia's. "Except I got a busy schedule to keep so maybe I don't have time."

"Are you Mr. Cordova?"

"Call me Luis." A squirrel dashed past their feet, raced up a parkway elm, and sat in the branches chattering down at them.

"Well, Luis, I'm putting together a pictorial essay of people doing physical labor." She held up the camera strapped around her neck. "And I'd like to snap some photos of your crew at work."

"Why you want pictures of those ugly guys? You take my picture instead." Clenching his fist to show off his biceps, he let out a booming laugh. "Make all the girls swoon."

"Well," she said, trying to inject a touch of sexual innuendo into her voice, "I'll take shots of you too. And when I put the exhibit together, I'll be sure to include a nice big label with your name and number on it. It'll be free advertising." She pulled a pen and small notepad from the pocket of her wine-colored slacks. "Can I have your phone number?"

He recited it.

"And the names of your men?"

He shifted his weight, then gave her a crafty smile. "You can use my name, no problem." He lowered his voice. "But these other guys, they're kinda shy. You get my meaning?"

She nodded. *You didn't really expect him to hand you Edwardo on a silver shovel, did you?* "These photos will make a wonderful study of men working at a hard, physical job."

"You talking 'bout jobs reminds me of a favor you could maybe do me."

"Oh?" A small yellow wasp flew near her face and she brushed it away. Her hair felt hot and heavy on her neck.

"Actually, it's for my daughter." A softness came into the dancing brown eyes. "I got this beautiful girl, Rosa. She just started eighth grade at St. Theresa's."

"The kids back in school already?"

"They start in August around here. Anyway, the teacher, she gave the class a pretty hard assignment. Rosa's gotta talk to somebody with a professional job and write a paper about it. You know, somebody with a college degree." His shaggy brows drew together. "Only we don't know no people with college degrees. So maybe you could think of somebody Rosa could talk to."

"What kind of girl is she?"

He smiled fondly. "My Rosa, she's got a lot of spirit. She doesn't let nobody give her a hard time. But she's pretty tender hearted too. She's always bringing home these stray animals, and then my wife has to throw them out while she's at school."

"Maybe Rosa'd like to interview me? I'm a social worker and she sounds like the sort of girl who might be interested in something like that." *Social workers, teachers, nurses—all carriers of the sappy, soft-headed gene that leads to the bringing home of wounded birds and the taking on of cat-rescue projects.*

"You got a job?" Cordova looked at her curiously. "But you don't have to be at no office today?"

"I'm a therapist. I see clients at home." A beat-up car rolled past, rap music blaring from the windows. "You think Rosa'd like to hear about my work?"

"Sure, why not? She's getting pretty worried 'cause she don't know who to talk to." He moved a little closer. "How 'bout I drop her off tomorrow at four? Maybe by then you talk your husband into signing up for Cordova so you get rid of all your weeds like that lady across the street."

She tossed her hair, hoping the gesture would come across as playful. Never having learned to flirt, she felt ridiculous pretending to encourage him. "I have used your services a little. Last summer I paid one of your men to carry something out of the basement for me. It's that guy over there with the mower. Edwardo, I think his name is."

For an instant Luis's jovial expression froze. Then the broad smile returned but in a semblance more strained than before. "Nah, you got the wrong guy. Edwardo quit last summer. But you need some job done, I'll take care of it. Then you sign up for my service." A young woman pushing a stroller came toward them from the corner. They stepped onto the grass to make room for her.

Luis looked at his watch. "You know what? I got so busy talkin' I lost track of the time. You better take those pictures right away 'cause I gotta get going pretty quick." He turned to walk briskly across the street, Cassidy trotting along beside him.

Her eyes on his face, she asked, "Did you hear about the murder?"

He halted abruptly. "What murder?"

"Olivia Mallory. The woman whose property you're working on now."

"That woman was murdered?" He frowned deeply. "I guess we might as well quit then, if nobody's gonna pay us."

"Oh, you'll get paid." Pulling Behan's number out of her pocket, she explained that Olivia's attorney was managing the property and would attend to all her bills.

"Well, okay, then." Luis turned his dazzling grin on her again. "You come take my picture now. Make all the girls swoon."

She moved from worker to worker, snapping several shots of each. The largest of the four, the one she guessed to be Edwardo, lowered his head every time she came near him.

Ten minutes later she was back on her own sidewalk watching the men dump a garbage can full of clippings into the bed of the truck.

Luis waved from the cab. "Tomorrow at four you get to meet my Rosa."

৪১        ৪১        ৪১

It was just past two when Cassidy closed the door on her afternoon client and went upstairs to prepare for her call on Evelyn. Studying her image in the bedroom mirror, she noticed the wrinkles in her dusty-rose blouse, the faded look to her cotton slacks. She remembered the way Evelyn had examined her on the previous trip and how her expensive violet dress had helped her stand up to the lab owner's scrutiny. Despite the unwritten rule against women appearing twice in the same clothes, she felt a strong urge to wear the violet dress again.

Evelyn impressed her as an iron-willed woman who would do her best to avoid admitting or explaining anything, and Cassidy's mission was to break her down. She would need every ounce of confidence she could muster. She went to her closet and took out the dress.

*I don't care if she does think it's the only outfit I own. If it helps me not wither under her stare, it's worth it.*

After changing clothes and packing her keys, wallet, phone and the roll of exposed film into the matching shoulder bag, she looked in the mirror again. Her cinnamon mane hung shaggily around her oval face. *Trip to the beauty parlor wouldn't hurt either.*

She pulled herself up tall. *No you don't.* She'd decided long ago that she would never allow her self esteem to ride on the maintenance of a slick facade. *You're not having your hair done just so Evelyn doesn't look down on you.*

The phone rang as she was going out the bedroom door. She returned to her desk and picked up.

"I thought you were gonna visit me today," Esther said in her whiny-child tone.

"I didn't say I'd be coming by any more. And this calling has to stop."

"But you wanna know about Olivia, don't you?"

"I doubt very much that you have anything to tell me."

"You asked why I was so mad. If you come see me, I'll tell you my secret about her trying to take me to court."

"I think you just make up stories to get attention."

"I got proof." Her voice grew agitated. "You come see me, I'll show you that paper 'bout her taking me to court. She was a mean, nasty girl and I'm glad she's dead."

"You actually have a document I could look at?"

*Don't fall for any of her tricks. The more you give in to her, the harder it'll be to get her out of your hair.*

Yeah, but isn't it always the unturned stone beneath which the winning lotto ticket lays?

"All right, I'll be there in a few minutes."

"Will you bring kolacky?"

Gritting her teeth, Cassidy clicked down the receiver.

ಬಿ    ಬಿ    ಬಿ

As she climbed Esther's porch steps, Cassidy noticed that the small purple car she'd seen before was not in the driveway. *Considering Esther still tootles around town, you're lucky she hasn't taken to dropping in instead of just calling.* She shuddered at the picture of Esther walking in on a therapy session, plopping down beside her client, and demanding kolacky.

Esther opened her door part way and stood in the gap to block Cassidy's view of the interior. "You can't come in till I pick up. I was looking for that paper and now there's stuff scattered all over the living room."

"I don't mind the mess." Cassidy started to step inside but the old woman didn't budge.

"I can't let you see these papers I got. It's nobody's business but mine."

"I'll give you one minute and then I'm taking off."

"I'll be right back."

The door closed in her face and did not reopen for nearly two minutes.

*What is the matter with you, standing out here in the hot August sun getting sweat on your nice dress in hopes that this dotty old lady who thinks her husband's still alive will hand you a big fat clue?*

The door opened again and Esther pulled her inside, then seated herself on the couch. "Now you just sit down here beside me, sweetie, and make yourself comfortable." She patted the cushion. "Did you bring me anything?"

The heat and stink of the house making her slightly nauseous, Cassidy perched on the opposite end of the ratty, claw-footed sofa. "Where's the paper you told me about?"

A worried look crossed Esther's horselike face. She patted the thin gray hair hanging limply to her jaw. "I know it's here someplace. Maybe if you come back tomorrow I can find it."

"Why don't you just tell me what it was about?" Cassidy's gaze was drawn to a sideboard overloaded with garish ceramic knickknacks. The standout was a two-foot high, pink and yellow pig sitting on its haunches.

"I got this paper in the mail that said Olivia was gonna take me to court. She said the judge'd make me leave the house to her. And if I tried to give it to Danny they'd take it away from me." Her voice went shrill. "How could my own niece treat me like that? She said if I tried to leave it to anybody but her, it'd be proof my mind wasn't sound. But I'm not crazy." Esther slid closer, her gnarled hands grabbing at Cassidy's arm. "You don't think I'm crazy, do you?"

Laying her palm on top of the knobby fingers, Cassidy said gently, "I don't think you're a bit crazier than any sly, crafty old fox."

*Don't be nice. It just encourages her.*

Yeah, but like Danny said, I'm planning to be old someday myself.

"I had to go to court before. I got this plumber to do some work for me and the bill was too high so I didn't pay. And the plumber, he took me to court. You know what the judge did? He told me I had to give that guy two hundred bucks. But I couldn't afford it. All I got is my social security and Danny makes me give him some of that."

"I guess nobody likes to be taken to court." Cassidy noticed the ubiquitous head-and-shoulders print of Jesus hanging near the door. *I'll bet this grasping old conniver thinks of herself as a good Christian. Well, why not? Most of the country's worst reprobates make that same claim.*

"Olivia wanted me to get rid of Danny so I wouldn't leave him the house. But I shouldn't have to fire him if I don't wanna."

"Well, Olivia's gone now so you don't have to worry about it any longer."

A malicious gleam came into the faded old eyes. "She had it coming. She shouldn'ta tried to make me go to court."

&#8478;   &#8478;   &#8478;

Outside, Cassidy inhaled fresh, clean air, relieved to have made her escape from the foul-smelling woman within. *How does Danny stand it? I'd rather be debt-ridden any day than have Esther whining at me all the time.*

We all have different tolerances. You're willing to let Starshine take advantage of you, but not old ladies. Danny does a better job of not allowing Esther to push his buttons than you do, and for all you know, his nose isn't as sensitive, either.

&#8478;   &#8478;   &#8478;

After dropping off the film at Walgreens, she drove into the city toward the laboratory, her mind on the meeting ahead. Her approach would be simple. If Evelyn did not answer her questions in full, Cassidy would call the Medicare hotline number she had acquired from the library and report the recalcitrant lab owner on the spot. Although she'd been nervous about the confrontation earlier, Cassidy now realized that, given all the aces she was holding, Evelyn really had no choice but to comply.

Cassidy, however, still had some tricky decisions to make about how to play her hand. She could not promise to give back the forms, even if Evelyn spelled out every detail. The lab owner would simply have to explain herself with the hope that Cassidy might choose, in the end, not to report her. The best scenario would be if Evelyn's story rang false, in which case Cassidy could, in good conscience, dump everything on Manny's desk and be done with it.

But if Evelyn's story was convincing, if Cassidy came away with serious doubts that Evelyn was the killer, she would be faced with the unpleasant task of deciding whether or not to report the fraud. That's where the dilemma came in. She wasn't sure that she could bring herself to make the hotline call. There were two voices with opposite points of view yammering in her head.

*The woman's cheating Medicare. You can't ignore it just because it's a crime against the government. She's stealing from all of us and you have to put a stop to it.*

How can you use threats to get her to talk, then turn around and report her anyway? That'd be an incredibly slimy thing to do.

The thought of calling the hotline brought up an enormous feeling of resistance. *Everyone knows snitches are the lowest form of bottom-feeding life.*

Cassidy parked in front of Med Tech's small window, positioning herself so Evelyn could look out and verify her location. She called the lab on her cell phone. The receptionist answered, running her words together in a mushy voice.

Cassidy said, "Put me through to Evelyn Wentworth."

"Who may I say is calling?"

"The person who has what she was looking for last night."

After a brief pause, Evelyn came on the line. She said, her voice as arrogant as ever, "And who's this? Olivia's busybody little neighbor?"

"I'm parked directly outside your window. I have the Medicare hotline number here in front of me, which I may or may not call. So what say you and I sit down and discuss the pros and cons of my dialing that number? This meeting will have to be now, at my convenience, not yours."

"Well." Cassidy heard a long, indrawn breath. "You do make a persuasive argument. Give me five minutes. There's a new coffee house at the end of the block. I'll meet you there."

# 15. A Ruined Dress

Cassidy walked to the café, which sported a hunter green exterior, sparkling windows, and a glossy oak door. It was the kind of storefront that abounded in trendy neighborhoods but looked completely out of place on this particular block, a lonely outpost of gentrification having nothing in common with the taquerias, produce stands, and super mercados that surrounded it.

After ordering a latte from the fresh-faced girl behind the counter, she took a marble topped table near the window. The gurgling of the espresso machine briefly drowned out the quiet strains of classical music in the background. There were no other customers.

Evelyn, clad in a champagne-colored silk tunic and pants, appeared minutes later and sat across from her. The coffee house was sparse and airy, with white walls, dark woodwork, and a fig tree in the rear corner. Although modern track lighting illuminated the counter area in back, an elegant Tiffany lampshade hung above their window table.

The lab owner's green eyes appraised Cassidy coldly for several seconds. "So, what exactly do you have?"

"The papers you broke into Olivia's house to search for. I was in her backyard when you went out the door."

"The forms she took from the lab. Now how might they have gotten into your possession? You happen to go through her house ahead of me?"

Cassidy smiled. *Yeah, but not having gotten caught, I don't have to admit it.*

The girl from behind the counter served Cassidy's latte. She had tawny hair pulled back from her face except for the few obligatory strands left to dangle in her eyes. "And what can I get for you?" she chirped to Evelyn.

"Black coffee."

"Irish cream, hazelnut, or French roast? And would either of you ladies like a freshly baked scone?"

"Just bring coffee." She bit off the words. "I don't care what kind."

The girl glanced down at Evelyn's tightly drawn features, then scurried back behind the counter.

"So, you say you've got the forms. Which, by the way, are stolen property. How much do you intend to charge for their return?"

Cassidy kept her face blank, not showing her surprise. *Should have seen this coming. Of course she'd think you're out for blackmail.* "How much were you paying Olivia?"

"She hadn't gotten around to asking for anything yet."

"So what did you do when she threatened to report you?"

The girl approached their table with a streaming styrofoam cup. They leaned back in their delicate, wrought iron chairs to wait until she was gone.

Evelyn's finely arched brows pulled together in a frown. "What is all this bullshit, anyway? You obviously don't know how to conduct a simple business transaction. If, in fact, you do have the forms, you need to prove it by showing me copies. Then we negotiate. If we strike a bargain, you hand over the paper, I give you money, we never see each other again. A discussion of what Olivia or I did is not part of the deal."

Cassidy laughed, a forced laugh, not entirely believable, just a loud snort intended to throw Evelyn off balance. From the lab owner's startled expression, Cassidy could see she had succeeded.

"You're not dictating the terms here. I am. Whether or not I have the actual papers, a call to the hotline will get you investigated. The forms, as a matter of fact, are locked away in my safe-deposit box." She stiffened her back and looked Evelyn directly in the eye.

"What I want is information. If I don't get straight answers, I'll call the hotline now and turn the forms over later. You tell me everything I want to know *and* manage to convince me it's the truth, I might not report you."

"I don't get it? What are you up to?" She stared hard at Cassidy. "You're not suffering under the delusion that you're Jessica Fletcher, are you?" She barked out a harsh laugh.

"You're not listening," Cassidy said, her voice gentle. Pulling her shoulder bag off the back of her chair, she extracted the phone and the sheet of paper with the hotline number on it. She placed the two items on the table in front of her. "I think Olivia threatened to blow the whistle and you killed her."

Evelyn laughed again. "You really *do* think you're Jessica Fletcher."

"Tell me what happened." Cassidy tapped a burgundy fingernail against the paper with the number on it.

"You're going to report me anyway. Why should I talk to you?"

"The possibility exists that I won't. But only if you tell me everything."

Her jaw clenched, Evelyn gazed toward a group of Hispanic children in Catholic school uniforms jostling their way past the window. "Olivia wasn't able to handle the job. She was slow. She made a lot of mistakes. She couldn't manage the new software." The lab owner turned her icy green eyes on Cassidy. "When she came up for her last review—around six weeks ago, I guess it was—I put her on probation. I said I'd work with her but we both knew it was hopeless." Shifting her gaze to the window again, she wrapped one blue-veined hand around the other.

Cassidy sipped her latte and waited.

"After I told her about the probation, she said she'd been taking work home, and she was sure that once I gave the matter more thought, I'd realize it wasn't in my best interest to fire her."

Evelyn drew in a long breath through slightly parted lips. "I knew what she meant, of course. She was blackmailing me to keep her on the payroll. And the worst of it was, I figured if she got away with that first demand, she'd be back later to ask for money." Ignoring the lack of ashtrays, Evelyn removed a pack of Winstons and a gold lighter from her purse. She touched the flame to her cigarette and inhaled deeply, then blew smoke out of the side of her mouth.

"What did you do?"

"What could I do? I had no choice. I had to keep her on, even though it meant hiring a part-time person to help with her work load." Glancing around, she walked over to the counter, argued briefly with the girl behind it, then returned with a pretty ceramic saucer, the rim sky blue, small red apples in the center.

"You obviously didn't like Olivia."

"What was there to like? She was a non-entity. A pathetic little mouse who couldn't do her job." Evelyn flicked ashes into the saucer. "The truth is, I didn't like her but I didn't exactly relish the thought of canning her, either." She puffed at her cigarette, sipped coffee. "I felt sorry for her. I know what it's like to lose everything and I wouldn't wish that on my worst enemy."

"But that wouldn't have stopped you from firing her."

Evelyn met her eyes. "You've never run a business, have you? You've got no idea what it's like to lose your ass over a couple of wrong decisions."

*She's right. You've never viewed life from the other side of a bankruptcy.*

"Look, the reason I'm doing what I'm doing is not because I enjoy contemplating the possibility of jail time. The guy I bought the lab from doctored the books to make it look like the business was turning a nice profit. It was only after I'd gone in hock up to my eyebrows to buy it that I discovered he'd had to skim Medicare to make ends meet." Anger flared in her eyes; the corners of her mouth turned down.

"The entire staff is a waste. The place needs a complete housecleaning but I can't afford to pay the kind of salary it would take to bring in competent help. And the role of grim reaper doesn't exactly appeal to me, either. If you were ten years away from retirement and had to either submit false claims or go broke, what would you do?"

*I wouldn't commit fraud, that's for sure*

*And what makes you so certain? It wouldn't be the first law you've broken. How can you possibly know what you might do if you were as desperate as this woman?*

"Where were you Sunday night?"

"At home, and no, I don't have an alibi."

"What about the gun?"

"What gun?" A muscle pulsed at the edge of her cheek where her blond hair brushed against her face.

"The gun you used to own." *Before you left it next to Jake's unconscious body.*

She shook her head slightly. "You don't know about any guns. You're just guessing."

"But you did have a gun, didn't you?"

She blew out smoke, then shrugged. "Since I frequently work late at the lab, I wanted a gun for protection. But I don't have it any more. It was stolen out of my car several months ago."

"Did you report it?"

"It wasn't registered."

Staring past Evelyn at the fig tree in the corner, Cassidy wondered whether the woman had started twitching over the gun question because it was her firearm that killed Olivia or because she'd broken gun laws as well as Medicare laws. Cassidy also wondered how much of what she'd heard was the truth.

"So," Evelyn said, grinding out her cigarette in the ceramic saucer, "are we done? What are you going to do with the forms?"

*Good question.* "Why don't you work on finding a way to turn a profit without cheating Medicare while I decide whether or not I'm going to report you."

৪৩      ৪৩      ৪৩

On the hike back to the Toyota, Cassidy felt heaviness settle over her. The heaviness of desperation and futility, the main threads running through the lives of both Olivia and Evelyn. Although the lab owner hadn't liked Olivia, she'd felt sorry for her, and Cassidy could say the same about her response to Evelyn.

The woman was cold, bitter, ruthless, as hard to warm up to as a snake. But Cassidy could understand how being hammered by failure might have made her that way. If she'd lived Evelyn's life, she couldn't be certain she would have come out any better.

*What's worse, I haven't a clue whether or not she was telling the truth.*

Cassidy was by no means ready to remove the lab owner's name from her list of suspects. But neither was she pinning all her hopes on proving the woman guilty.

*The other problem is, I can't bear to even think about reporting her.*

৪৩      ৪৩      ৪৩

Cassidy drove south on Western, then west on Augusta, stuffing her purse into her lap as she turned onto the boulevard. Waiting at a light, she watched three small black girls jump rope on the sidewalk. A slump-shouldered, drugged-out looking guy shuffled past the girls. On the opposite corner a cross-shaped sign announced the New Hope MB Church.

As she pressed the accelerator, the engine coughed, coughed again, and died. *What? The Toyota never quits on me.* Her stomach jittery, she twisted the key and listened to the starter grind. Somebody honked. Glancing in the mirror, she saw a man flip his finger at her in the car behind hers. She cranked the key again and the engine caught.

The car ran smoothly for half a block, then the motor choked, stopped briefly, started up again. *Please don't die. Not here. If you're going to break down, please get me across Austin Boulevard first.*

The motor kept spluttering. *Thank God it's not rush hour. Traffic's still light, parking lane's nearly empty. If the engine cuts out, at least I won't be left sitting in the middle of the street.*

Another two blocks and her engine quit again. She wrenched the wheel to the right, pulling against dead power steering, and hauled the car over to the curb before it came to a complete stop. Looking around, she realized she was not on one of Augusta's better stretches.

She cranked furiously, the jumpiness in her stomach getting worse. The grinding went on and on. Afraid of wearing the battery down, she finally stopped. She made herself breathe deeply. *Doors are locked. Still several hours before dark. Not really so bad. Lot of streets worse than Augusta.*

Ahead of her two mothers pushed strollers and an innocuous group of teens leaned against a beater car. Behind her three males in their early twenties lounged on the corner. She assumed they were drug dealers, although a nervous little voice reminded her that they might be gang-bangers, a more dangerous breed than dealers.

She dug out her phone and called Triple A. The operator informed her that a tow truck would arrive within an hour and a half.

Her anxiety revved higher. She remembered Zach's making her promise to call if anything happened.

The old resistance rose up in her again. *Hate feeling like some helpless little Jane who has to go running to Tarzan every time she's in a jam.*

*Grow up, kiddo. You forced Zach to let you go with him, side by side into the inferno. Now it's your turn to accept a friendly assist.*

She called his cell phone.

"Yeah."

She told him about the breakdown and her location. "I'm not in any danger, so if you're in the middle of something there's no reason I couldn't wait it out."

"I'll be there in . . . oh, let's see, about twenty minutes."

"Which direction will you be coming from? I'm going to have my eyes peeled for your car."

"I'm at this bar in Cicero, so the best route'd be north to Augusta, then east to where you're sitting."

Clicking him off, she mulled over the cause of the breakdown. *Why now? How come after nearly ten years of faithful service, your Toyota has a sudden coronary? Because you told Esther to stop calling? You climbed George's tree? You backed Evelyn into a corner?*

*Evelyn knew you'd be occupied elsewhere for a while. She could easily have told one of her people to do the deed while she was gone.*

As Cassidy stuffed her phone in her purse, she noticed a middle-aged man staring at her from the opposite side of the street. Worrying that he might go after her expensive handbag, she pulled the strap over her left shoulder, flattened it in her lap, and laid both forearms across it.

He ambled over, leaned close to the window, and spoke through the glass. "This ain't no place for a lady to be sittin' in her car. You want me to call somebody?"

"Thanks, I'm waiting for a tow truck. And my husband'll be here soon."

"I hope for your sake he gets his ass on over here pronto." He gave her a wave and went on his way.

She stared straight ahead, hoping to see Zach's car even though it was too early for him to be there yet. At the next intersection nearly a block away, a traffic light hung overhead and a small, dilapidated grocery stood on the corner. The store was yellow, its windows bricked up, a burglar bar gate standing open beside the door. A jumble of hand painted words in various colors cluttered the front of the building: WIC, Food Stamps, Soda, Cigarettes.

As the heat built up, the air became almost too thick to breathe. Her skin felt slimy and the armpits of her dress were soaking. *No getting out of a trip to the cleaners now.* Remembering the warnings about animals suffocating in closed cars, she cracked her front windows. As she leaned into the rear seat to open the other two, she looked back at the three dealer-types who inhabited the corner behind her. Two, in baseball caps, seemed deep in conversation. The third, bareheaded, stared in her direction.

*What's the matter with them they haven't come over and tried to do a deal? Where's their spirit of enterprise? No wonder they're stuck on Augusta Boulevard, haven't moved up to the night club circuit yet.*

She looked at her watch. Almost twenty minutes since her call to Zach. Fingers drumming on the steering wheel, she focused intently on the intersection ahead. Minutes later a blue sedan resembling Zach's Cougar stopped at the light.

A sudden explosion rocked her car and sent bullets of glass hurtling against the right side of her body. Letting out a shriek, she turned toward the large male whose hands were reaching through the shattered window to grab at the bag in her lap. Hanging on tight, she pulled it away before he could quite get hold of it.

"Gimme that, bitch." His fist pounded her right shoulder and arm. He clutched at her sleeve, ripping it halfway off.

She flailed out with her right arm, swatting at him, trying to beat his hand away from her bag. He got a firm grasp on it and started yanking, but the strap was anchored around her left shoulder and he couldn't pull it off.

Hearing a screech of brakes, she looked up to see the Cougar jerk to a stop nose to nose with her Toyota. Leaving his door open, Zach jumped out, got behind the man who was pounding on her, and hauled him away from the car. Staring through the broken window, she saw Zach throw a punch in the face of her attacker, a man with bulging weight-lifter arms.

She also saw the two baseball-capped buddies begin to move in their direction. The bareheaded guy swung at Zach. He ducked, took a glancing blow to his cheek, then shoved his fist in the weight-lifter's face again.

Cassidy grabbed her phone and started to dial 9-1-1. *Oh shit. Don't want Chicago cops rescuing Johnny Culver.*

She took her keys, leapt out of the Toyota, and shouted, "The cops are on their way."

Zach yelled back, "Get in my car."

*You've gotta get him out of there.* She gauged the width of the parkway and sidewalk. *Room for the Cougar.* Racing between the bumpers of the two cars, she jumped into the driver's side, slid the seat forward so she had her feet planted solidly on the pedals, then reached over to unlock the passenger door.

Zach slammed her attacker up against the Toyota but one of the buddies clamped a hand on Zach's shoulder and pulled him away.

Cassidy screeched backward, then jammed the car in drive, tore up on the sidewalk, and headed straight at the three guys who had Zach surrounded.

All four males turned to stare at the approaching car. Zach lunged into the baseball-capped thug who stood between him and the Cougar, broke out of the huddle, and threw himself into the passenger seat.

Backing off the curb, she sped into the eastbound traffic lane, then glanced across at Zach. He was hunched forward and breathing heavily.

Wiping his forehead with his arm, he said, "You okay?"

"Yeah, what about you?" She raked glass out of her hair and brushed at her clothing.

"I should've left that bar sooner. I made the mistake of talking a couple minutes longer. If I'd fucking got out of there right away, this wouldn't't've happened."

She reached with her left hand to finger the sleeve that was ripped away at the shoulder. "He tore my dress. You know, I really loved this dress and now it's ruined."

"We can buy another one," Zach said gently.

She was silent for a full minute. Noticing how badly her hands were shaking, she drew up to the curb, rested her arms on the wheel, and laid her forehead on her arms. Her breath came in short gasps. "I don't think I can drive any more."

"That's all right." Zach picked pieces of glass out of her hair. "We can sit here as long as you like. Then, when you're ready, you can get in the passenger side and I'll drive."

"I didn't really call nine-one-one. I figured you wouldn't want to be dealing with any Chicago cops right now."

"I'm pretty amazed you thought of that. Actually, I knew you didn't report it because you can't get through to nine-one-one on our cell phone."

She raised her head and took a deep breath. "Okay, I think my legs are steady enough now."

Changing places, she studied his face. "You've got a bruise up high on your right cheek. How much damage did he do you, anyway?"

"Nothing as serious as a ruined dress. A few bruises'll be fine. Just the ticket for somebody like JC."

"What're you going to do with all that adrenaline you've got pumping through your system?"

"What I'd like to do is drink. But the way you get pissed off, it's not worth the hassle. I'll have to think of something else. Maybe I'll go beat the shit out of that punk gangbanger. I expect that'd do the job."

Warmth flowed through her chest at the thought of all the changes Zach had been willing to make so they could live peacefully together. Changes like reducing the amount he drank because it worried her to see him overdo it.

"What're we going to do about my car?"

"I'll drop you off, then go wait for the tow truck." He crossed Austin Boulevard.

She immediately felt safer at the sight of green leaves floating all around them. "But then you'll be sitting on Augusta."

"Considering my new look, I don't think anybody's going to mess with me. Besides, I have a car that works. If anybody comes near me, I can drive away." Parking by their back gate, he turned to face her, his eyes troubled. "What worries me is why it happened in the first place."

"Me too."

"You know how I feel about coincidences. I hope we find out this is a case of unassisted mechanical failure, pure and simple. But I have to tell you, that's not what I'm expecting to hear. Your having an accidental breakdown at the same time you've been talking to all these people who weren't overly fond of Olivia doesn't seem likely at all."

Her first response was to feel pleased at his concern. Her second, to feel guilty that she was making it difficult for him to maintain his undercover persona, possibly even endangering him. She remembered his I-don't-need-this-now reaction when she'd told him about her plans to investigate, followed by her own glib assurance that she wouldn't be looking for any help.

"I think you're right. The car may well have been vandalized by one of the people I've talked to." She paused. "But I promise to be very careful in the future. Now I want you to turn yourself back into a hoodlum, go be JC, and trust me that I won't go driving alone on Augusta Boulevard again."

He shook his head. "How can I just forget about this?"

"You're the best person I know at not thinking about things. Now you go do your job and let me do mine."

&#10086;   &#10086;   &#10086;

She went inside and took a shower, then picked up her violet dress from the floor, a few more shiny nuggets shaking loose as she lifted it. When she saw it was not just the seam but the fabric itself that had been torn, she carried it out and dumped it in the alley trash can. The heaviness she had first noticed after her meeting with Evelyn gathered itself into a lump in her stomach.

*It's only a dress. Your happiness does not depend on the piece of fabric you wrap around your body.*

But it wasn't just a dress. It was the fact that Zach, who cared not at all about clothes for himself, had taken her to Lord and Taylor's and insisted that she purchase the best outfit in the store. He'd said at the time that she should always keep one dynamite dress in her closet in case she caught another psychopath and had to go on TV. Before Zach, no man had ever wanted to spend money on her or pressured her to buy nice things for herself or even cared very much if she was happy.

The lump, however, went beyond having to throw the dress away. *It's not calling the police when Olivia first raised the blinds. It's going behind Manny's back to meddle in things you should leave alone. It's forcing people to tell their sordid stories and not being able to use anything they say. It's bringing Tigger into the house and losing her. It's dragging Zach away from his investigation when his safety depends on maintaining his hoodlum role.*

Feeling one part guilty and two parts sorry for herself, she decided the best medicine would be to coax Starshine into some heavy-duty, motor-throbbing, slant-eyed cuddle time. Wandering through the house, she called "Kitty, kitty," but the calico failed to appear. She ran a cat food can through the electric opener and almost immediately heard paws thumping up from the basement.

Starshine leapt on the counter and buried her face in her bowl. Afterward, as she sat happily washing her face, Cassidy tried to scoop her up and cart her off to the bedroom. But the cat wriggled free and disappeared into the basement again.

*There's no way you can compete with Tigger. You're just going to have to be lonely, rejected and cuddle-deprived until you get the feral out of here.*

Which would not be anytime soon. Getting her out meant driving to Wisconsin, and Cassidy wasn't willing to sacrifice half a day to do it. She was, in fact, as hot in pursuit of her own quarry, Olivia's killer, as Starshine was of Tigger. For the time being she would simply have to live with the two cats chasing through her house and hope to hell the feral maintained her civilized use of the litter box.

An hour later she sat in her desk chair, feet propped on the radiator, a yellow pad in her lap. The pad bore a list of suspects, the information she had learned about them jotted beneath their names. She also had drawn a cartoon face for each depicting the person's demeanor: a bitter face for Evelyn, long- suffering for Danny, greedy for Esther, angry for Edwardo, vulnerable for Shelby, unstable for Brenner.

Having written everything down she could think of, she now stared out the window, hoping to shut off the chatter in her conscious mind so her unconscious, with its computerlike abilities, could assimilate the information and spit out the answer. Her gaze rested on a red, barn-shaped house across Hazel, a bright new banner hanging from its porch. Emblazoned on the banner were three autumn leaves, red, orange, and gold, a reminder that summer was coming to an end.

The phone rang and she swiveled to answer it. Zach's voice said, "The Toyota should be up and running with a brand new window by tomorrow afternoon. A clean window on the passenger side'll make the others look so bad by comparison you might need to run it through a car wash to even things out."

She smiled. Neither of them was overly fastidious about their cars or anything else. *Imagine what it'd be like if Zach was a neat-freak. You wouldn't have survived the first month, that's what.*

He added, "I'm getting sick of bar food. How 'bout I pick you up and we go out for a nice, relaxed dinner?"

Feeling a sudden, intense yearning to have their normal life back, she had to grit her teeth to keep an eager *yes* from jumping out of her mouth. *Oh no you don't. You've already disrupted him once today. You're not getting him even more distracted by making him bounce back and forth between being Zach and being JC this evening.*

"Every time something bad happens you want to come home early and pamper me."

"Why assume this is about you? Maybe I'm the one in need of pampering. I haven't been socked in the face like this since I was ten years old."

"Sorry, but JC is not the type to put his drug-buying operation on hold to take his wife out to dinner."

Zach chuckled. "Just because Johnny's highest aspiration in life is to make coke more accessible to the youth of Athens, Illinois, you can't assume he wouldn't like to spend a little quality time with his wife."

"Your task right now is to forget you even have a wife. No, wait, I don't want you going quite that far. Tuck the fact of my existence into the back of your mind and then get on with the job of worming your way into the confidence of those dealer-cops."

She hung up the phone and drew a happy-face cartoon representing the lift of spirit Zach's call had brought her. Earlier in their relationship she had fought against his caretaking urges, fearing they would undermine her independence and diminish her. But she had moved past that, and now found herself basking in the little kindnesses he offered. She had come to realize that the pleasure they both derived from being good to each other was fundamental to the bond between them. And she also realized that even though Zach seldom accepted any physical caretaking from her, she was nonetheless instrumental in meeting his emotional needs in some mysterious way she didn't fully understand.

She glanced at her watch. The pictures of the lawn service crew were waiting at Walgreens, but she didn't have a car to go get them. Another little job her grandmother could do. *Which'll make her even happier.* She smiled as she picked up the phone, thinking how lucky she was to have Gran in her life.

After requesting a picture delivery, Cassidy filled her grandmother in on everything that had happened during the day. "I went into the Evelyn meeting with the totally irrational idea that I'd somehow be able to turn myself into a human polygraph and come away with a fix on whether or not she was lying."

"But don't you do that in therapy sometimes? Figure out when people are fudging a little?"

"I can usually tell when somebody's slanting or distorting, which is probably what made me think I'd be able to catch Evelyn in some kind of lie. The giveaway is when people are evasive or inconsistent, or when their story sounds pretty implausible. None of those things happened so maybe every word out of Evelyn's mouth was the truth."

Cassidy bit her lip, remembering how the woman had badgered the waitress into giving her a saucer to use as an ashtray in a no-smoking establishment. "Except that, given Evelyn's level of desperation and her self-centered way of getting what she wants, she still tops the list for winner of the most-likely-to-commit-murder award."

"Maybe she's just a better liar than your clients are."

"The other thing is, I feel so torn about reporting her. Gran, why don't you just tell me what to do and make it easy?"

Gran let out a cackling laugh. " 'Cause whatever I'd say, you'd want to do the opposite."

"Well, no problem there. You can use reverse psychology, I'll be oppositional, and we'll both be happy."

"Don't you worry. We'll figure this out somehow. Oh, and by the way, my friend Irma said she could get Olivia's phone records for us. Maybe that'll help us come up with something new. She's gonna give them to me Saturday morning when we get together for breakfast."

As Cassidy hung up, she heard Starshine clattering up the staircase outside the bedroom. Moments later the calico was ensconced on her lap, front paws kneading, a raucous purr rumbling through her body.

"Well, what do you know? I guess your cuddle alarm hasn't totally ceased to function, even if Tigger does have more to offer in the fun and games department than I do."

Starshine's slanted eyes gazed rapturously into her human's as Cassidy bestowed a gentle cheek scratch. With Zach interrupting his undercover zealotry to check in on her, and Starshine returning to her lap, Cassidy's world slid back into place.

ຂຽ ຂຽ ຂຽ

A short time later Gran dropped off the pictures and Cassidy sat down at her desk to go through them. The photos were not bad. She had at least one clear shot of each of the men's faces, including a decent profile of the larger guy who'd tried to avoid her camera. Pulling Behan's card out of her top drawer, she left a message on his machine: "I took photos of Luis and three of his men, and I bet one of them turns out to be Edwardo. Let me know when you can come by and look them over."

Later that night she was brushing her teeth for bed when she heard a piercing shriek from the basement again. Even though she knew it signaled nothing more than a pretend war between cats, it sounded so much like a child's cry it made her breath catch and goosebumps rise on her arms.

She went downstairs, grabbed Starshine, and locked her in the extra bedroom. "If you won't play nice, you'll have to do a time out."

ຂຽ ຂຽ ຂຽ

The next morning, Thursday, Cassidy sat at the dining room table, her purple mug at her elbow, the photo of the man she thought was Edwardo in her hand. The last time she'd talked to Olivia's attorney, he'd said that once they knew for certain the deported Mexican was back in the country, he would use his influence with the prosecutor to get the charges against Jake dropped.

*Which is all you really need. You've been knocking yourself out trying to identify the killer—a ridiculous undertaking in the first place. Nobody's going to sit down over coffee and say: I did it. It's me. I'm the one.*

*But it isn't necessary to hand Manny the* right *guy. All you have to do is get the* wrong *guy out of jail.*

This train of events would be set into motion as soon as Carl confirmed that the man in the photo was Edwardo. *He should've called by now.* Recalling that her machine had skipped two messages in the past week, she tip-toed into the bedroom where Zach was asleep, took Behan's card down to the kitchen phone, and repeated her words on his recorder.

The day stretched emptily ahead. She had two clients from ten till noon, Luis's daughter Rosa at four, and Shelby at eight. None of these activities seemed destined to advance her investigation, and her other choices, yard work, cleaning, and laundry, interested her not at all.

*All you want to do is show the photo to Carl. And staring at the phone has never yet made it ring.*

She did not hear the chirping sound she was waiting for until after one. Seated at her desk, she grabbed the receiver.

"This is Jim Foley over at Firestone. Your car's ready to pick up. What with putting in a new fuel line and replacing the window, the bill comes to two seventy-five."

Wincing at the cost, she asked, "The fuel line? What was wrong with it?"

"You know, I've been in the business a long time and run into all kinds of vandalism, but I've never seen anything quite like this before. The line was crimped to keep the gas from getting to the engine. 'Course there was enough gas already in the line on the engine side to take you a mile or so, but after that, nothing could get through."

"Are you sure it was done deliberately? There's no chance it could've gotten crimped by itself?"

"When you come in, I'll show you the pinch marks left by the pliers."

She put down the receiver. *Well, it's not as if this comes as a big surprise.* Tapping a pen against the managed care form she was filling out, she pondered the who and the why and the reason for crimping a fuel line as opposed to slashing tires or pouring sugar in the gas tank.

Evelyn, who'd seen the Toyota parked outside her window, was far and away the likeliest candidate, although it was always possible someone else had followed Cassidy to the lab. Evelyn's motive was obviously revenge. Cassidy had called her on the cell phone, and the lab owner, presuming the agenda to be blackmail, had requested a five-minute delay. Five minutes to hand down the order to damage Cassidy's car. And wanting to lash out and retaliate certainly was consistent with the ruthlessness Cassidy had seen in the woman. The crimping of the fuel line also made sense. It removed Cassidy from Evelyn's doorstep, stranding her far enough away that she could not walk into the lab owner's office and demand help.

*You need to remember this is all assumption. You've built a great case against Evelyn, but the case the police have against Jake is every bit as good.*

Identifying Evelyn as the probable vandal helped her investigation not at all, however, because the lab owner's spiteful actions had been based on her fear of being charged with fraud, not murder.

*Stop trying to figure everything out. You need to go pay the damn bill and get your car back.* Cassidy hitched a ride with her grandmother, handed over her credit card, and reclaimed her Toyota. She even stopped at a car wash on her way home.

&#8270; &#8270; &#8270;

Rosa, a young girl slightly shorter than Cassidy's five-two, arrived at her rear entrance at a quarter past four. Her thin boyish body was clad in jeans and an orange knit top, a knapsack strapped to her back. Her hands and skinny arms moved constantly.

"Pops said you'd let me interview you."

Cassidy opened the screen door. "Come on in."

The girl entered the waiting room, her lively brown eyes scanning everything in sight. She had smooth light brown skin, a pug nose, a friendly, smiling mouth and a pointed chin.

"Would you like something to drink?"

"Sure. You got any Coke?"

Sticking her head in the fridge, Cassidy did not see much beyond beer for Zach, wine and yogurt for her, some fruits and vegetables, and the usual array of staples. When she was in her obsessive stage, shopping fell by the wayside. As she rummaged around, she heard Rosa wander into the dining room. Finally locating a lone can of Diet Pepsi, she handed it to the girl.

"This is a pretty nice house. And you got so much room." Rosa, her glossy hair pulled into a banana clip, loose strands crinkling around her face, stared at Cassidy curiously. "You got any kids?"

"Uh uh."

"I don't know what it'd be like to have a big house like this with no kids. We got eight in our family—well, some of them are cousins— and we're all on top of each other."

"When it comes time for cleaning, it seems like too much space." *Not that you actually* do *cleaning.* "But it's nice to be able to work at home. So, let's go sit in my office and talk." She pointed her head toward the rear of the house.

Cassidy settled in her chair. Rosa plopped down on the sectional and took out a legal pad.

"Okay, why don't you start telling me 'bout your job?"

Cassidy provided a general explanation of therapy.

"You know, the thing that's hard for me to understand is why these dudes'd go to a stranger to talk. I mean, I know what therapy is. I've seen it lots of times in the movies. But it always seems pretty weird to me to pay somebody to give you advice."

*She's right. It is pretty weird. Maybe you ought to go find some honest way to earn a living.*

"When your friends have problems, what do you do to help them?"

"I listen real good and then I tell them what they should do. And I always give really good advice—everybody says so. If they'd just pay attention better, they wouldn't get in so much trouble."

"The reason people talk to therapists is that therapists *don't* give advice." *Mostly you don't. Sometimes you can't resist. Giving advice is so much easier and more fun than doing what you should be doing.*

Rosa jiggled her pencil. "But therapy's only for Anglos with lots of money. People like us, we wouldn't need a therapist. We got plenty of friends to talk to, and we all help each other."

"You're right. It's usually middle class whites who go into therapy. But I don't agree that having lots of friends means you don't need it." She glanced at a flock of starlings eating berries in the small tree outside her window. "I bet you know people who have drug and alcohol problems. Or get in trouble with the law. Or find themselves pregnant before they're ready. Or maybe just feel sad and overwhelmed most of the time."

"Oh sure. Lots of people have stuff like that. But those dudes who come see you—even though they spend all that money on therapy, it doesn't mean they never have problems anymore, does it?"

"No, but when therapy works, it enables people to handle their problems better."

A horn honked twice from the street outside the office, and Rosa jumped up to look out the north window. "Pops's here." She turned an impish grin on Cassidy. "Thanks for telling me about therapy. I'm not sure I believe in it very much but it's fun to see in the movies."

"Well, who knows? Maybe someday I'll decide you're right and then I'll have to go find something more useful to do." *Like flipping burgers or checking out groceries.*

"You know that lady across the street? Pops told me she got murdered. Did you get to see the body or anything?"

*This is not the time for honesty.* "Um . . . I just heard about it."

Her pert face suddenly drew into a tight, angry frown. "That woman, she was a real witch. She deserved to get killed. You know what she did? It was because of her my cousin Lupe died." Rosa started bouncing toward the door.

"Wait! Can't you tell me what happened—"

"Sorry, gotta go." The girl scurried through the waiting room and was gone.

Cassidy watched Rosa climb into the pickup, then headed for the stairs. If Luis's daughter held Olivia responsible for the death of a child, the whole clan—Luis's side as well as Edwardo's—must have deeply resented her. Cassidy needed to get the bombastic, talkative Luis to tell her about the cousin's death. What had worked with him before was flirting. As awkward as it felt, she would have to do it again.

*His place or yours? His. That way he can't drive off in his pickup when he gets tired of answering your questions.*

She dialed and his machine came on. In a voice laced with sexual suggestiveness, she murmured. "This is Cass McCabe. I've been considering what you said about signing up for Cordova's lawn service and I'd like to come by your office tomorrow to discuss it further. Why don't you pick a time when we won't be interrupted?" She gave him her number and clicked off.

*Do you realize what you've just done?* She pictured herself in a Xena costume, a dagger sticking out of her boot, backed up against Luis's desk, the lawn service guy breathing down her neck and peering into her cleavage.

Cassidy had no clients to see that evening, just Shelby, who was due at eight. The past two nights she had gone to Olivia's to avoid dealing with JC. But Zach had been so much his old self yesterday it raised her hopes that he might be getting better at moving in and out of his undercover persona. She decided to stick around this evening and see if he was able to return from his day's wanderings and treat her in a normal fashion.

At six-thirty she was at her desk, a stack of bills and the checkbook in front of her, the register showing an insufficient balance to cover the month's expenses. Hearing Zach's footsteps, she turned toward the doorway. He came into the bedroom, glanced at her coldly, then sat in his chair and swiveled it toward his own desk.

*Just turns his back, acts like I don't exist.* Although she recognized it as typical JC behavior, she still experienced the old sinking sensation she'd felt all her life when someone she loved abandoned her.

Still not facing her, he said, "I need to catch a couple of hours sleep. So, if you don't mind?"

*Even the voice is different. Zach has this kind of drawling, bemused tone. JC always sounds clipped, terse, almost growls when he's forced to actually talk to you.* She had seen this kind of thing in therapy. A perfectly normal client would be overtaken by a different part, and the person's whole demeanor would change right in front of her. But even though she'd encountered it as a therapist and been living with it in her own house for nearly a month, she still felt a sense of shock every time she bumped up against this churlish stranger in her husband's skin.

*What if Zach reaches the point he can't make JC go away?*

Look how fast he came running to the rescue yesterday. He's not going to let this thug control him.

She went to lean against the doorjamb. Arms folded across her chest, she addressed his profile. "Shelby's coming at eight. I'll meet with her on the porch so you and I don't have to cross paths."

He looked up, his face opaque and humorless. "Is she a babe? Maybe I'll join you."

"You're trying to start a fight, aren't you? I suppose you'd like it if you could goad me into throwing a fit, and then you'd have even more of an excuse to mess around with that little bimbo friend of yours."

He stood. "I don't need an excuse."

She went downstairs and took out the vacuum. Pushing it furiously, she tried to work off her anger. It sucked up thick clumps of cat hair, the fur accumulating twice as fast with two felines in the house.

The madder she got, the more she wanted to crash Zach's party at

The Zone. Her imagination had been working overtime, conjuring pictures of orgies under the tables. *Reality's usually not half as bad as the scenarios you paint in your head.* The thought of sneaking in to get a firsthand look was tempting. *But if he caught you, he'd think you were spying. Well, you would be.* The balance between them right now was too delicate. It wasn't worth the trouble it would cause if he found her out.

&#8526;    &#8526;    &#8526;

Cassidy opened the front door and said, "Hey," to Shelby, who stood outside the screen on the opposite side of the enclosed porch. The evening was dusky, but illumination from the picture window created a soft glow on the porch. Cassidy pulled the screen door wide and invited the young woman in.

"Let's sit out here." Cassidy gestured toward the wicker couch. "The weather's just perfect." The August heat had abated to a warm-bath temperature, a mild breeze wafting the perfumed smells of late summer through the porch's open window.

"Look, are you sure we have to do this?" Shelby wore tan shorts and a white tee, HILFIGER inscribed on the front, a black bag suspended from her shoulder. "I almost called to cancel."

"But you didn't. So why not make yourself comfortable while I get us something to drink?" Cassidy waved toward the couch again.

Stiffly lowering herself onto the cushion's edge, Shelby ran a hand over her thick, dark curls. Her face, with its high cheekbones, smooth planes, and straight, fine features, was lovely.

"What would you like? Wine, beer, nonalcoholic?"

"Wine, absolutely. If you're really going to make me do this, I should get the biggest glass you've got. Better yet, the whole bottle."

Cassidy headed inside. *Sounds like loosening her tongue wouldn't be too difficult. Especially since she's clueless about your hidden agenda.*

*You can't get her drunk*, a shocked voice jumped in. *This is therapy. Well, almost therapy. Shelby's been bruised and battered by all that rejection, and the only way for her to get past it is to understand why it happened. Since you knew Olivia, you're the one who needs to work with her on this.*

Cassidy took two long-stemmed glasses down from the rack in the dining room and opened a bottle of chardonnay.

*Can't fix everything in a single session, but at least you can get her started. She's got to be a client first, a suspect second, and you can't let her drink too much or the therapy won't work.*

Sitting on the opposite end of the couch, Cassidy handed the young woman a half-filled glass. "So, how've you been doing since we talked?"

"I'm all right. Keeping myself busy, not thinking about it."

"Except?" The chimes hanging from Cassidy's eaves clanged melodiously.

"How'd you know?"

"There's always an except."

Shelby sighed. "I'm not sleeping too well." On the other side of Hazel a woman sat on the porch of her Victorian home, her radio tuned to a blues station, the wind blowing rifts of wailing music across the street.

"What are all the unanswered questions?"

"Well, we already talked about the first one—why she didn't keep me. You said she couldn't handle it, and I guess I can go along with that. But even if she wasn't up to raising me, why weren't there ever any phone calls or birthday cards?" Turning diagonally to face Cassidy, she leaned back into the corner and crossed her long legs at the ankles.

"The other question is, after I came to Chicago specifically to get to know her, why'd she refuse to talk to me for so long? The way she kept hanging up—I felt like she hated me." Setting her glass on the floor, she fished a Kleenex out of her puffy black bag, dabbed at the corners of her eyes, then wrapped the tissue around one slender finger.

Cassidy watched a black sedan park in front of the Victorian. A man got out and joined the woman on her porch. It reminded her of her dating days with Zach, the bad old times before these current bad times.

She turned to face Shelby. "The driving force in your mother's life was fear. Many of the simple, ordinary things the rest of us take for granted were so frightening for Olivia she couldn't do them." Cassidy put her glass aside and rested her hands in her lap. "I'd like you to think of a time when you wanted to do something but you were so scared you couldn't get yourself to go through with it."

Shelby sat straighter. "I'm never like that. If I want something, I make myself do it. I just keep at it—the way I did when I forced Olivia to talk to me."

*That tough, strong exterior to hide the vulnerable little person inside.*

"Everybody's had some time in their life when fear stopped them."

Shelby was silent for several moments, her fingers twisting the tissue. "Well, okay. I remember once when I was a kid. I climbed up to the highest diving board, but when I got right up to the edge, I couldn't jump off. I had to give up and go back down that ladder."

"I want you to make that memory as real as possible. Let yourself feel exactly what it was like not to be able to make yourself jump off that board."

Shuddering slightly, she gazed into her lap and began shredding the tissue. "It was . . . creepy. Like cold chills. I stood there, totally paralyzed, and then I started inching backward. I didn't plan on climbing down that ladder, I just did."

"And how did you feel about the fact that you had to go back down the ladder?"

"It was awful. There were all these kids in line making fun of me and they all had to get off the steps so I could come down." Shelby's deep blue eyes caught Cassidy's, then dropped to the torn tissue in her hand. "I felt really dumb."

"Okay, now imagine Olivia as a twenty-year-old girl taking her baby home from the hospital, then getting so frightened she couldn't go through with being a mother. So she had to go back down that ladder, which meant giving her baby away. And just like there were all those kids who witnessed your defeat, Olivia had your father and grandmother who'd witnessed hers. Who knew she was incapable of raising her own child."

Cassidy paused. With Shelby's head lowered, she couldn't read the younger woman's expression. "Now if you put yourself in that situation, how would *you* feel about contacting your child later?"

Stuffing the torn tissue in her purse, Shelby took out a new one and began twisting it around her finger. "I don't know. I suppose I'd be embarrassed. I'd feel like everybody thought I was a failure."

"Now fast-forward twenty-three years. Imagine that your whole life has been one episode after another of backing down that ladder. You haven't succeeded at your job. You never married. You don't have any friends. You've never even been able to leave home. How would you feel if your daughter wanted to get to know you?"

Shelby sighed. "I wouldn't want her to see what my life was like. I'd be afraid she'd think I was pathetic." She shifted, crossed her legs, then stretched them out in front of her again. "I suppose I wouldn't want to be reminded of the mistake I'd made getting pregnant." She swiped at her eyes. "And I guess it'd be pretty hard to see my daughter having a successful life when I hadn't done one thing with mine."

"Does that answer your questions?"

There was another long silence. "But how do you know it wasn't just lack of interest? I always assumed she was totally indifferent to me."

"Do you know anything about her cats?"

"They seemed pretty important to her. Sort of like her babies." She rubbed her left palm against her cheek. "More important than I ever was."

"Olivia loved her cats. Taking care of them was probably her only real source of gratification. I think the feeling she had for her cats came out of a strong maternal instinct. She just couldn't direct that instinct toward people because she was too afraid of them." A few strains of bluesy saxophone floated by.

"I never thought of it that way."

"I'd like for you to see her house."

She shook her head. "I really don't want to."

Cassidy waited.

"You've already forced me to feel things I don't want to feel. If I see her house, I might end up feeling sorry for her."

"Would that be so bad?"

Shelby's shoulders stiffened and the cords stood out on her neck. "What about me?" Venom flashed across the beautiful face. "Why should I waste sympathy on her? She never gave me anything."

"Not even her ring."

Shelby took out a third tissue and began shredding it furiously.

"What happened the last time you saw her?"

"I don't want to talk about it."

Cassidy said in a low voice, "You had a fight. A really bad fight. And then you never saw her again." She paused. "If you keep it inside, it'll eat at you forever."

# 16. Newspapers

"I told her she had no right to keep the ring," Shelby said angrily. "That she'd manipulated my father into giving it to her, and she was a selfish bitch not to give it back. Then she accused my father of cheating her out of marriage. She said he'd strung her along with promises he never meant to keep, and that being an unwed mother was the worst thing that'd ever happened to her." Shelby lowered her head, her dark hair falling forward.

"I was so pissed at what she said about my dad, I just lost it. I grabbed her hand and jerked the finger backward. I think I might've been trying to break it, I'm not sure." She covered her face, then dropped her hands and looked at Cassidy. "I went home and stewed about it for a few days, then I wrote a letter and put every mean thing I could think of in it. It just seemed so unfair, her blaming my dad like that when she'd dumped a kid on him and he had to quit school because of it. I hate her for saying that. I just hate her."

*This girl's got a lot of rage. Borderline rage? Borderlines are the ones who stalk people and go all out for revenge. Could Shelby have shot her mother and taken the sapphire?*

"I'm surprised you haven't asked about the ring. Her godfather's managing the estate and he might want you to have it."

"That fight was so awful. After I finally cooled down, I felt like I never wanted to see her or the ring again."

"I can understand why it seems all wrong for you to feel sorry for her. She was supposed to take care of you, not the other way around. But I still think you should see the house. This is likely to be your only chance to get a first hand sense of her." Cassidy paused. "Will you come?"

     ജ   ജ   ജ

On the way over, she prepared Shelby for the foul odors that awaited them on the other side of Olivia's door. Stepping into the foyer, Cassidy felt her body tighten as the fetid air surrounded her.

Bamba came mewing to greet them. "This is the tom." Cassidy bent down to scratch his rump. "He's the pushy one. After he eats, he always demands that I sit on the floor and pet him."

In the kitchen she pointed at the two orange females sitting next to the food bowls. "And these are Barbra and Ella, named after the singers, I guess. They're shyer than the tom, but when I sit quietly on the couch, they climb into my lap and purr."

Squatting down, Shelby extended a hand for Bamba to sniff. "We had a bunch of barn cats in Maine but they never let you pet them."

*Do a sales pitch on the cats? That's really pushing it. But still— might be good for her to have something of her mother's.* "I have to find a home for Olivia's babies." She watched Bamba rub his face against Shelby's hand. "I know it's taking care of her again, but what do you think?"

Shelby stood, her mouth twisting into a cynical smile. "Is that what this is all about? Did you put me through this whole song and dance just to get me to take her cats?" She shook her head emphatically. "Olivia wouldn't do one damn thing for me, but I'm supposed to get all dewy-eyed over her poor little kitties? Now you might be able to manipulate me into feeling sorry for her. You might even be able to con me into coming over to her house. But there's no way you're getting me to adopt her animals."

*Of course she feels manipulated.* Taking a half step back, Cassidy said mildly, "My only purpose was to help you understand your mother." *Well, and do a little pumping.* "If you don't want the cats, that's fine with me."

    ဆ   ဆ   ဆ

After Shelby left, Cassidy found a message on the machine from Luis. "I'll be at my office tomorrow around ten. You wanna see me, you come by then." His voice was flat and uninviting, a complete turnaround from yesterday's buoyant, teasing tone.

*What's happened here? He must've guessed that something's up. Something other than a secret liaison.*

Remembering the way Luis's face had changed when she asked

about Edwardo, she suddenly realized how clumsy she'd been. By bringing his name up, she'd made it obvious she was after something other than either yardwork or a Lady Chatterly tryst.

More bothersome, however, was the fact that she still had not heard from Carl. Up until now, he'd been prompt about everything, and she couldn't understand why he hadn't returned her calls. She wanted him to look at the photos. Especially now that it had dawned on her that her chances of uncovering the murderer herself were about as great as the Bears' chances of winning another Super Bowl.

*If it turns out this guy in the picture isn't Edwardo, you are going to be majorly disappointed.*

&#8286;   &#8286;   &#8286;

The first thing she did the next morning was check the answering machine. No new messages. It was Friday, and she had nothing scheduled all day except her meeting with Luis, which she doubted would net her anything.

*Why isn't Carl phoning me?* She remembered thinking earlier that if her clients did not receive a return call, she hoped they would assume her answering device had failed.

*Maybe his machine is in worse shape than yours.*

The most sensible recourse, she decided, would be to put the photo in an envelope and drop it off at Behan's house after she saw Luis.

In choosing her attire, she decided to go for sexy on the outside chance that testosterone might win out over family loyalty. She hunted through her closet, finding almost nothing that qualified, then finally selected a clingy, scoop-necked, lavender top to wear above her black jeans. As she slid her feet into low heeled sandals, she considered the possibility of danger.

Picturing the jolly, swaggering Mexican she'd chatted with earlier, she could not bring herself to imagine that she would be in any real peril, but she stuffed her pepper gun in her tote just to be on the safe side.

She drove to Cicero, a deteriorating, largely Hispanic suburb south of Oak Park. Trolling slowly to check addresses, she spotted the Cordova sign, then noticed a man sitting across the street in an ancient sedan, the windshield cracked, a leprosy of rust destroying the metal. She tapped the brakes lightly and peered into his car, trying to get a good look at his face. The man instantly raised a newspaper to block her view.

She cruised around the block, returned, and parked next to the storefront office, placing her car directly in front of the window so she could keep an eye on it from inside. The man behind the sedan's wheel positioned the paper so his face remained hidden. *Edwardo. I'd bet money on it.*

She glanced around. Adjacent to the lawn service office was an empty lot containing the red pickup, the trailer, and an old truck on blocks, the lot enclosed by a chain link fence topped by concertina wire. Across the street was a children's clothing store, the window crammed with frilly dresses encased in plastic bags.

*So what now? Go inside and take the chance of getting your car vandalized again? Or worse—of having Edwardo follow you in and shoot you? Except he wouldn't want blood all over the office. Or are you, for once in your life, going to do the smart thing—turn tail and go home.*

She could not face returning to her house to spend the whole day obsessing about the case. Especially not with one more unturned stone right in front of her.

She got out, locked her car door, and went inside. Luis stared at her from behind a painted metal desk at the far end of the room. A lumpy couch was backed up against the wall to her right, three wooden armchairs stood in front of the desk, and a TV sat on a rickety stand in the corner, the top of the television scarred by cigarette burns, the picture playing but the sound off.

Luis folded his burly arms on the desk. "Well, pretty lady, you decided to come see me after all. But you don't wanna talk about signing up Cordova." He shook his head, his face morose. "You got something else on your mind, don'tcha?"

She took one of the wooden chairs, angling it sideways so she could glance back at her car. "I'd like to talk about Edwardo."

He shook his head disapprovingly. "Why you wanna talk about things that are none of your business?"

She hated that question. There was no good answer. "Because I'm a busybody. I found Olivia after the murder and I'd like to know what happened to her."

"What's that got to do with Edwardo? He's back home in Mexico taking care of our mama and papa."

*No he's not. He's right outside this office.*

"What tipped you off that I wasn't here to sign up for the lawn service?"

"That other day after I left I got to thinking 'bout you bringing up Edwardo, then taking all those pictures. The more I thought about it, the more I didn't believe you were really gonna show off photos of those ugly guys. Then Rosa told you 'bout blaming that murdered lady for Lupe dying and right away you wanna come talk to me. So I figured it was something to do with that lady getting killed."

"Why is one of your workers sitting in a car across the street?"

"He's just worried you wanna make trouble. He thinks maybe you're crazy or something." He made a circling motion next to his head. "He argued with me I shouldn't see you but I figured you might make more trouble if I don't."

"Look, I really don't want to cause any problems." She turned to check on her car. A group of gangbanger-type teens shuffled past on the sidewalk, but they weren't paying any attention to her Toyota.

She gazed directly at Luis, his ridged brow lowered gloomily, all trace of his previous ebullience gone. "Somebody killed my neighbor. I know Edwardo threatened her last summer, and then a couple of days ago I see him working in her yard again. So I can't help thinking that maybe he was still mad at her. Mad enough to shoot her, especially if he blamed her for the death of his child."

"You didn't see Edwardo. You rich Anglos can't tell the difference, one dumb spic from another."

"Luis, that's not true. I like you. I think Rosa's fantastic. I could've taken my photos straight to the police but instead I came here so you could explain to me if I'm wrong."

"You wanna beer?"

Glancing at the tall waste basket full of empty Bud cans, she shook her head. *You may not think he's dumb but you do think he starts drinking a mite early in the day.*

He reached into a small refrigerator next to his desk, pulled out a can, and popped the top. A colorful serape and two framed pictures of Mexican villages hung on the wall behind him.

"Okay, I tell you what happened, then you throw those pictures away."

She nodded. *Nodding is not a promise.*

"It wasn't your neighbor's fault that Lupe died. It was Edwardo's. He started the business and I worked for him, but he got to messing up pretty bad. The problem was, he liked the girls too much." He flashed a grin as if to say, "Who doesn't?"

"How was that a problem?" *These therapy questions sure do come in handy.*

"Edwardo, he was six inches taller than anybody else in the family, and being bigger always seemed to make him the boss. Well, after he got to meeting all these ladies through the business, he wanted to beef up his muscles even more. He wanted all the Anglo ladies to admire him." Luis's voice dropped into a deep, heavy tone. "So he got to taking some stuff to build up his muscles."

"Steroids?"

"He started getting hard to work with. Picking fights with people. A lot of times he'd yell at the guys in the middle of a job and they'd just walk out on him. But the worst of it was when he got into fights with customers. Then he might do something to wreck their lawns. I tried to get him to stop the pills but he wouldn't listen to nobody."

"What happened to his little girl?"

Luis shook his head glumly. "Poor little Lupe. She was only three. After Edwardo's family went back to Mexico, she got this terrible sickness and she just died. There wasn't no hospital in the village. It never woulda happened here. Edwardo's wife and kids, they blamed that lady for getting him deported. But I knew he did it to himself. There were a lotta people pissed off at him. If that lady hadn't got him sent back, somebody else would've."

"How'd you feel about his getting deported?"

He shrugged. "He's my brother so I didn't like it. Rosa used to take care of Lupe and she loved her uncle so I never told her 'bout the steroids." He frowned darkly. "But in a way I was glad he left before the business got completely wrecked. I had to work twice as hard, building it up again."

"But he's back now and this time he's working for you."

He glared at her. "I told you—he's not here. The whole family agreed. He got himself in too much trouble. It's better he stays back home."

ಐ       ಐ       ಐ

As Cassidy left the office, her gaze zoomed in on the man in the rusted-out car across the street. This time he met her eyes. It was the guy from her photo. She reached into her tote and grabbed both her keys and the pepper gun. Although he did not leave his sedan, he continued to stare. *Trying to scare me. Letting me know I better not mess with him.*

Glancing in her rearview mirror as she drove away, she saw him go into the office. *Even though Luis sees his brother as a major screw-up, that doesn't mean he wouldn't lie like a used car salesman to protect him.*

She headed toward Behan's home in Riverside, an elite, planned community about ten miles southwest of Oak Park.

Driving into Riverside was, in a small-scale way, like going from Kansas to Oz. Most of the surrounding streets were seedy commercial or rundown residential, but once Cassidy crossed into Riverside, the landscape turned picturesque. Although the houses were old, they were attractive and well maintained, with meandering streets, a river through the middle of town, and large squares of meadowlike grass.

She drew up next to a small, ivy-covered brick house. The tiled roof was sharply peaked, with another tall peak above the arched front door. It had a low concrete porch, a wrought iron railing along the sides, and a shrub-bordered walkway curving out to the street.

Looking at the house through the car's side window, she felt a small sense of dread start up in her stomach. Her gaze locked on to two plastic-wrapped newspapers lying on his porch. *Something's wrong.*

Legs going stiff, she walked from the car to the foot of the steps, her eyes never leaving the newspapers. The feeling in her stomach got thick and black, began oozing up into her chest. Her gaze jumped to the mail slot. If he hadn't picked up the newspapers, the mail would be uncollected too. She pushed the doorbell and heard chimes ringing within.

*Yeah, but you know he's not going to answer.* People who were able to open their doors did not leave newspapers on their porches. Even though she was certain the mail would be there also, she could not resist raising the brass flap and peering into the chute. The lower section was clogged with envelopes and brochures.

*Either two or three days' worth.* Cassidy had talked to Behan Tuesday morning when he stopped over to report that the two lawn service guys had seen him watching their office. She had then called him Tuesday night to inform him about the broken window, and Behan must have contacted a workman the following morning to get it repaired. He'd taken in his Wednesday paper, but her phone call that afternoon had gone unanswered.

*Could be out of town. It's not as though he's obligated to tell you if he goes away for a few days.* Knowing it was useless, she jabbed the doorbell again the way people press lighted elevator buttons in an attempt to stave off feelings of helplessness. *Maybe he's sick. Hasn't been able to get out of bed for three days.*

The thick black feeling rose into her throat and she had to swallow it back to keep from gagging. This scene was too familiar, one she had encountered countless times in fiction. *In movies you know something scary is about to happen because the music goes boomedy-boom, thumpety-thump, crashing toward a climax.*

*Right now, it's this awful feeling in my gut that's telling me this is bad.*

The way the scene usually ran, the unsuspecting heroine found the door unlocked, walked in, and stumbled over a dead body. *Even if the door was wide open, I wouldn't go inside that house. And I'm definitely not unsuspecting.* Nonetheless, she couldn't stop herself from reaching out to turn the knob. *Locked! Thank God, thank God, it's locked!*

Starting to feel queasy, she sat down on the top step. *This is all your fault. You convinced Carl he needed to investigate and now the odds are he's dead. And in addition, Zach's probably headed toward widowhood because you stupidly convinced yourself that good, old, jolly Luis didn't present any danger. The only one with anything to gain from all this is JC, who may well turn Zach into a bimbo-groping dope dealer if you're not around to prevent it.*

*Stop this. You have to think.* If Carl were dead, she needed to get the cops to go inside and find his body, because nothing in the world would induce her to take on that task. But as far as she knew, the police would not break in on the strength of newspapers, mail, and the feeling in her gut.

*If Carl's been murdered, the chances are he didn't invite the killer in for tea.* So there might be signs of forced entry. If she could show that to the cops, they would go inside. Circling the house, she inspected each window for damage. In the back she came across one that was open. As she moved closer, the stench hit her.

She had smelled death before, but the deaths had always been fresh ones. This death was older, riper, the stink of decay intermingled with the more familiar odors of blood and bodily waste.

Her stomach twisted but she did not throw up. She was not the vomiting kind. Instead, she got weak in the knees, had difficulty breathing, and went cold and shaky all over. Stumbling back to the porch, she dropped down on the top step again.

She closed her eyes and gritted her teeth. *I can't stand this. I can't. Not two bodies in one week.*

*You haven't seen it. You could walk away and let somebody else find him.*

*Then I'd have to pretend I don't know what I do know and that's how people make themselves crazy.*

*Call it in anonymously.* She felt an almost overpowering urge to run, to not face the police, to not answer questions. The prospect of sitting in a cop car for hours, then sitting in the station for more hours, then telling her story ten times over made her want to scream. The police would think her cursed, finding two bodies in less than a week. Or worse—a psychopathic social worker who murdered people, reported their deaths, then made up elaborate stories about them.

*Why not make the call, then skip out?* Zach had done that once, and she'd been furious, even though she'd understood his reason.

*You're not permitted to go against your conscience. The only time you're allowed to commit illegal or unethical acts is when you firmly believe it's the right thing to do.*

Remembering that Zach had told her she couldn't reach 9-1-1 on her cell phone, she drove to a service station and called from there.

&#x204A;   &#x204A;   &#x204A;

The police broke in and found Carl dead of a gunshot wound to the head.

Hours later Detective Dickensen, an easygoing guy in his mid-thir-ties, took her in to the Riverside police station. She laid out every bit of the story that seemed connected to Carl: Olivia's murder; Cassidy's efforts to convince Carl that the police had arrested the wrong man; Carl's suspicion that the killer was Edwardo; his stakeout of the lawn service office.

She paused, trying to determine if she was obligated to reveal anything else. *You should tell him about the files. Investigating on your own was a bad idea from start to finish, and now Carl's dead because of it. This is your chance to unburden yourself and bow out.*

*Gran, Zach, and I are the only ones who know the files exist. That means I don't have to tell anybody.*

Dickensen asked, "What else have you done to identify this alleged person you saw in your neighbor's living room?" She heard a tinge of sarcasm in his voice.

*And who can blame him? Just think how ludicrous it must sound, a social worker running around trying to solve a case the police have already closed. It's a wonder he hasn't sent you off for a psych eval.*

They sat in a small, well-lighted room similar to the interview room at the Oak Park station, except this cubicle had three straight-backed chairs instead of two. Dickensen had listened closely and taken notes, but she'd picked up a dismissive tone that made her think he might not put too much effort into tracking Edwardo down.

She described her own experience at the lawn service office. "Since Carl was shot shortly after they caught him watching the building, I'm worried my visit this morning might put my name on their hit list too."

"You definitely need to take precautions."

*Like what? Borrow my neighbor's Uzi?* She looked into the detective's opaque blue eyes. "Are you going to interrogate Edwardo?"

"We'll certainly try, although he may be halfway back to Mexico by now. But he won't be our only suspect. Carl Behan was a powerful attorney. He made a lot of enemies during his career. His death may not've had anything to do with your neighbor getting shot."

"Doesn't it seem awfully coincidental that he'd be investigating her murder and then get killed himself?"

Dickensen shrugged. "The biggest problem with your theory is no forced entry. If Behan considered this Mexican so violent, why let him into the house? This is an attorney who worked with a lot of dangerous people. A very savvy guy."

"Maybe Edwardo went in through the open window."

"The screen hadn't been removed." He glanced at his watch. "I invited Detective Perez over to join us. I thought it might be useful for the three of us to put our heads together."

*What a nice way of saying he wants Manny to get me out of his hair.*

Five minutes later Perez came in and straddled the empty chair. His lips were tightly clamped. His brown eyes, always warm toward her in the past, were cold and disapproving. "Well, I hear you've been keeping yourself busy."

*I hate being judged by others. Especially considering how much of it I do to myself.*

"You knew I was certain Jake didn't do it, but you wouldn't listen. So I told my story to Carl Behan, a defense attorney, and he agreed that the evidence against Jake was lousy. He'd had a run-in with this lawn service guy last summer and was aware of the kind of temper Edwardo had. So Carl tried to locate him—which is what you should've been doing—and now he's dead."

The detectives exchanged a look, both faces showing disgust at Cassidy's diatribe.

Dickensen said to his colleague, "These civilians watch cop shows, they're all instant experts. Everybody knows how to investigate a murder better than the people paid to do it."

Manny looked her straight in the eye. "Is there anything else you haven't told my friend here?"

She gritted her teeth. "No." *Oh shit. If he ever finds out the rest of it, you'll have to leave the village 'cause he'll be out to get you every time you roll through a stop sign or shoot a light that's just turning red.*

Perez's eyes narrowed. "Ms. McCabe, I am taking you off the case."

ॐ     ॐ     ॐ

It was six o'clock before they allowed her to leave the station. Driving slowly through rush hour traffic, she tried to think where to go. What she wanted most was to curl up in Zach's lap and have a good cry. But it wouldn't be Zach walking through the door tonight; it would be JC. And JC would not be offering any laps to crawl into. Since Zach had told her that the easiest time for him to shed his hoodlum persona was when he came home at dawn, she decided to wait till then.

In the meantime, she needed a refuge as badly as Tigger had needed her radiator, and the only place she knew to go was Gran's. She called and said she was on her way to grandma's house to get her stomach filled, her spirit propped, and her self-esteem kissed and made better.

Gran said she would get right on it.

     ဆ    ဆ    ဆ

Her grandmother, wearing a red Scarlett O'Hara wig, shooed Cassidy out of the kitchen and into the living room, where two stemmed glasses and a bottle of Merlot stood on the glass coffee table. Cassidy sank into one of the armchairs.

Gran picked up the bottle. "How 'bout I pour you some of this light sun-kissed red with just a hint of cherries?"

Cassidy sighed deeply. "The way I'm feeling tonight, I think I should skip the wine."

"Sounds like some of this soothing, sun-kissed vino is just what you need."

*Much as you'd love to guzzle that nice sun-kissed wine, one glass'd probably send you off on a crying jag.* "I'll be better off if I limit myself to the soothing effects of your wonderful company and good home cooking."

"Well, I'm sure you know what's best." Disappearing into the kitchen, Gran returned with a tray of lasagna, garlic bread, and green salad.

Between bites of rich cheesy pasta, Cassidy filled her grandmother in on the day's events.

"I hope you're not feeling guilty over Carl's murder too?"

"I did at first but then I got hold of myself. This is different from Olivia. Carl was an astute, knowledgeable guy. He wouldn't have gotten involved in the investigation unless he believed it was worthwhile. He made his own decision, so I can let myself off the hook where Carl's concerned." She swallowed lasagna. "Of course, that doesn't keep me from wishing fervently that I'd stayed out of it and Carl was still alive."

*And your own longevity a tad less in doubt as well.*

Her small face looking determined, Gran said, "I hope you're not gonna let that bossy cop make you drop our investigation."

"I haven't done anything illegal—well, except for taking the files. As long as we work within the law, we can do whatever we want."

"Good, 'cause I'm getting those phone records tomorrow and I want us to go through them."

Cassidy decided not to think about the legality of obtaining un-authorized phone records.

ℬ     ℬ     ℬ

She remained at Gran's until after ten. Back at home, she left a note for Zach telling him about the murder and letting him know she needed to talk. Tigger was behind the wall unit again, with Starshine posted at one of the exits. Cassidy tried to lure the calico away from guard duty, but Starshine laid her ears back and sent her a don't-touch-me look. Cassidy gave up and went to bed.

ℬ     ℬ     ℬ

She was dozing lightly when Zach came into the bedroom, asleep enough not to sit up and greet him, awake enough to know he was there. She waited, expecting that he would either turn on the light or come over and kiss her. He did neither. He left the room dark and, from the sounds that he made, seemed to be standing on his side of the bed undressing.

She heard the whump of his body colliding with the dresser. Zach, quite sure-footed, generally did not bump into things. Fully awake now, she sat up and turned on her reading lamp.

He regarded her fuzzily. "I know you wanted to talk but I'm too beat. I gotta get some sleep." He spoke slowly, making an effort not to slur.

"You're drunk." Her first reaction was surprise. She had not for a minute doubted that he would make himself available now just as he had the night Olivia was murdered.

"Yeah, so what?"

"You said you had to hold a tight rein on yourself, keep everything under control."

"Look, what do you fucking want from me? Here I am doing this killer investigation, and then you have to go get yourself involved in a murder, put yourself in danger, get fucking attacked on Augusta Boulevard."

His words pummeled her, made her feel small and hurt. *No, damnit, he has no right to talk to me like that. He's the one out of line here, not me.* She stared at him, speechless.

"So here I am stuck worrying about you when I've already got more than I can handle myself. What's the big deal about having a few drinks?"

"A few?" The instant it was out of her mouth she knew it was the wrong thing to say.

"So, you want to follow me around and count drinks? Tell me when I've had enough? Just what the fuck is wrong with a guy getting sloshed on his own front porch?"

"Nothing." She remembered his saying how important it was for them not to let anything come between them. "Except I really needed you tonight."

"Yeah? Well, I can't always be who you want me to. Sometimes I just need to get good and roaring drunk, and if that's too much for you, I'll get out of your way."

"Zach . . . " She didn't know what to say, and even if she had there was no point saying it when he was too drunk to listen.

"I believe I'll sleep on the couch tonight."

# 17. Sleeping Alone

*Oh shit.* Feeling an ice cold sense of aloneness, she hugged herself tightly against the shivery spikes running across her skin. She heard him take a sheet from the extra bedroom, then walk down the stairs. She did not want him near her but did not want him leaving, either. Throughout their time together, they had fought sporadically, usually during periods of high stress. Some of their fights had been bad, but they hadn't spent a night apart since Zach moved in.

She wandered into Tigger's room to gaze out the window toward the Chicago skyline. The sun was just beginning to show above the treetops. Returning to bed, she pulled her knees up tight, wrapped her arms around them, and tried to make sense out of what had just happened. *Think like a therapist.*

Zach had always displayed a strong protective side, an urge to be comforting. And even though he still drank more than she liked on occasion, she'd seldom seen him intoxicated, and when she had he'd never been either slurry or belligerent. It wasn't Zach who'd gotten drunk to avoid being with her. It was JC. The last time Zach had needed to pull out of his persona so they could talk, he'd accomplished it by having a drink on the porch. Tonight Zach hadn't been able to put aside his undercover role. JC had refused to relinquish control.

*This is getting scary. The closer Zach comes to the end of his investigation, the more desperate JC's going to be to hang on.*

*Get a grip. Zach and JC are not two different people, just separate aspects of the same personality. You are not a believer in woo-woo, mystical kinds of phenomena.*

*Yeah, but you've been working with parts for years now. And you know we all have parts that are not so nice and sometimes these parts take over.*

◊    ◊    ◊

She lay in bed a couple of hours longer, not sleeping, then put on jeans and a purple tee and went downstairs. Zach was sprawled out on the blue paisley couch, a lavender sheet wrapped around him. Staring down, she was aware of a welter of contradictory feelings. She was still angry at the things he'd said, but seeing him so undefended in sleep, she also felt a surge of love, and right beneath that, an oppressive, grinding fear that his undercover work might shift the balance inside him, might change who he was.

She shook him awake. He looked up at her a moment, his eyes confused, then dragged himself into a sitting position.

Running a hand over his face, he said, "Sorry 'bout last night." Leaning forward, he put his elbows on his legs, his chin on his hands.

She sat in the powder blue armchair next to him. "What happened?"

"I went out on the porch to have a drink and didn't stop." He shrugged. "The stress is getting to me."

"How you feeling?"

"Like shit." He put his hands to temples. "I'm out of practice. I used to be able to drink twice as much and not feel it the next day."

"I'm worried." Curling her fingers over the end of one armrest, she rubbed small circles in the nub of the velvety fabric.

"You're not starting to think I'm an alcoholic again, are you? You know how much I'd cut back before this investigation."

"I'm worried that it's getting harder for you to shift out of being JC."

He gazed at the floor a moment. "Yeah, it is. But the end's in sight. Heather introduced me to her cop friends a couple of days ago and I've already started wearing a wire. Which has really upped the ante in the stress department." He rubbed his face. "I gotta tell you, this is one investigation I'm ready to be done with. I could go my whole life without stepping foot inside another club."

"Zach, what if JC takes control?"

"You're getting weird again. I don't believe in channeling, crystals, or vampires out roaming the streets. I also don't believe that a persona I've created could take over my life." He paused. "I admit there are times when it's hard to pull out of, but that doesn't mean it could just grab control." He reached over to pat her knee. "Now I have to go upstairs and get some more sleep 'cause I really do feel like shit."

Zach did not, at the moment, sound like a man who'd turn hostile and mean on her. But once he was up and moving he'd have to go back into his hoodlum part, and who knew what he'd be like by tonight.

*Get your mind on something else.* The one good thing about investigating Olivia's murder was that her obsession over finding her neighbor's killer had blocked out her obsession over Zach. Remembering that Gran was due to arrive soon with phone records, she assembled the numbers of everyone connected to Olivia, then added the reverse directory number to her list.

&#8478;    &#8478;    &#8478;

"Look at this." Gran placed a stubby finger beneath a line of print on the paper on the dining room table in front of them. Cassidy sat in a chair with Gran hovering near her right shoulder. Reading from the paper, Gran said, "Somebody made a forty-five-second call from Olivia's place at nine thirty-three Sunday night."

"I was getting out of my car at about nine-fifteen. She answered the door a minute later, and then I never saw her again. So this call could've been placed by the killer."

Gran, long blond ringlets dangling around her shoulders, plunked down in a chair kitty-corner from Cassidy. A diffuse, late morning light filtered through the window on the north wall. Outside, Cassidy saw a number of small black children playing in the middle of Briar.

She checked the mystery number against her list. "This doesn't belong to anybody we've talked to." She gazed at her grandmother admiringly. "I think you've just reactivated the investigation."

Gran smiled and patted her hair, taking a moment to bask in Cassidy's praise. Turning serious, she remarked, "That poor lonely woman. It looks like she didn't use her phone more than five times a week."

"And all the calls were between Olivia and her aunt, which, considering my experience with Esther's wheedling, couldn't've been much fun." Stepping into the kitchen, Cassidy lifted the receiver from the wall and dialed reverse directory. "Here's hoping it's not unlisted." She listened to the mechanical voice at the other end, then wrote down PAM GARDINER, followed by an address.

"You got it!" Gran pounded her tiny fist on the table. "Now we know who she is and how to find her."

"This could be a real break." Sitting down again, Cassidy stared at the name, aware that sleeplessness had left her foggy and dull-witted. "The only problem is, I have no idea in the world how to approach her."

Gran studied her intently. "You don't seem quite yourself today."

"Just tired." She stared at two small boys holding hands and spinning in a circle. *Like I've been doing. Spinning, spinning, getting nowhere except maybe closer to a bullet in the head. And now Gran's come up with a new lead, only I can't figure out how to use it.*

From the look on Gran's face, Cassidy had the sense that her grandmother was about to dig deeper. Not wanting anyone to know about Zach's recent bout of scurrilous behavior, she said, "Um . . . I'd just as soon not go into it right now."

"Any time I start getting too personal, you just tell me to back off. I don't ever want to go sticking my nose in where it doesn't belong." Wrapping her fingers around her chin, Gran stared off into space, then stood to clap a hand on Cassidy's shoulder. "I'm going to reconnoiter. I'll go talk to people on Pam's block. Then tomorrow, when you've had a better night's sleep, we can figure something out."

ଷ     ଷ     ଷ

At a quarter to five Cassidy prepared the porch for her pizza date with Bryce. She pushed two picnic benches together to make a table, covered it with a red and white checkered cloth, then brought out a pile of napkins. The air on the porch was hot and sticky, but there was no other place for eating that would be any better.

*How much you going to tell him about the undercover work?*

*You want him to form a bond with his father, he has to understand him. Just like Shelby needs to understand Olivia. So Bryce has to hear what Zach's been up to. Not the hoodlum part, but at least the investigation.*

Minutes later Bryce carried a large flat box onto the porch. The smell of oregano and cheese sent Cassidy's stomach into a hunger frenzy.

Bryce disappeared into the kitchen, then returned with two Red Dogs. "You can't refuse to serve me now that I'm eighteen."

"It's twenty-one in Illinois, but I'll let it go this time."

He opened the flap of the pizza box and they set about to do some serious eating. The boy was long and lanky, his face angular, his eyes dark and sulky. The only physical feature he had in common with his father was his deep bronze skin.

Bryce scarfed down three-quarters of the huge pizza, then pushed back his molded plastic chair and slid lower on his spine, his knees jutting high in the air. "Okay, so tell me—why all the secrecy about Zach's story and how come he hasn't called?"

Leaning back in the wicker couch, Cassidy licked her greasy fingers, scrubbed them with napkins, then told him about the undercover investigation.

He scowled but she did not take it personally. Bryce's MO was to get instantly angry about almost everything, think about it further, then eventually come around.

*Considering his girlfriend OD'd, I suppose it's inevitable he'd have a reaction to Zach's getting anywhere near drugs. Even though Zach's whole intention is to nail the dealers.*

Bryce sat up straighter. "He shouldn't be doing this as a private citizen. The chances are he'll start using again himself. Or get busted. Or, more likely, get himself killed. He can't even do the buy without breaking the law. How could the *Post* authorize anything as illegal as this?"

"Well, they didn't exactly. His editor gave him a tacit go-ahead, but if Zach gets arrested, they'll take the position he was freelancing. However, if he pulls it off, they'll be happy to print the story and maybe even reimburse his expenses." *You sounding a tad bitter there?*

Several wasps had come in through the open window to hover over the pizza. Shooing them away, Bryce refastened the floppy lid. "How big a buy is he going for?"

"Ten grand. His story to the dealer cops is that he wants to set up his own operation downstate. He has a buddy at the *Post* with a fully rigged surveillance van. Zach'll get the transaction on tape, deliver the evidence to the feds, then head for his computer." Taking a long swig of cold beer, she held the sweaty bottle to her forehead.

"You mean Zach has to put up ten K of his own money and he doesn't even know for sure if the paper'll expense it off?"

*As if we had ten K.*

"He found a backer. Zach's Uncle Martin is an attorney with a lot of clout, and he's also something of a philanthropist. He thought busting those cops had sufficient merit that he was willing to put up the money. Besides, if all goes well the feds'll arrest the cops, collect the marked bills for evidence, and then eventually the money will get returned to Martin."

Bryce tapped his left heel on the floor. "It was stupid of Zach to do this on his own. He should've taken that tip directly to the FBI."

*Kid's right. That's exactly what he should've done.* "Well, he thought he could handle it and so far he's doing okay. He wants to use the experience to write a first person series on drug trade in the clubs."

Bryce turned his head sharply away to stare out the porch window for almost a minute. Two men in business suits walked past the house. It was the time of evening when commuters returned from their city jobs.

The boy shifted his gaze back to her face. "You said Zach wasn't screwing up, but I think he is. I know you always defend him, but having him out partying—or pretending to party—every night can't be doing your marriage any good. Don't you start to wonder what he's really up to?" He furrowed his brow. "I know I would."

*Since when did this kid develop ESP?* "Okay, I probably shouldn't be telling you this, but I don't want to lie either. You're right, this has been hard on our marriage. The odds are we'll get back on track as soon as this is over. But—worst case scenario—even if we don't make it as a couple," her chest tightened as she said the words, "you aren't getting rid of me. I expect to have a pizza date with you once a month for the rest of my life."

Bryce stood and stared out the window. Speaking with his back to her, he said, "I hate how selfish he is. He's such a grandstander. Always has to go after these big stories, always putting himself in risky situations. And he doesn't give a shit how much he hurts you or anyone else to do it." He turned and glared, daring her to disagree.

"Bryce, that's not fair. Zach and I are both the kind of people who can't just walk away from something like dirty cops setting up their own drug ring. You're right—he is a risk-taker. It's a core part of his personality and he can't change who he is just because you and I get scared when he puts himself in danger."

"I don't care what he does."

"I understand how it makes you feel to have your father take on something that could get him killed. But it's not true that he doesn't care about us. It's just that Zach never planned to have any wives or children. He intended to go through life with no ties to anybody, no one who'd be hurt if he got himself into something he couldn't get out of."

"Yeah, but now he does have a wife and kid."

"You came as a seventeen-year-old surprise, remember? And I'm every bit as bad as he is, so we deserve each other. He doesn't want to hurt either one of us, but there's no way he could stifle all that drive and ambition he has. And if he didn't have it, I'm not sure I'd want to be with him."

"Doesn't matter what he does," Bryce grumbled. "You always stick up for him."

"It just occurred to me—I'm going about this all wrong. I should reel off this long list of complaints and then you'd have to switch sides and go on the defense."

&#8477;    &#8477;    &#8477;

As soon as Bryce was gone, Cassidy went to a movie to make sure she didn't run into JC. Afterward she slipped into a deep sleep, not rousing until she was jolted awake Sunday morning by a sense that something was wrong.

She was lying with her head on the pillow, lids still closed but the lights gradually coming on in her head, when suddenly, for no reason she could think of, that black viscous feeling was back in her stomach. Her eyes flew open. Zach was not in bed nor had the covers on his side been disturbed. *Sleeping on the couch again?*

She pulled on a long tee and hurried downstairs. No sign of him in the living room or anywhere else. *Damn him! Didn't come home. Where the hell is he? What if those killer cops found the wire?* Racing into Zach's office, she saw the red light blinking on the answering machine.

Zach's voice played back on the tape: "I won't be making it home tonight. Don't worry. Nothing's happened. I'm not with Heather. I'll catch you up later."

Except it wasn't Zach's voice. It was the terse, growly tone of JC.

*Not with Heather? Is that true? Zach never lies to you but JC's in control now and nothing's the same.*

Cassidy went downstairs to sit at the dining room table, both hands wrapped around her purple mug, a half empty bag of Reese's in front of her. Starshine trotted up from the basement to eat, then, amazingly, came to join her on the table instead of returning to her Tigger-games.

"This is it," Cassidy announced to the calico. "I'm not playing good supportive little wife one minute longer."

Mwat. Starshine pricked her ears and gazed at her human out of large black pupils.

"So, you're probably wondering what else I can do besides wait around for Zach to appear. Whenever that might be."

Starshine, who liked Zach and never wanted Cassidy to disrupt the status quo, struck at the Reese's bag, knocking three candies out onto the tabletop. Losing interest in the conversation, the cat scooted one peanut butter cup around the teak surface until it fell to the floor.

*Is Zach going to follow his usual routine, show up early this evening and feed you some bullshit excuse for last night's dereliction?* "I hope he doesn't. And even if he does, staying out all night is beyond the pale. There's nothing he could say that'd make it all right."

Unwrapping one of the two other candies, Cassidy rested her elbow on the table, held the Reese's aloft, and stared at it. *You're not going to see Zach this evening. Or maybe not for days. JC's in the driver's seat now and he's not about to check in with you.*

"So then, if Zach won't come to me, the obvious thing is for me to go to him."

*You've been dying to do it. A chance to observe first hand what he's really up to with his clubby little girlfriend at their clubby little playground.*

*Yeah, but you're not going to like what you see. You already know JC's a pig who handles Heather. This is not going to make you one bit happier.*

*Happy's not the goal here. Angry is what you need to be. Angry enough to fend off those insidious memories of the good times, as well as your feeble-minded urge to take him back. Angry enough to override all the subversive feelings that make you weak. You need to crank up the anger till you're strong enough to do whatever it is you need to do.*

Starshine began a hockey game with the last piece of loose candy, a cat-sized puck. When it went the way of her first Reese's, she followed it to the floor, then zipped back down to the basement.

Cassidy bit into her own peanut butter cup and chewed slowly, her resolve hardening. The day before she'd felt jittery, faded, useless from lack of sleep and anxiety over what was happening to Zach. Up until this morning, she'd viewed his thuggish behavior as short-term and marginal: almost, but not quite, beyond her ability to tolerate. *Which means pretty bad, because as you well know, your tolerance for abuse is way too high.* But now he'd gone clearly over the line and that had freed her up, energized her. *No need to worry about escalating or making matters worse, because his not coming home is as bad as you're ever going to put up with. And it justifies anything at all you might decide to do in return.*

She watched George Brenner come out his front door with his two Dobermans.

First she would attend to her own case. She would strategize with Gran and visit the woman whose number had turned up on Olivia's phone records. After that, she would wait at the house until eleven to see if Zach appeared, although she was certain he wouldn't. When eleven, an eternity away, finally arrived, she would go down to The Zone and see how JC comported himself in his natural habitat.

&O    &O    &O

Answering her front doorbell around noon, Cassidy found Gran on the porch, the birdlike figure wearing a coppery pageboy and an elated smile along with her usual shorts and tennis shoes. Despite the over-heated air inside the porch, Gran plopped down on the wicker couch. "Boy, did I ever hit paydirt. Any time you want something reconnoi-tered, you just send your super-snooper grandma out to do it."

Taking the plastic chair at the end of the picnic-bench table, Cassidy clapped her hands in appreciation. "Hear, hear."

Gran bowed her head twice in acknowledgment of the applause, then straightened her wig. "What I did was, I told some kids I was looking for an old friend about my age and they put me on to the neighborhood gossip."

"Not bad." The wind chimes jangled. A car pulled up across the street, a family dressed in church finery disembarking and parading up the walk toward a gracious Queen Anne.

"I knocked on this woman's door, and when she answered, I pointed at Pam's house and said I'd been born there. I told her I was back in town for a visit and curious to find out who was living there now."

"What a great scam!"

"Well, this old lady—she must've been close to ninety—she couldn't grab onto me fast enough. We sat on her porch with a pitcher of lemonade and that old woman answered every question I could think of, and then some. So now I got all the lowdown on Pam Gardiner."

Cassidy leaned forward, her arms resting on her legs. "Is it juicy? What is it?"

"You know," Gran said in a satisfied tone, "there's nothing to beat a good gossip session. Those soaps, they don't have anything on real life." She propped her feet on the checkered tablecloth. "Okay, it turns out Pam is in the middle of a very nasty divorce. Her husband is this big bucks corporate guy who lives in Oakbrook and is giving Pam a really hard time over custody. He wants to keep the kids, *but*," Gran paused for dramatic effect, "the wife says he molested their daughter. The problem is, Pam can't prove it and he's got all this money to pay slimy lawyers to take the kids away."

*Bastard abusers! If they've got big enough bucks, they get access to the kids they're abusing. Okay—not all men who get accused are guilty—but some are and sometimes they get custody.*

"The courts never take children completely away. But they might let the father keep them during the week, limit Pam to weekends." A bluebird flitted past the row of casement windows fronting the porch.

"So anyway, when Pam found out about him molesting the girl, she grabbed a bunch of money out of their joint account, bought this dinky house in Brookfield, and moved into it with her kids. That was two years ago, and the divorce is still going strong."

"Divorce hell. I've seen a lot of my clients go through it." Cassidy shook her head. "So what's her life like? Does she work?"

"At first she was going to the U of I, but then she had to drop out. She works part-time but doesn't like to leave the kids too much 'cause the divorce has been so hard on 'em. This old lady I talked to thinks she's a real nice girl who just had bad luck in the husband department."

*Wouldn't it be nice to chalk up bad husbands to misfortune? Well, you see, the reason I married two losers is, I broke a bunch of mirrors back in the eighties.*

"But that's not all." Gran swung her feet to the floor, leaned forward, and slapped her palm against the red and white tablecloth. "Pam has a frequent visitor who drives a small black car and usually shows up after dark."

*Small black car. You saw one recently. Where was it?*

"This old lady I talked to is just going nuts 'cause there's no way for her to see who the visitor is. He drives up to the attached garage, uses an automatic opener, and never gets out of his car. So my friend can't even get a peek at him. Or her. I suppose it could be a woman." She paused. "It's just driving that old lady crazy, not being able to see who's in the car."

"Gran, you are fantastic."

"And I even figured out how you can get Pam to talk to you. There's a school referendum coming up, and the district's got volunteers out surveying parents to see what all they want in their schools. Well, Pam's got herself a six and an eight-year-old. She probably wouldn't think twice about letting a volunteer into her house."

"So my job is to dig up a clipboard, go knock on Pam's door, and weasel my way in as a surveyor."

&#8526;  &#8526;  &#8526;

"Well, that just about covers it." Cassidy jotted a final note on the clipboard in her lap. "Thanks for being so nice about answering all the questions."

"I want the best possible education for my kids, don't I?"

Cassidy heard a forced brightness in Pam's voice, read tension in the pinched lines around her mouth. The thirtyish woman sat opposite Cassidy on a flat-cushioned plaid sofa loaded with Barbies, books, trucks, and action figures. She had weary gray eyes, high cheekbones, and a sprinkling of freckles across the bridge of her thin nose. Cassidy thought she probably had been quite pretty before the tightness and exhaustion set in.

As Pam picked up a Barbie from the pile of toys and began nervously straightening the doll's pink prom dress, Cassidy kept her eyes glued to a thin gold band on the fourth finger of the woman's right hand. It was the only piece of jewelry Pam wore, and from the way she'd kept her fingers curled around her palm throughout the entire interview, Cassidy was convinced she'd turned the ring around to hide the setting.

*Wouldn't you love to march over there, grab her hand, and force it open? Yeah, but then what? She'd order you out of her house, the ring—if it's Olivia's sapphire—would disappear, and there'd be no evidence. Besides, your socialization has made you incapable of attacking innocent people.*

Pam gazed at her curiously, probably wondering why she hadn't started toward the door yet.

Using her most empathic voice, Cassidy said, "You mentioned a custody battle. Well, I went through one myself a couple of years ago. I had horrendous anxiety attacks over it, and the attorney bills just about did me in. But I was lucky. I met this really nice guy who stuck with me through the whole ordeal. Anytime I needed a shoulder to cry on, he was there to give it to me." *Right up until four weeks ago.* "I just hope you've got somebody like that in your corner."

"Oh no." Pam shook her head emphatically. "I couldn't do that. If my husband thought I was seeing anybody, he'd make my life even more miserable than it is already."

"He wouldn't have to know."

"I couldn't take the chance."

Two tow-headed children yelling at each other came through the back door into the kitchen. Since the kitchen was not quite a separate room, merely the rear section of a long rectangular space with the living room in front, Cassidy could see the kids clearly. The girl, slightly taller than the boy, was slender and delicate, with a stoop-shouldered, depressed look to her. Cassidy felt a heaviness around her heart as she watched the child squabble with her brother.

Pam went into the kitchen, talked to the children in a soothing mother-tone, then ushered them back outside.

*Looks like it's time for plan B.* She had thought ahead about what she would do if empathy failed her, but her fallback plan required a level of deceit and confrontation that felt highly unnatural. *You have to do it.*

As the woman returned to the living room, Cassidy slid her clipboard into her tote and stood to face her. "I'm not really doing a survey for the school district. I'm a private investigator hired by the family of a murder victim, Olivia Mallory.''

Her face going pale, Pam pressed both hands together against her throat. "What? I never heard of her. What does she have to do with me?" She frowned, "You know, I really don't appreciate being manipulated like this."

"I'm sorry I had to do this, but according to Ms. Mallory's phone records, a call was made to you from her house right around the time of her death. That was nine thirty-three a week ago Saturday night."

"But I don't even know her."

"However, the fact remains that a call originating from the Mallory house was answered here on August twenty-fourth."

Her brow furrowing, Pam stared into space for several seconds. "I seem to remember getting a wrong number that night. A man's voice. He sounded drunk."

"You're sure it wasn't someone you know?"

Patches of red appeared on Pam's cheeks. "I think you better leave now."

Straightening her back, Cassidy maintained eye contact. "Thank you for the information. And I'm sorry I had to lie." *Sorry for which lie? The one before or the one now?*

Cassidy held out her right hand.

Pam folded her arms beneath her breasts, her own right hand tucked out of sight. Shaking her head, she stepped backward.

Cassidy left the house and drove toward Oak Park. *A wrong number. Sounded like a drunk. Oh shit—what if it really* was *Jake? What if your innocent-man-in-jail theory is nothing more than rationalization and denial? What if you drummed up the whole thing just to appease your conscience over Olivia and get back at Zach.*

She knew she normally maintained a good grasp of both reality and her own motives. But it was possible her guilt over Olivia's murder and her anger at Zach had combined to make her lose her sense of balance, just as Zach had lost his.

*But what about that ring she was trying so hard to hide?*

*More guesswork. You don't know it's the sapphire. The possibility exists that you've been wrong about every single thing this entire week, and now you're wrong again about the ring.*

❧    ❧    ❧

At ten-thirty that night Cassidy changed into black leggings, black low-heeled sandals and a purple silk blouse. Checking her wallet, she recounted the bills she had withdrawn from their joint account just a few hours earlier. *Fifty bucks. Should be more than enough for parking and the cover.* Her chest tight, she got in her Toyota to drive to the River North area of Chicago.

*This is not going to be fun. The flight path you're on has a decidedly kamikaze feel to it.*

*Yeah, but at least I'm doing it. If our marriage is going to crash and burn, I want to be in the pilot's seat.* An odd feeling of exhilaration surged through her, then sputtered off into anxiety.

She stopped at Austin Boulevard and glanced in her rearview mirror at a white commercial van that had pulled up behind her. Seeing the van jiggled something in her memory but she couldn't get hold of it. *A van and a small black car.* Pam's mystery guest drove a black car similar to one Cassidy had seen recently. *Still can't remember where.* And there was something else about a van she also couldn't recall.

*Zach's deranged behavior is not only messing up our marriage, it's also disrupting my memory banks.*

Turning south she looked back to see the van moving along behind her. Two blocks later she checked again and it was gone.

❧    ❧    ❧

Cassidy scanned the raucous, ear-splitting room. The lights were low, the denizens of this netherworld so glittery and snakelike she felt as if she'd been transported to an alien universe—the Planet of the Party People. The music was deafening, the whole place seeming to throb. She slid around the perimeter of the room, moving a few yards, then halting to search the dance floor and bar again.

On the third stop she spotted him. As much as it was what she expected, seeing the real life version hit her like a fist in the stomach. He stood with his back to the bar, Heather snuggled under his left arm, a glass in his right hand. He was flanked on both sides by clubby creatures, two males with slicked down hair and silky shirts that looked as if they'd hatched from the same egg as Zach.

She inched closer. At about ten feet she stopped to observe, taking cover behind a large male and peeking out around him. Heather had her twitchy body pressed up against Zach, his arm beneath her bosom, his fingers cupping one small breast. Cassidy felt creepy and voyeuristic, her face growing hot with shame, as if she were the offender, not him.

Heather wore a sparkly gold dress, the skirt ending at mid-thigh, a delicate blue tattoo extending beneath it. She was tall and rail thin, all except her face, a softly rounded countenance that would have appeared childlike were it not for the stoned look in her darkly circled eyes. Her hands moved constantly, rubbing her mouth, tugging at her nose. Her hair was silver-blond, tumbling around her face in a shaggy, urchin cut. Cassidy didn't know whether to hate her or feel sorry for her.

*Not her fault. She doesn't have a clue. Definitely not responsible for anything except her own blighted life.*

A fortyish woman, walking unsteadily, brushed against Cassidy's shoulder. Someone jostled her from behind, knocking her into the man in front of her, who stepped aside. She moved quickly to lose herself in the crowd again.

She wondered briefly why Zach, who was not even what she would call handsome, had a history of getting just about any woman he wanted. *No mystery there. Same reason he got you.* One part was the challenge, the fact that he'd never made himself totally available until a year ago when he'd decided he wanted to marry her. A second part was his toughness, his ability to stand up to anybody and never back down. A third was his caretaker side, his willingness to listen and try to understand. Taken altogether, it made for a combination generally in short supply among the single male pool, a category Zach no longer belonged in but probably would be reentering shortly.

He removed his hand from Heather, extracted a pack of Camels from his shirt pocket, and lit up. *Oh God!* Seeing him with a cigarette in his mouth shocked her even more than seeing his hand on Heather's breast. *Damn him. This marriage was the best thing that ever happened to either one of us, and he's bound and determined to rip it apart.*

Hardly aware she was doing it, she started across the room on a path that took her directly in front of him. If the voice in her head had not been drowned out by the background roar, as loud as a storm at sea, she would have heard it say, *He's busted and I'm going to make sure he knows it.*

Once she'd moved past him, bile rose in her throat and she felt a sudden urgency to get away. But just as she veered off toward the entrance, a hand clamped down on her arm and jerked her around. Having expected Zach to ignore her, she was caught completely off guard. He dragged her up close and said, his voice tight with anger, "Do you come here often?"

# 18. A Second Divorce

"I was just leaving."

"Come on over. I'll introduce you to my friends."

"As what? Your wife? Or, more accurately, soon-to-be ex?"

"How 'bout—the girl I used to date in high school."

"Get your hands off me. Why are you doing this, anyway?"

"A better question would be, Why are you here? Only the answer's obvious, isn't it? You're here to check up on me. So why not come over and meet the people I spend my nights with? You can get a good close look at the little chickie who shares her stash with me." Turning back toward the bar, he yanked her arm so hard she felt a stab of pain in her shoulder.

"Stop it! You're hurting me."

He let go. "You're going to be rude and refuse to join us?" Giving her an unpleasant smile, he added, "Guess I'll just have to console myself with Heather-baby then." He turned abruptly and walked away.

She stood rooted to the spot, feeling like a small animal who'd been hypnotized by one of the snake creatures, not able to flee though her life depended on it. Zach leaned against the bar, retrieved his cigarette from an ashtray, inhaled, and blew out smoke. Staring straight at Cassidy, he made some comment that caused the other two males to chuckle. Heather, perhaps too far gone for humor, wriggled her skinny little butt up against him. Cassidy watched as Zach wrapped his hand around the girl's neck the same way he'd always done with her.

⊱       ⊱       ⊱

That night she slept only a few fitful hours. At ten o'clock the next morning she sat in her swivel chair, feet propped on the radiator, her body achy and hollow. Gazing through the window at children playing in the yard across the street, she contemplated the implications of a second divorce. *Means you're a two-time loser. Hopeless judgment about men. Lousy relationship skills. Means there's something wrong with you. Means you're a reject.*

It was the kind of litany she heard frequently from clients but seldom indulged in herself. However, a second divorce—that was worth wallowing over.

A squirrel sat for a moment outside the window, its hind legs on the porch roof, its front paws scratching the glass.

*You know lots of perfectly fine people who've had two divorces.* Her therapist voice tried to inject a note of common sense but the part bent on self-pity overrode it.

*After two failed marriages, you couldn't even do therapy. With your own life such a mess, there's no way you could pretend to know anything about what other people ought to do.*

She heard Zach's footsteps on the stairs. Her stomach churned. She heard him come through the doorway but refused to turn in his direction. He sat in his chair and she still did not look.

"I'm so sorry, Cass. God, I'm sorry. I feel so incredibly stupid."

*Not feel,* are. *You* are *stupid.* Finally she turned. He looked as if he'd gone without sleep for a very long time.

"I was just thinking about what a second divorce will do to me." Venom sluiced through her. She wanted to claw at his face, tear out his eyes. "Damn you. Getting married was your idea. You actually talked me into it. Do you realize, if we hadn't made it legal you could just slink away in the dead of night and I could pretend you never existed?"

He rubbed both hands over his face, then dropped them onto the arms of his chair. He looked so whipped she had to pour gasoline on her rage to keep it burning.

"If I were an objective bystander, I'd tell you to run like hell. I'd say, 'Didn't your mother ever teach you to stay away from reporters and other forms of lowlife?'" He pulled himself straighter. "But I'm nowhere near objective and I don't want to lose you. Even though there's damn little I can say for myself right now, I'm not going to let you give up on us."

"Yeah, right. I could see you didn't want to lose me by the way you acted last night." She paused. "So you're smoking. But you weren't going to do anything you couldn't tell me about."

"I was going to—"

"I was going to tell you," she mimicked nastily. "God, do I ever know *that* line well."

He sighed. "What happened at the club—that's the least of it. What I did afterward," he ran his hand over his face again, "that was the major fuck-up."

Cassidy said, her voice going low and soft, "You slept with her."

"Not quite."

"Not quite? What does 'not quite' mean?"

"It means, I came way too close." Walking to the window, he leaned his hands against the frame and looked out. After a long moment, he turned to face her. "I told you you didn't have to worry. That I wouldn't do anything you couldn't live with." He paced over to his chair and dropped into it. "I feel like such a shit."

She said through clenched teeth, "So why'd you do it?"

"I can't even explain."

She waited in silence.

"It started the night before last. Some time around midnight I took my little bag of white powder into the john and sucked it up my nose. I didn't see it coming. I didn't know I was going to do it. I just did it."

"And did you keep doing it? Have you been doing coke for the past thirty-four hours?" *Oh shit. This is worse than just losing him. I have to watch him lose himself. No you don't. You just have to get him out of your life.*

"I crashed at Reno's yesterday, started again last night, then stopped about eight hours ago. I didn't want to come home till I got myself straightened out."

"And where did you accomplish that goal? At your little kewpie doll's apartment?"

"About two a.m. I told Heather I wanted to take her home. Every other night I've put her in a cab. But last night I said we'd go to her place to celebrate the fact that she'd hooked me up with her friends."

Cassidy turned her face away. Her eyes were dry and gritty. *Tell him to stop. Don't put yourself through this.* "Go on."

"As soon as her apartment door closed, she started stripping. She went straight for the refrigerator, and by the time she got there she had all her clothes off. She pulled a bottle of vodka out of the freezer and took this long drink." He ran a hand over the top of his head, squeezed the back of his neck.

"That's when it hit me. It came slamming down like a ton of bricks. The fog suddenly cleared and I heard this voice in my head saying— Moran, what the fucking hell are you doing here? And then I thought about you and how I was breaking every promise I ever made to you just by being there." He let out a long sigh.

"She was so skinny and undeveloped. She looked like she could've been twelve years old. I felt like a dirty old man. Like some pervert taking advantage of a kid."

Closing her eyes, Cassidy bit down hard on her lip. "You asshole. How could you do this to us?"

"I don't even know. When I came to my senses, it felt like I'd been completely out of it since before I went into that john. It really did seem like JC just taking over. Like going into trance or something. I could see myself doing these things, and on some level I knew I was out of control, I knew I was doing things I didn't want to do, but I couldn't stop. It was as if I'd turned into some kind of wind-up toy." He shook his head, his face bewildered.

"I warned you this could happen."

"Yeah, and now I wish I'd listened."

"So the fact that she looked like a twelve-year-old shocked you into getting yourself back into control. And if she'd been more filled out, if she'd had a woman's body, you would've gone ahead and slept with her. Although the primary issue isn't whether you had sex or not. The real issue is, you've made it impossible for me to ever trust you again." She took a deep breath. "I don't know why I even care, but go ahead and tell me the rest of it."

"I got out of there right away, drove to the lake and took a good long hike to work all that shit out of my system. Then I came home."

She studied him for a couple of beats, noticing how worn down and gray around the edges he looked. *Don't you even think of feeling sorry for him. Or giving him a break. Or putting it behind you.* "So what are you here for? To get your clothes?"

He looked directly at her. She avoided his gaze for several seconds, then allowed her eyes to meet his. What she saw in them was his steadiness, his resolve, his determination to have what he wanted. And at the moment what he wanted was her. She found it hard to resist—that sense of his wanting her so intensely.

"A year ago when the police were all over my ass, I said I thought I should move out and you kept telling me we'd get through it. Now I'm the one saying we have to find some way to stay together. I know what I've done is beyond shitty. But before that hoodlum part showed up, you and I were very good together. We have to find a way to get through this."

Until this instant she'd felt as dry as a desert. But now the tears started, not full force, just enough to clog her throat and sting her lids. *Stop that. You're not allowed to cry. You can't just roll over because he wants you back. He has to pay for what he's done. He has to suffer.* She swallowed. "Will you drop the investigation?"

He went to look out the window, hands on hips.

"I guess that means the answer's no."

He turned back around. "It's all ready to go. Last night we started nailing down the details."

"You want to hold onto me but not enough to give up your story."

"The drop's set for Thursday night. It's only four more days."

"In other words, don't put you to the test. Don't make you choose."

"If I throw it in now, everything we've both been through will be a waste."

"And if you don't, our marriage will be a waste." *How could you even think of giving him more chances? He'd like to keep you around but you'd never be number one, never top of the list. That spot's reserved for his investigations and his front page exposés.*

"It's not just the story. These are two very bad-ass cops and I want to see them go down."

"Before you ever started this investigation, you promised me you wouldn't do anything you couldn't tell me about. I trusted you, and look what happened. Now you want to go back out there for four more nights and I'm supposed to be the kind of idiot who'd make the same mistake all over again? I thought you liked your women to show some degree of intelligence."

"I won't lose control again."

"And you expect me to take your word for it?"

He rubbed his hand over his face. "I either drop the investigation or it's over?" He sounded uncertain, as if the decision were a coin standing on edge that could go in either direction.

Seeing him so torn, her anger began to drain away, leaving her unprotected from the scorching pain in her chest. "Can you give me one good reason to believe that hoodlum part wouldn't take over again once it's back in it's home territory?"

An intense look came over his face. "I've figured it out. I know what it wants." He gazed at her, then away. "This is a rebel part. The part that smoked dope and refused to go to classes when I was a teenager. All it wants is to break rules and stay high." He paused. "If I hadn't gotten a wake-up call when I was arrested back in my twenties, Johnny Culver is who I might've become."

"And I'm in his way so he wants to get rid of me."

"That's the only reason I ended up at Heather's. Not because I have any interest in her. I never did. None."

She believed him. She had not seen any evidence of his being drawn to women who were less than his equal.

"That rebel part was trying to give you so much crap you'd have to throw me out. It doesn't want to be accountable to anybody."

"Well, it looks like it's going to win, doesn't it?"

He blinked, then shook his head. "Is that what I'm doing? Letting it win?" He paused. "When I came home this morning, the only thought in my head was to get you to forgive me. I don't think it ever occurred to me that you might not be willing to." He shook his head again. "For once this isn't arrogance. It's just this feeling that there's something so strong between us that neither one of us would ever let it go." He gave another long sigh. "You know, I think it's just beginning to dawn on me that I could actually lose you."

Returning to his chair, he rolled it around to face her, then rested his hands on her knees. "I won't let that part win." He gave her a weak smile. "For one thing, I'd look pretty ridiculous—a strung-out, over-the-hill reporter turned cokehead."

He inched his hands up her thighs. "I'm not going to let my pig-headedness over catching bad guys screw up both our lives. If I stop right now, would it be possible for us to get through this and be fine like we've always done before?"

Then the tears came for real, pouring out of her eyes, causing her to gasp and choke and grab for tissues. Zach guided her to the bed, sat down and pulled her into his lap. She leaned her forehead against his shoulder and cried for Olivia and Carl and the cats. And for all the ways Zach had hurt her and their near loss of each other.

When the tears were over, she looked up blearily. "Now what?"

"All I can think of is a shower and a few hours' sleep." His arms tightened around her. "But I don't want to let go of you. Do you have any clients? Maybe we could take a nap together."

"No clients till six. A nap sounds wonderful."

Twenty minutes later she snuggled up against his shampoo-scented body. Just as she was falling asleep, his burry voice whispered in her ear, "I'm so glad I have you."

The next thing she knew he had his hand on her shoulder to wake her. She rolled over. Zach was raised on one elbow looking down at her.

"It's after five. We overslept. We won't even get to make love until later."

She sighed. "This is one time I wish my clients would all go away and leave me alone."

"Before you start getting ready, there's something I want to run by you." He paused. "I just realized I could do the buy without going to the club more than one more time."

Her body went rigid.

"Look, if the answer's no, I won't say another word. But just hear me out, okay? I could go down tonight and finalize the plan, then tell Nate I'm heading back to Athens to set up my network. Once the details are nailed down, there's no reason for me to hang out at the club anymore. Could you live with that?"

She got up, donned her long tee, and sat on the bed, Zach settling in beside her. "Tell me again. Why should I put up with this?"

"Because it would gladden my heart to put Barry and Nate away for a good long time. Obviously, busting two dealers won't change anything in the grand scheme of things. Ten more will spring up to take their place and we won't be saving any future Heathers or Tiffanys." Tiffany was Bryce's girlfriend who'd overdosed. "But cops who kill small-fry street dealers and set up their own drug ring deserve to get theirs."

"If this were your last night out, JC'd be desperate to cause trouble. Why wouldn't he suddenly have you bingeing on coke and screwing Heather?"

"Well, for one thing, after last night Heather's going to think I'm pretty pathetic. The story'll probably be going around that I can't get it up."

She giggled. "Are you sure you even *want* to go back?"

"I could take you with me."

She looked at him as if he were nuts. "Yeah, right. After you made fun of me in front of those cops."

"I told them I'd dated you in high school and you still remembered that the last time we went out I borrowed money from you to take your best friend to the prom. I was making myself look bad more than anything."

"Jerks like that'd admire you for getting away with it."

"I could say I tracked you down, paid off my debt, and sweet-talked you into going out with me again. You could sit at one of the tables while I worked out the arrangements at the bar."

"Why'd you try to drag me over to meet your friends, anyway?"

"Just to piss you off. It was the hoodlum trying to split us up." He paused. "Would you come with me? I'd like to have you there."

ಬ    ಬ    ಬ

Cassidy had been sitting at the small table for almost an hour, her lungs filled with smoke, her eardrums hammered by noise. She tried to keep her gaze focused on the dance floor but couldn't stop from sneaking occasional peeks at the bar, where Zach stood with the two men she'd seen the previous night. Heather had not made an appearance. Zach had no cigarettes in his hand but he did seem to have a fresh bourbon every time she looked.

She gritted her teeth and drummed her heel, staring fixedly at the apparently double-jointed twenty-year-old bodies jerking around in front of her. After what seemed like a slow-moving week, she felt Zach's hand on her shoulder. Standing, she gazed up at him.

The old lazy, slightly amused Zach-expression was back in place. Putting a hand beneath her elbow, he spoke close to her ear. "Now's the time for me to lead you out on the dance floor. But not here. I want to clear out of this place as fast as possible. I'd much rather dance with you in the bedroom where it's just the two of us and we have the floor to ourselves.''

Reaching the lot where they'd left the Cougar, Cassidy halted next to the driver's side of the car. On the hike from the club, she'd noticed that Zach had achieved an exuberant alcoholic glow.

As he unlocked the door, she asked, ''Don't you think you better give me the keys?''

''I know I've had a lot to drink but I can get us to Oak Park.'' He gave her a direct look. ''These past few weeks—having to be somebody else—have been pretty awful. Tonight I need to feel like I'm back in charge and I don't want to be driven home.''

''You're sure?''

''I'll be careful.''

''Okay.''

It was close to midnight when they arrived at the house. Zach went inside, then closed the door to turn off the alarm while Cassidy stood under the porch light gazing across Briar. Zach reopened the door and Starshine came racing out to play jungle cat in the unmown backyard. *Guess she's ready for a break from her self-appointed job as Tigger-guardian.*

Looking back at Olivia's house one more time, she suddenly noticed a large, stub-earred cat sitting erect on the ledge beneath the front window. *Milton.* As good as she was feeling already, her spirits lifted further. *It's an omen. Everything's going to be fine.*

She called Zach back outside. ''This is the first I've seen of Milton since the murder. I'm so glad he's all right.'' The three indoor cats flashed into her mind. ''Oh shit. I was so busy planning my divorce this morning I forgot to feed Olivia's animals.''

''Not now.'' Taking her hand, he led her into the waiting room and kissed her soundly. ''This time it's us first, the cats second.''

Recalling how Brenner felt about his wife's cats, she wound her arms around Zach's neck and kissed him back.

He bent his head down so that it touched hers. ''You go put on something black and slinky. I'll be up in a minute.''

In the bedroom she dug through her underwear drawer and came up with a black slip and panties. Appearing seconds later, Zach handed her a cutglass brandy snifter full of amber liquid. ''Grand Marnier.'' As she sipped the smooth, orange-flavored liqueur, he slid a CD into the player, removed all but his white jockey shorts, took a long swallow from the snifter, and pulled her into his arms. "Do you remember drinking Grand Marnier out of the same glass that first night you came to Marina City?"

"I remember everything about that night."

Their bodies touching from her bosom to her hips, they swayed to the sound of Ray Charles' gravely voice. "Georgia, Georgia . . ."

"I remember drinking Grand Marnier, you trying to ask about condoms, making love, and then having to take you home because you couldn't leave your cat alone overnight." She felt his chin grazing her forehead, her breasts brushing his chest, his hands sliding down her back.

"Considering you didn't call afterward, I'm surprised it registered."

"There've been so many times I nearly lost you. I almost didn't see you again after that first night because I knew you weren't the kind of woman I could just walk away from. Then I screwed up that newspaper story and you quite rightfully threw me out of your life. And now, over this last month, I've been acting like such an ass you were ready to file papers."

He stepped back, drank down half the liqueur, then handed the glass to her. "Do you have any idea how much I need you?"

"Needing me is something you usually keep pretty much to yourself."

"Not tonight." He led her to the waterbed, slowly removed her slip and panties, then drew her down on the sheet beside him.

After they made love, he stretched out on his back and said, "The thought of losing you terrifies me."

She wrapped her body around his. "Then stop doing things to make it happen."

"Being stupid and self-destructive has never been my goal in life." He paused. "At least, not for a lot of years it hasn't." Laying his wrist across his forehead, he added. "God, I'm tired. I'm tired and I'm drunk and I don't think I could move if the house was burning down around me. But this was a night when I needed a little excess and I needed you to share it with me." He gave her a light kiss. "Now I'm going to roll over and get a solid eight hours' sleep, and when I wake up tomorrow I'll be back to my normal self."

&#8478;   &#8478;   &#8478;

Remembering Olivia's unfed cats, Cassidy dressed in a shirt and shorts, stuffed her neighbor's key in her pocket, and headed out the back door. As she started across Briar, Starshine abandoned her stalking games to trot along beside her. Stepping onto the curb on the far side of the street, Cassidy stumbled slightly. *Guess half a snifter of Grand Marnier's got you a little light-headed too.*

*But it was worth it. Not often you get to celebrate your husband's return after four weeks of alien abduction. Plus all that great sex and getting to hear for once in your life that he couldn't stand to lose you.*

Deciding to check the trap first, she slipped past the Cavalier and quietly approached the gate. Even if Milton wasn't in the steel box, he might be hanging around Olivia's backyard. She wanted to get a good look at him, see how well fed he appeared. If it turned out he was there, she might be able to slip up fairly close. Of all the ferals, Milton was the least afraid of humans. *Just slide in gently. Don't startle him.*

She passed through the gate into the backyard, then stopped to let her eyes adjust to the greater darkness inside the tall fence. As Starshine sniffed the stoop for other cat smells, Cassidy peered into the bushes around the edge of the property. A moment later the large tom emerged from behind a shrub at the rear of the yard. He took a couple of steps in her direction, then sat down to stare at her.

*Probably thinks I'm here to feed him. Except the food jug's inside and the bowls are long gone.* As she gazed into the cat's glittering eyes, she once again had the bizarre sensation that he was reading her mind. *You've definitely over-imbibed here.* Starshine, hunkered into stalking position at her feet, growled softly.

She heard something from above, a soft thwap like a fat book hitting the floor. Looking up, she felt her stomach lurch. A window near the east corner of Brenner's house was backlit, a soft light reflecting off the ceiling. Silhouetted in the dim glow, Brenner stood at the window. All she could see of him was a curved portion of his profile, and beneath that, a wrist and hand. In the hand was a pistol and it was pointed at Milton. *Gunfire! Silenced gunfire!*

# 19. Adrenaline Junkie

Milton sat in the same place as before. *Brenner's aim must be way off.* The gimpy old tom began strolling toward her.

Her eyes flew upward. Brenner appeared to be positioning his gun for another shot. *Hasn't seen me. Totally focused on the cat. Shit, he's going to try again.*

"Stop," she yelled. "Don't you dare. I'm reporting you for shooting cats."

He turned the gun in her direction. *Thwap.* A spurt of heat grazed her right shoulder.

"Ow!" Clapping her hand to the wound, she started racing out of the yard, Starshine streaking along beside her. She bolted through the gate and was running past the garage when the calico swerved abruptly, dashed between her legs and sent her crashing headlong toward the driveway. She caught herself with her hands, the rough surface burning her palms, the jolt of the landing shooting red-hot flashes through her wrists and arms.

Rising to her knees, she put her left foot on the ground and tried to push off, but a sharp pain in her ankle caused her to lose her balance and go down again. *He's sure to come after you. He'll be here any minute.*

She got to her feet, reached out for the car to steady herself, and took a step forward. Her ankle hurt but she could walk on it. She heard Brenner's door slam, his footsteps coming toward her. An instant later he sprinted around the back of Olivia's car, raised his arms, and held the pistol about a foot in front of her face.

*Oh God!* With trees blocking the light and the gun so close, all she could see was a shadowy figure standing behind the weapon. The smell of sweat and gunpowder set off surges of panic in her gut. *Breathe. Keep breathing.*

"What the hell were you up to, making me shoot at you like that? What a stupid thing to do, yelling at me from her yard. Just look at the trouble you've caused." He talked too fast, the words tumbling over each other to get out of his mouth.

*Hyper. Extremely hyper. What's it mean?*

"Get in my house right now before somebody sees us."

She swiveled her head, looking desperately for help, but no one was there. She opened her mouth to scream. *No, don't. He's too crazy. He'd probably shoot.*

"Get moving!"

She sucked in air and started toward his house. *Have to think like a therapist, talk him down.*

She went inside, the doggy smells assaulting her. In the soft light flowing from beneath fringed lampshades, she studied Brenner's deeply lined, ashen face, the feverish light in his eyes.

"What am I going to do with you? I've gotta figure this out. But now you've got me so manicky I can't think straight."

*Manicky! That's it! The guy's bipolar.* Brenner flopped heavily on one of the Victorian sofas. She perched on the other, her stomach twitching wildly. She knew how unpredictable and dangerous people in a manic state could be.

He pounded his fist on one of the pillows. "You had no business getting involved with that woman and her cats."

*Gotta be a therapist. Don't let him see how scared you are.*

Clearing her throat, she made an effort to keep her voice steady. "You seem pretty agitated, Mr. Brenner. I'd have to guess you haven't been taking your meds." Her left hand clutched at the wet, sticky wound on her shoulder.

"Just like a woman. Women have always been my problem. My wife made me take those damn pills. They slowed me down. That's what she wanted. Made it easier for her to control me. It was because of the lithium she was able to talk me into buying this house right next to Austin Boulevard. Right where all the crime is. A place where you have to protect yourself, have to have guns. She got me to let the cats sleep with us. She even made me be nice to that weird lady next door."

He jumped up, went to stand at the window, then returned to sink down on the sofa again.

"My wife died, you know. Couple of years ago. At first I was lost without her, but then I realized I didn't have to take the damn meds anymore. I could get me a couple of dogs, have all the guns I wanted. If my wife hadn't messed with my mind, making me take that damn lithium, I could've been a famous general like my father."

Cassidy said in a low, soothing voice, "It must've really startled you when I yelled like that out in the yard. You couldn't think of anything to do but bring me inside so we could straighten things out."

"Had to keep you from telling. Can't let anybody know about the guns."

"Yes, but now I see it was all my fault and I really do apologize. So don't you think we could be friends again?"

He shook his head vehemently, got up, paced, sat back down again. "I can't let you go. You'd tell the police about my guns."

A chill ran down her spine. "If I'm missing very long, my husband will come looking for me." *After a lot of hours of sleeping it off, he will.*

"I'll have to lock you in the trunk, drive you some place else. Need to set it up so nobody knows you were here." Laying the gun in his lap, he pressed both hands against the sides of his head. "You've got me so confused, I can't think where to take you."

*He's a little nuts, but not nuts enough to fall for any promises not to tell the police.*

"Zach knows about your guns. If I disappear, the police will search your house. You'd be better off letting me go now, before you commit any really serious crime."

"How do you know what crimes I've committed? The only thing that makes sense is to lock you in my basement room until I can figure out how to get rid of you."

*Oh shit. Can't get anywhere with him if I'm locked up.* The chill crept from her spine down through her arms, causing her hands to tremble. "No, please. We need to talk. We have to work things out."

He crossed to where she was sitting and held the gun to her head. "You're trying to confuse me, just like my wife used to do. Now shut up and do what you're told."

"Please don't—"

"If you say one more word, I'm pulling this trigger." He grabbed her left arm, jerked her to her feet, and pushed her toward an archway leading into the dining room.

She stumbled ahead of him, breathing shallowly through her mouth. He took her downstairs into a finished basement, opened a heavy wooden door and gave her a hard shove, propelling her several feet forward into a dark room. Pivoting, she saw him flip on the fluorescent lights and close the door, then heard the soft thud of a bolt sliding into place.

Adrenaline flooded her system, her muscles knotting and her nerves stretching way too tight. She wanted to throw things, break things, stamp her feet, tear the place apart. *Pull yourself together!* She squeezed her eyes shut, took a deep breath, then opened them and looked around. The small, windowless room was knotty pine, located near the front of the house. Racks holding a variety of firearms lined one wall. She saw pistols, rifles, shotguns, strange looking weapons she couldn't put a name to. *Bazookas? Missile launchers? And, of course, an Uzi or two.*

Although she didn't think he was crazy enough to leave her in a room with loaded guns, she searched out a Beretta, the only pistol she was familiar with, and verified that the magazine was in fact missing. She then examined several other firearms, confirming that none had ammunition.

The space seemed tiny, airless, claustrophobic. Wrapping her arms tightly across her chest, she rocked on her toes. She saw herself clubbing Brenner with a shotgun, heaving a pistol into his face when he opened the door. *Pathetic. There's nothing you can do.*

The adrenaline eventually drained away, leaving her shaky and exhausted. She sat on the cold asphalt floor, elbows on her knees, chin on her fists. Remembering the way Zach had fallen instantly asleep, she wondered how long it would be before the widower came to get her. The image of Olivia's body popped into her mind. Brenner had to be the one who'd killed both Olivia and Carl, which meant he wouldn't hesitate to kill her. And even as confused as he was now, he undoubtedly would recognize the necessity of getting her out of his house before dawn.

An hour later the doorbell rang. She glanced at her watch. Three-thirty. *Zach? He wouldn't be awake yet, would he? And how would he know where you are?*

Four more staccato rings.

*Here's hoping Brenner's too confused to realize he shouldn't open the door. Or too agitated to sit and ignore it.*

The bell kept ringing. She held her breath. A minute dragged by.

Footsteps and the skittering of claws sounded overhead. The door opened.

"What the hell—"

She caught a voice from outside. *Oh God! It is Zach!*

She started screaming, kept screaming, couldn't stop. She threw herself at the door, beating her fists against the wood until they were red and raw.

Even with all the noise she was making, she heard the click of the bolt. She stopped in midstream, gulped, and began gasping for air. As she stepped back, the door swung inward. Brenner stood in front of her, the dogs at his side, Zach behind his right shoulder. Zach pushed past him and grabbed her.

"It's all right. Everything's going to be all right. The police are on their way."

She clung to him for a moment, then leaned back and said, "I don't understand. How'd you know where to look?"

"It was the cats. I'll explain later."

Several squads arrived. The police handcuffed Brenner and deposited him in the back of one of the vehicles. They separated Cassidy and Zach, took their statements, then allowed them to sit together in a squad car.

Cassidy's legs were weak, her forehead damp with sweat. She rubbed the back of her wrist across it. "Oh God, it's over. The whole thing is over."

Zach squeezed her hand.

"I kept trying to think where I'd seen a small black car and now I remember—it was in Brenner's driveway." She went on to explain the connection between Olivia's murder, Pam Gardiner, and the visitor who drove a small black car. "So that means it has to be Brenner."

"I hope so."

She sat quietly, going over the night's events in her mind. "But you still haven't told me how you knew where I was."

"It was a team effort. Tigger and Starshine worked together to lead me to you."

"You're making this up."

"True story." He patted her knee. "With all that booze on top of the sleep deprivation, the odds are I would've stayed zonked till noon. Except this horrendous cat shriek from the extra bedroom woke me up. So I went running in and there was Tigger sitting in the open window."

"That's amazing. She actually screamed with no other cat chasing her?"

"I think she may've been trying to find a way out. But wait—it gets better. I was conscious enough at that point to notice you were missing, so I went outside to look for you, and there was Starshine sitting on Brenner's porch. She came running across the street as soon as she saw me, but before she noticed I was there, she was just sitting on the porch waiting for you to come out."

"Waiting for me?"

"Why else would she be there? The guy's got dogs. She never hangs out on his property. Well, since I knew Brenner was a nutcase, I figured he must've grabbed you when you went over to feed Olivia's cats."

"Not bad." She laid her hand on his leg. "But since you'd already called the police, why take the chance of coming inside when you knew he had all those guns?"

"I probably should've held off." He paused. "I guess I was trying to make up for being such a jerk this past month."

ಶಿ    ಶಿ    ಶಿ

The next day Cassidy saw clients in the morning, then refilled her mug in the kitchen and went to join Zach at the dining room table where he sat with the paper spread out in front him.

"I clipped a cartoon for you." He handed her a strip in which a turbaned Sylvia was typing her response to a personal advice question: "Dear 'Miserable unless I'm in love,' Please forgive yesterday's out-burst. I do take your problem seriously. I suggest joining an aerobics class . . . not being in love will seem pleasant by comparison."

She smiled. "This is perfect for the refrigerator."

He studied her face, his eyes concerned. "I've been thinking about Brenner. Just because the guy's crazy doesn't mean—"

"No, wait. He really isn't crazy. I know that's what I said last night but the truth is, bipolar's a very treatable disease."

"Yeah, I know. People who're bipolar—manic depressive—whatever you want to call it—if they stay on their meds they're fine. But a lot of them don't, and then they get nuts."

"It's really a shame about Brenner." She closed her eyes briefly. "And even more of a shame that Olivia died because Brenner went off his meds. Apparently he was able to live a normal life as long as he took his lithium." She gave Zach a small cat-smile. "Just like you're able to be a decent human being as long as you stay out of clubs."

"Anyway, as I started to say, we can't assume Brenner murdered Olivia."

"Of course he did. He's got guns all over the house. He's hated her for years. He's psychotic enough to take a shot at me. And even though I had myself convinced Evelyn was behind the car vandalism, I can see now Brenner must've followed me around and done it while I was in the coffeehouse. He taught shop. He'd know about crimping fuel lines. And it happened shortly after he saw me in his tree." She gazed at a man riding his bike down Briar, a lab on a leash running along beside him.

"You're not listening." Picking up her hand, Zach rubbed his thumb across the back of her fingers. "There's nothing to connect Brenner with Carl Behan. Don't forget, you've still got Edwardo out there. He's the only one we know of with a reason to be extremely pissed at both victims. It could be Brenner, but it also might be Edwardo or somebody else we haven't even thought of."

Pulling her hand away from his, she pressed her thumb and fingers against her forehead. "I want it to be Brenner. I want this all to be over."

"But there's a good chance it isn't. If Edwardo killed Behan and he knows you've got those pictures, he could be planning to do to you what he did to the other two victims. This is not a time to get careless."

Gazing into space, she pictured Olivia's body at the bottom of the stairs, Carl's porch with the newspapers on it, the lawn service guy staring at her from his rusted-out car. *Friday you were convinced Edwardo was going to come gunning for you. This morning you were convinced you were in the clear*. She shook her head, no longer sure of anything.

"Hey, where'd you go?" Zach took her hand again. "I have three items on my to-do list, and two of them require your presence."

She looked at him suspiciously. "Now that you're back to your old self, are you going to start ordering me around again?"

"Consider it gentle persuasion. The first thing we need to do is take you over to West Sub and get that wound looked at. The second is to go shopping and replace the dress that got ruined."

"What's the third?"

"Trap Tigger and take her to Wisconsin. I was perfectly happy to have her get me up at three this morning, but I don't need screams in the night on a regular basis."

Cassidy nibbled her bottom lip. "I was sort of hoping we could work with her, turn her into a pet."

"Work with her? You can't get near her. Besides, she's an outside cat. She isn't happy here."

"What about Milton?"

"Considering he's stayed clear of the trap all week, he's obviously decided to decline your invitation to go winter in Wisconsin. He's probably found some other cat lady on a different block and is doing fine."

*So Zach wants to take over your cat rescue project. You going to let him get away with that?* Her lips tightened.

*What he says makes sense. There's no use fighting it.* She frowned, feeling irritated, defensive, and relieved all at once. She glanced at Olivia's window ledge where Milton had appeared the night before. *But at least you'll get a peek at your old buddy now and then.*

&#8474;   &#8474;   &#8474;

They stopped at the emergency room to get her wound cleaned and rebandaged, then drove to Oakbrook Center for lunch. After eating small pizzas with pineapple, spinach and chicken teriyaki toppings at the California Pizza Kitchen, they held hands and wandered the outdoor mall. They strolled past fountains and flower gardens, stopping to admire a vivid display of red salvia, pink zinnias, and yellow marigolds. Her wrists and shoulders ached and she still felt an occasional twinge in her ankle, but these complaints were minor compared to the heady sense of freedom she experienced at taking a break from her worries over the cats, the murder and Jake. At Zach's insistence they headed for the dress department at Nordstrom, an upscale department store where a tuxedoed pianist played old favorites. After trying on several garments, Cassidy was ready to make her selection, but Zach urged her to keep looking until she found one she liked as well as the one she'd lost. He went with her, up and down aisles, pulling hangers off racks whenever he saw something he thought she'd like.

She finally reached the point where everything was starting to look alike. "I'm in overload. I've got three terrific outfits here and I don't know which to choose."

"Take them all."

"Have you looked at our checkbook lately?"

"It's a temporary shortfall. We'll be fine in a couple of months." He placed his hand on her arm. "I want you to have them."

When they returned to the house, Zach helped her carry the bags up to the bedroom, then said, "I'm going out for awhile."

She looked up curiously.

"Just some things I need to think about."

She watched as he headed toward the stairs. Although he'd clearly wanted to take her shopping, she'd noticed that he had become quieter over the course of the afternoon. *Whatever it is, it's not the return of JC or a problem with us. He'll tell you when he's ready.*

Sliding into her desk chair, she jiggled a pen between her fingers. Even if Brenner did turn out to be the killer, she wouldn't be finished until she'd dealt with Evelyn and the Medicare fraud. She had decided what she was going to do but she still had to inform Evelyn. Not a call she was eager to make.

She looked up the number and dialed.

"Well, Cassidy McCabe—or should I say Jessica? Have you found your murderer yet?"

"I thought so, but maybe not."

"If the killer is still on the loose, I hope the police find him. Olivia was a pain in the butt but nobody deserves to end up the way she did."

"Aren't you talking about yourself here? Isn't the real message— even though you cheated Medicare, you don't deserve to lose every- thing?"

Evelyn's voice turned somber. "I've been thinking about both things—Olivia's murder and the possibility of losing the business. And it sure as shit doesn't seem to me like the punishment fits the crime."

"Well, I'm inclined to agree with you. I wouldn't want to be the cause of anybody's financial ruin." *Whatever happens, she's responsible, not you.* "But I also can't stand by and allow the fraud to continue. So I'm giving you six months to clean up your act. At the end of February I'll report you to the hotline but I won't give them the forms. If your business is totally on the up and up by then, you shouldn't have a problem." She swiveled her chair toward the window and stared at trees growing so thickly they blocked out the sky.

"So what're you going to do with the forms?"

"Keep them in my safe-deposit box." *Life insurance. Just in case it wasn't Edwardo or Brenner.*

Evelyn sighed. "I wish you'd tell me how I'm going to stay in the black without that little source of extra income."

"Not my problem." *God, that feels good. You should say it more often.*

"The only way I could possibly get out of this hole is by dumping half the staff and bringing in fresh blood." She sighed again. "You probably think of me as a real hardass, but the truth is, I've seldom been able to actually can anybody."

"Do what you have to do." She clicked down the phone. *Even if she fires every last one of them, it's not my problem and I don't have to feel guilty.*

As Cassidy walked away from her desk, it occurred to her that she hadn't checked the answering machine all day. Detouring into Zach's office, she pushed PLAY.

"There's one other lead that might be worth following up on."

*Oh my God! It's Carl!* The hair rose on her arms.

"At first it seemed like such a long shot I didn't bother mentioning it. But now that I've looked into things a little further, I think there may be something here. A couple of months ago, Olivia asked me to draw up a petition . . ."

Beep.

*I can't believe this! First the machine loses the message for a whole damn week, then it cuts off the ending.*

Frantically rewinding the tape, she tried several times to retrieve the missing portion, but finally had to admit to herself that it was gone.

*Shit!* She pounded her fist on the Formica table. *There's somebody out there Carl started checking on just before he was murdered, and I have no idea who that person is.*

ജ     ജ     ജ

After her last client left for the night, she went upstairs to the bedroom where Zach was opening mail at his desk. She sat on the bed and he swiveled to face her.

"Where'd you go this afternoon?"

"Just drove around. I had some things to sort out."

"Well, I'd like to hear about the sorting, but there's something else I need to discuss first. Something I want you to do that you're not going to be thrilled with." She paused. "Why don't you come sit beside me so I can wrap my legs around your body and otherwise beguile you."

He settled in next to her. "So what is it you have in mind for me that I'm not going to like?"

Lacing her fingers through his, she laid both their hands on his denim-covered thigh. Her skin looked pale against his dark pigmentation. "I want you to let Bryce and me ride along in the surveillance van when you do the drug drop."

"You're right. I don't like it."

"Bryce is really pissed at you. First, for disappearing on him without warning, and second, for putting yourself in a situation where you could get killed. He's lost everybody else. He can't afford to lose you."

Zach disentangled his hand from hers and ran it over his face. "Well, he's got a right to be pissed. I'm pissed at myself."

"What about?"

"Going undercover. Just look at all the damage I did. To you. Our marriage. Even Bryce." He shook his head. "When I was out driving this afternoon, I kept asking myself why I thought I had to do it in the first place." He gave her a rueful smile. "Not a question I would even have considered before you came along."

"That's a good question. One I probably ought to ask myself more often. So, what did you come up with?"

He patted her leg. "You and I have talked before about my tendency toward addiction. Well, I'm beginning to wonder if adrenaline isn't my real problem." He paused. "When I was going out there every night, getting away with something, beating those cops at their own game—I was really pumped up. Now I'm just flat, sort of in withdrawal."

"An adrenaline junkie?" *And what about you? The two of you addicts together, like two drunks finding each other in a bar.*

"Going undercover all on my own was really stupid." She glimpsed self disgust in his eyes.

"Maybe I should schedule you in for a session. Better yet, we should find some other therapist and go in together, since I seem to have a similar proclivity."

He smiled grimly.

"Seriously, if you're seeing this as a problem, is there anything you want to do about it?"

"Lock JC in a cage and make sure he never gets out again."

"You know, as much as I can't stand him, it was JC who made you tough and independent enough to survive growing up with a mother who hated you and a big brother who wanted to turn you into his personal slave."

"Well, anyway, JC has one more job to do and then I'm done with him. Now as to riding in the surveillance van, I know why you want to do it. You always want to get in the middle of everything. But why Bryce?"

"So he can feel more a part of things. See you in action, see you doing something worthwhile. Maybe even find something he could admire in you."

"Yeah, but right now I'm not sure it *was* worthwhile and I certainly don't want him admiring this hot dog behavior of mine."

"He'll decide for himself what he likes and doesn't like. So far all he ever does is find fault, but I think that's because he doesn't feel like he's got any real place in your life." She stared at their wedding picture, Cassidy in the middle, Zach and Bryce on either side, the three of them looking absurdly happy.

"You know, this undercover work you've been doing takes a lot of courage."

"Foolhardiness," he grumbled.

"Courage. If Bryce watches from the van, maybe he'll see you as the strong, competent person you are. So what if you screw up some-times? At least you always try to do the right thing." She reached around to kiss his cheek. "You're his father. He needs to feel proud of you."

"Even if I'm not proud of myself?"

"Beating up on yourself is not your style. I'm the one whose job it is to feel guilty around here." She intertwined her legs with his. "This mood of yours won't last. By Thursday night you'll be as arrogant as ever."

ℬ    ℬ    ℬ

Wednesday afternoon she picked up a call in the kitchen. "Next to Olivia, you're the most exasperating woman I ever met," Shelby said, her good-natured tone taking the sting out of the words.

Cassidy pictured herself dragging Shelby, dog-collared and chained, over to Olivia's house. "Have you been having an emotional reaction to that talk we had the other day?"

"No, actually, I went home and got my first good night's sleep since you appeared out of nowhere like the wicked witch of the west. Honestly, I'm beginning to think you're an instrument of the devil, someone I should definitely steer clear of."

Cassidy remembered her seance dream, Olivia's ghost handing her a mirror that revealed a series of faces. *No, I'm just channeling your mother's spirit is all.* "If you're sleeping better, what's the problem?"

"Well, first of all, the way you get me to do everything you want. Whenever I'm around you, I act like some weak-willed little wuss—definitely not my normal personality."

"I couldn't get you to do anything unless some part of you agreed with me." Leaning against the doorjamb, she gazed out the dining room window at a smoky, overcast sky. "What else are you mad about?"

"You changed my image of Olivia and I'm not the least bit happy about it. I used to see her as this tough-as-nails person who didn't give a shit about anybody. Now, I keep picturing her as this helpless little kid walking around in a woman's body."

"Why unhappy about that?"

"There you go again, making me say things I don't want to say."

"You don't have to say anything." *Give people permission not to talk, they almost always do.*

A moment of silence. "This is something I hate to admit even to myself." She sighed. "It's taken away all my excuses. Every time I start to feel sorry for myself, I think of . . ." she paused, then got the word out ". . . my mother, and I can't."

"I can see why you'd be angry. I've taken something away that's been a big part of your life for a long time."

"And the other thing that's even more annoying—I sleep fine now but I can't stop dreaming about that damn cat. I have the same dream over and over. I'm just getting home from work, I open the door, and this big white tom comes running up to greet me. I can't get it out of my mind."

*What's this? A home for one of my orphans?* "Are you actually telling me you want Bamba?"

"Well, at first I thought I'd take just him. But then I couldn't stop thinking about those poor, shy little females. They're sort of like Olivia, aren't they?"

Cassidy's eyes widened in amazement. "You want all three?"

Her voice going small and thin, she asked, "You suppose I could come by tonight and get them?"

&#8278;   &#8278;   &#8278;

When her doorbell rang an hour later, Cassidy was surprised to find Manny Perez standing on her front porch. Wondering if he might have found out about her visit to Pam, she said, "I'm not talking without an attorney present."

He smiled, the warmth back in his dark-coffee eyes. *So he hasn't heard about your latest transgression.*

"I thought you should know that Brenner made bail."

"What? He was full-blown manic Monday night. He should be in a hospital. There's no question he's a danger to himself and others."

"Look, I happen to agree with you but it's not my call. The only way he could've been hospitalized is if the prosecutor'd presented a case for commitment at the bail hearing, and he wasn't about to do that because it would've handed Brenner his defense."

"So this psychotic neighbor of mine who sees me as the cause of all his woes is out on the loose."

Perez shifted his weight. "It's not as bad as it sounds. We confiscated the guns and Brenner tells us he's back on his meds. We also issued dire warnings not to go anywhere near you. He gives you any trouble, just call 9-1-1 and we'll haul him in again."

"Did you interrogate him about Olivia's murder?"

"He admits to pinching your fuel line but denies shooting the Mallory woman, whom he refers to as the cat lady."

"You still convinced it was Jake?"

Perez gazed at the floor, then looked up. "The possibility of a link between the Mallory and Behan murders has raised some questions. We checked out that lawn service guy you mentioned. He's definitely back in the country but we haven't been able to run him down yet."

She pictured Edwardo staring at her darkly from his rusted-out car.

"But regardless of whether or not Jake's guilty, there's no excuse for your meddling." Some of the warmth went out of his eyes. "Look what happened to Carl Behan—possibly because you talked him into doing surveillance."

"It might not have been Edwardo." She described the partial message from Behan she had found on her machine.

Perez jotted it on his pad. "Now back to the point I was making." He gave her a stern look. "Can you honestly say you think it's okay for citizens to investigate each other whenever they think the police are wrong? If you have a problem with how we've handled a case, you can talk to us about it. But it is *not* okay to go prying into the lives of everybody you consider a suspect. Vigilantism is never acceptable." He paused. "You got that?"

She clenched her teeth to restrain herself from reminding him that she'd talked to him and he hadn't listened. *Keep your mouth shut. This is a fight you can't win.* She forced herself to speak mildly: "I can see that it's not a good idea for private citizens to involve themselves in police matters."

"That's better." He smiled, the friendliness back in his face.

Voices clamored in her head as she watched him get into his blue Ford and drive away. *Yes, but Jake would've been convicted if you'd left it alone. However, when it comes right down to it, you really* don't *believe in vigilante action. Yeah, but look how many times you've been convinced you had to run your own investigation.*

*There's no way you're ever going to get this reconciled. One part of you believes you shouldn't do what you've been doing. But this other part believes just as strongly that* not *to do it would be wrong.*

ಬಿ    ಬಿ    ಬಿ

Thursday morning Cassidy and Zach discussed the drug drop, scheduled for midnight that night. At ten p.m. he came into the bedroom and held her for a long time.

"I have to go. Sam—he's the surveillance guy—he's gotta get me wired up, test the equipment, do all the prep work." He ran the back of his fingers along the side of her face. "I'll see you when it's over."

# 20. A White Van

Cassidy watched Zach's image on the seven-inch screen attached to the partition in the back of the van. Sam resided in a captain's chair in front of the control panel, with Cassidy and Bryce on a seat behind him.

Ten minutes earlier the Cougar had pulled up half a block ahead of the van. Five minutes passed, then a Chevy sedan parked just behind the Cougar. A man stepped out on the passenger side. Her chest tightening, Cassidy recognized him as one of the two dealer cops from the club. Coming around to join the newcomer on the sidewalk, Zach said, "Right on time."

"You think I wouldn't be?" The cop's voice came thinly through the wire.

The cop opened the Chevy's trunk and the two men leaned into it. She assumed the cop was counting the bills in the envelope Zach had picked up from his Uncle Martin earlier that afternoon, and Zach was testing cocaine from the brick in the dealer's trunk.

He turned to the cop. "You satisfied, man?"

"Looks okay."

Cassidy glanced at Bryce, who was leaning forward, elbows on knees, eyes glued to the screen.

"Well, bro," Zach removed a package from the trunk and saluted the cop, "I'll be back next month for another load."

The cop slid into the Chevy's passenger seat and the sedan drove off. Zach returned to the Cougar and left also.

"Way to go, Zach!" Sam made a thumbs-up gesture.

"Well shit," Bryce said. "The driver never got out. You only caught one of them on tape."

"Don't worry." Sam fiddled with the controls to blank out the screen, then rotated his chair to face them. "Zacho's already got several tapes with the three of 'em discussing the buy. He could probably nail both fuckers even without the video." Sam had a fleshy face, black brillo pad hair, and a large paunch. "Man oh man, this is going to be one sweet story."

"What's so great about it?" Bryce demanded. "I see stuff like this all the time. Cops get busted for burglary, robbery, assault, you name it."

"Yeah, but there's a witness saw one of these mopes whack a dealer. A cop charged with murder one—now that's a story."

Bryce shrugged, attempting an attitude of indifference, although the gleam in his dark eyes told Cassidy he was far more hooked than he'd ever be likely to admit. He asked, "So what happens next?"

"I drop you two off at your cars, then I meet Zacho to give him the tape . . ." he glanced at his watch ". . . about forty-five minutes from now."

Bryce asked, "Why the long wait?"

"We're going to drive around a while, make sure we're not followed."

Cassidy explained to Bryce, "Zach'll put the coke, the tapes, a written statement, and the numbers from the bills into a briefcase, then hand it over to an attorney who'll deliver everything to the federal prosecutor. If all goes well, the DA will strike instantly, and those two guys in the Chevy'll be locked up before morning."

"Yep," Sam said. "Just a couple more hours and Zach'll be home in bed."

"That's all there is to it?" Bryce said, a hint of disappointment in his voice. "All that buildup for what—five minutes of tape?"

"You know, you're right," Cassidy said. "It would've been a lot more dramatic if the dealer'd ripped Zach's shirt off, found the wire, made him go down on his knees and executed him."

Bryce gave her a big, phony grin. "Yeah, it would have."

          ಲ     ಲ     ಲ

Rain started on the drive home. Dashing through a light shower, Cassidy went into the kitchen where Starshine sat by her food bowl. After dishing up a catly snack, Cassidy thought briefly of Tigger and the trap in the basement, but the idea drifted away before she could motivate herself to go see if the feral had made it into the steel box yet. She went upstairs, Starshine trotting ahead of her, to wait for Zach. Settling on the bed, she watched wet, shimmery images slide down the north window. The calico curled up beside her and made her chin available for scratching.

"I'm really glad you took some time out from your busy Tigger-chasing schedule to come sit with me. I'm not going to stop being a wreck till I see Zach walk through that door."

Two hours later he did just that, his hair wet from the rain, a bourbon and soda in each hand. He gave her a glass, then sat facing her in his desk chair.

"I just went down to check on the trap and Tigger's in it."

Cassidy broke into a wide smile. "Two drug dealers and a feral cat all in one night."

"Quite a haul, isn't it?" He took a long swallow. "Now all I have to do is unwind enough to catch a few hours' sleep. Tomorrow's going to start early and end late and I need to be as sharp as possible."

"What's going to happen?"

"First I get to shave." He ran a hand over his stubbly jaw. "Then I have an eight o'clock meeting with my editor to discuss exactly how we're going to play the story. After that I'll probably get called over to the DA's office for several hours of debriefing. When I leave there I'm likely to run into a mob of TV newshounds sticking cameras in my face." He started taking off his shoes. "I'd guess that by tomorrow night we'll be watching my performance on the ten o'clock news."

"I'd even be willing to forego my boycott of the news if you're on it." She paused. "So you'll be too busy to take Tigger to Wisconsin. And I've got several clients scheduled for tomorrow and Saturday."

"Tigger has lousy timing." He rubbed the back of his neck. "Any suggestions?"

"I know. I'll donate more money and get Harve to provide trans-portation."

"Good. One problem down." He rolled his chair up close to the bed. "The other thing that concerns me is, I won't be around much over these next few days, and I don't like leaving you alone when the guy who killed Olivia and Carl is still out there."

She drew her brows together, thinking how unfinished Olivia's murder still was. "I don't see anything to worry about. Nothing's happened since Brenner forced me into his house Monday night. Besides, we have no indication that the murderer considers me any kind of threat." She moved her head from side to side. "Well, why would he? I spent days and days mucking around in everybody's dirty secrets and I don't know anything."

He rose out of his chair, leaned over, and planted a kiss on her forehead. "Promise to stay inside and keep the doors locked?"

She laughed. "No, of course not."

ര     ര     ര

The next morning Cassidy handed Tigger and another check over to Harve, then returned home to see clients. Finishing at six, she went upstairs to play the new answering machine Zach had purchased, which sat in the spot on her desk the old one had occupied until they moved it into his office. Every time she saw it there, her spirits lifted, the machine's presence signaling a return to normalcy.

Starshine, dozing on the bed, started murping the instant Cassidy entered the room. The cat scrambled across the pile of books on the nightstand, trotted the length of the radiator, then leapt over to the desk, arriving before Cassidy could cover the distance between the door and her chair. She sat down and took out a pad.

Starshine, having had no companionship for the past two hours, walked back and forth in front of Cassidy's face, waved her tail in Cassidy's eyes, rubbed her cheek against Cassidy's chin, and took tiny mincing steps on the pad.

"No one would ever say that your communication skills were less than stellar." Cassidy scratched behind the calico's ears. "In fact, every one of my clients could take lessons from you on how to better make their needs known."

Standing to reach over Starshine's wriggly little body, Cassidy pushed PLAY, then used her left arm to fend off the cat so she could write.

Gran's voice said, "It looks like our investigation is out of gas. But I sure do want to thank you for letting me play junior detective. Snooping around in other people's business beats out swimnastics any day."

Her mother's voice said, "I'm getting sick of having to watch extravaganzas all the time. Only three more days and then I finally get to come home."

Esther's voice said, "Danny's at school all day today and I haven't had a single person to talk to this whole week long." Her tone was flat and lifeless. "I really miss Olivia. She used to visit every week. And Danny, he won't be around forever. I just don't know what I'm gonna do when he's gone."

Swiveling to prop her heels on the radiator, Cassidy created a lap for Starshine, who instantly hopped aboard. Purring riotously, the cat kneaded Cassidy's chest as if she, like Esther, had been deprived of human contact for a week.

Cassidy glanced out at a gloomy, gusty, rainy day, then looked down at the blissful cat. "Even though I know you're only using me, I can't help falling for it."

Starshine settled into a neat bundle on her chest, their chins a mere two inches apart.

"As long as you had Tigger, I was nothing more than a feeding machine. But now, with your preferred playmate on her way to Wisconsin, I'm suddenly number one on your hit parade again."

Starshine gazed at her out of slitted luminous green eyes.

"But at least you're upfront about it. I know how fickle you are, and I can either accept the affection you offer when there's nobody better around, or I can do without. And since I'm sitting here accepting it, I must still be operating under the something's-better-than-nothing principle that's governed most of my life."

Mrup, Starshine said, attempting to change the topic.

"You want to talk about something else? Okay, let's discuss Esther. That woman's even more maddening than you are. Half the time I want to smack her, the other half I feel sorry for her and want to go feed her kolacky."

Starshine bestowed a love bite on her hand.

"I suppose you'd prefer that I forget about Esther and devote myself to you. But the problem is, I still have Olivia's key, and Esther's the logical person to palm it off on, even if she doesn't want anything to do with Olivia's property. Besides, it would be much more mature of me to go to her house, kolacky in hand, and explain why I won't be coming over any more instead of avoiding her phone calls for the rest of my life." She remembered chastising a client once for disposing of an unwanted boyfriend by going into deep hiding instead of telling him directly that the relationship was over.

Sitting up, Starshine patted her cheek with a velvet paw.

Although the feline touch was pleasant, it reminded her of Esther's gnarled fingers stroking her arm. Cassidy shuddered, thinking of the bad smells and grasping hands.

She stared out at the dirty sky, drops spattering against the window. *Be so much nicer to stay inside your dry, comfy house and cuddle your newly ardent cat.*

Zach wanted her to avoid risk. Was there any danger in going to Esther's? *You can't rule out the possibility she's the killer.* But Esther was not a high-ranking suspect and Cassidy had done nothing to incur her anger. *Besides, I hate being afraid all the time. I'll pack my phone and pepper gun, and I'll be fine.*

"Sorry Starshine." She touched her lips lightly to the cat's nose. "I have to go break up with Esther."

&#x285;   &#x285;   &#x285;

Cassidy donned a plastic jacket, grabbed her tote, and ran out through the blowing rain to her garage. Driving south, she peered intently through her splotchy windshield, the light so low it could have been nightfall instead of early evening. She headed east on Cermak, located the bakery, then circled around to the lot in back, a wide strip with perpendicular slots abutting the sidewalk. Half a dozen cars were strung along the length of the block. She dashed into the bakery's rear entrance, purchased kolacky, then came back outside. In the short time she'd been gone, a white commercial van had pulled in next to the driver's side of her Toyota.

She stood beneath the building's eaves and stared into the unoccupied van, a partition behind the front seat blocking her view of the back. It held no signs or racks, so she assumed it was privately owned. A white van had appeared behind her, then disappeared, the night she'd driven to Zach's club. She also had heard something about a van from one of the people she'd talked to but she couldn't retrieve the memory. *What kind of investigator are you? You don't even write everything down in a notepad.*

A tingly, pins-and-needles sensation started in her chest. *This is ridiculous. There are vans all over the place. You're imagining things the way Olivia did, looking for an excuse to avoid visiting Esther.* She shifted from one foot to the other, then circled the van to make sure no one was lurking on the other side. *Not a soul anywhere. I suppose it's possible that somebody's hiding in the back, but most people would consider that a highly paranoid thought.*

Taking a deep breath, she gripped the pepper spray in her left hand, the keys in her right, and marched into the yard-wide strip between the two vehicles. Dropping her gaze to the small round lock, she inserted her key. Rain gusted into her face. Thunder boomed in the distance. She heard a small metallic creak but before she could turn around, something came down hard on the right side of her head. Pain bloomed behind her eyes in dazzling sunburst colors.

        ဢ      ဢ      ဢ

A prickly feeling against her cheek. Not cat whiskers. More like carpet. A pounding in the back of her head, dust in her nose, hands tied behind her. From the sticky feel of the bindings around her wrists, she thought they were taped together. Rolling over, she pulled herself upright and scooted backward to lean against the wall.

The van's interior was almost completely dark. She heard rain pinging against the roof, a clatter of cans rolling on the floor. The traffic sounds were so muffled she thought the van walls must be insulated. She considered screaming but felt certain it would be a waste of energy. If there was any possibility of making herself heard, the killer would've taped her mouth as well as her hands.

The van jerked to a brief halt, knocking her sideways. Realizing it was easier to stay on her stomach, she remained where she was and put her attention into trying to free her hands. After struggling for several minutes, she allowed herself to just lie quietly and think.

Stray wisps floated through her mind. She pictured Zach, stretched across the waterbed, admitting that the thought of losing her terrified him. She recalled his irritation at her for taking on a solo investigation, his urge to protect her, his request that she stay inside and keep her doors locked. What she had done, allowing the killer to capture her, was consummately unfair to Zach. If she ended up dead, he would be the one to suffer.

Zach had spent his whole life not letting anyone get close. Then she had come along and hammered at his defenses until she knocked them all down and he had no way left to stop himself from needing her. And now, if she got herself killed, he would be so much more bereft than if she had never bulldozed her way through his walls.

The backs of her lids started to sting. It was too much to bear, imagining what it would be like for Zach if she were to die. She had to force her woolly thoughts elsewhere.

The van. Something about a van and a small black car. Pam and the ring. Esther with a savings account under her maiden name. Carl fixing things for Olivia. Esther's insistence that Olivia was taking her to court. Carl's message that there was someone else he'd begun to check into.

Suddenly all the pieces started falling into place like marbles in a small plastic puzzle, each smooth, round ball rolling around the box to find its own cup. Clink. Clink. Clink.

She now knew who was sitting behind the wheel of the van.

# 21. The River

The van went up and over something that felt like a curb. On the other side, it swayed more, the terrain seeming mushier. *A park? Forest preserve?*

During the time her mind was wandering, Cassidy had been too distracted for panic. But the thought of being taken into a forest preserve, a favorite Chicago dumping ground for bodies, made her breath stop and her hands go cold.

She couldn't think of a single plan. Zach was still at work. Her tote was missing. She was like a cat who'd been using up lives way too fast. How many near misses had there been? She couldn't even remember. *What if this is number ten? What if all the lives are over?*

The van halted and she quickly pulled herself into a sitting position against the rear wall. The door to her right jerked open, a sprinkling of rain hitting her face. The light outside was murky but there was enough of it to distinguish the figure, an unlit flashlight in hand, climbing into the van.

Gritting her teeth, she pushed back the fear and spoke in a voice strong enough to carry over the storm. "This was a mistake, Danny. If you hadn't grabbed me, I'd never have known it was you."

"You should've stayed away from Pam." He looked straight at her, then started to shut the door.

"Don't close it. It's too claustrophobic in here."

"The rain'll blow in."

"You're planning to kill me, right?"

"I have to do it." His voice despairing.

"At least let me sit here and look at the trees as long as I can." She could see their huge, leafy tops, the wind whipping through them with a lion-like roar.

He sat on the floor opposite the open door. "I guess there's no harm. It won't be much longer anyway." He switched on the flash to check his watch, the beam illuminating the gun in his waistband. "It's seven-thirty now. With this storm, we should have full darkness by eight."

"I'm surprised you didn't just knock on my door, walk in, and shoot me the way you did Olivia and Carl."

"I couldn't keep doing the same thing. It'd be too obvious the deaths are connected."

Her voice trembling, she asked, "So what's the plan?"

"Look, I'm really sorry about this. I know, 'sorry' is completely inadequate." He drew his knees up tight, laid his arms across them. "It's going to be a drowning. Your body will wash down river, I'll park your car a couple of miles upstream, and there'll be no real evidence to prove whether it was an accident, suicide, or murder."

Zach would know. Gran had the files and Zach would figure out it was Danny and come after him. Maybe even kill him. But explaining this to Danny wouldn't help her.

"You don't want to do this, that's obvious. You probably didn't want to murder the other two either."

"Of course not." A harsh note came into his voice. "I never imagined anything like this could happen to me. I was always the good kid, the one who did everything right."

Another gust of rain howled through the van. A branch banged down on top of it.

"Then don't. It won't do you any good anyway. The police have reopened the case and they're bound to catch up with you eventually."

"There's no way out." He took a ragged breath. "Did you see Pam's daughter, Jannie? A beautiful little girl, looks just like her mother."

"Only a glimpse."

"Her father rapes her. Jannie told, and Pam did everything she could to keep the girl away from him, but the bastard wants joint custody. Now he's forced Jannie to recant, and there's nothing Pam can do." Danny took in another deep breath. "I'm the only hope they have. I'm going to kill you *and* I'm going to get away with it because I have to."

Her throat contracted. "You're taking Pam and the children and going underground?"

"As soon as I empty out all the accounts. I can't withdraw it all at once—it might flag somebody's attention."

"It's Esther's money, isn't it? Squirreled away in small accounts under different names and security numbers. And you get her to hand it over by threatening to withhold the little treats and favors you provide. I saw you manipulate her that way the first time I visited."

"It's amazing how much she and her husband were able to stash away fifty years ago, when you could give bank officers any name and number you wanted and nobody checked anything. They both worked, she inherited the house, every spare cent went into those accounts of hers. She probably had close to a million, never paid taxes on any of the interest. That's why Olivia couldn't report me—if anybody'd found out about it, the fines on her inheritance would've been enormous. And Esther, even with all her money, she still sees herself as that impoverished little girl from the depression."

"So you figured you'd put Esther's fortune to a better use." Cassidy wasn't being sarcastic. She herself would go to great lengths to save a child from sexual abuse. "If you hadn't killed two people, I could understand it. But murder—there's no way you can justify murder." *Especially you can't justify murdering* me.

"When I went to Olivia's house, I was hoping I wouldn't have to do it. I thought maybe if I explained why I needed the money . . ." The storm raged louder, drowning out his words.

Cassidy scooted over next to him so she could hear better. "Olivia tried to get guardianship, didn't she? You went to her house hoping to convince her to drop the petition. But incompetency is really hard to prove. You didn't have to kill Olivia—you could have beat her in court."

"Carl was very good at getting what he wanted, and Esther was in a panic over the whole thing. She would've fired me before taking her chances on a hearing."

*So that's another thing Carl was fixing. Olivia wanted Danny gone and Carl was going to arrange it. Although I bet Carl didn't know about the money or he would have zeroed in on Danny right away.*

"You tried to talk to Olivia and she probably flew into a rage and started screaming." *Like she did with Brenner and Edwardo.*

He lowered his chin onto his arms. "God, it was awful. I never imagined anything could be so bad. And afterward I had to find the file. I knew she kept a record of all Esther's accounts. And while I was searching, Pam started sending me this SOS message on my beeper, and my cell phone battery was dead so I had to make a quick call on Olivia's phone. Pam was in a panic because her husband hadn't brought Jannie home on time, but then he showed up a little while later."

"Why leave your file?"

"I figured nobody'd take Olivia's allegations seriously. I also thought it might seem strange if she kept a file on everybody she knew except me. I had to take Esther's but I didn't want to disturb anything else."

"You took the ring."

"I shouldn't have. To tell you the truth, after I shot Olivia I almost went to pieces. I saw the ring and just grabbed it. I wanted to give Pam something nice. So far, all the money's gone to her attorneys." He looked outside. "It's dark enough now."

"How did you justify it? How were you able to set it up in your head so you could live with yourself?"

He turned toward her, his face haggard. "Olivia never had a life. Never any joy or happiness. She had so little to lose. And Carl, he was an old man. His life was behind him." He paused. "Jannie's just a little girl. If we don't get her away from her father, he'll destroy her. Jannie, Pam, and I—we deserve a chance."

Cassidy's voice grew somber. "How are you going to justify killing me?"

"If they arrested me, I could get through it. But they'd drag Pam into it. All I ever told her was what to say if anybody asked about the phone call. We agreed that whatever I had to do, she didn't need to know about it. But they'd interrogate her and force her to testify, and I don't think she could survive all that on top of what's happening to Jannie."

He turned on the flashlight and stepped out of the van, then reached back in to haul her toward the opening. "So you see, what it comes down to is—it's Pam or you."

Dragging her outside, he held her wrists with one hand while he snagged a roll of duct tape out of the van with the other. Rain beat against her shoulders. The treetops lashed furiously and lightning streaked in the distance. She tried to pull away but he jerked up on her arms causing so much pain she immediately stopped. *When're you going to make a run for it? Not yet. Be docile now, wait till he's distracted.*

Tearing off a piece of tape, Danny stretched it across her mouth and pushed her forward, the flashlight beam extending along the ground in front of them. To her left was a dropoff, to her right the trees. Moving in the direction the van was pointing, they stumbled along a narrow dirt track that paralleled the river a few feet from its edge.

They covered a short distance, then he pulled her up close to the dropoff and looked down. The distance from the top to the river below was only about five feet but the descent was steep. Negotiating it in dry weather would not be difficult but the rain had turned the bank to mud.

*He's going to have trouble getting himself down, much less hanging onto you.* She wondered if she ought to make her break when he tried to take her down to the river, then realized that with her hands tied, she'd never be able to keep her balance. The mud looked slimy and disgusting. It made her skin crawl to think of going down there.

He jerked on her arms. "Not here. Just keep moving."

She leaned into the wind, rain stinging her face. Water trickled down the neck of her jacket. Her tennis shoes squished. Chilled to the bone, she couldn't stop shivering.

"Move it along," Danny shouted above the storm. "We have to get this over with."

She tried to yell back but the tape held her mouth closed.

He yanked up on her hands. *God that hurts.* Gritting her teeth against the pain, she trudged faster, amazed at the degree he could control her just by pushing or lifting her arms.

They walked for several minutes, then he veered up close to the edge and looked down again. The bank was just as steep here as the place they'd looked before. A few yards beyond where they stood, a dead tree extended at least twenty feet out into the river, its tangled, snaky branches protruding in all directions.

*He's not paying attention.* She reared back against him, then lunged sideways. Her shoes slid in the mud and she went over the edge, bumping and crashing downward. With her hands fastened behind her, she had no means of controlling her movement. Her body rolled part way over, dragging the side of her face across sharp roots, then her legs went zooming through a thicket of weeds and she splashed into the river.

Panic flashing through her, she thrashed around, got her feet under her, and stood up.

The river was warm and shallow, extending a few inches above her knees. She had mud in her lashes, water in her nostrils, and tape across her mouth, making it difficult to see or breathe. *This is awful, I can't stand it.* She dropped to her knees, rinsed her face in the river, blew water out of her nose. At that instant the mud in her eyes and the lack of air in her lungs seemed worse than a bullet in her brain.

"I wasn't quite sure how I was going to get you down the bank but you solved the problem for me." She looked up to see Danny, his body not coated with mud, standing three feet away.

*Oh shit, oh shit, he's going to hold my head underwater.* She twisted and pulled at her bindings, frantically trying to free her hands. This time she could feel her wrists sliding inside the tape, the mud greasing her skin.

Danny stepped in front of her, put both hands on top of her head, and pushed it down. Digging the toes of her tennis shoes into the river bottom, she rammed her head against his legs, then yanked away in the opposite direction, breaking his hold.

She jerked her face out of the water and stood up, her lungs bursting. He jumped her again, his hands grabbing at her jacket, tearing it off her body in his attempt to get a firm grasp on her. As she turned to run, he wrapped one hand in her hair and yanked her back. Pushing her down on her knees again, he forced her head back into the water.

Pulling as hard as she could on her wrists, she finally wrenched one free, leaving the tape to flop loosely on the other arm. She placed her hands on the riverbed, stretched out flat as if she were floating, allowed her body to sink lower, then slid out from under him. As she came up out of the water, she stripped the tape off her mouth and hauled in air. Pivoting, she saw him reach for her, but he was unprepared to have her coming at him with her hands. She moved in close, flailing her arms to prevent him from getting a grip on her, and thrust her knee in his groin. As he folded inward, clutching himself, she went slogging through the water away from him.

She dragged air into her burning lungs. The ankle she had twisted on Olivia's driveway nearly gave out under her. The muddy riverbottom sucked at her feet, holding her back. She didn't dare look behind her but knew he was there, knew that at any moment his hands would grab her, push her down, shove her head under the water again.

A twig scratched her arm. She looked up to see the dead tree right in front of her, completely blocking her path. *Oh God. No place to go.* But her legs kept moving, she kept trying to run as if she could barrel her way right through the enormous trunk. Her foot hit something. She stumbled forward, hands grasping at a thick branch. She heard a loud crack, felt the branch come loose from the tree. Suddenly she was holding a club. Stepping backward, she anchored both hands around one end and whirled, the branch extending out in front of her.

She saw him moving toward her, shoulders bent, head lowered. She heard the dull thunk, watched as the branch plowed into the side of his head. He wavered, then went over sideways, crumpling in slow motion.

She wiped a hand over her face, clearing the dirt out of her eyes, and made a dash for the riverbank. Digging around in the mud, she clutched at exposed roots and hoisted herself up. She stopped for a moment at the top, disoriented, then turned right and ran back to the van, parked about twenty yards from the place she'd come out of the river.

She got inside the cab, turned on the dash and headlights, then yanked off the tape still dangling from one wrist. The keys were in the ignition. Her tote was on the floor. She moved the seat forward, locked the doors, and started the engine. With trees on one side and the river on the other, there was no room to turn around so she began moving forward.

She was only a few yards from the spot where she'd climbed up the bank when she saw Danny standing near the edge. He stepped out in front of her headlights, pointed his gun at the van, and fired. She closed her eyes briefly. The windshield didn't shatter, the tires didn't blow.

Fixing her gaze on Danny, she clenched both hands around the wheel, pressed hard on the accelerator, and drove straight at him. The van lurched forward. He lunged closer to the edge but did not go over the bank, the only way he could have removed himself from her path. *Wants me to kill him.* At the last instant, she jerked the wheel to the right, grazing Danny with her fender and sending him flying toward the river.

She hit the brakes and sat for several seconds, trembling and gasping for air. When she was finally able to move, she backed down the track until she could see the road about a hundred yards off to the right, then drove straight across the grass, over the curb, and onto the highway shoulder. Hands shaking, she removed the phone from her tote and called home.

"Moran here." Zach's voice, worried.

"Oh God," she sobbed. "You told me to stay home and lock the doors and I didn't do it."

"Where are you?"

"I don't know. You can't come get me 'cause I don't know where I am. Danny took me in the back of his van to the river and tried to drown me but I got away and hit him with the car. Then he fell over the bank and I don't know if he's dead or alive but he might need paramedics. Oh God, I hope I didn't kill him. I don't want to kill anybody ever again."

"I'll find you."

# 22. The Burning of the Files

"I figured we had to have the file burning party tonight," Gran said. "Your mother's due home tomorrow and I wouldn't want her to get wind of what we've been up to while she was away."

Bright flames crackled in the stone fireplace opposite the square glass coffee table, the heat neutralized by the cold breeze blowing out of Gran's AC vents. The silver bucket stood in the center of the table, a bottle of sauvignon blanc sticking out at a jaunty angle, a second bottle of cabernet standing nearby. The stack of files sat on the side nearest the hearth.

Cassidy leaned back against the plush cushion of her armchair. As long as she didn't move, she could almost ignore her sore muscles and bruised flesh. But whenever she stood, sat, or walked, her body let her know it was paying her back for failing to stay inside and keep her doors locked.

"Another celebration." She smiled at Zach, seated in a matching armchair kitty-corner to hers. He sported a new black tee with a bright yellow inscription across the front: SAVE WATER, DRINK BEER. His face wore its normal, easy-going expression, his jaw cleanly shaven, his hair freshly cut and combed to the side.

The doorbell rang and Gran hopped up to admit Bryce, who halted in the entryway to gape at the purple bruises on Cassidy's face. "Jesus, Cass, what happened to you?"

"As soon as we all get settled, I'll tell you about it."

Picking up a glass from the table, Gran looked at Zach. "Does he get wine?"

"I'm eighteen now. You have to serve me," Bryce said aggressively, the same line he'd used on Cassidy.

Zach chuckled. "There shouldn't be any problem since Cass never lets anyone drive if they've had more than a sniff of alcohol."

Standing tall, Gran patted her dark ringlets and preened. "So what'll it be? The light, supple sauvignon or the robust, raspberry-scented cabernet?"

Bryce opted for the red, then sat on the floor to lean against the side of Cassidy's chair, his face toward the fire. All she could see of him was the back of his dark crew-cut head.

"So," he said, "did you really drag me all the way over here just to burn a few files?"

"First you get to hear why Cass's face currently matches her wardrobe, then we're going to dispose of a lot of dirty secrets by performing a fire-burning ritual." Removing the sauvignon from the bucket, Zach topped off Cassidy's glass and refilled his own.

Zach knew all of it, Gran most of it, Bryce had no idea what she'd been doing. She started at the beginning and recounted the entire experience. *Therapy for me. I'm always surprised how much it helps just to tell your story.*

Bryce responded angrily. "You didn't mention a word about any of this when I came over that night."

She started to say she hadn't wanted to worry him but realized that was an evasion. *The bullshit excuse people use to get out of explaining themselves.*

"You were already mad at Zach for putting himself in danger. I didn't want you mad at me too."

Gran said, "But what about the little black car? If Danny drove a van, how could he be the one that neighbor saw sneaking into Pam's garage?"

"There were two small cars, a black Honda in Brenner's driveway and a deep purple Dodge in Esther's."

"I bet the purple car looked black at night," Bryce said.

"Right. Brenner told me he'd seen a van in the alley the night of the murder. Well, that was obviously Danny's car. But I knew he sometimes drove Esther's because the purple car was missing that time I stopped over when Danny wasn't home. Pretty easy to see why he'd rather drive Esther's snazzy little Dodge when he visited his girlfriend instead of his dinged up old van."

Zach asked, "Didn't you see Danny today at the hospital? How's he doing?"

"He'll live to stand trial, although he said he wishes I hadn't swerved. He's not giving up Pam's name and I promised not to volunteer any information about her either." Sipping her wine, she stared into the dancing orange flames.

Gran rose from the settee across the room and tossed in another log. "It just breaks my heart to think what that little girl is up against. Zach, if you get me a gun, I'll go shoot that bastard father of hers myself. At my age I'd die of natural causes before they ever finished up with the appeals and all." She cackled. "Wouldn't you just love to write the story? There I'd be on the front page in my Farrah Fawcett hair holding a big old cannon."

"I can see the headline now. 'Pistol Packin' Mama Shoots Molester'."

Cassidy shifted in her chair. "Danny told me Pam's planning to take the kids and go underground."

Bryce moved over to sit against the wall, presenting his face instead of his back to Cassidy and his father. He said to Cassidy in a challenging tone, "Don't you have to tell the police about the ring?"

"Why? So Pam'd be forced to testify? To make it harder for her to get Jannie away from her father? So Esther—who inherits everything— would get a ring she has no use for?"

Bryce frowned. "If Danny wanted to shoot somebody, why not the father? He's the one who deserved it."

Cassidy gazed into the boy's dark, angular face. "Because Danny wanted the money. He tried to make it sound so altruistic, but you take somebody like Danny who's spent his whole life doing for others, he's got to have a sense that the world owes him. He probably saw the money as his reward for all the years he spent taking care of old ladies."

Zach picked up the top file, went to the hearth, and began tossing pages into the fire. "Well, here goes Danny." Sitting on his heels to watch it burn, he added, "A basically decent guy who couldn't withstand the temptation of all that money." He paused. "Isn't that what tragedy is? An essentially noble person with a fatal flaw? He commits one wrong act and then he's doomed."

Putting her glass on the table, Cassidy waved one hand in the air as she talked. "Of course Danny's responsible for his own actions, but it was Esther who set the whole thing up. She found two people, Danny and Olivia, both so needy and deprived they made prime targets. Then she dangled her money in front of them like a carrot and gloated over her ability to play them off against each other."

Zach said, "And now she's got nobody."

"Not even me. I stopped at her house today and officially broke up."

Gran took the second file. "No more dirt on Shelby." She threw the pages into the flames. "I get the idea you all feel sorry for Olivia, but after reading about the spiteful things she did, I don't think I like her very much."

Despite aching muscles, Cassidy forced herself to carry Evelyn's file over to the fire. She handed it to Zach, then returned to her cozy chair. "I admit Olivia sometimes treated people badly, but I think she was so fragile and scared she just couldn't help herself. Jake's metaphor of Sleeping Beauty and the prince had a lot of appeal for me."

Zach, sitting cross-legged in front of the hearth, turned to face her. "She didn't need a prince. She needed Prozac."

*He's right. As much as you'd like to believe otherwise, love never cures mental disorder.*

"So," Gran said, "What's Jake gonna do now?"

"He's moving back to Indiana. He's got grown kids there and he wants to start rebuilding his relationship with them, making amends."

Gran picked up another file. "Well, now it's Brenner's turn to burn." Standing in front of the fireplace, she fed the pages to the flames, then looked down at Zach.

"Where do you stand with the feds? They gonna give you any trouble?"

"My attorney says they're too busy building their case against the cops to bother with me."

Bryce went to the coffee table and picked up the last file. "Hey, Edwardo old buddy, time to vamoose."

Squatting next to his father to throw the pages in, he continued, "That was a pretty cool story you had in the paper yesterday. But I don't see why drug trade in the clubs is such a big deal. Why shouldn't people be able to buy coke along with their martinis? I mean, you used to get high all the time, didn't you? Matter of fact, I'd be surprised as shit if you were able to hang out there a whole month without taking a few snorts yourself.''

Cassidy felt the room go tense. *How's Zach going to field that one? I don't know which'd be better—the truth or a lie. God, I hope the next question isn't about Heather.*

Zach stood to lean on one side of the fireplace. Bryce stood also and leaned opposite him.

"I did start using for a short period. Then I came to my senses and remembered that I wouldn't be able to stay married or keep my job if I got hooked again.''

"A lot of people use drugs recreationally and don't have any trouble with it.''

Cassidy sat forward. "How can you say that after what you saw Tiffany go through?" *Thought he hated drugs. Wouldn't go near them. But you can't count on it. You've seen people hated their parents' drinking, grew up to become drunks themselves.*

"Tiff overdid it. It wasn't the drugs, it was her not being able to control it. It's just like alcohol. You all drink and don't have a problem with it.'' He leered at his father. "At least as far as I can tell, you don't.''

*Has to needle Zach every time he's with him. Normal kid stuff? Or because he feels so disconnected?*

Zach said, "Can I take this to mean you're doing drugs?''

"Yeah, sure. Well, mostly just at parties. Everybody drinks and drugs at parties.''

"I hope you're able to keep it recreational, that you never have the kind of problem I did.'' He shifted slightly. "I'd find it very hard to see you getting self- destructive.''

Hunkering down in front of the fire again, Bryce gazed for several seconds into the flames. "I don't use that much," he muttered. "I just wanted to see if it makes any difference what I do.''

"It does." Zach ran a hand over his face. "I'm sorry I wasn't around when you were a kid." He paused. "I probably wouldn't've been a very good father. I always get wrapped up in other things, don't pay enough attention to the people I care about.'' Bryce looked up to meet his eyes. "I missed out on the first part of your life but I'd like to be around for a whole lot of the rest of it.''

ဗာ    ဗာ    ဗာ

In the car on the way home Cassidy said, "You've started saying the strangest things. When JC had control, you hardly spoke to me at all. Now you sound as if some kind of Phil Donahue part's taken over."

"Donahue? I hope I haven't gone as soft as that."

"What you said to me that night after the club was wonderful. Something I've always wanted to hear and never have. And then tonight with Bryce—the words that came out of your mouth were exactly right. Just what he needed from you."

"It's sort of like a pendulum swing. I went too far in the direction of being an insensitive thug, now I'm overcompensating. Don't worry, I'll work my way back to the middle and resume my normal, noncommunicative style."

Smiling, she reached for his hand. He wrapped his fingers around hers and didn't let go until they were home.